Anne Grace Prestwich

Life and Letters of Sir Joseph Prestwich...

Anne Grace Prestwich

Life and Letters of Sir Joseph Prestwich...

ISBN/EAN: 9783744719063

Printed in Europe, USA, Canada, Australia, Japan

Cover: Foto ©Raphael Reischuk / pixelio.de

More available books at **www.hansebooks.com**

LIFE AND LETTERS

OF

SIR JOSEPH PRESTWICH

M.A., D.C.L., F.R.S.

FORMERLY PROFESSOR OF GEOLOGY IN THE
UNIVERSITY OF OXFORD

WRITTEN AND EDITED BY

HIS WIFE

WILLIAM BLACKWOOD AND SONS
EDINBURGH AND LONDON
MDCCCXCIX

PREFACE.

THIS Memoir was not undertaken without anxious misgivings : it might not have been attempted but for the encouragement and prompting of Sir John Evans, who urged that I could best tell of the home life, and that the scientific publications, by the subject of the Memoir, had already spoken for themselves. I accordingly decided to do my utmost in what, it is needless to say, has been altogether a labour of love.

I have to acknowledge my special indebtedness to Sir Archibald Geikie for his great kindness in writing the Summary of the Geological Work accomplished by Joseph Prestwich, as well as for the use of letters in his possession. A debt of gratitude is also due to Sir John Evans, who not only placed numerous letters at my disposal, but undertook the critical supervision of the MS., and was the helper and adviser throughout. To Professor Rupert Jones my warmest acknowledgments have likewise to be made for his ever kind co-operation ; and to Mr Horace B. Woodward, of the Geological Survey, I must record my gratitude for his invaluable assistance, without which it would not have been possible for me to accomplish what has been done : to him also is due the arrangement of the List of Published Papers.

On account (except in a few cases) of the scarcity of original letters, those from friends and correspondents have been inserted when they have served to elucidate the subjects under discussion at the time. To M. Albert Gaudry, of the Institute of France, I am indebted for his sympathy and encouragement, and also for allowing me the use of letters. To Professor Capellini of Bologna, and to Professor Louis Lartet of Toulouse, I have likewise to record my grateful acknowledgments.

Professor Jules Marcou of Cambridge, Massachusetts, who took an eager interest in the preparation of this Memoir, has, alas! not lived to witness its completion. Mr William Colchester, an old and attached friend who so lately wrote expressing his wish for the speedy publication of this volume, has likewise passed away. The recent death of Sir Douglas Galton, the dear friend and companion of Joseph Prestwich in geological excursions at home and abroad, has been a personal grief, and is the severance of another link with the past.

Among the friends to whom I am indebted for letters and data may be mentioned the Rev. R. Ashington Bullen, the Rev. Osmond Fisher, Mr Benjamin Harrison, Sir Joseph D. Hooker, Professor Judd, Sir John Lubbock, Mr Mansel-Pleydell, Mr S. R. Pattison, and many others. I have also to express my thanks to Dr

Henry Woodward for his ever-ready helpfulness, and for the use of the Plate for illustration of the group of the four friends—Joseph Prestwich, Professor John Morris, Mr F. E. Edwards, and Mr Searles Wood. The kindness of Mrs Lyell (author of the 'Life and Letters of Sir Charles Lyell') has made it possible to introduce several letters to Sir Charles. I have also to thank Mr Roderick F. Murchison for the loan of several letters to Sir Roderick I. Murchison; and Mrs Mason Hoppin of New Haven, Connecticut, U.S.A., for so kindly obtaining information about the Great Seal of the United States. To none am I more indebted than to my three sisters, Isabella, Margaret, and Louisa E. Milne, who have given constant and loving aid in the preparation of the MS. for the printer.

G. A. P.

Darent-Hulme, *May* 1899.

CONTENTS.

CHAPTER I.

1812-1830.

ANCESTRY AND YOUTH.

CHAPTER II.

1830-1834.

CITY AND HOME LIFE—ZETETICAL SOCIETY—VISITS TO SHROPSHIRE —NATURAL HISTORY SOCIETY.

CHAPTER III.

1834–1849.

GEOLOGY OF COALBROOK DALE AND GAMRIE—TERTIARY MEMOIRS.

CHAPTER IV.

1849–1858.

EASTER EXCURSIONS—'THE WATER-BEARING STRATA'—'THE GROUND BENEATH US'—FURTHER TERTIARY MEMOIRS.

CHAPTER V.

1858–1859.

BRIXHAM CAVE—FLINT IMPLEMENTS—VISITS TO ABBEVILLE —GOWER CAVES.

CHAPTER VI.

1860-1863.

ANTIQUITY OF MAN—FIELD GEOLOGY—GEOLOGICAL MAPS.

CHAPTER VII.

1863-1870.

HUMAN JAW OF ABBEVILLE—ROYAL COAL COMMISSION—ROYAL WATER COMMISSION—PRESIDENCY OF THE GEOLOGICAL SOCIETY.

CHAPTER VIII.

1870-1874.

MARRIAGE—VISIT TO PARIS—ITALY—RETIREMENT FROM THE CITY—AIX-LES-BAINS—PROFESSORSHIP OF GEOLOGY AT OXFORD.

CHAPTER IX.

1874–1878.

OXFORD—FIELD GEOLOGY IN ENGLAND, FRANCE, WALES, AND SCOTLAND.

CHAPTER X.

1878–1888.

PRESIDENT OF THE *RÉUNION EXTRAORDINAIRE* OF THE FRENCH GEOLOGI-CAL SOCIETY AT BOULOGNE — TEXT-BOOK ON 'GEOLOGY' — PRESIDENT OF THE INTERNATIONAL GEOLOGICAL CONGRESS.

CHAPTER XI.

1888–1895.

PLATEAU IMPLEMENTS OF KENT—LETTERS ON POST-GLACIAL SUBMERGENCE —CORRESPONDING MEMBER OF THE ROYAL ACADEMY OF THE LINCEI —VICE-PRESIDENT OF THE GEOLOGICAL SOCIETY OF FRANCE.

CHAPTER XII.

1895–1896.

LAST DAYS.

ILLUSTRATIONS.

"And Nature, the old nurse, took
 The child upon her knee,
Saying, 'Here is a story-book
 Thy Father has written for thee.'

'Come, wander with me,' she said,
 'Into regions yet untrod ;
And read what is still unread
 In the manuscripts of God.' "

SIR JOSEPH PRESTWICH.

CHAPTER I.

ANCESTRY AND YOUTH.

THE family of Prestwich of Prestwich [1] and Hulme, from whom the subject of this memoir was descended, were holders of land in the county of Lancaster at a very early date. In the end of the twelfth century they possessed estates in this county, and the name occurs as Prestwych or Prestwich again and again, now in one reign, now in another of the early English kings, chiefly in records touching tenures of land, marriages, &c. In 1301, among the nine witnesses to Thomas de Grelle's charter to the burgesses of Manchester, are the signatures of Adam de Prestwiche, the fifth witness, and Jōhe de Prestwyche, the ninth.

A curious document among the family papers is the copy of a letter now in the British Museum, and dated 2nd April 1573, from Queen Elizabeth " To our trustye and well - beloved Edmunde Prestwyche Ar." After recounting the necessity of putting the kingdom in a state of defence, " the Queene " requires from him

---

[1] The village of Prestwich is situated on the Coal Measures, about three and a half miles north-west of Salford.

A

the loan of "a meane porton of monye Untill some
further reasonable ayde may be given Us by the whole
realme, . . . and therefore having made Choyese of
you ffor your Abilitye good will youe beare to us and
our Realme wee requyre you to pay to our use The
summe of fiftye pounds," &c., &c.   "The Queene"
makes provision for its early repayment.

    Hulme Hall, the home of the family for many gen-
erations, was a picturesque half-timbered house on the
banks of the Irwell, situated about two miles south-
west of old Manchester : at one time it was surrounded
by a moat, and it is believed to have been occupied
by John de Hulme in the reign of Henry II.   Aikin,
in his 'History of Manchester,' published in 1795, says
of the Prestwiches :—

    This family, by embarking in the royal cause in the Civil Wars
of Charles I., lost much of their property, so that in the reign of
King William, Hulme Hall and estate were sold, and purchased
by Sir Edward Moseley, who left it, together with his other
estates, to his daughter Ann, wife of Sir John Bland, Baronet,
who made it her chief residence.   At the death of their son, Sir
John Bland, Baronet, it was sold to G. Lloyd, Esq., and it now
belongs to the Duke of Bridgewater.

It would appear that the last-named owner broke up
the venerable pile of buildings into thirty or forty
cottage-tenements, of which but little if any vestige
now remains.   The carved oak panels, which decorated
the best rooms, were purchased by the Earl of Elles-
mere and removed to Worsley Hall.   The actual site
of Hulme Hall was about a quarter of a mile west of St
George's Church, Manchester, in a tract now traversed
by the Manchester South Junction and Altrincham
Railway.

    Although the estates of the family are now all owned
by others, and although so few survive to bear the

name, yet it will never pass into oblivion. For several centuries it had been handed down in the Prestwich gallery in the Cathedral or Collegiate Church in Manchester, where many of the race found their last resting-place. The gallery itself no longer exists. It is, moreover, remembered in Manchester that the gift of its first free library was made by the Rev. John Prestwich, Fellow of All Souls', and brother of Sir Thomas of the Civil Wars.

A baronetcy was conferred on Sir Thomas Prestwich, on the 25th April 1644, by Charles I., on the field of battle outside Oxford, as an acknowledgment of his services to the royal cause, and in especial for having raised a troop of horse at his own cost. Several small gold medals or badges were then struck off bearing the effigy of the ill-fated king. One of these badges, given to the new-made Baronet at Oxford, is in the keeping of the writer.

Medal given by Charles I. to Sir Thomas Prestwich.
(Twice the actual size.)

As may be understood, the Prestwiches were greatly impoverished by the sacrifices they had made on behalf of the

Crown. At the head of the [Royalist] party in Manchester we find the names of Holland, Egerton, Prestwich, Stanley, &c. Sequestration and confiscation were put in force against the conquered in a manner most revolting. It was after this that in 1660 the sale of Hulme Hall took place, and this sale was confirmed by Act of Parliament in 1673. Towards the close of the Civil War, Sir Thomas refused to give further assistance to the royal cause, but that his mother prevailed upon him to continue his allegiance, telling him that she had hidden treasures wherewith to supply his needs; but unfortunately the old lady was seized with apoplexy, and died before she could reveal her secret.

It was supposed that this treasure was buried in the neighbourhood of Hulme Hall, and for a long time afterwards gipsies wandering about the country made considerable profit out of this by selling the secret, which they pretended to know.

The baronetcy had been for many years in abeyance, when it was assumed by John Prestwich (a cousin of our geologist's father); but his claim to the title was not legally acknowledged : he was not descended from the first baronet, but from his cousin, and from a younger son of that cousin. The father and grandfather of the geologist repeatedly stated that they were in possession of papers showing their descent. One day, however, the father went to an election with the said papers in his pocket; on returning home the pocket was empty, and the papers have never since been heard of.

Sir John, who left no family, was greatly interested in the Prestwich genealogy, and many volumes in MS., containing extracts from documents in the British Museum, heralds' visitations, deeds, &c., which related to the subject, were written by him with extreme care. He was a Fellow of the Society of Antiquaries, and a manuscript by him on Earthquakes was published in

1870 by our Joseph Prestwich in the 'Geological Magazine' for that year. In 1775 his book on 'Mineral, Animal, and Vegetable Poisons' appeared; but he is best known by a work published in 1787, entitled 'Respublica, or a Display of the Honours, Ceremonies, and Enseignes of the Commonwealth under the Protectorship of Oliver Cromwell,' &c.

It is interesting to note that it is to this Sir John Prestwich that the United States are indebted for the design of their Great Seal. Three committees had been appointed, one after another, to prepare a seal, but as none of their designs gave satisfaction to Congress, on June 13th of the same year (1782) the whole matter was finally referred by that body to Charles Thomson, its secretary.

He procured several devices, among them an elaborate one by William Barton of Philadelphia; but none of them met with approval until John Adams, then in London, sent him a design suggested by Sir John Prestwich, an Englishman who was a warm friend of America and an accomplished antiquarian.

It was described in 1782 as follows :—

Arms.—Paleways of thirteen pieces, argent and gules; a chief azure; the escutcheon on the breast of the American eagle displayed proper, holding in his dexter talon an olive branch, and in his sinister a bundle of thirteen arrows, all proper, and in his beak a scroll inscribed with this motto: *E Pluribus Unum.*

For the Crest.—Over the head of the eagle, which appears above the escutcheon, a glory or breaking through a cloud proper, and surrounding thirteen stars, forming a constellation, argent on an azure field.

Reverse.—A pyramid unfinished. In the zenith an eye in a triangle, surrounded with a glory proper. Over the eye these words, *Annuit Cœptis* (God has favoured the undertaking). On the base of the pyramid the numerals MDCCLXXVI., and underneath the following motto: *Novus Ordo Sœculorum* ("A New Series of Ages"), denoting that a new order of things had commenced in the Western World—or freely translated, "A new era."

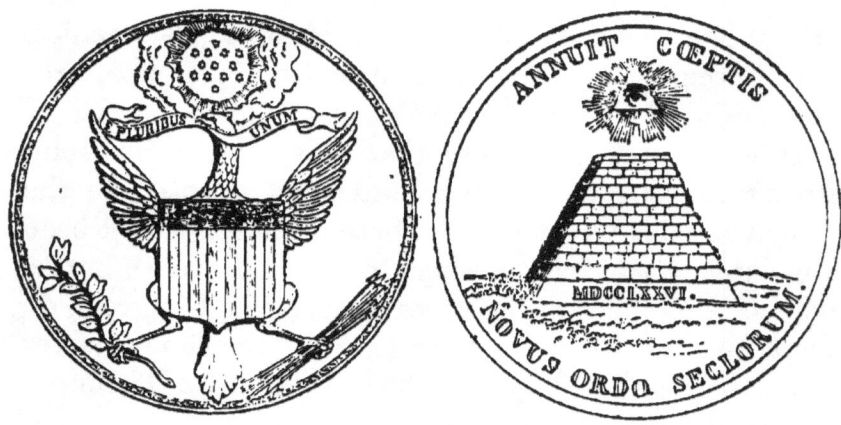

The Great Seal of the United States.

This design of Sir John Prestwich's, which was adopted as being the simplest and most significant of any submitted, still remains the arms of the United States. "It was strange" (as the writer of the paragraph in an American paper observed) "that after six years spent in deliberation, Congress should have finally adopted a design by one of a nation with whom America was then at war."

But all our interest centres in the Prestwich whose life we shall now attempt to trace. His father, Joseph, after whom he was named, was one of a firm of wine merchants in Mark Lane, who imported, and supplied the trade in the provinces as well as in Scotland and Ireland. Joseph Prestwich, senior, was the only son of Elias Prestwich of Broseley in Shropshire (whose grandparents had migrated there from Ireland, one of the family having taken refuge and settled there during the Civil Wars); and his wife was Catherine, the only surviving daughter of Edward Blakeway, the squire of Broseley. It was in Clapham, and amid its then rural surroundings, that the father and mother of our Joseph Prestwich began their married life.

Early in the century Clapham and its neighbourhood were very different suburbs of London from what they are to-day. The fields and green lanes of those years have vanished, and their place has been invaded by ever-extending blocks of brick and mortar. At that time comfortable houses stood in their own grounds or gardens, the gardens generally merging into productive orchards. Now coal-trucks and sheds cover sites which were noted for their heavy crops of fruit. Then railways were unknown, nor had tram-cars, which run in rapid succession in the now noisy thoroughfares, ever been heard of. In short, the aspect of the place is altogether changed.

Of the parents of Joseph Prestwich it may be remarked that his father was a man of ability, widely read, with a knowledge of art, who enjoyed nothing more than his tours and journeys in France and Holland, when he was occasionally accompanied by his wife. Foreign travel was then for the few, and was not made easy for the many. He was of a sanguine temperament, racy and witty—"very good company," as a relative explained, when describing his ever-ready repartee.

The mother of our geologist, to whom throughout life he was tenderly attached, was the eldest of seven. Three of the little Blakeways died in childhood, and the survivors were Catherine, Edward, John, and James. Catherine (Mrs) Prestwich was greatly beloved by her family and friends : she was entirely domestic, sweet-natured, and refined—a good wife and an affectionate mother. She made a happy home, and her distinguished son in after-years often acknowledged that he could not have accomplished the work that he did but for the advantages of this quiet and cheerful abode.

Mrs Prestwich was cast in a different mould from her mother, whose maiden name was Prytherch. Mr Blakeway of Broseley had been some time a widower when he confided to his friend the Rev. Stephen Prytherch, the vicar of Leighton (who had a bevy of very handsome daughters), that his home was lonely and that he wished to marry again : would he give him one of his daughters? The vicar was delighted, but the question was, Which? His advice, "Better take the eldest," was followed. It was a wooing not long a-doing, and Catherine Prytherch soon became Mrs Blakeway of Broseley Hall. Although there was great disparity in age, the squire being thirty years the lady's senior, she made an excellent wife, and they became an attached couple. But she was a strange mother : she made a point of sending all her children out to nurse soon after their birth, so as to have no further trouble with them. They were placed with a much-respected Quaker family, and their father, who was fond of his children, rode daily over to see them. Mrs Prestwich used to say that the amusement which she and her little brothers liked best was sitting on the banks of the river and listening to the sound of the water. Their mother took no more concern about them until they were sent home old enough to be packed off to school. Thus mother and daughter were very unlike : Mrs Blakeway with her marked individuality and strong will, — her daughter, Mrs

Prestwich, all unselfishness and gentleness, and full of thoughtfulness for others. The Blakeways had been connected with the Church for many generations, and a kinsman, the Rev. John Brickenden Blakeway, rector of St Mary's, Shrewsbury, was joint author with Archdeacon Owen of a 'History of Shropshire.'

Mr and Mrs Prestwich had ten children, three of whom died in infancy. The eldest surviving was our geologist, who was born at Pensbury, Clapham, on the 12th March 1812, and whose death took place at Darent-Hulme, Shoreham in Kent, on the 23rd June 1896. He was the second of the name, the first-born Joseph having lived only a few months. Thus the two sons and five daughters were Joseph, Isabella Civil, Catherine, Eliza, Emily, Edward Elias, and Civil Mary. The two survivors are Eliza (Mrs Tomkins) and Emily Prestwich.

Among the family papers there are forty-two little volumes of pocket-books containing brief diaries which were kept by our Joseph Prestwich's mother, and which date from the year of her marriage, 1809, to 1850, the year of her death. The entries are short, being only a few sentences recording the events of each day. But the volume for 1812 has a pathetic interest: when a second little Joseph had arrived to replace the first-born, the daily entries betray the constant motherly anxiety, and every symptom of the health of the infant is recorded. We give no extract: the reading was intended for a mother's eyes. In the diaries of the next few years there is only occasional allusion to little Joseph, since other children had been born to share in and claim the maternal care. It is evident, however, that the boy was, like most healthy little boys, restlessly active, with a tendency to lead his

small sisters into trouble.   At the tender age of
five the child was placed as a boarder at a school
about a mile distant.   This early launching into life
will be told in his own words, in a few pages of an
autobiography which nearly eighty years later Joseph
Prestwich had been urged to write, and which had
only just been begun in those last months when he
was attacked by fatal illness :—

I must have been a mischievous boy. At five years of age
I was sent to school. The last misdemeanour which led to it
was this. Our house at Lavender Hill stood in a large garden
and orchard in which was a fish-pond. One fine summer's day
the nurse was, I am told, sent to fetch us children and put us to
bed. Preferring an outdoor life, I persuaded my little sister,
who was eighteen months younger than myself, to hide in the
pond, where I felt sure they would never seek us. Accordingly
we marched in until the water was up to our necks, and there
we might have remained, heedless of the cries of the nurse, until
what I judged would be a fitter time for bed, had not my sister
betrayed us by an uncontrollable fit of laughter.

The school to which I was sent at Wandsworth was about a
mile distant from our home, and was kept by a Madame Saqui,
I presume a French emigrant. She suffered from dropsy, and
adopted a mode of exercise which I have never since seen. At
the end of the schoolroom was a tall seat formed by thick
cushions with springs, and having arms to hold on by on either
side. On this she bobbed up and down, while she could see
all that was going on in the schoolroom. It was very comical,
but to laugh we dared not. I do not remember what I learned
—I imagine it was but little. I remember better our amusements. At that time (1817) fairs were held in all towns and
villages around London, which had its own great central fair
in Smithfield. To the Wandsworth fair we never failed to be
led, and were then each presented with a bun. We had also
our daily walks. On one of those we passed by the lodge of
our house, and the gate being open, and having an innate
dislike to school, I ran off down the avenue until stopped by

the barking of a little dog which fronted me: whence possibly my subsequent want of affection for the species.

This school being found too near home, I was sent to one on Forest Hill. Again the fairs on Peckham Rye and Camberwell Green are the objects which cling most to my recollection. We were, I think, treated kindly, though our fare was at times somewhat hard. On Saturdays, the servants being much occupied, the ordinary dinner was replaced by a more simple meal of bread and cheese, the bread being not unfrequently speckled green. Our playground was a field on the top of a hill of bare London clay. I then had a small garden in which I dug what I was pleased to consider a well, London clay being water-tight. I had the satisfaction of frequently having it full of water. How little I thought then how much I should subsequently be connected with the structure and geological history of that formation. When the field was too wet we were allotted 200 to 300 yards of the public road which ran in front of the house for our playground, and occasionally levied small blackmail on the few passers-by.

In the meantime our family had removed from Lavender Hill to "The Retreat," South Lambeth. It was a three-storeyed house surrounded by a parapet wall. A favourite amusement was to walk all round the wall followed by the most fearless of my sisters, but the amusement not being considered safe, it was stopped. I was now sent to a day-school adjoining, where I fear my book studies progressed no more rapidly than before. Nature had more attractions for me. With my sisters we used to walk along the Wandsworth Road as far as Lavender Hill, and I well remember the interest with which I noticed two springs which then existed on that road. One was on Rush Hill, where it broke out from beneath a bed of gravel lying on the London clay. The other was at a lower level, and at the base of the gravel covering Battersea Fields. How well I remember wondering where the water came from: it was a mystery. These springs have long since disappeared from sight, for the road is no longer the quiet country road it was then, with only an occasional vehicle passing, but had been, when I last saw it, transformed into the resemblance of the Whitechapel Road, paved and street-like.

Our clergyman was a man of the world and of society. At his house I saw among many public characters Rammohun Roy, whose conversion to Unitarianism made at that time a great stir in London. He was a tall, striking-looking, grave man of about forty. Barnes, the editor of the 'Times,' was also a frequent visitor there.

It was now decided that I should be sent to school in Paris. Accordingly, early one fine summer morning, escorted by both parents and with my eldest sister, we started in the basket of the Union coach for Dover. Arriving in the evening, we had to wait till next day for crossing. Starting at ten, Calais was reached at about twelve. The rest of the day was spent in passing our luggage through the custom-house, getting our passports viséd, and securing places in the diligence. Before leaving Calais, I took the opportunity of going down one of the shallow wells which were then to be found in most of the courtyards of the town, and came up, I imagine, not much the wiser. Diligences started for Paris morning and evening. We left on a morning by the Messageries Royales, and after spending two nights and part of two days on the road, arrived in the great yard in the Rue Notre Dame des Victoires. I was now eleven years old, and the interest I felt in all I saw was excessive. I was never tired of seeing the streets — which then, with the exception of the Rue de la Paix, had no footpaths—and of watching the traffic and listening to the many cries.

The school selected for me was at the top of the Rue des Martyrs, at the foot of Montmartre. It was a large school, kept by a M. Colin. I was placed more particularly in charge of Mme. Colin and their only daughter, Mdlle. Fannie, who was two to three years older than myself. M. Colin was a man about forty, with only one leg—a sight at that time very common in Paris, when men with one leg or arm were constantly met with. I was the only English boy in the school, and nothing could be kinder than their treatment of me. I was a little bullied by the boys, for Waterloo was then of fresh memory, but I always found a few to take my part: there was the *cachot* if they were caught in the act [of bullying me], so I got on very well. The place was barrack-like and the fare simple. The floors were all tiled and the dormitories without furniture. . . . The breakfast was

very simple: the boys marched into the *réfectoire*, where long
loaves were run under a sort of chaff-cutting machine, and as
the great hunks fell on one side they were snatched up by the
boys—played at ball with, and then eaten and washed down
with a little water. Dinner consisted of *bouillon* and *bouilli*
followed by a dish of vegetables, the beverage being what the
boys called *abondance*—that is to say, one bottle of *vin ordinaire*
to one bucket of water. But all seemed contented, whilst I, as a
stranger, was allowed a few indulgences. The school, however,
soon broke up, and M. Colin removed to a small house, with a
few boys, lower down the street.

Education in Paris was at that time (1823) very cheap. As
extras I was taught, besides Italian, drawing, dancing, and fencing, at one franc per lesson. Our school was attached to the
Collége Bourbon (changed to the Lycée Condorcet), but I was
considered too young to profit by the connection. Amongst the
students attending the Collége was the Duc d'Orléans, son of
Louis Philippe, who a few years later was killed by a fall from
his carriage. We had two half-holidays a week, when we were
taken generally either to play in amongst the chestnut-trees of
the Tuileries gardens, or to the top of Montmartre with its
swings and quarries. The fossils were then unknown to me, but
I took great interest in the fine crystals of gypsum, which we could
cleave into plates as thin as a wafer and as clear as glass. In
summer we were frequently taken to one of the large baths on
the Seine, and there, wrapped in a *peignoir*, would spend long
hours. On Sundays I was taken to the French Protestant
church, or else went to spend the day with my sister in the Rue
de Valois. Occasionally Mdlle. Fannie would take me with her
in early morning to the great central markets. Nothing, in fact,
could have been kinder and more considerate than the treatment
I received, and I shall ever hold the memory of M. Colin and his
family in affectionate remembrance. Mme. Colin treated me as
a son. In fact, Mdlle. Fannie used to exclaim, "Oh! qu'il est
gaté ce petit Joseph!" But with all this my studies were not
neglected, and I learned easily and quickly.

He was petted and caressed, but was not spoilt,
and the happiness of school-life in Paris was never

forgotten. Perhaps in later years the very remembrance of it unconsciously acted as a magnet, and drew
him.to France and to his many friends there. A few
months after his arrival the boy had an illness, and
such was M. and Mme. Colin's kindness that they
had him then to sleep in their own room. The reason
that Madame Colin alleged for her devotion to the
little English boy was always, "Il est si raisonnable,
le petit Joseph!" It is not surprising that Mademoiselle Fannie became jealous. This jealousy, however, on the part of the young daughter was short-
lived, and when in later years she became Madame
Nyon, her eldest child was named after the sister of
" le petit Joseph."

The letters which he sent to his father at this time
—always in French—are very amusing. The following
is a specimen :—

PARIS, *Mars* 9, 1824.

MON CHER PAPA,—Je ne vous ai pas écrit plutot parceque je
voulais attendre jusqu'à la fin du carnaval pour vous dire tout ce
que j'ai vu. Le premier dimanche appelé le dimanche gras, j'ai
été voir le bœuf gras qui est le plus beau qui se trouve dans tout
Paris, il est suivi d'un char dans lequel il y a un joli petit enfant
habillé comme un amour, le char est conduit par un homme qui
represente le temps, tous ceux qui l'entourent et tous les musici-
ens qui l'accompagnent sont déguisés en soldats romains. Après
avoir vu cette mascarade qui attire toujours la foule, j'ai été me
promener sur les boulevards pour voir les masques, mais comme
il faisait un très mauvais temps je n'en ai pas vu beaucoup.
Lundi je suis allé au spectacle où j'ai vu Pierre de Portugal,
tragédie de Mr Arnauld, et les rendez-vous bourgeois travestis,
cette dernière piece est une farce de carnaval dans laquelle tous
les hommes sont déguisés en femmes et toutes les femmes dé-
guisées en hommes. Mardi j'ai vu dans les voitures beaucoup de
masques très droles qui allaient à un bal masqué. Le soir chaque
élève a mis quinze sous nous avons acheté du cidre, une tarte àla

frangipane et d'autres choses. Madame Colin nous a donné une crème, des crêpes, des cerises, du vin, et du jus de la fleur d'orange et avec cela, nous avons fait une jolie collation après laquelle nous avons été nous coucher. Je n'ai recu votre lettre que six semaines après qu'elle avait été écrite car vous l'avez écrite le 19 Janvier, et je ne l'ai recu que le 7 Mars. J'ai appris de Madame Thiebaut que j'avais une nouvelle petite sœur cela m'a causé beaucoup de joie. Je donnerai mes dessins à Madame Billin qui les enverra en Angleterre par l'Ambassadeur. J'ai presque fini celui qui est destiné à Monsieur Colin. Je n'ai pas encore commencé le paysage mais je m'[en] occuperai bientôt si vous le desirez. J'ai un nouveau maitre de danse qui est bien meilleur que le dernier, car il me fait faire beaucoup d'exercices. J'ai été voir le spectacle franconi avec ma sœur, Madame Thiebaut et Mademoiselle Victoire. On donnait la prise de trocadéro et le petit tambour. Je vous remercie bien des dix francs que vous m'avez envoyés mais je les devais pour le panier que j'ai donné à ma sœur et je les ai payés tout de suite. Isabelle et moi nous nous portons très bien. J'espere que vous, Maman, mes sœurs et mon frere et ma [bonne] se portent bien. Adieu, mon cher Papa.—Je suis votre fils soumis,　　　J. PRESTWICH.

After this date his father stipulated that all his letters were to be sent as they were written—uncorrected.

The boy delighted in Paris, and entered with keen enjoyment into the life and amusements of the school. He made great progress in drawing, for which he had unusual talent, and the crayon heads, &c., which he sent home from time to time, were remarkable as the work of a schoolboy. This faculty for drawing proved of great service to him in after-life when sketching sections in the field.

In reading these few pages of autobiography we have to bear in mind that this MS., alas! was never re-read, never corrected by its writer.

And now began my education in earnest. I soon mastered French, and carried away various prizes—amongst others that for *Cacographie*, which consisted in rendering into correct French a paper of text badly spelt. My translations of Latin into French were approved, and my reading of Dante and Ariosto gave satisfaction to my Italian master, who recorded his approval in the following lines [1] :—

"Al Gentilissimo Signor GIUSEPPE PRESTWICH in attestato di verace affetto il servo suo divoto FREDERICO BROGLIO.

SONNET

(of which a free translation is here given).[2]

" PARIS, *8th July* 1825.

" When now, as wont, you turn and leave behind
Fair France, at this last moment, in words brief,
Full of esteem and love for you, I find
Expression for my thoughts and for my grief.
Benign One ! hearken to my loving lay.
May not these accents to the winds be sent,
But in my heart for ever may you stay,
There find a home and soften my lament.
On your return midst household gods again,
With troops of chosen friends around you, then,
Upon that man unknown to fame, ah ! deign
Upon him, far removed by seas, as when
He taught you Tuscan tones in bygone days,
To think, for he will ever love and praise !"

Amongst the public events which I witnessed during my residence in Paris were the return of the French army from Spain and the arrival of the Duke of Northumberland as ambassador to "Louis Dix-huit." The procession of carriages and military in the latter case was very gorgeous, and the most extravagant reports were circulated of the great wealth of the Duke. I was in the crowd in the Rue du Faubourg Saint Denis, and the people around me were speculating, not upon his yearly income, but upon how much he was in receipt of

---

[1] These were evidently farewell verses addressed to him when leaving school in Paris.

[2] By the writer's youngest sister.

per day, per hour, and per minute. At the other striking
scene I climbed on the pedestal of the great statue at the
entrance to the Tuileries, where I could command a view from
the Arc de l'Étoile down the Champs Elysées, the whole length
of which was filled by squadrons of foot and cavalry marching
in from Neuilly. I think it took them about two hours to
defile by. They were a fine body of men, much stained and
weatherbeaten. The exhibition of fireworks at night was on
a large scale, and very effective.

At the end of two years, during which I had once visited
England, I returned home. My French costume created some
amusement. I wore a long blue swallow-tailed coat with brass
buttons and a tall hat. I found that in the meantime the
family had removed from "The Retreat" to "The Lawn"—
the house No. 8, afterwards occupied by Mr Fawcett. I was
now sent to a school at Norwood. . . . I here received my
first introduction to science—one master giving us occasional
lectures on chemistry, which fascinated me; but my home-work
was confined for a time to chemical experiments.

I was also instructed in history, geography, arithmetic, and
book-keeping. On holidays we played hockey with the masters,
as I had done in Paris. In the autumn we were allowed a day's
run in the wood, which then extended from Norwood to Penge,
to gather blackberries, which afterwards appeared on the table
for three days in the shape of blackberry puddings. I then
made my first and last appearance on the stage in the " Bourgeois
Gentilhomme" of Molière; but though I was a good French
scholar, my performance was not such as to encourage for me a
repetition of it at this annual festival.

At that time Guy Fawkes' Day was religiously kept by all
boys. We were allowed to gather sticks in the woods, and
these, with the aid of a tar-barrel, made a large bonfire, on
which a guy was burnt to the accompaniment of many squibs
and crackers.

I was now sent to Dr Valpy's school at Reading, who considered that my education had been greatly neglected, as I
knew nothing of Greek. Here I went through the usual course
of classics, with a little geography in the shape of a paid
extra. I managed to escape flogging for the two years I was

there, though I was occasionally called upon to hoist better scholars than myself. The doctor was noted for his flogging propensities; but having the authority of my father to run away in case I had to change places in this performance, the thought of it gave me but little anxiety, otherwise the discipline was not strict. In fact, it was too much the contrary—at least on the side where I was boarded.

Dr Valpy was a noted classical scholar, and doubtless found that the boy's education had been sadly desultory. We do not hear of Joseph having taken a good place in the school; his dancing, drawing, and fencing, his Italian and French, could not have helped him much. He was said to be "a quiet, shy boy, but full of energy, and always the leader of his companions." His letters from Reading find him invariably in the same financial position as he found himself when in Paris: when pocket-money was sent it was spent directly in presents for those at home, and always included a gift for his old nurse, thus leaving him penniless. The thorough way in which in one Reading letter the schoolboy makes a financial statement to his father, when he had not the means to pay his debts, and the method by which he shows every side of the case quite dispassionately, either for or against himself, were characteristic of him throughout life. He entered with zest into all the fun among the boys, who used to buy of the day-boarders blackbirds and thrushes, which they roasted and ate with relish. They also made custards in private, and excellently well they made them.

The urgency of the postscript in this Reading letter will provoke a smile :—

READING, *May* 1827.

DEAR FATHER,—I received your letter about three weeks ago, which I intended to have answered the next day had not a cricket-ball knocked off the top of my little finger, which has hindered me from writing till the present moment: it is not well yet, and I have only just begun to write. I am very much obliged to you for the pound you ordered Mr Knight to give me, but which I am ashamed yet forced to own I have spent; for there are an old man and woman that live on the Forbery who sell to us all sorts of things that we want. When you sent me the money I owed them about 15s. I went to pay her directly I got the money, but she said that I must wait till she made my bill. The next day being the fair day, I spent a great part of it in books, but I did not buy any trash, nor go into any shows; with the rest I paid my debts to the boys, and before she had finished my bill (which was a day or two ago) all my money was gone. But why I wish you to send me some now is because yesterday one of the Doctor's sons, a clergyman, went into the shop, and seeing a great many bills lying upon the table, took them up, and perceiving that the boys owed her a great deal, some of them £2 or £3, and others only 6d. or 9d., went to the Doctor and told him of it, who said that he would put all the boys on the obstinate list (when any one is on it, he has to do a long imposition every day, has to say almost all the lesson when his class goes up, generally gets caned if he says a word wrong, and seldom escapes a flogging during the week) till it is paid off, which he does by giving the woman sixpence a-day for those that owe her anything until they are out of her debt, so I should be on the list for a month. So, dear father, it would be the same to you whether you send it me now or had it put down on your bill. Please, if you send the money at all, send it before the end of this week. I was rather surprised when you said I was not to have any parcels; but since it is your desire that I should not have any I will submit to it, though I should prefer having them continued, for though it is a great school, most of the boys don't despise having wine, cakes, fruits, &c., sent them. I have not bathed yet, for I do not think it warm enough. Please to excuse the writing on account of my finger, which I find very awkward still. I hope you, dear mother, sisters, and brother are quite well; and with my love to you and them, I remain, dear father, your dutiful son,   J. PRESTWICH.

N.B.—Please to answer this letter directly, if it is convenient to you. Mr and Mrs Hornbuckle desire their compliments to you.

The autobiography continues :—

On the occasion of the battle of Navarino, where the combined fleets of England, France, and Russia managed to destroy the Turkish fleet, greatly to the advantage of the latter Power and little to the profit of the first two, the boys were given a half holiday, and naturally looked upon the battle as a glorious victory. A great event was a general election, for as elections then lasted three weeks, the boys shared in the excitement by siding with the blues or the yellows, finding it a pleasant break in the monotony of school-life. Boating and bathing we had in plenty in the Thames at Caversham and Pangbourne. Among my contemporaries there was Jackson, afterwards Bishop of London, a studious tall lad, who joined but little in the school games. Reading was then a quiet country town without railways, and with little trade except its breweries; [Huntley and] Palmer and Sutton were still below the horizon.

Leaving school, I was entered at sixteen years of age at University College, London, then recently opened. Having partly my own choice of subjects, I selected Chemistry under Dr Turner, a popular and excellent teacher; English under Mr Dale; Latin, Prof. Key; Greek, Prof. Long; Natural Philosophy under Dr Lardner; and Mathematics, Augustus de Morgan. As I had to walk four miles daily to and from South Lambeth, I found my *curriculum* rather too extended; and as I had little liking for the classics, I fear I neglected them in favour of chemistry and natural philosophy.

Unfortunately I missed the first few mathematical [lectures], and then feeling discouraged in being unable to follow, I ceased to attend, much to my subsequent regret. All my spare time, spare pocket-money, and spare thoughts were spent on chemistry. I also entered the practical class, then under the direction of Robert Warington, a most kind and painstaking teacher. In this subject I passed a good examination and obtained a certificate [with honours, *Ed.*]

At "The Lawn," at the foot of a few steps leading down from the breakfast-room, there was a small dark room, which was our student's laboratory, and known as his "Den." When at home he was usually to be found in it at work amongst his minerals, acids, &c. Here he manufactured the laughing-gas which he administered to his companions (and he had always a following), with occasionally alarming effects; here he blew glass and set himself to make philosophical instruments. The five young sisters hung upon his words, and looked up with admiration at their clever elder brother, sharing in the delight and often in the danger of some of the experiments. Frequently in later years he urged that every boy and girl should be taught at least the elements of chemistry.

In appearance the thin tall stripling, now 5 feet 10 inches in height, resembled his mother's family. He had strongly marked features, a clear fresh complexion, a thick crop of hair which was nearly black, and an unusually fine forehead. But his eyes were the great feature of his face,—luminous hazel eyes which mirrored every emotion, now liquid, yet always with a light in them, or when indignant or angry (and he could be both) flashing fire. Naturally he was quick in temper, and on one occasion when his anger lasted, and when reminded that this was possibly the temper of his ancestor, the old knight-banneret, cropping out, he burst into laughter, and the anger, like a lightning-flash, went as it came. Nothing stirred his indignation so much as when he met what was false, or a sham, or underhand, and then he spoke out his mind. He could not conscientiously join in repeating the Athanasian Creed, so he made no feint of an open prayer-book, but deliberately shut it, whereas when the "Benedicite omnia opera" was sung, no one in the congregation joined with greater fervour. He delighted in that song of praise.

At this period of his short college course he was in the habit of versifying, writing rhymes to his companions, or penning sonnets to his pretty partners at dances,—and he had always many pretty partners, being quite what is termed "a lady's man." Later on we hear of his escorting his sisters and elder cousins, and also daughters of friends, to school in France, a responsibility which rested very agreeably on his shoulders. His poetry consisted chiefly of Odes in blank verse on Nature's varying and changing moods, of which he was the watchful observer. Although never a talkative lad, he was eminently sociable, his father and mother were both hospitable, and in all the exuberance of his young life he enjoyed to a degree the evening parties and gatherings of relatives and friends.

Yet underlying all his delightful buoyancy of spirits there was that intense earnestness—that determination to interpret for himself the records of the rocks. He was preparing for that work, the obstacles to which at one period seemed overwhelming, but to which he was steadfast throughout life, and which held his heart to the very end.

It is evident that while at University College every subject was neglected for the sake of chemistry and natural philosophy. It is evident, too, that he took the direction of his studies into his own hands: Latin and Greek were set aside; mathematics also were neglected, though most unwillingly. On leaving college he worked at mathematics with a private tutor, but never ceased to regret that he had not attended the college course. In the intervals between lectures he frequented the British Museum: he also found time for lessons in oil-painting and lithography from Mr Waterhouse Hawkins. Subsequently the sale of his paintings enabled him to purchase materials and apparatus for experiments.

The economies which he practised during those college days, in order to provide himself with money for the purchase of chemical materials, were carried to excess, and involved no little self-denial. An ample allowance was given to him for dinner in town, but, conscious of his parents' liberality, he never confessed to the family that most frequently dinner consisted of a bun or a roll, or occasionally a sausage-roll. "The Lawn" at South Lambeth was four miles distant from University College, so that daily he had an eight miles' walk, which was lengthened by his making a long round by Doulton's factories, to save the toll on Vauxhall Bridge, which was the direct road. One ingenious device to put him in funds was the sale to his mother of arrowroot made from potatoes at so much per lb., she having presented him with the potatoes! Then there was a great demand for arrowroot in the household, the young sisters petitioning for its daily consumption.

In jottings for 1831 there is an entry of three oil-paintings being given in part payment for a mountain barometer and sextant. The only specimen of his painting which escaped conversion into money is the copy of a small picture by Wouvermann.

The system of working hard day after day on stinted food must have had a bad effect on his health, and it is a question whether it did not tell injuriously on him in after-life. Supper over, whether tired or not, he repeated some experiments to the small

appreciative family audience, which was often increased by one or two old school-fellows, who were
always welcome.

At that time geology was not taught anywhere in London.
The only nominal instruction then in geology and mineralogy was
to be had in three lectures by Dr Turner at the end of his course
of forty lectures on chemistry. Parkinson's ʻOrganic Remains'
in three quarto volumes and his small octavo in one volume
constituted the student's stock-in-trade.[1]

I had a *Conularia* from Coalbrook Dale. It puzzled me, as it
did the Professors of my acquaintance.[2] Chemical analysis led
me to the study of rocks and minerals, so it was on that side that
I approached geology. The variety of paving-stones which I
passed in my daily walks to college caught my attention, and led
me to inquire what they were made of and how made. I used
also to go to the British Museum in Great Russell Street to inspect the organic remains, and pondered especially over the
well-preserved and attractive series of the *Calcaire Grossier*.[3]

The following years my holidays were spent at Broseley in
Shropshire, a market-town celebrated for its tobacco-pipes and
iron- and coal-works. The latter soon attracted my attention,
and I spent hours at the heaps of ironstone, the seam worked
being the Pennystone, so rich in marine remains. My chief
work there was, however, on a subsequent and longer visit.

It is pleasant to find that on one of these journeys to
Broseley he was most kindly and hospitably received by
his grandmother, who, as he reports in a letter to "The
Lawn," "entertained me sumptuously." An anecdote
is told of her, that when on a visit to Mrs Prestwich,

---

[1] Sowerby's ʻMineral Conchology,' then in course of publication, was
beyond the student's reach.

[2] The true relationship of *Conularia* has not yet been established,
although it is regarded as a Pteropod, belonging to an order of pelagic
Mollusca.

[3] A richly fossiliferous series of limestones, &c., equivalent to our
Bracklesham Beds.

her only daughter, to whom she was greatly attached, the young Prestwiches were all away from home. Kate, the second grandchild, happened to arrive one day at "The Lawn" before the departure of her grandmother, whose exclamation, "Snow in harvest," testified to anything but pleasure when she was told of the home-coming of the young girl. Doubtless Mrs Blakeway felt disappointed at the interruption to the quiet of her visit, and at the distraction that a child in the house must cause to the mother. On her visits to "The Lawn," Mrs Blakeway's custom had been to give a present in money to each of her Prestwich grand-children; but to Joseph, the eldest, when a boy, she only gave half of what she bestowed on his sisters, saying she knew "that his money would be all spent directly"!

Yet although she would have nothing to say to chil-dren, this very original old lady had keen pleasure in the society of her grandson when he was no longer a child. His name must have been made widely known throughout the Broseley district by the miners. His youth, his enthusiasm in descending and working among their coal-pits, and his characteristic courtesy to all with whom he came in contact, must have won their hearts.

His grandmother often declared that she intended to live as long as her husband, who died in his ninety-third year, and she actually attained that age.

CHAPTER II.

1830–1834.

CITY AND HOME LIFE—ZETETICAL SOCIETY—VISITS TO SHROPSHIRE—NATURAL HISTORY SOCIETY.

WHEN Joseph Prestwich entered upon his City career, which was to last over forty years, he was about eighteen years of age. It was not the career he would have chosen, it was not congenial, but circumstances were such that it was his duty to adopt it, and therefore he applied himself to business with all the conscientiousness and earnestness of his nature. Perhaps there are few endowed as he was, who would have had the moral courage to resist the fascinations of science. At the outset he planned out his life and resolved that there should be no interruption to his geological work. The hours at his own disposal he allotted, as before, to the identification of fossils and to the analysis of minerals. Time for that work, and for practical chemistry as well as for his mathematics and reading, had to be found in the early morning before breakfast and after his return from the City at six or seven in the evening, when each hour had its appointed subject. By this method he was able to accomplish much; yet one is at a loss to understand how he found leisure also for painting and for his very successful lithography. As will be seen by the table on page 28, he gave a stated time to read with his sisters, who were respectively fourteen, fifteen, and nearly seventeen years of age.

This unobtrusive little table is strongly significant. It was planned by no promptings from without. The youth seemed to have had an intuitive consciousness that there was something for him to do, that he himself might aspire to demonstrate some truth in God's nature, and henceforward every hour he could call his own was set apart to train and gird himself for the task. He had an uplifting purpose in life from which he never swerved, and hindrances seemed to be stimulants instead of deterrents. Yet with all this stern and persistent devotion to close study, no one more enjoyed with gladness of heart the Christmas dances and family parties. There was constant and affectionate intercourse between the Prestwiches and their young cousins, the children of Mr John Blakeway. One of that large family of ten cousins was Mrs Rouquette, with whom there was close intimacy throughout life; another is Mrs Mushet; and one is Mrs G. Murray Smith, wife of the publisher. Young Prestwich had a passion for waltzing, an exercise which suited his active temperament, and as quadrille-parties were also then in fashion, there were frequent opportunities for this welcome relaxation from incessant desk and head work. Music was always a great pleasure to him: the only instrument, however, that he played was the flute.

Eventually he found that there was time for little else but geology. Saturdays and Sundays came to be regarded as his own, when he went out to observe and learn, and when the foundation was laid of his

	Rise at a quarter to 6.	6 to 7.	7 to town time.	7 to ten at a quarter past 8.	Half-past 8 to 10.	10 to 11—bedtime.
MONDAY .	.	Arranging my cabinet.	Attend to mathematics.	German.	Works on natural philosophy.	Miscellaneous reading.
TUESDAY .	.	Chemistry.	Give one hour and a half to Kate and Lal, then miscellaneous reading.	Chemistry.	Read mathematics with Bella.	Do.
WEDNESDAY	.	Miscellaneous experiments.	Attend to mathematics.	Geology.	History.	History.
THURSDAY	.	German.	Chemistry.	Chemistry.	Chemistry.	Miscellaneous reading.
FRIDAY	.	Label, trim, and arrange my fossils and minerals.	Give one hour and a half to Kate and Lal, then to miscellaneous reading.	Natural philosophy.	Read geometry with Bella.	History.
SATURDAY .	.	Miscellaneous experiments.	Attend to mathematics.	German.	Miscellaneous reading.	Natural history.
SUNDAY .	.	Rise at 7; then read Paley's 'Natural Theology,' Milton's works, Bible, &c., until church-time.		To Nature's God through Nature's works.		

knowledge of the geological structure of the London basin. Dr G. Owen Rees,[1] his friend from boyhood, was a frequent companion in these Saturday and Sunday walks, when he often laughingly declared that Joseph always starved him. The same complaint was made in after years by one or two other friends, who grumbled at the hard and scant fare, yet who were always eager to accompany him. One in especial was Edward I'Anson,[2] the eminent architect, whose wife was Catherine, the second daughter of Mr John Blakeway, the uncle of our geologist. They had been brought up together as children—nay, as infants (having been near neighbours), and throughout life they remained the same attached friends. When veterans with a long retrospect of years, it was touching to hear them address each other as "Edward" and "Joseph," which they did to the last. Rees told humorous anecdotes of their geological adventures. Once, late on a Saturday night, the two young men arrived at a village inn not far from Prestwich's future home, and asked for quarters. Dusty and worn, and in clothing not improved from visits to pits, and one of them probably with a rough bag of fossils and sundry specimens of clay or gravel slung over his shoulders, they were looked upon as suspicious characters, and refused admittance; so they had nothing for it but to trudge on several miles in the dark to a more hospitable house, which was not reached until midnight.

When the family in 1830 were at Boulogne for the holidays, we hear that Joseph took his brother Edward, a boy of ten, to inspect certain quarries which were

---

[1] G. Owen Rees, M.D.; born in 1813, died 1889.

[2] Edward I'Anson, F.G.S., President of the Royal Institute of British Architects; born in 1812, died in 1888.

fifteen miles distant.   An account-book for that year is
chiefly a list of small disbursements for fossils and many
varieties of minerals, showing the strong bent of his
mind.

A large scrap-book of printed geological sections, and
quaint, crude views of coal-mines, volcanoes, basaltic
rocks, minerals, skeletons of Plesiosaurus, &c., and with
descriptive letterpress, is very interesting.   In its pages
are occasional verses, entirely geological, gleaned chiefly
from 'An Old Fragment.'   A quotation from Milton is
given in the first page :—

> " He the world
> Built on circumfluous waters calm, in wide
> Crystalline ocean."

This scrap-book also contained a coloured map and
sections of the Boulogne district, which were evidently
drawn during the summer sojourn of the Prestwich
family there, as they bear the inscription in his handwriting : " Carte et Profils géognostiques du Bassin du
Bas Boulonnais, par M. Rozet, J. Prestwich fecit.   July
1830."   He was then eighteen years of age.

The last portion of the autobiography touches upon
another favourite holiday resort :—

I soon had the opportunity of studying the subject in the field,
my holidays being [again] spent at Broseley in the Coalbrook Dale
Coalfield, where Pennystone iron-ore was [still] largely worked,
and where I revelled day after day.   I was shown by Mr John
Anstie his fine collections from the Madeley pits, and he kindly
gave me every facility to study or make use of his specimens.
They had already attracted the attention of Dr Buckland, who, I
was told, coming one day to see the collection with bag and much
mudded, went to the back door and experienced some difficulty
from the servants in getting admitted.   I also descended a large
number of the pits to see the underground structure of the fossil
plants *in situ.*

His father naturally did not like those descents into coal-pits, and in a letter (when the young Joseph had gone to Broseley, accompanied by the son of their friend Mr Newton) writes : " Mr Newton, senior, has nothing to communicate. On my part I have to request that you would not allow his son to go into a coal-pit. I do not like the exploit for yourself, and as you have already descended into them you will not be accused of a superficial knowledge of your subject if you make your further researches by deputy."

But Joseph Prestwich's work was never done by deputy.

For a small remuneration (for then the wages of the working miners were only 2s. for a long day), I enlisted the services of several working men. The overlookers were also generally very willing to assist, so I returned night after night with my bag full. The pits were not large, nor were they very deep. From 150 to 500 feet was the general run. Descending them, however, was often a rough task. Sometimes we descended on trays; at other times we stood on the platform; a chain loop attached to the main rope was handed to each man, through which we placed one leg. At a given signal the rope was drawn up a few feet, when we all (generally there were seven or eight men) swung together like so many herrings at the end of a bunch, and then holding on to one another we were let down to the bottom. Sometimes the descent was in an up shaft which would be full of smoke and like descending a chimney. However, I considered myself well rewarded by the sight of the strata and especially the faults, nor did I overlook the surface. The one-inch ordnance map of the district was just then published, the cost being 16s. a-sheet. On this I laid down the surface geology, and with the aid of the pit sections, which were ever here readily given to me with permission to copy, I drew up my Memoir on Coalbrook Dale, which, later on, was published in the 'Transactions of the Geological Society.' Sir Roderick Murchison, who was working in

the adjacent Silurian district, kindly gave me the benefit of
his advice respecting the latter, and led me to make a considerable collection of Wenlock fossils. My kind friends the
Pritchards of Broseley also placed a room at my disposal, which
I soon filled.

Lindley [1] was then bringing out his 'Fossil Flora of Great
Britain,' and I was able to furnish him with several new species,
and to profit by his suggestions. I had now made the acquaintance of my lifelong friend, [Professor] John Morris,[2] who undertook to describe and figure the plants for my Memoir, while the
shells were taken in hand by Mr Sowerby. It was some time,
however, before the paper appeared in the Transactions. My
works of reference were Artis's 'Phytology,' and Lindley and
Hutton's 'Fossil Flora,' then in course of publication.

Thus the results of his work among the Shropshire
coal-pits under and above ground, and on the adjacent
country, were embodied in a memoir read before the
Geological Society. The first part, "On Some of the
Faults which affect the Coal-field of Coalbrookdale,"
was read in February 1834; while the second and
principal part, on "The Geology of Coalbrookdale," was
read on two successive meetings of the Society, in
April 1836. Although not published in the 'Transactions of the Geological Society' until 1838, the memoir
was in great part written when the author had just
completed his twentieth year. His friend Sir John
Evans, with whom he was on terms of brotherly
affection until the end of life, with whom indeed he
shared every joy and sorrow, remarks of this paper in
an obituary notice to the Royal Society, "It at once
established his reputation as a geologist, and it has
ever since been numbered among our British classics."

[1] Dr John Lindley, Professor of Botany in University College, London;
born 1799, died 1865.

[2] John Morris, F.G.S., Professor of Geology in University College, London; born 1810, died 1886.

Photo by C. Essenhigh Corke, Sevenoaks.

Professor JOHN MORRIS.

CALIFORNIA

Another friend,[1] the writer of a biographical notice, remarks :—

Looking at it now, it may be regarded as a model of what a memoir should be on such a subject as the coalfield and its associated strata. The Silurian and Carboniferous rocks, the New Red Sandstone, the Igneous rocks and the drifts, were all duly described, and, what is more remarkable, considering the youth of the author, the superficial extent of the various rocks was shown on a map of the scale of one inch to a mile, in a manner differing in no very important particulars from the subsequently published map of the Geological Survey. . . . So highly indeed would we speak of this work, that had the author done nothing subsequently, we believe it would have entitled him to a permanent place on the roll of those geologists who have rendered distinguished service.

In a diary which he kept for the first few months of 1832, while practically a City clerk, we are startled to find how often his midday meal was sacrificed in order to provide money for the purchase of philosophical instruments and materials for chemical experiments. This practice had become a regular system. In the first week of January there are four days on which the entry occurs " dined on biscuits." On the 19th we find his dinner consisted of " oranges and biscuits." His usual routine appears to have been at least two hours' work before breakfast, and on his way into the City he seldom missed calling at " Smith's," a shop where he purchased, or had made, much of his chemical and other apparatus. A few extracts from this diary, touching only on his geological and chemical work, will give some idea of its scope.

Jan. 5.— . . . Bought a lot of tubes, bottles, &c. Usual routine of business. Called at Smith's for some apparatus to explain

---

[1] Mr H. B. Woodward, F.R.S., 'Natural Science' for August 1896, p. 90.

C

the laws of the radiation of heat. Found E. T. and E. G. at home; the latter favoured us with several songs. Remained some time in my laboratory to prepare some apparatus; afterwards I played two games at draughts, &c. . . .

6.— . . . Called at York Street to order an air-pump and sextant, the former second-hand. . . .

15.— . . . Arranged my blow-pipe. Went to church. Uncle John called, . . . likewise J. Noble. I made two differential thermometers and several other [things] before dinner. After dinner we had reading and singing, *both of which I avoided.* I shirked to bed at ½-past 10.

21.— . . . I wrote some verses, No. 6, for Maria or Louisa—neither would accept them. Spent the evening in my rooms; filled the eudiometer with oxygen, and made several jars of hydrogen, and likewise an eudiometer,[1] &c.

22.—Made a siphon during the evening (had seen Dr Mitchell's[2] fossils in the morning).

23.—Went to an "at home" at Miss Gordon's [school]. . . . After supper I prepared a few jars of oxygen and hydrogen, with which I gave a lecture on the principal characteristics; and likewise a few striking examples of chemical affinity. The experiments went off well, and I believe pleased.

26.—Called on E. Evans, giving him two small bell-jars of my making. E. lent me his galvanic trough. . . . I remained until 12, making an eudiometer, differential thermometer, &c.

29.— . . . After dinner I made some laughing-gas at T. W.'s earnest solicitation. It made me very obstreperous, but had little effect upon Tom or Edward.

31.— . . . Made a gold-leaf electroscope.

Feb. 1.—I spent the evening in my rooms. . . . Burnt my fingers badly. _____

[1] An instrument for the volumetric measurement of gases.

[2] James Mitchell, LL.D., F.G.S.; born 1785, died in 1844. A zealous worker on the geology of the London area, and an early friend of Prestwich's. Mitchell's observations on the strata and wells around London were carefully recorded in five MS. folio volumes, and these were deposited by Prestwich, in 1889, in the library of the Geological Society of London. There is no doubt that Prestwich owed much to the help and encouragement of Mitchell, as acknowledged by him, Quart. Journ. Geol. Soc., vol. x. p. 141.

3.— . . . Called on Carey. Goniometer not yet finished. Went to the Geological Society to see the museum ; introduced myself to Mr Denis, who politely offered to show it to me at any other time, but Mr Lonsdale and some other gentlemen were then upstairs; he likewise invited me to the general meetings.

*7.—*Took my eudiometer to have it graduated ; blew glass. . . .

18.— . . . I gave a lecture (of one hour) on electricity to my father, sisters, &c. ; succeeded pretty well ; got on as far as the development of the two theories—audience well pleased.

20.— . . . At $\frac{1}{4}$-past 9 gave a lecture on electricity (1$\frac{3}{4}$ hour)—went on as far as the laws of distribution—managed very well.

*21.—*Down at $\frac{1}{4}$-past 8. Read. Mr Brooke brought me Biot's 'Géométrie Analytique.' . . . Went to Oeller and Green's to have an electrical flask blown ; saw it made myself.

23.— . . . Got home at $\frac{1}{2}$-past 6 ; gave them a lecture on electricity one hour long—rather tired.

March 4.— . . . Excursion from Gravesend to Northfleet ; went round to all the cottages ; bought all the fossils we [E. I'Anson and I] saw.

*13.—*Down at $\frac{1}{2}$-past 7. Read mathematics. Went to the lecture on chemistry at the London University ; asked Dr Turner to take me to the Geological Society, which he promised to do. . . .

14.— . . . Read mathematics. . . . At $\frac{1}{2}$-past 8 went to the Geological Society ; heard a very animated and interesting discussion on the Oolitic formations [paper read by Murchison on the Cotteswold and Cleveland Hills]. Messrs Murchison, Conybeare, Sedgwick, De la Beche, Lyell, Greenough spoke ; asked Dr Turner to propose me as a member.

*20.—*Down at $\frac{1}{2}$-past 8. Read ; cleaned some chalk fossils. . . . Walked home. E. Newton was there. Made some laughing-gas— E. I'Anson, Edward, and myself. Nearly threw E. I'A. into convulsions—all of us much frightened ; had little effect on E., very little on me and my sisters ; E. I'A. and E. Newton ran away when I took it. Read, and retired at $\frac{1}{2}$-past 11.

21.— . . . E. I'Anson studied with me at the goniometer.

22.— . . . Called at the Geological Society; saw young Denis.[1] He offered to propose me as member. Copied a section of Murchison's. Bought 10d. worth of plaster of Paris. Took casts of my sisters and E. I'Anson. Stuck to Emily's eyelashes—$\frac{1}{2}$ an hour coming off; read; retired at $\frac{1}{4}$ to 12.

23.— . . . Read. Wrote part of my ' Geology of Shropshire.'

28.—Down at $\frac{1}{4}$ to 7. . . . Bought some objects for the microscope. . . . My father came; went with him to see the doublesighted Scotch child—very well managed and ingenious, surprised both of us. . . . At $\frac{1}{4}$-past 8 went to the Geological Society, where I spent a very pleasant evening; left at $\frac{1}{4}$-past 11; home after 12.

29.— . . . Found G. Grant at The Lawn. Spoilt my evening; very weary; played at *écarté* with G. G.; read; retired at 11.

April 4.— . . . Went to Pastourelli's, where I bought a siphon-gauge, &c., for 2s. 6d.; bought a map of England for 3d. . . .

5.— . . . No breakfast. Read all day magazines, reviews, &c. . . . Read, microscopised. . . .

6.— . . . Down at 10. Read as before; blew more glass. Read until 11; got through a great deal.

7.—Much better; down at $\frac{1}{4}$ to 9. Went to an auction of a medical man in Conduit Street, where I bought a fine galvanic trough for 16s., then left for fear of spending more.

9.—Down at $8\frac{1}{4}$; read. . . . T. Turner called; walked with him nearly an hour to the Seven Dials, where I had an electrometer made. Home at 7; tired. Intended to lecture on electricity. G. Grant came—played at *écarté.*

11.—Down at 8. Read. Went to Mark Lane, then to Dr Mitchell's, who had received the fossils from Norwich, of which he gave me a large portion, and also some lias specimens. . . . Intended to lecture on electricity, but E. I'A[nson] came; spent a pleasant evening with him; . . . retired at $11\frac{1}{4}$.

14.—Down at $8\frac{1}{4}$; read. Wrote a letter to Mr Anstie and an-

---

[1] The only Fellow of the Geological Society of the name at this period was Nicholas Dennys, of 4 Cambridge Terrace, Regent's Park.

other to Mr Rose,[1] to each of whom I sent about 50 or 60 chalk fossils. My father came: he told me that Meredith had sent me some fossils from Lyme Regis. . . .

With the practice of rigid, and to us painful, economies, it must not be thought that young Prestwich was parsimonious or illiberal. His nature was the very reverse: he was generous to a fault; and although throughout life it was a principle with him to exercise strict economy in his own personal expenditure, we believe it was carried out to enable him to spend more upon others. Deeds of unselfish kindness, involving on his part no little self-denial—perhaps known only to the writer—cannot be spoken of; to do so would be a violation of his wishes. In later years we come upon a touching letter from one who was a stranger, saying that he had the undying gratitude of a family for his generosity in saving one member of it from disgrace which would have overwhelmed one and all. The circumstances were made known to Joseph Prestwich, and although a stranger, and his income at the time circumscribed, he at once came forward with a sum of money which the family was unable to provide, and which he gave unreservedly. Acts such as these were unknown to the world.

An example of young Prestwich's patient industry is shown in a quarto volume of MS. in his handwriting, giving copies of geological papers and their accompanying illustrations from the 'Transactions of the Geological Society,' the 'Magazine of Natural History,' the 'Annals of Philosophy,' and the 'Edinburgh New Philosophical Journal.' He was thus enabled to study memoirs by Englefield, Sedgwick, Buckland, Webster, &c., whose writings he could not then afford to pur-

[1] C. B. Rose, F.R.C.S., F.G.S., of Swaffham; born 1790, died 1872.

chase.   In the same volume are copious extracts from
Dufrénoy and Elie de Beaumont, Cuvier, Galeotti, &c.

In 1833 Prestwich established an association for
mutual aid and self-improvement named the " Zetetical
Society "[1] among young men of his own age, and all of
whom were his personal friends, one of their number
being [Dr] G. Owen Rees.   The rules were set forth in
a small pamphlet.

According to Rule II., " The object of this Society
shall be the cultivation of scientific and literary knowledge, by placing at the disposal of the members a
library, museum, and apparatus; and its proceedings
shall consist of lectures, essays, and discussions upon
all subjects save those of a theological nature."   Each
member had in turn to give a lecture, or propose a
subject for discussion, under the penalty of a fine.   The
society started with fifteen members; the weekly meetings were held first at "The Lawn," and afterwards
alternately at the homes of some of the other members,
until, owing to their increased numbers, rooms and a
small laboratory were taken for the Society in Surrey
Street, Strand.   The list of chemical apparatus lent by
its president for the use of the members was very comprehensive, comprising a small French furnace, blow-
pipe, retorts, &c., and all sorts of chemical appliances
—in short it was a complete laboratory equipment.   It
included a good microscope and a cabinet of minerals.
On looking over the list sent to him by the hon. secretary, of some seventy items, one cannot forget the
effort, the self-denial, and the care that had brought
each piece of that laboratory equipment together.

The Zetetical Society flourished for only a few years.
Joseph Prestwich soon found that his position in the

---

[1] The term "Zetetical" implies the *direct search* after knowledge.

City compelled frequent absence from London for
several weeks, and sometimes months at a time, as in
the case of Epernay, where he remained one winter.
The other members of the Society were likewise
summoned away one by one to their professional or
business avocations, and the Zetetical Society, after
its brief term of useful and improving work, was
broken up.

Its members formed an interesting group. All were
steady, earnest young men entering upon life — all
animated by the same spirit — all eager for self-
improvement. Not one, alas! survives to tell the
tale, but old letters which come to light reveal that
their affection for their young leader was life-long, and
did not cease with the breaking up of the Society.

There is no doubt but that Joseph Prestwich was a
remarkable man, endowed with remarkable gifts. But
for that extreme diffidence, that constitutional shyness
which he had inherited from his mother, and which
prevented him from ever possessing the confidence in
his own powers necessary for every public man, he
might have come much more prominently to the front.
Although always and everywhere very popular, that
distrust in himself interfered with his career as a
public man and a speaker. This lack of self-assertion,
however, did not lessen the number of his personal
friends, for no one ever possessed a greater gift of
attracting and winning the regard, and retaining the
attachment, of those he valued and who knew him
intimately. They found in him a kindliness, or rather
a brotherliness, peculiar to himself. To comparative
strangers he appeared reserved. As Prestwich's old
friend Mr S. R. Pattison justly remarked, "He was
free from assumption of any kind, and always began

talking on a subject with great simplicity and humility."
Perhaps the most prominent feature in his character
throughout life was his truthfulness and love of truth.
He had also a strong sense of justice. He abhorred
"the falsity of exaggeration," and although no student
was ever more fired by enthusiasm for his subject, even
when a youth his words expressed the exact sense,
justly and carefully weighed. This habit of severe
accuracy has assisted in no small measure to give to
his writings the high place which has been assigned
to them.

It was in 1833, the year of his coming of age,
that Joseph Prestwich's wish was fulfilled, and he
was elected, while Greenough was President, a Fellow
of the Geological Society of London, a fellowship that
was to last for sixty-three years.

At this date also he attained a more responsible
business position, and began to travel for his father's
firm, as we find letters addressed to him at Falmouth,
Worcester, and other towns, &c. These journeys to
all parts of the country, and often abroad, were full
of interest, and were prosecuted during a large portion
of his life, contributing in a great measure to his wide
and rapid acquisition of geological knowledge. From
his accustomed seat on the top of the coach he was
able, like William Smith in earlier days, to scan the
landscape on every side, and his trained quick eye,
like that of the "father of English geology," enabled
him at a glance to grasp the physical features of a
new district. He thoroughly enjoyed this healthy
out-door life, and the traversing of ground so often
new.

Yet there is another aspect to these journeys, and
a very pathetic one. They were very solitary; he was

thrown upon himself, as, although always courteous to his fellow-travellers, there were none who sympathised with his tastes and with that ardent desire for knowledge—none with whom he could hold scientific converse. After dinner at a small table his note-books were opened, and the evening was spent in registering the work of the day, and in entering any fresh geological facts, and in drawing sections. His nature was eminently genial, and as years sped on this lack of companionship pressed hard upon him. He had never been talkative, and this isolated mode of life made him more silent and more self-contained, whilst at the same time he pined for fellowship. He rarely complained, yet again and again during long absences he wrote to some member of the family, reiterating that he kept counting the days until he should again join "the dear home circle," or be back in his "dear home."

His geology had become all-absorbing, and had grown to be the passion of his life; yet if on those long country tours there had been one sympathetic soul to whom in the evenings spent in the "commercial room" he could have communicated new points made out, new lights thrown on some hitherto obscure relation of the geological strata, his pleasure would have been intensified tenfold. He was realising the truth so graphically expressed by the veteran geologist, the Rev. Adam Sedgwick, for whom he entertained the warmest admiration and regard, that "pleasures would be withered things if we could not impart them, and our joys would be but lamplight in a dungeon if there were no friend to rejoice with us."

In a charming letter written in French to "mon cher ami," one of his old Paris schoolfellows at M. Colin's, Joseph Prestwich repeats that never had he

been so happy in any school, and that he had often
wished to return to Paris. He confides to this friend
that although engaged in commerce he aspires to be
a geologist, and mentions a business tour in Devon
and Cornwall.

Cornwall, qui est célèbre pour ses mines de cuivre et d'étain,
offre des attractions bien grandes pour le géologue et le minéral-
ogiste, et je me place dans les rangs comme un humble étudiant.
Que mes vues sont changées depuis que je t'ai vu! j'étais content d'étudier ma vocabulaire latine et de construire des thèmes;
à présent je voudrais tout savoir — tout voir — tout analyser.
C'est dire beaucoup—tels sont mes désirs. Oh, si j'avais le temps
à lire et à étudier tout ce que je voudrais!

No words could more fitly express his fervent aspira-
tions.

It was in all probability about this date that young
Prestwich projected a plan for a Natural History
Society, the object of which was thoroughly to work
out the geology, botany, &c., of the London Basin by
the personal observations of its members. We do not
hear of the formal establishment of this Society; but as
its members were self-elected, consisting of those who
could contribute to the knowledge of the natural history
of the country round London, and as in its beginning
there was no subscription, it is possible that there may
have been many meetings at the London Coffee-House
in St Paul's Churchyard, where the members were to
assemble until they could afford the expenses of a fixed
establishment. The scope of this "Natural-Historical
Society of the Neighbourhood of London" is somewhat
ambitious, and is given in his own handwriting. Norfolk and Suffolk were not included, but the boundary
line of the country to be examined was to extend from
Harwich westward along the northern extremity of

Essex, whence it would range " in a south-west direction
by Henley-on-Thames to near Hungerford, when, turn-
ing abruptly eastward, it bends by Guildford, Croydon,
and thence in an irregular line near Chatham and
Canterbury to the South Foreland. The reason for
adopting so large and irregular a district is that the
zoological and botanical distributions are materially
influenced by geological superposition, and that the
development of the latter would be extremely incomplete were the limits more restricted."

The following extract is from a letter to an old Reading schoolfellow, Mr Edward Hurry, at Bogota :—

J. Prestwich to E. Hurry.

BIRMINGHAM, *Oct.* 1834.

MY DEAR EDWARD,— . . . I must again return you my best
thanks for your kind endeavours to procure for me such minerals
and fossils as you may meet with. The district in which you are
now situated affords few or none of these, but the sea, I should
think, would abound with a great variety of corals, shells, sea-
weeds, &c.—specimens of all of which would be highly acceptable. That which to you appears trifling and valueless from
the circumstance of its being commonplace and abundant would
be of much interest here. No object of natural history will come
amiss.

The letter is a long one, giving news of Dr Valpy,
and reminiscences of schoolboy days at Reading.

Mr E. Hurry in reply deplored his lack of knowledge
of geology and mineralogy, and besought his old schoolfellow to put him in the way of acquiring it, adding
that he had sent to England for a book on the subject
for study. We find ten pages of large letter-paper—
a closely written document without date, beginning
" My dear Edward," which was the draft of a letter
of instruction sent to Mr Hurry at Carthagena. After

a warning that he must not expect to be able to read the difficult facts in geology until the alphabet had been mastered, he advises young Hurry to select one particular subject on which to exercise his observation, and suggests that he should study, for example, the action of water, not in reference to its chemical properties nor its stagnant state, but its powerful mechanical action when in a state of motion. We quote the sequel, as it may be a help and encouragement to some earnest young geologist :—

We are all endowed with reason and observation, of which it is your duty to avail yourself to the utmost extent. Geology is entirely a science of observation and comprehension; accustom yourself on all occasions to employ those talents—notice the effects of all you witness, study their causes, and you cannot fail to become a good geologist. And what can afford more delight than the free use of that reason wherewith nature has endowed us all! What infinite pleasure results from witnessing the powers and exercising the capabilities of your own mind! And above all with what ecstasy, with what gratification, with what feelings of admiration, of gratitude, and of enthusiasm, do you trace out the mighty works of the Deity, do you fathom their mysteries and unravel their intricacies! You read what must have been His thoughts, His ideas, His intentions, when you thus perceive the results of His wisdom and His power, for in everything will you find intent and purpose. When thus surrounded by and studying His works, how can you fail to look

"Thro' Nature up to Nature's God"?

This was the letter of a mere youth. Its influence on his friend in the land of exile can never be known.

CHAPTER III.

1834–1849.

GEOLOGY OF COALBROOK DALE AND GAMRIE—
TERTIARY MEMOIRS.

THE early part of 1834 was spent in Ireland, and the later spring months in Scotland. The result of the northern journey was a paper read in 1835 before the Geological Society, " On the Ichthyolites of Gamrie in Banffshire," which, though written subsequently to the Coalbrook Dale Memoir, was yet his first published work, as it appeared in an abridged form in 1835. This paper was supplemented by another in 1837, in which was first noticed the occurrence of shells in the Till at high levels and separate from raised beaches. The two papers were published in full in 1840.

We are unable to ascertain to whom the following letter was addressed. It is quoted merely to show the care which the young geologist evinced in replying to any inquiry :—

LYNN, *14th June* 1835.

MY DEAR SIR,—I have to apologise for not making this communication at an earlier date. I had expected that I should have been enabled to have done so upon my return to London last April, but I found my notes upon the subject so scanty, and my sketch of the specimen so imperfect, that I waited until another trip to Shropshire would enable me to afford you more minute details.

The fossil in question was found in a vertical position in a fine-grained sandstone, associated with numerous plants, principally of the genera *Calamites* and *Stigmaria*, lying in all positions. The stem was truncated about eighteen inches above the roots, which, to the number of four, were prolonged from it to a length of about four feet; but as the seams of the sandstone were continued through these roots, the lower parts of them were separated and lost upon the removal of the specimen, which, at the time that I saw it, had been so acted upon by the weather that the external marking was nearly obliterated.

This sandstone bed overlies a thick deposit of shale containing ironstone, and characterised by numerous exuviæ which are totally wanting in the sandstone. In this latter, in common with several other beds of sandstone, the larger fossils are generally in a vertical position, traversing several divisions of the rock, whereas the lesser specimens lie in all positions, but most frequently horizontally, and in the seams of the beds. . . . Trusting that this slight communication may be yet of some service, I remain, my dear sir, yours sincerely,

J. PRESTWICH, Junr.

As a worker not altogether unknown, for the value of his Coalbrook Dale paper (although not yet published) had been at once recognised, he was present at the meeting of the British Association in Dublin in 1835. In the same year he again made a lengthened tour in Scotland, when an extract from a letter posted at Inverness gives an account of a visit to Edinburgh :—

J. Prestwich to C. Prestwich.

MY DEAREST KATE,— . . . Now I must take you back again to Edinburgh, where I was detained much longer than was agreeable. However, some letters of introduction, with

which Mr Hutton of Newcastle [1] kindly furnished me, were
the means of making me acquainted with several pleasant and
celebrated men. Among others I had the honour of forming
Professor Jameson's acquaintance,[2] of which I hope to be able
to avail myself more upon a future visit. This time I merely
had the opportunity of spending a short half-hour with him, as
I wished to be in Edinburgh at eleven, and the doctor resides
about two miles from town. He received me very politely,
presented me with a few specimens, and expressed a hope that
I would visit him when again in Edinburgh. An interview
with Dr Robson, secretary to the R. S., enabled me to inspect
their collection of Burdiehouse [Carboniferous fossils] at their
rooms. A Mr Rhind was going to introduce me to Lord
Greenock, but he happened to be out of town. He is a great
coal-measure and ironstone geologist. I am anxious to compare
notes with him. The great analogy presented by the organic
remains of the limestone at Burdiehouse with those of the coal-
field of Shropshire made me very desirous to visit the spot,
which is distant five miles from Edinburgh. In order to find
time I walked out there with a Mr Charlton at six o'clock one
morning, arrived there before eight, and was much gratified with
the deposit and its elegant flora, still could see no proof of its
deposition in fresh and shallow water according to Dr Hibbert's
hypothesis. Many of our present geologists are too fond of
tossing up and down a few hundred square miles of country, as
though it were a carpet they were dusting: this terrestrial [crust]
is formed of no such pliable material.[3]

J. Prestwich to the Same.   CARLISLE, 14th Nov. 1835.

MY DEAREST KATE,—It is to me a source of infinite gratification to have once more crossed the Border, with a prospect of

---

[1] Joint author with Dr John Lindley of 'The Fossil Flora of Great
Britain.'

[2] Robert Jameson, Regius Professor of Natural History in the University of Edinburgh ; born 1774, died 1854

[3] The evidence of intermittent subsidence is, of course, admitted (see
Prestwich, 'Geology,' vol. ii. p. 3) ; the fresh- and shallow-water formation
of the Burdiehouse limestone is not now questioned.

a speedy return to our dear and happy home. You can scarcely, dear Kate, appreciate all the attractions of that delightful spot. Many and many an event which from its daily and habitual occurrence passed unnoticed in the pleasurable *mêlée* is now, by contrast with similar scenes, but scenes differently enacted, and with associations totally at variance, brought to my recollection with the most vivid freshness and delight. Still, Kate, not only are past events productive of much pleasure, but so also are those proceedings which are hourly and constantly taking place in my absence, and with a brief detail of which I had hoped to have been favoured rather more frequently than I have been latterly. . . . I shall fully expect to hear from you at Liverpool. . . . With best love to all, believe me, your very affectionate brother,   J. PRESTWICH, Jr.

Another paper on the Banffshire coast was written after his second long tour in Scotland, and was entitled " On some recent Elevations of the Coast of Banffshire, and on a Deposit of Clay formerly considered to be Lias." It was read at the Geological Society in 1837, and published in full in 1838.

A memoir in French, which likewise was written at an earlier date, was read in the 1837-38 Session of the Société Géologique de France, " Sur les débris de Mammifères terrestres, qui se trouvent dans l'argile plastique aux environs d'Epernay." This paper was long remembered in Paris as having given rise to an important discussion, in which Constant Prévost, Deshayes, Rivière, and others took part.

A letter to his sister Kate expresses his happiness to find himself again in his beloved France.

RENNES, *July* 1836, *Friday Evening*, 10.

At last, my dearest Kate, I am again in France : that long-anticipated visit is now performed, and I enjoy it most intensely. I like the country, the people, the living, and in fact I am inclined to be displeased with nothing. I only fear that I shall be satiated with the continuance of enjoyment. Every moment has its pleasure — some new scene is unfolded — some fresh variation in costume or in manners is exhibited, or another town is to be explored. But the very excess of my curiosity carries with it a drawback which, though trifling on any other occasion, is, at the present time, rather tantalising. I feel dissatisfied if everybody else does not exhibit the same enthusiasm and the same earnestness in viewing and exploring the country.

I could and would willingly at any time go without my dinner rather than not see all that may be worth examining in a town when we remain but two or three hours—and of course, in order to make the most of so short a time, it would be necessary to use some activity and despatch, or I have no objection to rise at four in the morning for the same object. . . .

In another letter to this sister, dated from Broseley, September 1836, he alludes to the meeting of the British Association at Bristol, and to its very hospitable reception there. " All the head men of the Association were received at private houses ; the lesser men were of course obliged to be content with the rascally Bristol inns. I was very well pleased to meet with Rees on Monday morning, more especially as I always feel myself rather solitary in so large an assembly where I am intimate with no one."

In a rejoinder to the above letter, we quote a passage to show the estimation in which his " den " was held by one member of " The Lawn " household :—

C. Prestwich to J. Prestwich.   Tʜᴇ Lᴀᴡɴ, *Sept.* 23, 1836.

. . . We have an Irish housemaid ; she is very ignorant and a Catholic—nothing will induce her to go into your little back room ; she does not much like arranging the breakfast room. She has taken into her head that you dissect dead bodies, and that the shark's jaw is what you take them up with. I should have told you that nurse took her to the door one day, when she saw all these things. She crossed herself, and was very glad to get away. It is said that the housemaid never passed the door without crossing herself. . . .

One of his earliest (Tertiary) geological expeditions was made from Norwich in 1836, where, under the guidance of Mr Samuel Woodward, the geologist and antiquary, he paid his first visit to the Thorpe Crag pits, and there obtained a fine molar of *Elephas meridionalis*, now in the Norwich Museum.

What with geology and what with business, 1836 was indeed a busy year : but could any year of his life be pointed to which was not busy ?

J. Prestwich to his Sister, Mrs Russell Scott.

LIVERPOOL, *Nov.* 25, 1836.

MY DEAREST ISABELLA,— . . . My letter to "The Lawn" will probably have informed you of my proceedings in Ireland— of my trip up the Shannon, and my visit to Ballinasloe. I thence went to Galway. As this is the most thoroughly Catholic town in Ireland I felt curious to see the monastic establishments, and having an hour to spare I applied to a Father Flynn for directions. He very civilly volunteered me his guidance. We proceeded to the Presentation Convent, a fine large building on the outskirts of the town. Its objects are religious seclusion and the education of the poor. I was much pleased with the schoolrooms, of which there were five, containing about five hundred girls from six to eighteen years of age. They were clean and tidy, and are taught reading, writing, arithmetic, geography, and needlework. In one room the children were working patterns on net, a large quantity of which is sent over by the Nottingham manufacturers for that purpose. I found the nuns very obliging. They showed and explained everything to me. Their dress somewhat resembles that of the Sisters of Charity in Paris. There were twenty-five in this convent ; some were young and pretty. One of them had a fortune of £10,000. Poor girl ! They all looked happy and healthy. We afterwards walked through the garden and visited the chapel, which contained three good Italian paintings. One presented that strange mass of incongruities so common to old religious paintings,—St John, in the wilderness, clothed in the skins of wild beasts, had his face decorated with moustaches and a chin piece, and was attended by two Franciscan friars in full costume!

We then went to the Franciscan convent—it is nearly extinct; there are only three old ladies there. The national school of Galway is large, and calculated to accommodate eight hundred boys: there were but four hundred there when I saw it. They are taught by the monks. The books are supplied by the Board in Dublin. From the cursory view which I took of them, they appeared to be good and appropriate. It was curious to see boys without shoes and stockings, and with their clothes all in rags, answering questions in geography, mathematics, astronomy, &c.— Believe me, my dearest Isabella, your very affectionate brother,

J. PRESTWICH, Junr.

A letter of January 2, 1837, written to him at Paris by his sister Kate, contains the following sentence: "Your account of your reception by Madame Colin was really quite affecting, and must have been very gratifying to you."

Very few original letters of the next few years are preserved, with the exception of those addressed to his brother-in-law, Mr Russell Scott, and these are not of general interest, being on family and business affairs. To our geologist Mr Russell Scott was the very kindest brother: he was a man of high character, and one who had the privilege of his friendship can only speak of him with reverence and affection. He saw and appreciated young Prestwich's talent, and appraised the difficulty of his leading two lives—the commercial and the geological—without detriment to health. Mr Scott, too, had had business experience, as he had amassed a very con-

siderable fortune in early life.   He invested a portion of
his capital in the Mark Lane firm, and thus became a
sleeping partner, which conferred on him the right of
giving his wise counsel and advice.   It is impossible to
over-estimate the importance of his now life-long affection for Joseph Prestwich, who was many years his
junior.

Later on, when Prestwich had moved into Mark Lane
and acquired the habit of working at his geology far
into the hours of the night, Mr Scott, who then lived at
Gaddesdon Hoo, Hertfordshire, often wiled him away
from the City from Saturday until Monday.   They
generally made a trysting-place between Mr Scott's
house and some rather distant railway station.   It was
characteristic of our geologist to choose a station several
miles from the house, so that he might have more
ground to go over, and the chance of making observations in a fresh and wider field.   He thus had a walk
across country to a given point where his brother-in-
law waited, the latter having put up the carriage at
some village inn.   These walks were delightful to both,
and most refreshing to the City man.   We find notes
written again and again by this devoted brother-in-law,
urging that it was high time for rest and a holiday,
little thinking that perhaps a holiday might mean the
closest working time of all.

Here we may observe that Joseph Prestwich delighted
in the society of children, and seemed to know by instinct what pleased each child most.   He had the gift
of fascinating and amusing them as no one else within
our knowledge ever had, and it was a joyous time for
the little Scotts when " Uncle Joseph " was at "the
Hoo."   Sophia, the eldest, was a child of unusual
promise, with a mind cast somewhat in the same mould

as his own—with that ardent love of knowledge, and that intense longing to seek after and know the truth. The following fragment of a letter, without a date, addressed to her when a child, shows the writer's ever-present consciousness of the Hand at the helm, and indicated the spirit in which he worked :—

Observe, my dear Sophia, the wonders which surround you. Study and admire every object of the natural world. In all that you see there is beauty and harmony, and in all that you examine order and design. There is nothing so vast and so complicated but what you may hope to comprehend, and nothing so insignificant but what is worthy of investigation. All has proceeded from the same hands, and all indicate the same wisdom and admirable adaptation. Wonderful are His works, and perfect and unerring are His laws. Oh, should we not be thankful that we are endowed with capacities to comprehend His works and to study His laws, and being thus endowed with the means, ought we not to avail ourselves of so great and happy a privilege, humbly to explore and strive to comprehend the wonderful works of His hands, and gratefully and earnestly to admire their beauty and perfection?

Be assured, my dear little niece, that such objects of study and contemplation will ever afford you the purest and most unalloyed pleasure. . . .

In Paris, on the 8th January 1838, he had the gratification of being elected a member of the Société Géologique de France, on which occasion he was introduced by two eminent members, Constant Prévost and Achille Delesse. This brought him into contact with geologists in France who had come to the front, and hence the foundation was laid of many lasting and delightful friendships. His dear friends Albert Gaudry and A. Daubrée became prominent members of the French Geological Society, likewise the lamented Edouard Lartet—but we are anticipating—and many other distinguished names will in due time be added to the list.

Again we hear of his spending some time about this date in Epernay, where he had made himself master of the geology of the district. It was his habit to meditate upon any observations on new ground, especially where the relations or conditions of the strata were difficult to decipher, and where he had to propound a theory and show facts to account for his views on their superposition. He often pondered upon some unsolved geological problem for years, and it is possible that during this protracted sojourn in France he was amassing materials for his important paper, "Sur la Position géologique des Sables et du Calcaire lacustre de Rilly (Marne)," which was not given to the French Geological Society until the session of 1852-53.

A notebook for 1840 gives the following entry :—

Excursion to Arran viâ *Ardrossan, September* 19, 1840.
British Association.

Skirted the island from north to south, Mr Murchison pointing out the superposition of a red sand and conglomerate, which he classes as the New Red, but which is supposed by Jameson and others to belong to the Upper Coal-Measures, on a series of impure reddish limestones containing the *Productus hemisphæricus* and other characteristic mountain-limestone fossils, overlain by a thin band of coal-measures and small coal. This limestone reposes upon a series of beds belonging to the Old Red Sandstone —a quartzose conglomerate preponderating. The beds of these formations dip northward until we arrive at Glen Sannox, where an anticlinal line reverses the dip to the south about 26°, again bringing in the limestones which are worked at Corrie and the overlying red sandstones and conglomerate, which continue to Brodick, frequently, however, traversed and much disturbed by protruded Trap rocks. Landed at Corriegill Point to examine a beautiful instance of the intrusion of pitchstone through the red sandstone. The pitchstone is compact, and contains a few grains of glassy felspar. A few of the red sandstones in contact with it are highly indurated.

This Glasgow meeting was a signal success, and its president, Mr (afterwards Sir) Roderick Murchison, wrote of "the glorious day at Arran, when I lectured to a good band of workmen with every peak of Goatfell illlumined." Prestwich contributed no paper, nor do we find his name specially mentioned. From what we can glean, he had only been able to snatch one day, or perhaps two, so as to attend the Arran excursion. He was the reverse of self-assertive, and his habitual diffidence often kept him in the background, where, nevertheless, the busy brain-work went on, and where he pondered and observed. Memoirs were soon to emanate from his pen which were to give him a European reputation.

Onward during several years he was occupied in following up those researches in England and France, which he embodied in the well-known series of Tertiary papers. Of these Sir John Evans remarks :[1] "He not only reduced the little-known English Tertiaries into proper system (establishing the separate existence of certain local beds to which he gave the name of the Thanet Sands, proving the synchronism of the Reading beds with those of Woolwich, and fixing the true position of the London Clay with respect to the Hampshire basin), but he succeeded in correlating the Tertiary beds of England, France, and Belgium in such a manner that his classification was accepted by most geologists, and has stood the test of time."

In 1840 and 1841 Prestwich resided at 10 Devon-

---

[1] Obituary Notice to the Royal Society, vol. lx., 1896, p. xiii.

shire Street, Portland Place, which was then the family home.   Early in 1842, when the scope of his geological work had opened out, and when several important memoirs were in contemplation, his business responsibilities became heavier.   His father had always been speculative, and it was decided, as being best for the interests of the firm, that Joseph Prestwich, senior, should withdraw, and that our geologist should take the head of affairs.   Aided by a partner, he agreed to this arrangement.   Thus henceforward business journeys were at an end, and travellers were appointed in his place.   But this increased responsibility did not stem the tide of geological papers, which flowed on apace. His business residence in 1843 was 20 Mark Lane, and here he continued until 1855.

His note-books 1840-1850 show the extraordinary industry with which he investigated the Tertiary deposits in every locality of our southern and eastern counties, in order to make out their detailed structure and origin, and to compare and correlate them with the foreign Tertiaries.   He literally went over every acre of ground.   The index in one note-book gives 133 places, the observations on each locality being frequently illustrated by sections.   An entry of quite a different character in a note-book for 1846 may be quoted, as it throws light on his frugal mode of life.   " 1846, ' The Three Crowns,' at Walton near Sarum—a capital house, excellent ale, home-brewed.   Dinner off a loin of South Down mutton, household bread, 1 pint ale, and butter —9d.   Conscience forbid, so paid 1s. 1d."

His habits, in short, were of the simplest.   He never indulged in smoking, but this probably arose from a dislike to tobacco in any form.   He scarcely ever rode on horseback, preferring to go to his sections every-

where on foot; and when in later years he took the
reins in driving a pony-carriage, he was so much engrossed with the very roadside banks that the pony
ran up hill and down hill as it chose, and his companion
felt that these drives were scarcely safe.

While out on field-work, letters from his mother
attest her constant solicitude about his health, and
her anxiety lest he should take unduly long walks or
over-tax his strength. It is not surprising that he was
an inveterate walker, as he was lithe and spare, light of
step, with little weight to carry. It goes without saying that he was an expert climber: he scrambled over
cliffs and rocks with a nerve which was never shaken
but on one memorable occasion, to which he scarcely
cared to refer. He made the ascent—and we presume
that it was about this date—of the sea-face of Shake-
speare's Cliff, yet never spoke of it without a shudder.
Situated about a mile from Dover, it rises to a height
of 340 feet, and, as is well known, presents a sheer wall
of chalk to the sea. He was overtaken by the tide,
when unaided and alone he began the ascent of the
cliff. He had climbed up half-way, when he felt unable to go a step farther. There was bare foothold, and
retreat was impossible. It was the most perilous moment
of his life. He made a desperate effort, and we can
imagine the slim tapering fingers so curiously delicate
grasping any and every projection. After several awful
minutes, the summit was reached, where during half an
hour he lay on his back on the grass, unable to move.
It is needless to say that this experience was never
repeated.

During the presidency of Sir R. I. Murchison in
1846 he was elected a member of the Council of
the Geological Society, when the veterans Sedgwick,

Buckland, Fitton, De la Beche, Lyell, and others, were his associates.

Meanwhile Mr and Mrs Russell Scott had moved to Summer Hill, near Bath, where Prestwich on his flying visits made good use of his time in studying the features of that neighbourhood.

The geology of the northern portions of the Isle of Wight had a special attraction for him, and year after year repeated visits were made by him to unravel the structure of the district. In 1846 he read a paper at the Geological Society, " On the Tertiary or Supracretaceous Formations of the Isle of Wight, as exhibited in the Sections at Alum Bay and White Cliff Bay." In this he showed more certainly than had been done before that the elevation of the chalk ridge was subsequent to the deposition of the Headon Hill series, and he pointed out the connection between the lower Eocene beds and those of Bognor. In the same year he wrote a joint paper with his old friend Professor John Morris, " On the Wealden Strata exposed by the Tunbridge Wells Railway." Both of these papers appeared in the Geological Society's Journal, vol. ii., 1846. He also gave a notice to the British Association Meeting at Southampton that year, " On the Occurrence of Cypris in a part of the Tertiary Freshwater Strata of the Isle of Wight."

Early in 1847, the Palæontographical Society had its rise, Joseph Prestwich having been one of its original members. From Dr H. Woodward's [1] interesting account of its foundation and progress we quote the following passages :—

The origin was mainly due to the prior issue of Sowerby's

---

[1] Geol. Mag., p. 385, September 1896.

'Mineral Conchology,' of which the first part appeared in June 1812, and was followed by other parts for over thirty years. The portions of this work were brought out slowly and irregularly, and rarely illustrated more than ten species at a time. During the publication of this contribution to geological science, an association was formed (about the year 1836), called "The London Clay Club," the members of which were enthusiastic collectors of shells of the Tertiary deposits in the neighbourhood of the Metropolis. At one of the meetings of the club, about the year 1845, the late Dr (then Mr) J. S. Bowerbank suggested that as the 'Mineral Conchology,' at its then rate of issue, could not possibly depict all the British fossils within a moderate period, it would be well to have recourse to a new method. . . . The idea was favourably received; Mr Sowerby was asked to undertake the copperplate engravings, and many geologists living in different parts of the country were communicated with. In the furtherance of this object Mr Bowerbank laboured with much zeal and energy.

It is also stated that at a meeting held at the apartments of the Geological Society, Somerset House, on March 23, 1847, with Sir Henry De la Beche in the chair, it was resolved that a society should be constituted, the object of which should be "to figure and describe, as completely as possible, a stratigraphical series of British fossils." A further light is thrown on the foundation of the Palæontographical Society, from a paragraph in the fascinating 'Memoir of Edward Forbes,'[1] in which it appears that the reading of a paper by Joseph Prestwich hastened the foundation of a projected Tertiary Publishing Society.

At a meeting of the Geological Society (February 3, 1847) a discussion ensued upon a paper by Mr Prestwich on the "Tertiaries of the London and Hampshire Basins." Forbes, in the course of his speech, remarked with regret how much information

---

[1] By George Wilson, M.D., and Sir Archibald Geikie, p. 412.

on this subject lay scattered in different books and periodicals. Mr Bowerbank followed, and, on the spur of the moment, suggested the establishment of a Tertiary Publishing Society. The idea immediately found favour, and afterwards, at tea downstairs, it was expanded into a proposition to found a society for publishing plates of fossils, not from the Tertiary deposits only, but from all the British formations. This was the origin of the Palæontographical Society.

In the autumn of this year Mr Russell Scott urged our geologist, who was fagged and worn, to accompany him to a water-cure establishment in Germany, and try a treatment which Mr Scott had been ordered. It proved of the utmost benefit to the latter, but the overworked City man was so much reduced by the diet and treatment that he never quite recovered from their effects. Extracts from one or two letters from Boppart show, however, that he had regained his spirits, which were no longer affected by his health :—

J. Prestwich to Mrs Russell Scott.   MARIENBERG, *near* BOPPART,
29th August 1847.

Here we are, my dearest Isabella, installed in our respective dormitories, with visions of the successive operations in wet sheets, sitzes, &c., which are to commence at five to-morrow morning. I presume I am in the cell of some former Sister Theresa, and I suspect with very little addition to the original simplicity of furniture. . . . The view from the window is most beautiful. Below me is the terrace in front of the house, beyond that orchards sloping down to the old walls of Boppart, high and ruinous, and now serving the peaceful part of supporting vines and peach-trees. Over them appear the high-pitched slate roofs and gable-ends of the picturesque old town, with its quaint towers and fine old church in the Early French style. Over the town I could catch a glimpse of the Rhine, on the other side of which rise abrupt vine-clad hills, whilst beyond and behind Boppart are delicious plantations of all sorts of fruit-trees, surrounded by high hills covered with wood, with here and there a

beautiful ravine running through them.   It is at the entrance to
one of these ravines that this house stands—at a slight elevation
above one end of the town, and about a quarter-mile distant from
the river.   This situation is one of the finest you can conceive—
the establishment upon a scale of size, elegance, and completeness such as could not well be surpassed (I am now speaking of
it as a water-cure establishment only).   The house was formerly
a convent with 150 bedrooms. . . . We have commenced operations.   We had our first meal here (supper), and a melancholy
piece of business it was, I can assure you, when the prospect of
its continuance for three or four weeks is considered.   My impression is that it is the worst part of the process.   I had to
get through as well as I could one round of coarse black bread
and a soup-plate full of *sour milk* and two tumblers of cold
water, and I can assure you that I think my performance did me
credit.   The sour milk is really very nasty.   Mr Scott was let
off easier, as he is not recommended sour milk, dry bread, and
water, but was allowed the luxury of "white bread and butter,"
compôte de pommes, and new milk.   Happy man!   I must tell you
how he puzzled the doctor to-day, shortly after our arrival.   We
were speaking of the weather, which, the doctor informed us, has
been very wet for a few days past—so much so that in two days
19 millimètres of rain had fallen.   To this mode of receiving
the information Mr Scott immediately dissented, and suggested
that the doctor should solve the problem into legitimate inches
and tenths of inches.   The doctor was floored.   As for me, I
shall become as expert a reckoner as the country boy. . . . Give
my love to Civil, and kisses to all the dear children.—Your affectionate brother,   JOS. PRESTWICH.

Another Boppart letter, addressed to his mother,
gives a comical account of the process of tubbing and
packing in wet sheets.   Again, later, he writes to his
sister, Mrs Russell Scott :—

MARIENBERG, Sept. 13, 1847.

MY DEAREST ISABELLA,—Your very welcome letter of the 8th
inst. reached me yesterday. . . . The effects of the cure appear to be
very variable. . . . On me the effects appear to have reached their

maximum on the second day. Since then I perceive no difference
in my health or feelings. In fact, after the first eight days I
did not feel quite so well, and I found myself 1½ lb. lighter—a
loss in weight I could ill afford. Nevertheless, I believe I shall
be benefited by the treatment, and trust that its ultimate effect
will be more apparent than that of which I am at present conscious. Of course I follow the rules carefully. It gives me,
however, very great pleasure to say that on Mr Scott the favourable effects of the cure are most apparent. He will inform you
of his general feelings and symptoms; I will tell you of his
visible condition and actual deeds. Of our daily walks you are
doubtlessly informed. He now takes them without fatigue and
with much regularity. Last week we took a walk of twenty
miles. Yesterday (Sunday) we walked from Braubach to Ems
and thence to Stolzenfels. The day was very hot and the distance about seventeen to eighteen miles, and yet this morning
no fatigue or weariness is perceptible. Even his sore feet, which
caused him to limp in a very suspicious manner through the
ill-paved town of Lahnstein, cause him no uneasiness to-day.
The fact is, his gait through that respectable town was anything
but decorous—being far from steady, and such as would cause
strong suspicions of our water-diet at Ems. The paving-stones
being very irregular—some small, others large, some flat, others
pointed, his attention was directed to his safe transit from one
large flat stone to another—a proceeding not quite compatible
with the straight course, or steadiness of movement, but performed with much proper gravity of purpose.

Having now stated your husband's powers of endurance, I will
now mention his powers of consumption. I am fond of facts:
they illustrate briefly and to the point. I will therefore give you
a practical illustration of the subject, taken at a late period and
indiscriminately. It shall be our dinner yesterday at Ems.
We breakfasted as usual at 8 A.M. At one we dined. *Primo*, A
plate of *consommé au riz*. 2ndly, I saw his plate *well* covered
with bouilli and potatoes (here I considered he stood no chance
for the more *recherché* meats at the end of the dinner, and so
intimated to him). 3rdly, A *côtelette panée* (not small), with a
spoonful of cauliflower and another of potatoes. 4thly, *Frican-
deau de veau au purée de pommes de terre* (of this all recollection

was subsequently lost). 5thly, A leg of a poulet *à la jardinière* (this was considered trifling with one's appetite). 6thly, *Pouding au biscuit sauce d'abricots* (admitted to be good, and eaten accordingly). 7thly, *Filet de chevreuil piqué* (excellent, but considered to be very tardily served). 8thly, *Gateau de pommes*. 9thly, Dessert of grapes—accompaniments, four *petits pains* and three tumblers of water. Now you will, I am sure, my dear sister, be as much pleased with your husband's performance as I was, indicating, as I believe it does, an excellent state of health. My own satisfaction I expressed half an hour after dinner, and what do you think? Why, he doubted whether he had really made a good dinner. He thought he could eat some more. In fact he seemed to consider my opinion as rather unreasonable. I must tell you, however, that my own proceedings were in keeping with his, with the exception of a limitation in the soup, the bouilli, the vegetables, and the bread. . . .

I regret much I have not my calotype with me. What a picture for the children—their papa packed: Adieu, my dearest Isabella. My best love to my mother; kisses to the dear children. —Your affectionate brother,   Jos. PRESTWICH, Jr.

In 1847 two important memoirs appeared, both of which were published in the 'Geological Society Journal,' vol. iii., for 1847. One was "On the Main Points of Structure and the Probable Age of the Bagshot Sands, and on their presumed equivalents in Hampshire and France," after the discussion on which the Palæontographical Society was formed. In this paper the author pointed out the immediate superposition of the Bagshot Sands on the London Clay, and their division into three series, of which the central one was synchronous with the Bracklesham beds and the *Calcaire Grossier*. The other was also one of his early correlation papers, "On the Probable Age of the London Clay, and its Relations to the Hampshire and Paris Tertiary Systems," in which he showed that the previously received opinion of the age of the clays of Sheppey,

Barton, &c., was wrong, and that instead of being of the age of the *Calcaire Grossier*, they were of older date.

An interesting letter to Mr W. Lonsdale, formerly the esteemed Curator and Librarian of the Geological Society, evidently refers to those two papers :—

20 Mark Lane, London, 21st Dec. 1847.

My dear Sir,—You may probably not recollect the circumstance of my bringing you, in the year 1839, a paper on some detached portions of the Tertiary series of the neighbourhood of London. The facts were incomplete, and did not possess much novelty. After reading the paper, you recommended me not to present it to the Society at that time, and suggested a further examination of the ground. At the same time you expressed a regret that the English Tertiaries had not met with the attention which the French Tertiaries had.

With a full conviction of the correctness of your opinion, I looked further into the state of our knowledge respecting the English Tertiaries, and endeavoured to make myself better acquainted with their structure. From 1839 to the present date I have continued without interruption at my limited leisure moments the work which I then thought would require but a few weeks, and have still, I find, much to do. On portions of the subject I have, after a careful examination of the district, been led to form different views [from] those held generally, and these I have now in 1847 communicated to the Geological Society. It gives me now, I can assure you, much pleasure to hand you for your kind acceptance a copy of my papers published in the last number of the Journal. If there is any merit in them, to you in a great measure do I attribute such a result. It was at your suggestion that I proceeded in the work, and it has been the cautious and philosophical spirit of careful investigation and comparison of facts which I so frequently experienced in you that has helped to guide me through it. With my best and sincere wishes for your health and welfare, and with a grateful recollection of your frequent kind advice and assistance in many a geological difficulty, I remain, my dear sir, very sincerely yours, J. Prestwich, Jr.

A few years previously Mr Lonsdale had resigned office on account of his health ; but the same happy relations continued and were ever maintained between him and Joseph Prestwich. In a farewell note of November 1842, written with "such expressions of friendly good-bye as a note can convey," Mr Lonsdale fervently wished that our geologist would be long spared for the sake of his friends and for the progress of science, and that every success would attend him through life. Letters from this valued friend in after years, on to 1861, testify to the pleasure it gave him to receive occasional geological papers. His acknowledgment of these "acceptable tokens of remembrance" are given in grateful words.

William Lonsdale was unquestionably one of the old masters of geology. His memoir "On the Oolite District of Bath" is one of the geological classics : moreover, as remarked by Prestwich, and acknowledged by others, his studies of fossil corals "led to the establishment of the Devonian System." It fell to the lot of Prestwich, while he was President of the Geological Society, to record the death of his old friend ; and this he did in affectionate and touching terms. Lonsdale was born in 1794, and died in 1871.

In 1848 Prestwich was elected a member of the Geological Society Club, a private dining club which was founded on November 5, 1824, by Greenough, Warburton, Buckland, Fitton, Lyell, and twenty-six other Fellows of the Geological Society.

A letter of 4th January 1849 was in reply to Mr Russell Scott, who wished to know on scientific grounds the reasons for and against trees being planted near houses. Prestwich begins by saying that he had never paid the subject more than general consideration, yet

he covers more than seven closely written pages of
foolscap describing the functions of trees and foliage
in purifying the atmosphere. He dwells on the wonderful part which leaves perform in decomposing the
excess of carbonic acid gas and setting free its oxygen.
The minute care and detail shown in this letter characterised all that he ever undertook.

In 1849, while Sir Henry De la Beche was President,
Joseph Prestwich was awarded the Wollaston Medal
of the Geological Society for his researches in the
coal district of Coalbrook Dale, and for those subsequently carried on in the Tertiary Districts of London and Hampshire. The President emphasised this
honour by remarking that he was aware that for these
geological researches the time which the recipient of
the medal had at his disposal could " only be snatched
at intervals from the cares of commercial life." We
cannot do better than quote the reply : it summarises
in happy terms the benefits derived from a study of
his science. After expressing his grateful acknowledgments, the medallist proceeded to say—

It is true that I entered upon this field as a student and for
relaxation, but the interest and difficulties of the subject speedily
induced me to take it up with more earnestness and determination, and eventually led me to extend the inquiry over an area
which I, at first, never contemplated.

The Tertiary geology of the neighbourhood of London may be
wanting in beauty of stratigraphical exhibition and in perfect
preservation of organic types, but in many of the higher questions of pure geology,—in clear evidence of remarkable physical
changes, in curious and diversified palæontological data, however
defaced the inscriptions, which is after all but a secondary point,
—few departments of geology offer, I think, greater attractions.

The pleasure I have derived from the study of the remarkable
phænomena which have come before me in the course of the in-

JOSEPH PRESTWICH.

vestigation, has far outbalanced the few obstacles I have had to contend against. I, in fact, feel deeply indebted to geology, as a source of healthful recreation, as an inestimable relief and abstraction in due season from the cares frequently attendant upon the active duties of life, for its kindly and valued associations, and above all for the high communing into which it constantly brings us in the contemplation of some of the most beautiful and wonderful works of the creation.

To have received this, the highest award of the Geological Society, when he was not quite thirty-seven years of age, was a remarkable testimony to the value of the work which Prestwich had then achieved.

In the memoir of Sir Andrew Ramsay [1] an incident is mentioned connected with the award of the medal.

Ramsay's account of this anniversary meeting was as follows : "Sir H.'s speechifying day—the Geological Anniversary. Prestwich was awarded the Wollaston Medal. In rising to present it, Sir H. upset two large oil-lamps that stood on the table before him, and made a prodigious smash. All the house laughed, and poor P. was a trifle discomposed. He has a glorious head."

Dr Owen Rees sent his congratulations in a humorous note :—

G. Owen Rees to J. Prestwich.

59 GUILDFORD STREET, *March* 10, 1849.

MY DEAR JOSEPH,—I heard just now from my friend Warington Smyth that the Geological Society had awarded the Wollaston Medal to you.

Firstly, allow me to express my great disgust at your villainy in not informing me yourself, as you have thus postponed a great pleasure to me, who, notwithstanding your numerous bad qualities, [am] absurd enough to regard you with some slight amount of esteem.

Secondly, allow me to express a conviction—a heartfelt and

---

[1] By Sir Archibald Geikie, F.R.S., p. 144.

honest one—that the Society never did themselves more justice than in this award; and thirdly, I must request you to believe that I am sincerely rejoiced at your well-deserved success. Don't be proud—because I consider you enjoyed *great* advantages in geologising with me. You surely recollect the varied and profound discoveries, the great principles of action and thought for the discovery of truth, which I so eloquently poured into your ears, and to all of which I mean to allude whenever your name is mentioned. I don't mean to let pass so good an opportunity for a puff. Believe me in all sincerity and seriousness most joyful at your honours so nobly acquired, and ever, dear Joseph, your sincere friend,   G. OWEN REES.

The next two letters are in reply to inquiries from Sir Charles Lyell :—

J. Prestwich to Sir Charles Lyell.   LONDON, 1st *August* 1849.

MY DEAR SIR,—I am hardly able to venture an opinion upon the subject of your inquiry. For some years past I have kept myself so exclusively within the limits of the Tertiaries, that I fear I am not yet in possession of facts sufficient to enable me to offer you an opinion of much value. I have, however, this summer made several excursions into the Wealden, and only yesterday returned from a short visit to Mr Austen, with whom I examined part of the country he described. In my observations on the Drift period I have taken Essex as my base, for I have there found the characters of the different deposits by far the best defined.

From this as a centre I have worked over the district to the north as far as the coast of Norfolk, to the west to Devizes, eastward to the Channel, and am now proceeding over the ground southward, for I feel that the phenomena, although presenting great variety and infinite modifications, must be viewed in connection over larger areas.

I quite agree with you that in the Eocene period, prior to the formation of the London Clay, shallow seas prevailed over a large portion of our Tertiary area; for we have distinct and positive evidence of *debouchure* of rivers, of the formation of shingle banks,

and of the existence of coast-lines, in the fluviatile beds of
Woolwich, Upnor, &c., in the banks of round flint pebbles of the
hills from Croydon to Rochester, and in the presence of rocks
bored by the *Pholas* in parts of Kent, Essex, and Middlesex.
Yet I should hesitate in placing the then dry land in the position
of the present Wealden, although it is probable that a large
eastern portion of this district may have been dry land. But
the system of hills and valleys is so uniform through the Wealden,
and, I think, so evidently the result of one system of forces, that
no partial or disconnected actions could possiby have produced
so harmonious a result.

I fully admit the force of your observations respecting the
obliteration of the older denudation by others of more recent
occurrence, and that there is every probability that some portions
of the Cretaceous (and possibly the Wealden) rocks were above
the sea during the Eocene period; but, nevertheless, I cannot
help considering the entire present surface of the Wealden as
resulting from causes of comparatively recent date, subsequent
even to the period of the Great Northern Clay Drift. I cannot
separate the denudation of the Wealden from the denudation of
the valley of the Thames and all the surrounding districts, yet
there are some strong natural historical facts to militate against
this view, and my acquaintance with the district is not yet
sufficient to allow me to form a well-considered opinion. With
the country around London I am better accuainted, and hope in
the course of the next session to have the pleasure of submitting
to you some papers on this subject. I have had them in hand
some time, but have hesitated to bring them forward until my
observations were much more extended. In the Tertiary district
the Drift must, I think, be separated by four or five (may be even
more) well-marked divisions, part of them older than the Great
Northern Clay Drift, and independent of the present configuration of the land, and part of them of date subsequent to the
denudation of the existing valleys. Thus I am rather inclined
to the opinion that the commencement of the Drift period cannot
be placed farther back than of Post-Pliocene age, and that the
denudation of the Wealden and the excavation of all the systems
of valleys of the south-east of England resulted from the operation of forces acting simultaneously throughout this area during

this Drift period. At the same time, I hazard this opinion in its extension to the Wealden with considerable doubt, although I have reason to hope that with regard to the other districts it will be found fairly grounded. I do not know whether in this short explanation I have made myself clear, or whether I have entered at sufficient length on the points you wish. In any case, I shall be most happy to communicate to you any other facts I may be in possession of, or to enter more fully into any of my views requiring explanation ; and believe me to remain, my dear sir, very sincerely yours,　　　　　　　　J. PRESTWICH.

To the Same.　　　　　　　　　LONDON, 20*th August* 1849.

MY DEAR SIR,—I had written the enclosed letter on the night of the 31st July, when on the 1st August I received your second letter with further inquiries respecting the Drift period. I postponed, therefore, sending it until I had again considered the subject, and seen more of the district in question.

Since the publication of my papers on the London Clay and Bagshot Beds, I have only communicated to the Society short papers on isolated facts, and have not therefore gone again into the general views of subsidence and elevation affecting large areas and requiring lengthened observation. This subject I am about to resume in a paper on the beds between the London Clay and the Chalk, as well as in a paper on the *Diluvial* period. With regard to ground where the many hundred feet of London Clay and overlying beds were derived, I yet feel at a loss to form an opinion. I have thought much about it, and have sought in vain for any transported *rock specimens* in the body of the beds to show their origin. I have only one such specimen from the London Clay, and that is not very distinct. It is, at all events, some old and distant rock. The clays of Sheppey indicate the proximity of land on some point, I think, southward of that island.

In the beds below the London Clay the evidence is, however, stronger and clearer. The fluviatile beds of Upnor, Woolwich, and Lewisham, and of Guildford appear evidently to have been local things—small rivers, and flowing apparently from a land on the south, as the deposits do not seem to have extended themselves far from the then existing shore, and they are lost

in the other strata as they travel northward. On no part of the
north side of the London Tertiaries am I aware that fluviatile
beds have been found. At the period just before the London
Clay commenced shallow seas and lines cf coast are indicated,
both by these river-deposits, and by the occurrence at several
places of rocks bored by the *Pholas*. These south-coast rivers
would certainly seem to have flowed over land now occupied by
the area of the Wealden, but whether the chalk then covered it
almost to the exclusion of the older beds or not it is difficult to
say. I am rather inclined to look to the chalk for the supply of
the greater part of the beds below the London Clay, but yet not
to this entirely. The London Clay is, I think, derived from
another quarter, and a more distant one. The first deposited
Tertiary bed was broken up, and its *fragments* scattered in some
of the beds but little younger; and, again, the London Clay, I
believe, swept over and denuded Tertiary beds older than itself,
for [to] this action only can I attribute the number of small black
flint pebbles thinly dispersed at places in the beds of the London
Clay. These pebbles, I believe, come from the shingle beds below
the London Clay, but whence they were originally derived it is
more difficult to say—probably, I think, from *upper* denuded
beds of chalk. This is a point I am looking to at present. The
movement which upset the Tertiaries of the Isle of Wight I
think long anterior to the denudation of the Weald as it now
exists; yet may it not be quite possible that the elevation of
the Weald existed before this period, and that the elevation and
denudation were independent of each other?

The amount of vertical subsidence in the Isle of Wight
between the Chalk and the first appearance of land above
the waters must, I think, have been nearly 2000 feet — and
that an uninterrupted, tranquil, and noiseless action. (Nevertheless I believe in paroxysms.) The green-coated flints next
the Chalk I quite agree with you in attributing to a large and
extensive destruction of the Chalk. This was the commencing
scene of our English Tertiaries. The plants of Alum Bay
and Bournemouth imply no doubt the contiguity of dry land,
but still probably not a very near one, and an open sea, whilst
the fresh-water Eocenes [Oligocene] indicate a closing up of the
seas and the extension near at hand of fresh water.

D'Archiac, in his ' Histoire des Progrès de la Géologie,' reviews the subject, but does not go very fully into it, nor am I aware that any of the French geologists have more than alluded to it briefly, excepting, however, M. D'Archiac, who has well and frequently discussed it in several of his works.—I remain, my dear sir, yours very truly,   J. PRESTWICH.

With reference to the range and thickness of the local Tertiaries, the following is the draft of a letter on the Metropolitan Main Drainage, addressed to Sir Henry De la Beche :—

20 MARK LANE, *Augt.* 1849.

MY DEAR SIR HENRY,—In the report of the meeting of the Commissioners of July last several points were raised connected with the geology of part of the neighbourhood of London, especially with that portion of it extending eastward from St Paul's to the marshes opposite Woolwich. The subject was discussed in connection with the question of Mr Phillips's tunnel scheme, on which it has no doubt an important bearing. As considerable doubt seemed to exist as to the extent of the range of the London Clay and its depth through Eastern London, and also as to the nature of the beds between the London Clay and the Chalk, I venture to take the liberty of communicating the few facts I am in possession of connected with the geology of the district. As I believe a series of borings is in the course of execution, the observations may probably be of no use, and it will be unnecessary to bring them forward. If, however, they should tend to throw light upon any one doubtful point, it will give me much pleasure, and I beg you will make any use of them you think fit.

The consideration of this question geologically has led me to examine with some attention the various plans proposed for the more efficient drainage of London, and at the risk of being probably thought by you very presumptuous in venturing to give an opinion upon such a subject, I have in paper " B " expressed some difficulties I cannot but foresee in Mr Phillips's plan, and have given a sketch of a plan which might possibly obviate some of them. I may be all wrong—if so, burn the papers; if not, I shall be happy to offer any further explanation. I should never have ventured to have submitted this to you unless a gentleman who has had great experience in sewers had intimated to me that he did not consider my plan more impracticable than the others, and advised me to lay it before the court.   May I claim your kind services in taking charge of these two papers, and believe me to remain.   .   .   .

In connection with this subject, Joseph Prestwich prepared a " Geological Map of the Estuary of the Thames for the Referees of the Main Drainage of the Metropolis." It was printed by order of the House of Commons, 4th February 1858.

Two more memoirs were in 1849 given to the world, both through the channel of the Geological Society— namely, one " On the Position and general Characters of the Strata exhibited in the Coast Section from Christchurch Harbour to Poole Harbour"; the other " On some Fossiliferous Beds overlying the Red Crag at Chillesford near Orford, Suffolk," in which latter he showed the existence at Chillesford of a peculiar Arctic group of fossils in undisturbed beds above the Red Crag. The excursion to the Crag district was made in company with Godwin-Austen, Morris, and Alfred Tylor.

During the forties there had been great intellectual activity, yet if we compare his published work with that in the decade of years to follow, it will be seen that it had not reached its maximum.

On August 7th Prestwich had paid a visit to his old friend Mr Wickham Flower[1] at Croydon, and a week later he was at Hastings, exploring Fairlight

[1] John Wickham Flower; born 1807, died 1873: best known for his studies of the deposits yielding palæolithic implements near Brandon and Thetford.

Hill and the structure of the surrounding country, with Dr Fitton, the veteran geologist. On September 7th, Professor Morris accompanied him to New Lewisham, where they were fully occupied with sections and notes, and on the 10th October Mr I'Anson was his companion on geological work from Marlborough through Manton to the Valley of Rocks (Devil's Den). Early in November Professor Morris was again with him when they proceeded to Hertford,—this excursion being only one of very many made to that locality. In short, the record in the 1849 note - book of the field-work done after the 7th August is extraordinary. The districts round Brighton, Epsom, Leatherhead, Stamford Hill, Sutton, Horsham, Esher, Basingstoke, Winchester, and Wimborne, were explored, and sections were noted at these as well as at many other localities too numerous to catalogue.

CHAPTER IV.

1849–1858.

EASTER EXCURSIONS—'THE WATER-BEARING STRATA'—
'THE GROUND BENEATH US'—FURTHER TERTIARY
MEMOIRS.

FOR several years Prestwich had been in the habit of
making a short excursion into the country at Easter,
when he was accompanied by two or three geological
friends. To him these expeditions were most beneficial: he was fagged by the end of the winter, and
invariably felt refreshed by the change of air and
scene. He delighted in geologising and exploring in
the society of personal friends ; and as time went on,
these Easter parties became very popular, and were
usually composed of four or five "brethren of the hammer"; Prestwich, from his knowledge of the ground,
being director and keeper of the common purse. It
soon became known that to be one of Prestwich's
Easter party was a very good thing indeed, and those
hard workers who joined it were like so many happy
school-boys out for a holiday. Mention is made in a
letter to his old friend Mr W. Cunnington of one of
these expeditions.

J. Prestwich to W. Cunnington.   LONDON, *25th March* 1850.

DEAR CUNNINGTON,—A party of vagrant geologists will alight on Friday morning next, somewhere on the Chalk Downs south of the Farringdon Road Station. On Friday night they will probably sleep at Farringdon ; on Saturday at Swindon. The party will consist of Austen, Sharpe, Prof. E. Forbes, Nicol (?), Tylor, Morris (? ?), and myself. Can you manage to join us ? It would give me much pleasure to see you. I expect we shall do some good work and examine a considerable tract of country, as we purpose walking about twenty miles per day. I intend to try to get them (or part of them) as far as Devizes. If so, we shall make a descent then on Sunday night or early on Monday morning, so as to meet with you at home on Monday as a likely day. Your collection is one which a man of the Greensand as Austen ought to see. If you can manage to join us I will give you fuller particulars where to meet. I leave town on Thursday night.—Yours very sincerely,

J. PRESTWICH.

In the early summer a great sorrow overtook him : in June 1850 he lost his mother, who had been in failing health for several years. To his loving nature this was a keen trial. He never spoke of her except with great reverence, and in accents which showed how tenderly he cherished her memory. Like a true mother, she had been in the habit of reading every word of her son's geological memoirs—no matter how technical. One of these bears the inscription, " To my dearly loved mother, the first and last thought of the writer." Her miniature, in a dress of white lace devoid of ornament, was always in sight : it hung above his library mantel-shelf.

Among letters of this date we find one to his interesting young niece Sophia Scott, labelled " my dear uncle," written when her health showed symptoms of fatal decline. Sophia died at Malaga, where she had been taken in the vain hope that her life might be lengthened by residence in a southern climate. This letter displays his attention to every detail of the observations he counselled her to make, and his solicitude to cherish in the fading young life an unceasing interest in the marvellous works of nature. In reading between the lines we are conscious that a tender sympathy is expressed :—

LONDON, 25th July 1850.

MY DEAR SOPHIA,—The plant in the bottle which I sent you yesterday is a water-grass, in repute for the exhibition of the circulation of the sap in vegetables. You will, I think, find it a very interesting phenomenon. It is easily shown, and the specimen can be preserved for any length of time in water. You can plant it in some washed vegetable mould, an inch thick, on the bottom of any open glass jar or vase filled up with water.

What I should recommend you to do would be to get any common glass jar, about 8 to 12 inches high, and 4 to 8 inches across; place at the bottom of it about 1 or 1½ inch of washed vegetable mould (washed, because it would otherwise make the water too muddy), and then plant it with this and any other water *ground* plants (mosses especially). Fill the jar to within an inch of the top with dirty *pond* water (which will soon become clear), and then put on the top of the water a few *floating* water-plants—such as duckweed and ranunculus. Introduce into the water any water-insects or fresh-water shells and small crustacea—as the *Planorbis, Lymnea, Helix, Cypris,* &c. The plants at the top will thus prevent evaporation, whilst the animal and vegetable life will (as long as they are alive) keep the water fresh and free from putrefaction. After a short time the water will teem with a most active population, whose habits and characters you can study at your leisure. The larger animals will be visible enough through the glass, whilst the smaller ones you can get out and place under the microscope by means of a small dipping-tube. . . . Your mamma will, I have no doubt, be able to assist you in all the manipulations, and will tell you what the genera are which I have referred to above; and your papa will be able to assist you in deciphering my hieroglyphics in case you are at a loss in any part of this letter, which I am writing as usual in a hurry. The study, my dear Sophia, of these objects, small as they are, is full of interest. As they are thus kept in the proper element, you will be able to watch all the changes which take place in them. Every day will afford fresh points for observation, and the more you see the more you will, I think, wish to learn, so beautiful are the objects and so wonderful is their variety. Once started, there is no trouble at all. Keep the jar in a light place, with occasional sunshine upon it. I have annexed a rough sketch of the jar, so as to indicate its form and general appearance to assist you in getting it up. Trusting that it may prove to you, my dear Sophia, a source of pleasant and profitable recreation in your close confinement,—I remain, your very affecte. uncle,

J. Prestwich, Jr.

One of the special subjects to which for some time Prestwich had turned his attention was the question of water-supply, especially with regard to the service of London. Eventually he became the leading authority on this subject, and furnished many reports to public bodies and institutions that sought his advice. In later years he occasionally received inquiries from private individuals, who only knew him by reputation, asking him to point out the best situation in which to build a country house (giving the range of a few counties), so as to ensure a good water-supply. The request of a stranger writing for information about the effects of sea-water on blocks of magnetic iron-ore received immediate attention.

His first public address on the water-supply of London was given at the Royal Institute of British Architects, 8th July 1850, and was published in its Proceedings. Its title was, "On the Geological Conditions which determine the Relative Value of the Water-bearing Strata of the Tertiary and Cretaceous Series, and on the Probability of finding in the Lower Members of the latter, beneath London, Fresh and Large Sources of Water Supply." His opinion, however, which was confirmed by the experience of later years, was that the growing needs of London would necessitate in the future an ampler supply, for which the far-off mountains of Wales might be the best source.

Before the publication of his book on 'The Water-bearing Strata,' the first of three important memoirs which will ever be associated with his name was read at the Geological Society—"On the Structure of the Strata between the London Clay and the Chalk in the London and Hampshire Tertiary Systems. Part I., The Basement Bed of the London Clay, 1850." This paper is illustrated by twenty admirable sections, and a table is given showing the general range and distribution of the organic remains of the basement bed of the London Clay through the Hampshire and London Tertiary districts. The line of range is taken from the Isle of Wight north to Hungerford, thence east to Herne Bay.

These three papers were the outcome of years of careful research: they defined the boundaries of individual beds which had not previously been discriminated, or had been confused with each other, and the relations of the Tertiary strata in the London and Hampshire basins were demonstrated.

It has been pointed out by Mr H. B. Woodward[1] that Prestwich, commencing in the London area, zealously traversed the country wherever the Lower

[1] Natural Science, Aug. 1896, p. 91.

Tertiary strata were to be found, and hardly an out-lier of any importance escaped his observation. Mr Whitaker, who more than any other man has followed in the footsteps of Prestwich over this large region, referred in 1872 to the literature of the subject, and remarked that the period 1841 to 1860 "might well be called the ' Prestwichian period,' from the author who first clearly made out the *detailed* structure of the London basin." [1]

Notebook entries for August 1850 record detailed de-scriptions and sections made when on a tour in France. The districts round Boulogne, Clermont, and Beauvais were again explored, and the repeated exhibition of " drift" at Beauvais, and its resemblance to that near Marlborough, attracted his attention. The Abbé Maill-ard was Prestwich's companion at Bracheux for an examination of its sands. Epernay was the locality from which he dated in September, where he was joined by " Morris and Haines," and on this occasion copious notes were made on the " Sables de Rilly." Those repeated visits to Epernay bore rich fruit.

With the growth of geological knowledge questions continually arise with reference to geological nomen-clature. Perhaps no names of formations have given rise to more discussion than those of Upper and Lower Greensand and Neocomian. The views, therefore, of Dr Fitton — one of the old masters of geology, and the chief English authority on the Cretaceous strata —will be read with interest :—

W. H. Fitton to J. Prestwich.

53 UPPER HARLEY STREET, 15*th March* 1851.

MY DEAR SIR,—I hope you are making good progress with your paper; and I wish to mention to you (as it may save you

---

[1] Mem. Geol. Survey, vol. iv. p. 395.

the trouble of preparing any *long* note upon the subject) that, after going through most of the French papers in the ' Bulletin de la Soc. Géol. de France,' I find that the term *Grès Vert* is so frequently used in a right sense for our L. G. Sand; whilst, as you know, the *French* geologists have already distinct and different names for the *Upper Green sand* (" Craie tufau," " Craie chloritée," " Glauconie crayeuse "), and thus have avoided the impropriety of *joining*, as we have done, the " Upper" and " Lower" Green sands, which have really no connection.   It would be very unlikely that the use of a *new* term would be accepted, and *thought necessary* (if that is the only ground on which new names can be acceptable) in France.

I think, therefore, after fully considering the subject, that I shall confine myself—at present—to proposing simply to *adopt the term "Neocomian"* for the lowest divisions of our Cretaceous deposits; making it a part of our *Lower Green sand*, and including only the groups I., II., and III. of my large Table.[1]   The groups next above IV. to XIV. of the Table will then be the *middle division*—distinguished and well known in England ever since 1824-25 by containing *Gryphæa sinuata*, and being *conspicuously the middle division* of my section at Hythe and Folkestone (Kent).   You will see in the Table that in XIV. (*b*, No. 45) there is a continuous line of fossils going out *there* in a very distinct manner.   This line is, I am very glad to find, also very distinct in the *Hythe section* (at Sandgate); and there also separates the middle division of the L. Green sand from the uppermost division (XV. and XVI. of the Table), which, both at Atherfield and near Folkestone, consists chiefly of pure whitish or buff and yellowish-gray sand, with very few fossils (yet with *some* shells, and these sometimes silicified!).   This *upper division* of the L. G. S. occurs in France (and I suspect also in *Switzerland*, where it has caused some perplexity).

The " Gault" is immediately above this upper light-coloured sandy division, and makes a strongly contrasted boundary.   I think of giving a short sketch of the progress of inquiry, so far as the *Neocomian* and our L. G. sand are concerned.   This will enable me to give an account of the orginal *Terrain "Neocomien"*

---

[1] See Quart. Journ. Geol. Soc., vol. iii. p. 289.

— or rather, as it was called at first, of the *Terrain crétacé inférieur.*

And I hope thus to make everything clear as to the identities and differences existing between our group and some of those on the Continent.

When the members of the Palæontological Society come to *Upper Greensand* they will be enabled to judge of the expediency of making a new name for that deposit. And this additional change will by that time have been rendered more easy — to introduce further alterations if they should then be desired. But in the meantime I should not republish my note about *Vectine.*[1]—Yours very truly,   W. H. FITTON.

One of the intimate friends who was frequently his companion in Easter expeditions was Mr R. A. C. Godwin-Austen, F.R.S., one of the most distinguished geologists of his day, whose acute reasoning was shown in his famous paper on the probable underground extension of the Coal Measures in the south-east of England. A warm friendship existed between them, which was only severed by the death of Godwin-Austen in 1884.[2] They often went abroad together, perhaps for a few days at a time, to France or Belgium, to work out the geology of some particular district—the route having been carefully planned. The following letter throws a light on our geologist's proceedings. He had indeed made for himself a position altogether unique :—

From R. A. C. [Godwin-]Austen to J. Prestwich.

CHILWORTH, *April* 7, 1851.

DEAR PRESTWICH,—Do you intend to take your geological pupils into the country this Easter? If so, I am ready for a

---

[1] See Proc. Geol. Soc., vol. iv. p. 406, and Quart. Journ. Geol. Soc., vol. i. p. 189.

[2] Mr Austen took the additional name of Godwin in 1854. He was born in 1808.

R. A. C. GODWIN-AUSTEN, F.R.S.

tramp over any formation, but the less argillaceous it is the better.

I will leave it to Sharpe to fight the battle about dinner. All I stipulate for (Farnham being my prompter) is, that you will allow us breakfasts. What do you think of Oxford, commencing with Cumnor Hurst, and so looking up the old Doctor [Fitton] over his Headington, Garsington, Hazeley, Tetsworth, and Thame sections, and so on to Tring?

I shall not be able to be at the next "Geological"; but should it be proposed to renew the walk of the last year or two, I will join the force any day, anywhere, you may name.

Do not let my suggestion as to the district influence you. I am such a wanderer in our wide field that any district will come alike to me.—Ever yours very truly,

R. A. C. AUSTEN.

The next letter is from another geologist, also with a request for Joseph Prestwich to join in an excursion :—

Sir R. I. Murchison to J. Prestwich.

16 BELGRAVE SQUARE, *April* 14, 1851.

MY DEAR SIR,—Would it suit your book to make a run of a day or two to the other side of the Weald, looking at a few points by the way, and at some of the transverse splits in the S. Downs?

I intend to look at the valley of the Cuckmere, E. of Brighton, and at the "Wealden Drift" of Barcombe, mentioned by Mantell and Lyell.

I think of going on Thursday next. I shall probably return by the other side of the county—*via* Pulborough and Guildford.

It would be gratifying to me to have a playfellow like yourself for a part, at all events, of my tramp; and if you have a little holiday, you may not dislike to employ it to some extent in this way.—Ever yours,　　　　　ROD. I. MURCHISON.

The careful research necessary for the elaboration of his Tertiary papers also aided him largely in the acquisition of his knowledge of the permeable and impermeable strata, and of the action of springs and

underground waters.   In 1851 his volume on 'The
Water-bearing Strata of the Country around London,
with reference especially to the Water-Supply of the
Metropolis,' was published by his friend Van Voorst,
and was most favourably received.[1]   His complete
mastery of the subject must have taken the public by
surprise.   The author used often laughingly to affirm,
that if he had only at that time set up as a consulting
water engineer, he would have become a rich man.

It was probably about this date, or it might have
been earlier, that a proposal was made to him to join the
late Mr Allnutt, father of the first Lady Brassey, in
business as active partner.   This partnership would
possibly have led the way to fortune, but Joseph Prestwich (who had been his own master from the time he
had assumed the headship of his father's firm) saw that
under such circumstances his City work would become
more exacting—that it would in a greater measure
interfere with and curtail his leisure for geologising :
on that account, and while fully alive to all the advantages offered, he declined.

It will be gleaned from the following letter to Mrs
Russell Scott that he had under consideration a plan for
exchanging City work for some other avocation in which
he felt that his talents might be turned to better
account :—

LONDON, 17th May 1851.

You have exactly expressed, my own dear sister, that which I
feel upon the subject of my work.   I care very little about any
pecuniary benefit it may be to me, provided the plan should prove

---

[1] This issue was limited, for the large plate which accompanied the
volume was accidentally destroyed before sufficient copies were printed
off.   In 1895, however, a new issue was published (without the plate),
and this contains much new matter and some corrections in the form of
a supplement.

of benefit and advantage to my fellow-men.—but more especially
do I hope and trust that it may lead to some amelioration in the
condition of those who, by circumstances, are placed in a position
of toil and hardship which we who are in a more fortunate position should as a duty alleviate as far as lies in our power. The
misery I see around me is indeed sad,—it makes my heart bleed.
It is on this account that I must feel my dependent situation—
my inability to assist more effectually in the improvement and
welfare of the poorer classes. Then again, with reference to
Clapham, I deeply feel the responsibility to maintain a proper
provision for them — such as they have been accustomed to.
It is these considerations, and not a mere question of £ s. d.,
that lead me to hope, as a possible contingency, that some change
in my present position may result from this work. Then again,
as a secondary consideration, I feel that I am out of place here—
that my time and labour are not employed in those channels in
which they might yield their proper return. I feel that I could
make more of them, not only for my own benefit, but also in that
of which I feel the paramount importance — the progress of
science and its application to our improvement, intellectual and
physical.

It is therefore with regard to the public advantage, which I
hope would result from the carrying out of my plans, that I
should feel disappointed if my calculations should not prove
correct. Their success would be an ample reward to me, and *no
disappointment* should I experience on my own account by that
proving the only one.—In haste, I remain, my dearest Isabella,
ever your affectionate brother, J. PRESTWICH.

Nothing came of the project mentioned in the above
letter. Before long Prestwich was again taking one
of those business journeys during which he contrived
to make fresh geological observations, as may be
inferred from the following letter :—

J. Prestwich to Sir Charles Lyell. DORCHESTER, 21*st June* 1851.

MY DEAR SIR,—I shall be most happy to take a short excursion.
I fear that we cannot reach the Reculvers or Sandwich, but there

is an intermediate section of great interest at Upnor, near
Rochester, which we might easily visit by means of a return day
ticket on the North Kent line; or, if you prefer, we can take a
day ticket to Maidstone, and examine the Drift and Greensands.
With regard to the Reculvers and Sandwich, I will give you full
particulars of the best localities and points, and mark them on
the Ordnance Map, in case you wish to visit them on your way
to Belgium. I forgot to mention the Abbey Wood cutting. It
is very interesting. The other section, however, which I mentioned, on Plumstead Heath, shows the same phenomena. I am
not going beyond this town. To-morrow I hope to spend in the
Isle of Purbeck, and expect to be in London on Tuesday. I shall
not, therefore, fail to be present at the next meeting, when I
shall be happy to arrange the excursion in any way that may be
most agreeable to you, and remain, my dear sir, yours very
truly,   J. PRESTWICH.

The date of publication of his paper " On the Drift
at Sangatte Cliff, near Calais," was 1851, while that
" On some of the Effects of the Holmfirth Flood "
was published in the volume of the Geological Society
for 1852. Reference is made to the latter in the
following note :—

J. Prestwich to W. Cunnington.   DERBY, *8th March* 1852.

DEAR CUNNINGTON,— . . . I went from Huddersfield to
Holmfirth and then on to the Bilberry reservoir. The effects of
the flood were most remarkable. The valley was in many places
literally strewed with *débris* of sand, gravel, and rock, 1 to 6
feet thick. Transported blocks of 2 to 5 feet were common.
One huge fellow measured 22 feet by 6 and $2\frac{1}{2}$ deep. Talk of
glaciers! it would have taken one fifty years to have done what
this water-power did in an hour.—Yours very truly,

                                              J. PRESTWICH.

The third of Prestwich's great Tertiary memoirs was
likewise published in the Geological Society's Journal

for 1852, thus appearing two years in advance of the second part. Its title was, "On the Structure of the Strata between the London Clay and the Chalk in the London and Hampshire Tertiary Systems. Part III., The Thanet Sands."

The entry in the note-book for this year is: "*Easter Excursion, 6th to 15th April* 1852.—Forbes, Austen, Morris, and myself started on Tuesday for Boulogne. D. Sharpe and Tylor joined us at Calais on Wednesday night." They were met at Tournay by M. Dumont and M. Lambert, who were their guides over the most interesting ground in the vicinity of Mons, Liége, Aix, &c.

Another letter to Mrs Russell Scott mentions the amount of time spent on two geological papers:—

LONDON, *22nd December* 1852.

MY DEAREST ISABELLA,—Notwithstanding the troubles I have gone through, I am happy to say that my views and feelings continue as fresh as ever. I have no feelings of disappointment, and an abundance of hope. As contributing to this desirable end, I find geology is a most important adjunct. You must not, however, judge of the amount of labour (one, by the bye, of love, and therefore not felt as a burden but as an enjoyment) by the size of the results. The paper on the Thanet Sands is part of the results of ten to twelve years' researches—that on the Holmfirth Flood is the result of one Sunday's walk on a fine day last February. You are very good to read my papers. I do not expect it. You form an honourable exception to the rest of the family. My poor mother used to be the only member of it who ever had the patience to get through them.

I shall be delighted to see the children in town. Kate and her children are coming up to-morrow. With my best love to all the absentees, and wishing them all a happy and merry Christmas, I remain, ever your affectionate brother,

J. PRESTWICH, Jun.

During the session of 1852-53 of the Société Géologique de France, a paper which excited great interest in Paris was communicated to the Society by its English member, Joseph Prestwich. Of the estimate of this paper among French geologists we quote the Notice to the Society in November 1896 by M. Albert Gaudry, the eminent palæontologist.

Il visite ensuite longuement l'Est du bassin de Paris et le Nord de la France; enfin, en 1883, Prestwich nous a donné des renseignements de première importance "Sur la position géologique des sables et du calcaire de Rilly près Reims" (Bull. Soc. Géol., I™ série, tome x., p. 300). Il avait reconnu que les sables de Rilly étaient placés à la partie supérieure des sables de Bracheux, sur le prolongement des sables de Jonchery et de Châlons-sur-Vesles, position qui est aujourd'hui hors de toute contestation, tandis que Hébert soutenait que ces sables et le calcaire qui les surmonte formaient une série distincte, antérieure à toutes les autres formations tertiaires du bassin de Paris.

La démonstration de Prestwich paraissait péremptoire, cependant elle ne fut pas admise par Hébert, qui, dans une note détaillé, publiée l'anée suivante, maintint ses vues et combattit son contradicteur avec une énergie passionnée, persistant à enseigner pendant plus de trente ans la même erreur dix fois répétée. Justement froissé de la réponse d'Hébert, M. Prestwich priva notre Bulletin de toute nouvelle communication, et ce n'est que tout à fait à la fin de la vie d'Hébert, que nous l'avons vu reprendre ses publications sur le bassin de Paris pour établir la comparaison des assises de ce bassin avec celles du bassin de Londres qu'il connaissait à fond et avec le tertiaire belge auquel il s'intéressait beaucoup aussi. Les recherches théoriques ne lui faisaient pas negliger les applications pratiques de la science et il s'est occupé activement des questions de recherches d'eau, de houille, et comme conseil pour les grands travaux publics. On peut résumer d'un mot son œuvre géologique en disant qu'elle restera pour nous tous un modèle.

Better than any words of ours, this quotation shows

the position that Joseph Prestwich held in the world
of science in France.

During this and the preceding year the subject of
this Memoir had been in close correspondence with the
lamented Edward Forbes.   They were both at work
on the geology of the Isle of Wight, yet there is not
a shade of jealousy on the part of either.   They were
both only eager to help each other — eager for the
elucidation of truth.   Among several letters from this
distinguished naturalist, one from Sandown, dated 17th
December 1852, begins :—

DEAR PRESTWICH,—Your letter is a most interesting one to
me, and I hope you will write another, stating objections and
suggestions, as it is of consequence to me that I should look to
all points whilst I am on the spot. . . . I have had your
note on Hempstead transcribed and sent down to me, and have
been much pleased with it. . . .

A second long letter from Sandown, of January 16,
1853, enters into detail on the arguments and facts in
support of the writer's divisions of the geological beds
of the Isle of Wight, and concludes :—

As you say, it is difficult to judge of equivalents owing to the
very defective French lists.   On the general questions discussed
at the end of your letter it will be better to talk.   I hope you
will let me join your Easter expedition—it is exactly where I
should like to go; and with all this fresh in my head, I may be
of use.—Ever, dear Prestwich, very sincerely,

EDWARD FORBES.

This next Easter trip is recorded very briefly.
" 1853, 25th March.—Lynn with Forbes and Austen."

The last letter from Edward Forbes was from Hythe,
25th August 1853. (He died in 1854.) He and our
geologist had arranged to make an excursion to France,

the former to be accompanied by Mrs Forbes. Prestwich was unable to cross with them, and followed later.
Forbes wrote :—

I see no reason from your note for deviating from the plans
we concocted. If you can leave town sooner than you say, so
much the better. Within the limits of being back in England
on the 27th of next month, I am in a manner free to move in
any direction, and so that we can manage to see all that we proposed together, I can spend the time pleasantly and profitably in
any direction that may be convenient. . . . If you should be
delayed longer than you at present anticipate, I would go on to
Fontainebleau, and you could pick us up there.

If you have any hints or advice to give about seeing points
about Paris, a line addressed here will find me until Saturday at
midday.—Ever, dear Prestwich, &c.,   EDWARD FORBES.

The biographer of Forbes remarks : " These few
weeks in France were weeks of thorough enjoyment.
He used to speak of them as his ' honeymoon trip,' and
as the very happiest time of his whole life. He made
work subservient to enjoyment, and the holiday was in
this way the first, not on duty, that Mrs Forbes and
he had spent together." [1]

Edward Forbes had found out too the charm of the
society of his other companion on this expedition—a
companion who was so modest and unassuming, so full
of knowledge, and ever so ready to impart it. In
rough notes for 1853 we read that on September 23rd
a visit (no doubt a joint one with E. Forbes) was paid
to the famous conchological collection of Deshayes,
when among a multitude of shells Prestwich detected
a *Cyrena semistriata* having a strong resemblance " to
the unexp. spec. at Deptford." [2]

---

[1] Memoir of Edward Forbes, p. 522.
[2] See Quart. Journ. Geol. Soc., vol. x. p. 138.

1853 was the date of his election into the Royal
Society, an honour prized by every man who has done
original work. Prestwich's certificate of candidature
for the Royal Society was signed by Lyell, De la Beche,
Murchison, Edward Forbes, Ramsay, Daniel Sharpe,
Bowerbank, John Phillips, W. B. Carpenter, George
Busk, and Huxley.

J. Prestwich to Sir Charles Lyell.   BRISTOL, *13th November* 1853.

MY DEAR SIR CHARLES,—I am hardly yet prepared to answer
your inquiries so distinctly as I could wish. "The Drift"
question is so beset with difficulties, and is of such extent, that
I cannot venture to bring it forward at one time, but I shall, as
with my Tertiary papers, discuss each stage of it separately. I
hope, therefore, that you will have returned before I bring forward the "Denudation of the Weald," as on that point I should
particularly wish to have the advantage of your discussion. In
many of Mr Trimmer's views I quite agree,—such as two or three
periods of gravel-spread, the more recent date of the mammaliferous beds of the Thames valley as compared with the boulder
clay, &c.,—but in many others I differ. The one to which you
allude—viz., the extent of denudation at this first period of subsidence—I cannot agree in. The denudation of the Chalk evidently commenced at the commencement of the Maestricht
period, and was continued through the period of the Thanet
Sands to that of the London Clay. During this long interval it
seems to me that the Chalk over the Weald was planed down to
a mere shell, and in many places worn away, so that the work
of denudation left to be done at the more recent "drift" period
was comparatively small. But even in this period I do not
believe that it was all done at once—there is, I think, on the
contrary, evidence of several successive clearances.

At the same time, unlike the slow wearing away of the older
Eocene period, I believe these recent changes to have been sudden
and violent in their operation. Not having my books with me,
I can hardly make the references which I could wish. My
section (No. 8, Quart. Journ. Geol. Soc., vol. viii. p. 258) is, as

you observe, merely a representative diagram. It probably conveys my idea as well as a more natural section. . . .

It seems to me evident that such a mass of materials derived apparently from the Chalk and Greensands, combined with the *distinct thinning off of the chalk, before it was covered by the Tertiaries,* as we approached the Wealden, indicates *clearly* the destruction and removal of a large portion of the Chalk within the Wealden area before the Drift period. Mr Trimmer in his diagram does not seem to allow for the facts. I shall be most happy on my return to town in a week or ten days to draw out a more correct section, and remain, my dear Sir Charles, yours very truly, J. PRESTWICH.

My first communication connected with this subject will be on the Red and Mammaliferous Crags. This I hope to have ready in the spring.

Many years elapsed, however, before his papers on these subjects were communicated to the Geological Society.

At Easter, in 1854, Prestwich, Austen, Daniel Sharpe, and Forbes paid another visit to France, to explore the districts called the Pays de Bray.[1]

This year was notable in the life of Prestwich for the production of several papers, but was most memorable from the fact of a proposition having been made to him, which, if it had been accepted, must have altered his whole life. Sir Henry De la Beche, the well-known founder of the Geological Survey,—his good and constant friend,—wrote to Prestwich offering him the Professorship of Geology at the Thomason College, Roorkee, adding as an inducement that it would be an opportunity for working out the geology of the Himalayas. In the kindest way Sir Henry gave him to understand that every facility would be afforded him for the furtherance of this

[1] Memoir of Forbes, p. 531.

object, with regard to leave, allowances, &c. The offer was tempting, but there was no hesitation in the answer. It was impossible for Joseph Prestwich to abandon the City firm which held the family fortunes. Besides, he was not a good subject to begin a career in a climate like that of India : he was forty-two years of age, and his health had suffered from overwork. Added to these reasons, each of which was imperative, there were others which drew and held him to his native soil. He had thrown himself heart and soul into the elaboration of his Tertiary papers ; he was thinking out the intricate problems which, until his Memoirs appeared, had never before been clearly made out. On all counts, therefore, he decided to remain and plod on as the hard - working City man.

A letter regarding his Tertiary papers from the illustrious Professor Adam Sedgwick [1] will be read with interest :—

A. Sedgwick to J. Prestwich.　　　　　　　Norwich, *May* 11, 1854.

My DEAR SIR,—During the single day I was in London I left one or two of my papers in a parcel addressed to you at the Geological Society. I hope you will accept them as a mark of my respect and gratitude for your very valuable services in disentangling the relations of our Tertiary series. It is nearly over with me as a field geologist ; for my health has failed me so that I am now incapable of the hard labour in which I once delighted ; and my eyes have so greatly failed that I am unfitted for the comparatively easy work of collecting specimens in the quarries. Indeed I never was a patient collector, though once I had intense pleasure in working among the difficult and puzzling sections of our older rocks: but that work is nearly over on my

---

[1] The Rev. Adam Sedgwick was a Canon of Norwich Cathedral and also Woodwardian Professor of Geology at Cambridge. Born March 1785 ; died January 27, 1873.

part, and others have taken it up with great effect. I should rejoice to see you in Cambridge any time that I am resident. For the next two months I shall be a prisoner in the Cathedral Close.—Very truly yours, A. SEDGWICK.

J. Prestwich to Sir Charles Lyell. NORWICH, *3rd July* 1854.

MY DEAR SIR CHARLES,—I shall be in town in a day or two, but write now to answer your question about the sand-pipes on the escarpment of the N. Downs.

I drew attention to the fact in my paper read in March, on account of its importance in showing at how very recent a date the last most important denudation of the Weald took place. The section I gave agrees with your sketch. The slope, whenever I have seen it, is quite bare, and shows no signs of an old cliff. There is, it is true, a little chalk rubble, but that might arise from pluvial action.—I remain, my dear Sir Charles, yours very truly, J. PRESTWICH.

In 1854 we have also an array of papers which appeared during that year. The one which stands first on the list is the second of his Tertiary memoirs, " On the Structure of the Strata between the London Clay and the Chalk in the London and Hampshire Tertiary Systems. Part II., The Woolwich and Reading Series." In this paper an account is given of the impressions of fossil leaves from a bed of clay in the railway-cutting for the Newbury branch line, through the hill immediately west of Reading. An excellent plate shows these beautifully preserved impressions of plants, and in a note by Sir Joseph D. Hooker, also accompanying Prestwich's paper, the botanist remarks that, " both in a geological and botanical point of view, the Reading fossils are of first-rate interest and importance, as presenting us with an association of forms so entirely analogous to those now existing, as to leave no grounds for assuming that the now prevalent forms of foliage amongst Dicotyledonous plants did not predominate before the glacial epoch, posterior to which all the existing British plants, except the alpines, were introduced into our island, as has been shown by Professor E. Forbes in his Essay on the Flora and Fauna of the British Islands."[1] The paper following it is a short one, "On some Swallow Holes on the Chalk Hills near Canterbury." That which succeeds it is "On the Thickness of the London Clay; on the Relative Position of the Fossiliferous Beds of Sheppey, High-gate, Harwich, Newnham, Bognor, &c.; and on the Probable Occurrence of the Bagshot Sands in the Isle of Sheppey." The memoir immediately next to the preceding, and which treats of the same geological formations from the palæontological side, is entitled, "On the Distinctive Physical and Palæontological Features of the London Clay and Bracklesham Sands; and on the Independence of these two Groups of Strata."

Of these Eocene memoirs, Edward Forbes wrote—and he was no mean judge: "These remarkable essays embody the result of many years' careful observation, and are unexcelled for completeness, minuteness, and excellence of generalisation."

It will be observed that in 1854 there was a great amount of published work. It is true that all this geological literature had been thought out and worked at before, yet the amount of patient labour is "amaz-ing," when it is remembered that his daily duties ab-sorbed what are usually deemed the working hours of the day.

Besides the writings which were brought out by the

[1] Quart. Journ. Geol. Soc., vol. x. p. 165, 1854.

Geological Society in 1854, Prestwich gave the first of three lectures on the 1st May at the Clapham Athenæum, on the geology of Clapham and of London generally. There was a particular fitness in his delivering these lectures, as he was a native of the place, and knew every inch of ground described; they were heartily received (the two other lectures being given in April 1856), and although not written with a view to publication, they were brought out (at the request of friends) in 1857 in book form, as the well-known little work, 'The Ground Beneath Us: Its Geological Phases and Changes.' There were then but few elementary treatises of geology, and none, like those at the present time, which combined the soundest instruction in the most simple and pleasing language, so as to make geology easy; therefore it supplied a real want. It was written with the terse clearness which characterises all his writings, and was deservedly popular. Letters of congratulation on the appearance of this booklet poured in from the old geological leaders, some of them couched in the most generous terms. It was acknowledged to be the best possible introduction to geology, and had a large sale. Twenty years later Professor Huxley was heard by the writer to single it out and recommend it to his class for study, as the best exponent of the geology of London and its neighbourhood.

Although the record of geological papers for 1855 is shorter than that for 1854, still 1855 is signalised as being the year which produced another of the Tertiary memoirs — those memoirs on which his fame as a geologist will to a certain extent rest. It bears the title, "On the Correlation of the Eocene Tertiaries of England, France, and Belgium."

It had been preceded by two papers of relatively less importance, namely, by that "On a Fossiliferous Deposit in the Gravel at West Hackney," and "On a Fossiliferous Bed of the Drift Period near the Reculvers." The two which followed it were, "On the Boring through the Chalk at Kentish Town," and a "Note on the Gravel near Maidenhead, in which the Skull of the Musk Buffalo was found." These were both read in 1855, and appeared in the Geological Society's Journal in 1856.

Reference is made to the last paper in the following letter to Mr Lubbock,[1] who subsequently was his companion in several excursions :—

MARK LANE, 10/7/55.

MY DEAR SIR,—I am rejoiced to hear of the discovery of the musk-ox in the Maidenhead gravel. . . . There are several other large pits in the valley gravel which may be worth examining. Could you also inquire whether any bones were found in the gravel cutting of the Wycombe Railway at the hill (Folly Hill) adjoining Maidenhead? I inquired, but was not quite satisfied with the answer I obtained, although it was in the negative and agreed with my general views on the subject. On Saturday last instead of going to Staines I went to Brentwood and Warley. I shall most probably therefore go to Staines on Saturday next, and in that case shall require the map which I herewith send. If you will let me have it on Friday evening or Saturday morning before 12, it will do. Sir C. Lyell and I went to Grays last week, but shall have to return to Ilford probably on Friday or Monday next. We shall not remain long at the pits, but would show them to you, and possibly, if you could accompany us, might have to leave you there, as I fear there might not be room in the carriage of Mr Meeson, who proposes to take us to some other pits in the neighbourhood. The Grays pits are, however, the great features, and these I shall be happy to show you, and to join you again there. Believe me to remain, yours very truly,

J. PRESTWICH.

------

[1] Now Sir John Lubbock, Bart.

MY DEAR SIR CHARLES,—Unless business calls me out of town, any alteration of the days will be immaterial to me.

I think you will certainly find work for more than one day at Pulborough. On Wednesday, the 18th, I am engaged. Thursday and Friday will do for Flower's and Ilford. When we go to Ilford, I should like to take you to Havering-Atte-Bower, Chigwell, and Hainault Forest, so that you may see the relation of the Ilford deposit to the surrounding drifts, which I think always essential.

No mammalian remains have ever been found in the high-level gravel, nor I believe in the mid-level, though the opportunities for finding them are almost equally good as in the valley gravel. The bones brought by Mr Lubbock from the valley gravel of Maidenhead prove to belong to the *musk-ox*,—the first found in this country,—a capital fact.

A newspaper paragraph which I have not yet seen announces the discovery also of bones and tusks in some gravel beds near Kingston.

The correction of my Correlation paper reminds me of some questions I had to ask you.

You give a list of shells from beds of sandstone in your section of Cassel Hill (Q. J. Geol. Soc., vol. viii. p. 331). May not these beds belong to the *Nummulites planulatus* series ? Although this fossil is not found at Cassel, M. D'Archiac alludes to fossiliferous beds of that age at Cassel. I have ventured to refer to that list (p. 3) as possibly belonging to the *Lits Coquilliers* zone. Can you now furnish me with a more complete list of the shells of the *N. planulatus* series than you possessed in 1852 ? Have you also increased your list of fossils of the *N. lœvigatus* (*Calcaire Grossier*) series of Belgium ?

If you can give me any information on these points I shall feel much obliged, and remain, dear Sir Charles, yours very truly,

J. PRESTWICH.

P.S.—I should much like to see Forbes's MS. about the gravels. He has, I see, adopted my term of high- and low-level gravels, and I believe agreed in several of my views. How deeply I regret he is not amongst us to continue the inquiry and description with us.

The following note, also to Sir Charles Lyell, gives a little glimpse of Prestwich's life in Mark Lane :—

MARK LANE, *Monday*, 1855.

MY DEAR SIR CHARLES,—I am not surprised that you complained of the exchanged coat. You have the best reason for doing so. On returning home this morning a red label on a coat on the sofa caught my eye. My housekeeper sometimes places there an old coat of mine that I use to read or work in. This is missing. When here on Thursday you must have placed yours on or by mine on the sofa, and in going away have taken up the wrong coat. I am glad to find that the exchange was made here and not in the railway carriage. . . . I hasten to return your coat, which I hope you have not wanted, and remain yours very truly,   J. PRESTWICH.

P.S.—I walked yesterday through a good cutting of the Lower Bagshot at Stroud Green and one good one of the Middle (Greensand) Bagshot at King's Beeches. I found no fossils, but traced the Wealden gravel over some extent of the ground. I have found the same gravel, but not quite so mixed with L. G. S., at Hazely near Strathfieldsaye.

In 1855 Prestwich was elected as one of the Secretaries of the Geological Society, Mr J. Carrick Moore being the other Secretary. This honorary post he occupied only one year, as in 1856 he became Treasurer of the Society, an office which he held until 1868. In this year he read his second correlation paper, " On the Correlation of the [Middle] Eocene Tertiaries of England, France, and Belgium." This was published in 1857.

The following letter from Sir Charles Lyell refers to this paper, and especially to the list it contains of those Bracklesham shells which occur also in the Paris

Tertiaries, showing their vertical distribution in the latter series. The table given in this paper of the Barton fossils, with their equivalents in France and Belgium, is also most elaborate.

MILDENHALL, SUFFOLK, *Janry*. 30, 1857.

MY DEAR PRESTWICH,—I only received your proof to-day, sent me here into the country.

It makes me very desirous to see more—please to send me other proofs: as I return to town to-morrow, I shall be able to let you have them again immediately. I have not sent to the press my pp. in which I adopt the term Lower Miocene as the name for what I have called in 5th edn. Upper Eocene, but I must send them in a few days.

Your paper interests me much—the tables at p. 10 [pp. 93, 118] in particular. They are well imagined and startling, and remind one of Barrande's Colonies, on which I am writing—two adjoining, contemporaneous, distinct natural-history provinces. You have brought out the difference well.

Darwin will make much of it. Some barrier there must have been, but I daresay the so-called species are permanent varieties, as you suggest, in many cases—like Lowe's varieties of many land shells in the different Madeira islands, which he makes into species.

If you give a general table pray send it to me, that I may see your divisions.—Ever, &c.,   CHAS. LYELL.

Perhaps Prestwich's mode of life at this time conduced to the marvellous amount of published work. Before he had assumed control of City affairs Mark Lane had been his home, where an old housekeeper ministered to his wants and provided—in conformity with instructions—his very simple fare. Soon after dinner, or about eight or nine o'clock, the note-books were by his side, with maps and sections; and with a sheaf of foolscap before him, it became his regular practice to write far on into the night. It was thus

in the hours robbed from sleep that the Tertiary
memoirs were penned. He pursued this course, this
"burning the candle at both ends," not without misgivings on the part of his friends—and they were
many. When practicable he went into the country
from Saturday until Monday, and thus had a refreshing change—a change which, it is needless to add, was
utilised for his geology. Also he occasionally spent
an evening with one of his married sisters, the three
nearest in age having then their own homes.

The genial nature of the man was shown by the
evening parties which he contrived to give in his
bachelor City establishment, when there was a goodly
muster of relatives and young cousins, whom he delighted to have round him, and amongst whom there
was always unanimity as to the great success of
"Cousin Joseph's party." Of course there was dancing
for the young people, no one joining in it with more
zest than the host himself. These parties made a
curious yet pleasant break in the monotony of his
evening work : in calculating the daily delivery of
springs and rivers ; in tabulating lists of fossils ; in
the careful drawing of maps and sections ; in thinking out, and in throwing new light upon, obscure
problems in geology.

The death of our geologist's father, which took
place in November 1856, made a great change in
his life, as it led to his return to the family home,
where his youngest sister, Civil Prestwich, was left
alone. Although his father was a man of culture,
he had little interest in science : but it was from him,
doubtless, that Joseph Prestwich inherited his artistic
power and fastidiousness in matters of taste. Collections of specimens of minerals, &c., which had grown

in bulk in Mark Lane,[1] of course accompanied him, the fossils and sands and clays going, as we can believe, without regret on the part of the worthy old housekeeper. Civil Prestwich was ten years younger than her brother, and they had a joint home until her death in 1866. She at once became his secretary and amanuensis, devoting her whole time to the furtherance of his scientific work, freeing his mind and time from all the wear and tear of petty distractions. He was eminently domestic: instead of the solitary City sitting-room and that daily Spartan fare, he had now all the comforts of a happy home. Civil was capable and intelligent, and under our geologist's guidance rough manuscripts were transcribed, registers were kept; and a folio volume of references which lies open before us is entirely in her handwriting, and is a model of method and order. There are four columns —for England, France, Europe, and other parts of the world—and the authors quoted imply a wide range of research, although chiefly on Eocene, Miocene, and later Tertiary geology. They include also subjects which were discussed in subsequent writings, such as Raised Beaches, Drift, Boulder Clay, Glacial Action, River Deltas, Wear and Tear of Land, Caves, Temperatures of Mines, &c., and Theoretical and Cosmical Geology.

J. Prestwich to Sir Charles Lyell.

2 SUFFOLK LANE, *2nd January* 1857.

MY DEAR SIR CHARLES,—The question is a difficult one. If Forbes is right in his synchronism of the Hempstead Beds with the Fontainebleau Sands, then I do not see where to draw the line of demarcation between those beds and the Barton Clays.

---

[1] The business house was subsequently 2 Suffolk Lane, Cannon Street, and, about the year 1862, 69 Mark Lane.

6
10
2
2
2

20

Slate
rubble

loose sand
cemented with
sands with
land shells

not exposed

cemented clay
with ...
clay with pebbles

schistose rocks

The rubble is also occasionally
(apparently) cemented. The
present sand & shingle also
occasionally cements a
land ...

The length of the beach (a
rather old shore & dunes) is
about 1 mile, & cannot be
...... 50 to 100 or 200 ft inland
at the broadest part.

The adjacent ~~shore~~
dunes present in place

RAISED BEACH AT BRAUNTON, 1855.

I am, however, not yet quite satisfied on the question of parallel-
ism, nor is it one on which I would venture on a positive opinion
without the few months' research I hope to be able to devote to
it this summer.   At present, however, I am inclined strongly to
place the Grès de Fontainebleau in the Eocene period.

I think it will be a great pity to break up these great time
divisions into small sections.   Let us have, if they like, Lower,
Middle, and Upper Eocene, and Miocene, &c., but not a multitude
of terms founded on that base. . . . —Yours very truly,

J. PRESTWICH.

J. Prestwich to Sir Charles Lyell.

[14] CLIFTON ROAD EAST [ST JOHN'S WOOD], 12th Jany. 1857.

MY DEAR SIR CHARLES,—The pressure of business, of family
engagements, and a visit to consult various books on the subject
of your inquiry, have been the cause of too long a delay in
answering your last notes.

The correlation by Forbes of the Hempstead series with those
of Limburg seems correct enough, but the English beds are so
much related to those beneath the Belgian beds also, tho' possibly
to a lesser extent; whilst, according to Hébert and others, the
Grès de Fontainebleau is so little, or is rather so very distinct,—
that I cannot yet feel quite satisfied that there is not an error
somewhere or other.

I cannot reconcile myself to the association in the same time-
division of the Faluns of Touraine and the Fontainebleau Sands.
It is true that if the former are to be excluded, the Miocene
period becomes reduced to very narrow limits, or rather exhibition, in France and England; but then there is the point to
which you allude, whether in other parts of Europe we may not
find the time marks, the strata of that period.   I think we must.

If the Miocene has yet to have its limits defined, and the
Fontainebleau Sands are to be considered as the commencement
of a new period of change, then I think we must look elsewhere
than in the French Faluns for the maximum development of its
peculiar types.   I should not at all object in that way to take
the Fontainebleau Sands as Lower Miocene, filling up the centre
and top with German or yet to be discovered beds, but then I
should feel inclined to take the Faluns of Touraine as part of

another time stage. I was not at all satisfied from what I saw at Bordeaux of the connection there said by some to exist between the equiv. of the F. Sands and the Faluns. The Fal. of Leognan are said to underlie certain freshwater limestones said to be synchr. with those of *La Brisé*—this was not at all clear to me. One fact was very [clear], that the Fal. of Sancats did overlie that limestone, and that the latter probably overlaid the Font. Sands; but then between the limestone and the Sancats Fal. I found no passage—on the contrary, I found a marked division. The limestone was all fresh-water, and its surface was worn and *covered with the holes of boring molluscs*. I think this had not been noticed before. . . . With regard to the other questions you ask me, I think the Barton Beds at Barton form quite an exceptional state of things. I have shown in my last paper that that series is exceptionally a sandy series, and that the clays set in in places, and I take the Headon Hill Sands as rather the type than the exception. Certainly the line should not, I think, be drawn between the Barton Clays and the Headon Hill Sands. I think I shall draw my next sub-line at the base of the old Upper Marine, but to this point I have not yet come.

I am most anxious to see Forbes's work on the Isle of Wight, to study more accurately the fossil evidence he has based his divisions upon. I hope shortly to have more leisure to resume geology and to attend to treasurership duties. In the meantime I am snatching a few moments to get a paper ready for the next meeting. The subject will, I think, interest you, "Crag on the North Downs."—Yours very sincerely,   J. PRESTWICH.

J. Prestwich to the Same.   SUFFOLK LANE, *Monday, 9th Feb.* 1857.

MY DEAR SIR CHARLES,—I do object very much to placing the Sables de Bracheux on the parallel of the Thanet Sands. It is possible, however, that the latter may come into some part of the French area; and in mineral character there would be so little to distinguish them that they would all pass under the name of the *Glauconie Inférieure*, but I think they would be found to pass under the S. de B.

I know of no solid argument adduced by Hébert. It is a point I worked out with great care, and it was only after a long time that I obtained evidence to be depended upon. It

could not be done in France — the evidence is wanting. At Richborough the one distinctly overlies the other. See my first paper on the "Correlation of the French and English Tertiaries." There are a few species in common, but the bulk are different. —In haste, ever truly yours,   J. PRESTWICH.

Before the date of the annexed note Joseph Prestwich made the acquaintance in the railway carriage of a fellow-traveller who had likewise been summoned as a witness, though on the opposite side, of a cause set down for trial at the Kingston Assizes with regard to a water question at Croydon. They had travelled to Kingston in the same carriage without interchange of a word; but, as for some reason the trial did not come off that day, they found themselves in the afternoon again in the same railway carriage, when they entered into conversation and found that they had many interests in common. This was our geologist's first meeting with Mr John Evans of Nash Mills, Hemel Hempstead, who in a letter to the writer remarks : "I took a great liking for him, and I think that he did not dislike me, and the result was that I called on him in Mark Lane and he returned the visit at Nash Mills, and thus began a friendship which lasted forty years, and which most materially influenced the course of my life. I cannot at present call to mind the exact year of our meeting, but our friendship was already of some standing when in 1857 he introduced me to the Geological Society." Much pleasant field-work was afterwards accomplished by the two friends, and when they differed on geological questions — as differ they did — it never caused the slightest abatement nor estrangement of the brotherly affection which had grown up between them, and which was ever the same to the end.

J. Prestwich to J. Evans.   LONDON, *Oct.* 24/57.

MY DEAR SIR,—Elephants appear to have been common at
Bedford in former days.   Last year, or the year before, the bones
apparently of a whole herd were found in the railway cutting a
few miles north of the town.   I have that place in view for a
trip next season, and shall be glad if we can manage it together.
—With kind regards to Mrs Evans, I am ever truly yours,

JOS. PRESTWICH.

My trip to the Alps is still *in nubibus*, as probably the Alps
themselves now are.

Dr J. D. Hooker to J. Prestwich.   KEW, *Sunday* [1857].

DEAR MR PRESTWICH,—I am very much obliged for your interesting, and to me most instructive, lectures to the Clapham
Athenæum.

I have had the Reading leaves in my mind very often, and
saw Dr De la Harpe when he was here.   He failed in persuading
me of the correctness of his views, from what in such cases is
too much the inevitable cause, namely, the preoccupation of my
mind with my own conclusions !

I cannot see even a probability (much less an evidence) of any
of the leaves being referable to laurels, Sapindaceæ, Eugenias,
Rhus, and Cassia, all of which Dr De la Harpe does not seem to
regard as tropical families, which they *most eminently* are.   It is
true that some species of each are extra-tropical, but plenty of
species of the European trees (amongst which I would prefer to
seek analogues for the Reading leaves) are also subtropical and
tropical.

No. 51 of your woodcuts can have nothing to do with *Rhus*,
though as species of *Rhus* have both simple and compound leaves
of all shapes and many varieties of nervation and texture, it
would be difficult to find a looser or less tangible affinity.

With regard to 52, which he refers to fig or mulberry, it would
be difficult to find a leaf that could not be compared with some
fig or other of the 200 or 300 known species of that genus ;
and as figs are eminently tropical and mulberries temperate
plants, nothing could be more vague than such an identification.

The long and short is that De la Harpe's conclusions do really indicate a very tropical flora. The one thing that De la Harpe and I agree in is that the leaves do belong to the very commonest forms in the vegetable kingdom of dicot. plants.—Believe me, ever most truly yours, Jos. D. HOOKER.

Besides "The Ground beneath Us," only one paper was contributed in 1857, namely, that "On some Fossiliferous Iron Sandstone occurring in the North Downs," and this under a slightly modified title was published during the following year.

J. Prestwich to Dr [Sir] Joseph D. Hooker.

CANTERBURY, *Janry.* 30/58.

DEAR DR HOOKER,—I am much obliged by your criticisms on my observations about the Reading leaves. You have, I suppose, seen Dr De la Harpe's paper recently published in the Bulln. Soc. Vaudoise. I feel that further evidence is necessary, and must try if the Reading cutting is still accessible. They were at work in the bed in a side cutting last spring. Could you possibly manage to run down some warm spring day, for the work is too sedentary for this weather? I should much like to go down with you. The leaves are most abundant, and you might see much that might escape me. First of all, however, I should very much like to look into the evidence myself to the small extent that I may venture by the inspection of the forms of leaves under your guidance. My sister also wants to look at some forms of ferns and a palm (?) that can be associated for cultivation in our smoky atmosphere—not as a botanist, but for the pleasantness of green leaves and beauty of form. We purpose, then, visiting Kew Gardens some Saturday (now a comparatively leisure day with me), and if you could kindly spare me an hour or two to put me in the way of looking right and at the right things, I shall feel particularly obliged. I shall be in town again after Tuesday, and am yours most truly,

Jos. PRESTWICH.

The following letter from the veteran geologist, Mr

Leonard Horner, father of Lady Lyell, expresses his interest in our geologist's work :—

L. Horner to J. Prestwich.   MANCHESTER, *7th March* 1858.

My DEAR PRESTWICH,—It is only within the last three days that I have had an opportunity of reading " The Ground Beneath Us." Here in the evening, when the spinning-jennies are at rest, and when there are few temptations of parties and learned societies, I get through some very agreeable reading, as we generally bring with us a good supply of books. I do not know when I have read anything geological that has pleased me so much as these three lectures. In a clear attractive style you have described the great and minute features of the area, not in the least descending to what is commonly called " a popular view," but a masterly sketch, that must be perfectly intelligible to every educated person who for the first time has had geological phenomena placed before him, and embracing those great generalisations which must awaken the deepest interest and wonder.

You will do a great service to the cause of philosophical truth, will awaken a widespread interest in geology, especially among those living in the district you describe,—you will give a death-blow among them to the nonsense of Mosaic geology now so widely disseminated, if you will publish these lectures, not by Van Voorst, but by some publisher of extensive connections, such as Longmans or Murray. You have no occasion to add anything. I would omit from the title-page "being three lectures on," &c., down to " 1856." You can tell this in a brief preface. If you will do this, the little volume will be translated, I have no doubt, both in French and German. It would be best in 12mo, and the two plates might fold lengthways. The only criticism I have to make is to request you to consider what you say at p. 77, that the alterations in the proportions of sea and land could not cause a heat sufficient for the tropical organisms of the London Clay, by reading again Lyell's chapters on Climate in the last edition of his ' Principles.'

But I have not done with you : follow up the sketch with a volume fully descriptive of the same period. You say, p. 37, " I could have said much more." I hope you will say all you have to say.—Yours faithfully,   LEONARD HORNER.

The above letter revives happy personal recollections of Mr Horner, whose kindliness and steady friendliness made a deep impression on the writer. Mrs Horner died at Florence on the 22nd May 1862, and about a month later a copy was sent from there of the pathetic inscription on her tombstone in the Protestant cemetery. The last lines run :—

> " Thus do we walk with her, and keep unbroken
> The bond which Nature gives ;
> Thinking that our remembrance, though unspoken,
> May reach her where she lives.'

The little message in his handwriting in the corner of the paper—" with much regard, L. H."—has been a prized memento of both. In less than two years he had rejoined her, his death having taken place early in March 1864. Mr Horner had been twice elected President of the Geological Society.

CHAPTER V.

1858–1859.

BRIXHAM CAVE—FLINT IMPLEMENTS—VISITS TO ABBEVILLE—GOWER CAVES.

PRESTWICH'S attention for some time had been occupied with fossiliferous deposits in the Drift and with raised beaches, his investigations of the latter leading to those wide generalisations which later he was to give the world in a series of papers to the Royal Society. As a whole, his work had been chiefly in stratigraphical geology : he had worked out in detail the structure of the London and Hampshire basins as no one else had done, and he had made himself the chief geological authority on water-supply. But his powers were now to be directed to a new field of research, in which he became an acknowledged pioneer, and which brought about a complete revolution of modern thought regarding the antiquity of the human race. In this new inquiry his extraordinary memory was of especial service. He never forgot what he had observed and written, so as years went on and fresh discoveries threw further light on unsettled questions, this gift of memory enabled him to bring all his accumulated knowledge to bear upon the subject immediately under consideration.

Dr HUGH FALCONER, F.R.S.

In his researches now on the antiquity of man, he went hand in hand with his friend, Dr Hugh Falconer,[1] who two or three years before had returned to England from a long career in the East, where for a time he had been director of the Botanic Gardens at Saharunpore, and subsequently of those at Calcutta. It was, however, as a palæontologist that Hugh Falconer was best known, and as joint author with Sir Proby Cautley of a work on the fossil fauna of the Sewalik Hills, the 'Fauna Antiqua Sivalensis.'

Ossiferous caves had from time to time been dis-covered in England, but after the publication of Dr Buckland's 'Reliquiæ Diluvianæ' in 1823, the subject long ceased to attract attention. Falconer and Prest-wich were, however, cognisant of the fact that the fossil contents of several caverns had been crowded together pell-mell in local museums, occasionally with-out any label to show where they had been found.

Both palæontologist and geologist were keenly alive to the importance of carefully working out any cave evidence, and the opportunity they sought soon offered for the systematic excavation of the contents of a cavern.

On the 10th of May 1858, Dr Falconer addressed a letter to the Secretary of the Geological Society of London, announcing the discovery of a new and un-disturbed cave on Windmill Hill overhanging Brixham village, near Torquay. It was situated on a slope in the same tract of Devonian limestone in which the caverns of Kent's Hole, Anstey's Cove, Chudleigh, and Berry Head are found. Mr Philp, a dyer, had bought the site with the intention of utilising the limestone and building cottages, when, in November 1857, a small hole was detected in quarrying. Further work revealed

[1] Born February 29, 1808 ; died January 31, 1865.

a wider opening, and in the spring of 1858 the work-men were no longer in doubt but that they had come upon the entrance of a cave with branches. Dr Falconer urged that, as the fossil contents of several important English caves had been extracted without care or atten-tion, and had been scattered piecemeal, the Council should take immediate steps to prevent this being repeated in the case of the Brixham cave, and should arrange for systematic investigation.

The consequence of this letter was, that a recom-mendatory resolution was passed by the Council of the Geological Society, with the result that " the Royal Society, on May 13th, gave a grant of £100 towards the exploration of the cave in the manner suggested by Dr Falconer. Miss Burdett - Coutts contributed £50 towards the same object. At Dr Falconer's sug-gestion, a committee was appointed to carry the design into effect. The committee consisted of Professor Ramsay, Mr Prestwich, Sir Charles Lyell, Professor Owen, Mr Beckles, the Rev. R. Everest, and Mr Godwin - Austen. Dr Falconer was entrusted with laying down the plan and giving the instructions upon which the exploration was to be conducted, and the works were carried on under the immediate superin-tendence of Mr Pengelly. The fossil remains were identified by Dr Falconer. On the 9th September 1858 a report on the progress of the operations, drawn up by Professor Ramsay, Mr Pengelly, and Dr Falconer, was submitted to the General Committee, and by them was forwarded to the Royal Society, which, from the importance of the results already elicited, voted an additional sum of £100 to prosecute the inquiry." Almost immediately afterwards Dr Falconer was com-pelled to proceed to the south of Europe on account of his health, but the explorations were continued with unflagging energy and enthusiasm by Mr Pengelly.[1]

Prestwich heartily co-operated with Falconer, and approved of all the steps taken. Several years later, owing to the death of Hugh Falconer, at the request of the General Committee he drew up the final report on Brixham Cave. The excavations in it yielded rude flint implements of human workmanship, associated with the fossil bones of Pleistocene mammalia, thus indicating the presence of early man.

It may not be out of place here to transcribe the following letter, which was published in the first volume of the 'Geologist' (p. 252). It shows the interest with which the discoveries in Brixham Cave were welcomed, and its date almost coincides with that of Dr Falconer's letter to the Geological Society:—

To the Editor of the 'Geologist.'   [10] KENT TERRACE, 11th *May* 1858.

SIR,—Amongst the many interesting problems we have to investigate, and that are, now in particular, attracting the attention of geologists, is that which relates to the character of the fauna inhabiting this land during some of the later geological periods. Those only who have worked at this subject can form any idea of the vast number of elephants, rhinoceroses, oxen, deer, &c., which must, at more than one period, have flourished in this country on surfaces now buried beneath drift and gravel. Occasionally their bones are met with in very large quantities, but their distribution is very irregular and uncertain. The fact of their occurrence, however, frequently remains unknown beyond the place where the discovery is made, and the knowledge of such facts is too often lost or forgotten for want of a convenient and ready record.[2] Your pages could afford, sir, exactly the

---

[1] Palæontological Memoirs : Hugh Falconer, vol. ii. p. 486.

[2] "There is a case in point in another communication I have sent you. In that instance I happened to visit a gravel-pit, opened only temporarily, and find remains of elephants, of which no record would have been preserved but for my chance visit. See 'Geologist,' vol. i. p. 252."

facilities required. Thus it would be of great use, and I, for my own part, should feel particularly obliged if any of your correspondents in different parts of the country could furnish us with information on this point. I would confine myself more especially to the occurrence of the bones of elephants (the teeth and tusks being so easily recognised), although, at the same time, any information respecting the bones of other animals would be very acceptable; and I would ask for a mention of their occurrence—naming place, character of deposit, depth beneath the surface, position, whether in valley or on hill, &c. Such information you might tabulate monthly or quarterly, mentioning the authority. Or what would form a still more valuable record would be, that resident correspondents should each take a county, and give a list of places where such remains are or have been found. We particularly require information in this respect with reference to Northumberland, Lancashire, Cumberland, Cheshire, and other northern counties, although in the more southern counties the same particulars are also in many cases equally required. An additional interest now attaches to this subject, from the circumstance that there are indications of each different stage of this Pleistocene period having been marked by different species of elephant, &c. If these can be distinguished by the aid of Dr Falconer's forthcoming paper in the 'Quarterly Journal of the Geological Society,' the information furnished will be the more valuable.—I am, sir, yours truly,   JOSEPH PRESTWICH.

J. Prestwich to H. Falconer.   10 KENT TERRACE, 7/5/58.

MY DEAR DR FALCONER,—I twice had Lartet's paper in my pocket to call on you with it, but was both times prevented by business. I should much like to hear more of your Western progress, and will take an early opportunity to call on you, if possible, before I leave town on Thursday. I shall be at the Royal Society to-morrow evening. If I do not see you there, I will try to call on you at $5\frac{1}{2}$ on Monday.

I am the more anxious to hear what you have seen in Devon as I am going there shortly, after first a visit to Rouen, Paris, and Brussels, and intend to visit Banwell and a few other places I have not yet seen.

I was at Grays a short time since, and have made a good beginning with the plants. I return there again in 2 or 3 weeks to reap, I hope, a further harvest, having set all the people to work, and Mr Meeson having kindly given all the necessary orders to his workmen, and taken charge of all specimens. I went also to Ilford for the same object, but at present without success. I am going again, having a pit opened in the meantime. —Yours very truly,　　　J. PRESTWICH.

Our geologist's movements were so rapid that the expedition to the Continent, and also that to Banwell (in Somerset) and Grays (in Essex), were doubtless made before he set out on the 2nd July 1858 on a journey of exploration in the Swiss Alps, which extended over several weeks. He was not accompanied by any English friend, but was frequently joined by Swiss geologists. Much as he delighted in working with friends and sharing with them his matured views, yet, on new ground or in face of any unsolved problem, he preferred to think out the difficulties and every aspect of the case—alone.

The contents of a note-book for July and part of August were intended to serve as data for projected papers on glacial action.

The first few days were occupied with railway cuttings and in quarries in the neighbourhood of Neuchâtel. Accompanied by M. Desor, the geologist, and by M. de Pury, the husband of his cousin Henrietta Blakeway, Prestwich visited the Val de Travers in the Jura. The great stratified beds of gravel on the way to Berne were of special interest, and M. Studer pointed out to him the most striking geological features in its vicinity.

At Basle he had the advantage of the society and advice of another eminent Swiss geologist, M. Peter

Merian, where the roughly stratified gravel over the
flats adjoining the Rhine engaged his attention. The
geology of Bex is given in a few sentences, which are
followed by a striking outline of Les Diablerets with
numerous notes. It was probably on this occasion that
he paid the visit at Gryon to M. Renevier, the eminent
Professor of Geology at Lausanne, who guided him to
Anzeindaz (Alpes Vaudoises), at the foot of the Diablerets, where our geologist made a collection of choice
little Eocene fossils. Professor Renevier writes that in
returning they were overtaken by rain, and arrived at
Gryon completely drenched. Chamouni was afterwards
Prestwich's headquarters, whence, day after day, accompanied by a guide, he went from glacier to glacier,
never attempting any great ascent. He had looked
longingly at certain boulders near the Talèfre glacier,
where, "perched on the top of this cliff, are several
blocks of granite — one just on the edge of the cliff.
Could not get at them to see whether foreign to the
place." He was intent on ascertaining the rate of
movement of the ice, the origin of the boulders, and the
composition of the moraine gravels.

The numerous notes and sections give the altitude
of the moraines of different years, the smoothening or
polishing of granite blocks—whether sharp or rounded,
angular or sub-angular, or striated—observations on
ice-action in every phase, which would chiefly interest
an Alpine geologist familiar with the high Alps. One
sketch is that of the "Éboulement" of Les Mossons,
which spreads over half the valley now covered with
fields and houses. A guide refers it "au temps du
Déluge." Visits to St Gervais and to Sallanches ended
this tour in Switzerland.

On his return to England it was to find that the

results obtained from the excavations at Brixham were of much importance. In writing to Falconer on 14th September 1858, he suggests that another cavern might well be explored, "such for example as one on the Welsh coast, or a portion of Kent's Cavern, or 100 yards square of some bone-strewed surface gravel, such as a section of the rich bone-bearing gravel at Bedford, or Brentford, or Clacton, or Herne Bay, or Bracklesham, or many others."

The caution expressed in this next letter is characteristic :—

J. Prestwich to H. Falconer.   LONDON, *21st Septr.* 1858.

MY DEAR DR FALCONER,—I have to-day read the report and returned it to Ramsay. It will do very well for the London Committee, or the Roy. Soc., but for my own part I should not like to have it read at the Brit. Assoc. A report of that sort comes with a degree of might and authority which a short notice would not have. The statement you make with regard to human industrial remains is one likely to give rise to so much controversy, and is one which you make so distinctly, that I do not like to see it embodied in a report which may be supposed to express the opinions of the several members of the Committee, and in which I see my name introduced.

Now, although you have so good a case with regard to occurrence and position of the worked flints, I yet hesitate to accept the conclusions, and many others will probably do the same. There may be possibilities of mistake which further working may serve to correct, or on the other hand further workings may bring to light other facts tending to prove indisputably the remarkable association you allude to.

I quite agree with you that there is now much evidence tending in the same direction—so much that there is hope that, if true, it may receive some unmistakable corroboration : but until we have that, and that I have myself *worked* on the ground and looked at all the bearings, I hesitate and wait.—My dear Dr Falconer, yours very truly,   J. PRESTWICH.

In a note to Falconer, dated 28th September, he remarks :—

I am glad you have been to Folkestone. The bones there were in brick-earth or gravel. Those at Dover in chalk rubble. I should fear from what you say and what I have seen that the ruminants are in a state of confusion. It is not surprising, considering that all the Drift deposits have commonly been shovelled together into one dirt heap.—Ever yours truly,

J. PRESTWICH.

Another letter, dated "Tuesday," refers to the Folkestone fossils.

J. Prestwich to H. Falconer.

See 'Quart. Journ. Geol. Soc.,' vol. vii. p. 261. You will there find a paper by Mackie on a Pleistocene deposit at Folkestone, and among the fossils the hippopotamus and megaceros.

Is it possible that the hippopotamus of these late Pleistocene deposits is of the same species as that of the Norfolk coast?

With regard to Shorncliffe, I heard of it too late to visit it. Intending, however, to go, I made inquiries about the where-abouts, and found that although the bones came last from Shorn-cliffe they came first from Folkestone. It is, in fact, the same bed as described by Mackie, and was reopened in enlarging or repairing some of the works connected with the small fort above the Pavilion. The collection is certainly of great interest. —Ever truly yours,   J. PRESTWICH.

Three of his geological papers appeared this year, the most important being that on the westward extension of the Old Raised Beach of Brighton. It was significant of work to be done in the future.

But the incident for which 1858 is to be noted was the receipt by Prestwich of a letter from Hugh Falconer, written from Abbeville, when on his way to Sicily for the winter. The results to which it led

M. BOUCHER DE PERTHES.

were so important, bringing about so suddenly a revolution of opinion in the scientific world, that we
transcribe it in full :—

H. Falconer to J. Prestwich.　　　　ABBEVILLE, 1st *Nov.* 1858.

MY DEAR PRESTWICH,—As the weather continued fine, I determined on coming here to see Boucher de Perthes' collection.
I advised him of my intention from London, and my note luckily
found him in the neighbourhood.　He good-naturedly came in to
receive me, and I have been richly rewarded.　His collection of
wrought flint implements and of the objects of every description
associated with them far exceeds anything I expected to have
seen, especially from a single locality.　He had made great
additions, since the publication of his first volume, in the second
—which I have now by me.　He showed me "flint" hatchets
which *he had dug up with his own hands* mixed *indiscriminately*
with the molars of *E. primigenius*.　I examined and identified
plates of the molars—and the flint objects, which were got along
with them.　Abbeville is an out-of-the-way place, very little
visited, and the French *savants* who meet him in Paris laugh at
Monsieur de Perthes and his researches.　But after devoting the
greater part of a day to his vast collection, I am perfectly satisfied that there is a great deal of fair presumptive evidence in
favour of many of his speculations regarding the remote antiquity of these industrial objects, and their association with
animals now extinct.　Monsieur Boucher's hotel is from ground-
floor to garret a continued museum filled with pictures, medieval
art, and Gaulish antiquities, including antediluvian flint knives,
fossil bones, &c.　If, during next summer, you should happen to
be paying a visit to France, let me strongly recommend you to
come to Abbeville.　You could leave the following morning by
an 8 A.M. train to Paris, and I am sure you would be richly
rewarded.　You are the only English geologist I know of who
would go into the subject *con amore.*　I am satisfied that English
geologists are much behind the indications of the materials now
in existence relative to this walk of post-glacial geology, and
you are the man to bring up the leeway.　Boucher de Perthes
is a very courteous elderly French gentleman, the head of an

old and affluent family, and, if you wrote to him beforehand, he would feel your visit a compliment and treat it as such.

I saw no flint specimens in his collection so completely whitened through and through as our flint knives—and nothing exactly like the mysterious hatchet which I made up of the two pieces. What I have seen here gives me still greater impulse to persevere in our Brixham exploration. . . . —Yours very truly,   H. FALCONER.

The following letter, which is dated London, 4th February 1859, and refers to Brixham Cave, is addressed to Falconer, who was then in Palermo :—

J. Prestwich to H. Falconer.

MY DEAR FALCONER,— . . . Austen is satisfied that the flint instruments occur with the bones. After my last visit I cannot deny it, but still I am not satisfied without seeking every other possible explanation besides that of contemporaneous existence. None of the evidence which has come before me during the last ten years has appeared to me conclusive, and now we have an opportunity of settling the question more satisfactorily, we cannot be too cautious.

Austen and I spent a day at the cave, and left Bristow [1] there to take a plan and sections. This was in November. From several causes we have not yet recd. these documents, but we are now positively promised them. I understand they were not quite finished. When we have them before us we shall, now we have the money in hand, decide how next to proceed. The works have not been interrupted except for a week at Christmas. For some weeks past but little has been found—the greater part of the loam has been removed, and we are down to the gravel. After our visit in November we decided not to purchase the adjoining right of search. It was a gallery traversing the next quarry, and the greater part of [which] was worked away. We have plenty to do in the body of the hill. We left instructions to have all the bones packed up and sent to the Geological

---

[1] H. W. Bristow, F.R.S., in later years Director of the Geological Survey of England and Wales ; born 1817, died 1889.

Society. They are not yet arrived. Pengelly has so much to do, and is, poor fellow, just now greatly troubled by the failing health of a daughter. We had an interview with Vivian, which ended amicably, and by his consenting to withhold the publication of his notes on Kent's Cave, to which are appended numerous notes respecting the Brixham Cave. Austen and I do not exactly agree about our report; but nothing less will satisfy me than a full and complete examination of every part of the cave (now worked), the emptying to the very bottom of everything in the several galleries.

I am very glad you stopped at Abbeville, and am thereby fully confirmed to visit that locality at an early opportunity, and, as you suggest, to make the acquaintance of M. Boucher de Perthes. I trust you are enjoying fine weather, good health, and many caves.—Believe me, my dear Falconer, very truly yours,

Jos. Prestwich.

The wish expressed in the last sentence of the above letter with regard to caves was literally fulfilled. It found Falconer at Palermo in ecstasy about his discovery of flint implements associated with fossil bones in the cave of Maccagnone. He was also zealously engaged in making collections of hippopotamus teeth, which lay scattered in great quantity, with a few molars and bones of other extinct animals, outside the "Grotto di San Ciro" or "Mare Dolce," near Palermo, and where the women and children gathered them on the field in front of the cave in the intervals between his daily visits. It was a comical scene when an infant in arms, prompted by its mother, held out a tooth of hippopotamus to Dr Falconer, clasped by its tiny fingers. On one occasion forty-two mothers and children awaited his arrival, each provided with spoil. The mothers thought themselves liberally rewarded with a few quattrini, the smallest Sicilian coin.

April was the date in 1859 when Prestwich proceeded to Abbeville to make the acquaintance of M. Boucher de Perthes, whom he found a hale, hearty septuagenarian, enthusiastic, as well he might be, about his collection of flint implements. In France he was well known as an antiquary and archæologist and a voluminous writer of light literature,—perhaps no man was ever more possessed by the *cacoëthes scribendi*,— yet in England few had ever heard mention of his name. Although not a geologist, his name is so inseparably associated with the discovery of flint implements in beds of Quaternary age in France, that a few notes to recount his discoveries may not be out of place.

With a far-seeing sagacity which cannot but excite our admiration, M. de Perthes had predicted the certainty of his finding traces of man in the gravels of the Abbeville and Amiens district, and had during several years closely watched the excavations for the construction of a canal at Abbeville. Hence when in 1846 he announced the discovery of an ancient flint implement in gravel of the "Drift," associated with bones of elephant, rhinoceros, and other extinct animals, and when again in 1849 he asserted that numbers of rudely worked and chipped flint implements had been found with remains of extinct mammalia in the same undisturbed beds of gravel, geologists gave no heed to his announcement, and he was regarded as an amiable visionary. He challenged his countrymen to put his startling theory of so high an antiquity for his flint weapons to the test and make excavations for themselves in unbroken ground, but he was only laughed at. Dr Rigollot of Amiens appears to have been the one person in France who came forward expressing his dissent from the universal unbelief. He had been a vehement opposer of the views of M. de Perthes until he had personally examined the ground and the evidence, when his opinions underwent a complete change, and he became one of the strongest advocates for the recognition of the worked flints.

Throughout the whole of this famous inquiry, which had been prompted by that letter of 1st November, 1858, from Hugh Falconer, with characteristic generosity the latter invariably assigned the precedence to Prestwich, saying, "What I did was to stir up the embers of your interest in the matter into a quick flame."

In a chapter on "Primeval Man and his Contemporaries,"[1] Falconer remarks of MM. de Perthes and Rigollot, that—

The observations of both were either scorned or discredited. At the same time a quiet observer, of matchless sagacity and indomitable perseverance, Mr Prestwich, was making the Gravels in England an object of special investigation. Engaged during a long course of years upon the study of the European Tertiaries, he gradually worked his way up to the superficial deposits. Mr Prestwich's researches upon the Tertiaries, which have only been partially published, have earned for him the reputation of being one of the ablest geological observers of his time. But in the Quaternary sands and gravels he was unrivalled. Men have been in the habit of saying, in mingled earnest and raillery, that "point out a broken pebble amongst a thousand others in a gravel pit, and there is one who will tell you the point of the compass from which it came, the stratum which yielded it, the distance it had travelled, the amount of rolling it had undergone, and the time it had occupied in the journey." The power thus acquired was soon to be applied with clenching authority to the proofs of the antiquity of man yielded by those deposits.

On his memorable visit to Abbeville in April, Prest-

---

[1] Hugh Falconer : 'Palæont. Memoirs,' vol. ii. p. 584.

wich had been joined a few hours after arrival by Evans;[1] and next day, on account of a telegram received, they went together to Amiens, where they saw an implement *in situ* in the gravel, and had the section photographed.   The great caution exercised by our geologist in accepting no evidence except that which he had himself personally investigated was proverbial. In this case his decision was quickly made.   On the 26th of May—one month after his arrival at Amiens —his great paper, " On the Occurrence of Flint-implements, associated with Remains of Animals of Extinct Species in Beds of a Late Geological Period, in France at Amiens and Abbeville, and in England at Hoxne," was read before the Royal Society.

Before the completion of this memoir he made a second expedition to the Abbeville district, accompanied by Messrs Godwin-Austen, J. Wickham Flower, and R. W. Mylne.   This again was followed by a brief visit from Sir Charles Lyell, who happened to be in Paris at the same time.

Sir C. Lyell to J. Prestwich.

45 Rue de Ponthieu, 4th *April* [*May ?*].

My dear Prestwich,—I will be in time for the 4 P.M. train, and shall have an opportunity of talking over what you have seen at Joinville as we go to Precy together, and compare notes, as I have already seen C. D'Orbigny's section.

I shall go direct to Amiens, as I cannot stand getting there in the middle of the night.   It would unfit me for next day's work at Amiens.   In case your letters prevent you starting, I may say that I shall go at any rate to Amiens to the Hôtel de France et d'Angleterre.

I shall hope at any rate to have the journey together to Precy and to work next morning at Amiens.—Ever most truly yours,

Cha. Lyell.

—— - ——

[1] Now Sir John Evans, K.C.B.

J. Prestwich to J. Evans.　　　　　　　London, 18th *May* 1859.

My dear Evans,—I shall be restless until I visit Hoxne, especially as I wish to see it before my paper is read (which must be next week, if at all). So I want you to be so good as let me postpone my visit for a day or two. Cannot you come to Hoxne with me next Saturday at 3 P.M. and return on Monday evening? At all events I will, if convenient to you, take an early afternoon train to Nash Mills on Tuesday and report progress, and return on Wednesday morning. I should then equally see you and have the pleasure of the introduction which you promised me. I would have gone to Hoxne last Saturday, but did not like going there without you if possible, so I went *en attendant* to Salisbury, but without any success.

I have found out three brick pits at or near Hoxne, and hope to find traditions of the discovery and to have a trench dug on the right spot.—I am, ever truly yours,　　　Jos. Prestwich.

I enclose you two letters just received from M. de Perthes. I shall want a few lines from you for the Royal. . . .

This expedition to Hoxne, in Suffolk, was the result of Mr Evans having come across some flint implements found there in the end of the last century by Mr John Frere, F.R.S.,—to be seen in the museum of the Society of Antiquaries. Mr Evans's attention had at the time also been called by the late Sir A. Wollaston Franks to a flint implement found in Gray's Inn Lane, and preserved in the British Museum, and of which he (Mr Evans) gave notice in a paper to the Society of Antiquaries. This flint implement is notable as being the first discovered in Quaternary gravels in this or any other country. The paper was read on 2nd June 1859, a week after Prestwich's communication to the Royal Society. This latter made a great sensation, demonstrating as it did that a large portion of the flints in M. de Perthes' collection were of human workmanship, and pointing out their undoubted geological position. We quote one or two passages from the abstract of this paper :—

At Abbeville the author was much struck with the extent of M. Boucher de Perthes' collection. There were many forms of flints, in which he, however, failed to see traces of design and work, and which he should only consider as accidental ; but with regard to those flint-instruments termed "axes" (*haches*) by M. de Perthes, he entertains not the slightest doubt of their artificial make. They are of two forms, generally from 4 to 10 inches long, . . . and were the work of a people probably unacquainted with the use of metals. The author was not fortunate to find any specimens himself,[1] but from the experience of M. de Perthes, and the evidence of the workmen, as well as from the condition of the specimens themselves, he is fully satisfied of the correctness of that gentleman's opinion, that they there also occur in beds of undisturbed sand and gravel.[2]

With regard to the geological age of these beds, the author refers them to those usually designated Post-Pliocene (Pleistocene), and notices their agreement with many beds of that age in England.

Finally, our geologist stated that he—

Purposely abstained for the present from all theoretical considerations, confining himself to the corroboration of the facts :—

1. That the flint implements are the work of man.
2. That they were found in undisturbed ground.
3. That they are associated with the remains of extinct mammalia.

_____

[1] This only refers to the large worked *haches*. On his first visit to Menchecourt, the day after his arrival at Abbeville, he was fortunate enough to obtain in one excavation he had made to a depth of about 20 feet beneath the surface, several fine flint flakes with large bulbs of percussion in a bed with abundant remains of the mammoth and other extinct mammalia.

[2] Subsequently, Prestwich was summoned by a telegram from Paris, to which he responded by going to St Acheul, and finding an implement *in situ*.

A CONFERENCE ON FLINT IMPLEMENTS.

Prof. John Morris.   F. E. Edwards.
Joseph Prestwich.   Searles V. Wood.

4. That the period was a late geological one, and anterior to
   the surface assuming its present outline, so far as some
   of its minor features are concerned.

He does not, however, consider that the facts as they at present
stand of necessity carry back man in past time more than they
bring forward the great extinct mammals towards our own
time, the evidence having reference only to relative and not
to absolute time; and he is of opinion that many of the later
geological changes may have been sudden, or of shorter duration
than generally considered. In fact, from the evidence here exhibited, and from all that he knows regarding Drift phenomena
generally, the author sees no reason against the conclusion that
this period of man and the extinct mammalia—supposing their
contemporaneity to be proved—was brought to a sudden end by
a temporary inundation of the land: on the contrary, he sees
much to support such a view on purely geological considerations.

Before writing this paper, Prestwich, together with
Mr Evans, had made a searching examination of the
flints and gravels of Amiens as well as of Abbeville.
Both being experts in different departments—one from
his practical knowledge of geology, especially of the
more recent deposits, and the other holding the foremost rank in archæology—their joint opinion carried
great weight. Thus when their belief became public,
that M. de Perthes had made an important discovery,
and that a large proportion of the flint implements in
his collection were what he had claimed them to be,
men of science on both sides of the Channel cast away
their doubts and unbelief. Geologists hastened to
Abbeville to give their congratulations to M. Boucher
de Perthes, whose letters of this date, addressed to
Falconer and to Prestwich, are expressive of lively
gratitude. This gratitude, however, had previously
been tempered. It devolved on his English friends
to point out to M. de Perthes several spurious flint

implements in his great collection, in the authenticity of which he himself had implicit faith. These carefully worked counterfeits lacked the vitreous glaze and the staining of true implements, now termed "palæolithic," which the dishonest fabricator had been unable to reproduce. M. de Perthes had recklessly held out too tempting rewards for every implement found, and had probably paved the way for these forgeries which were readily detected by the experts, but they did not for a moment invalidate the evidence afforded by the many genuine flint implements.

Among the letters addressed to Prestwich, none throw more light on the questions which at that date occupied the minds of geologists than those from Mr Godwin-Austen. One more example is given in which is expressed, as usual, his delightful sense of humour:—

R. A. C. Godwin-Austen to J. Prestwich.

CHILWORTH, *June* 13 [1859 ?].

MY DEAR PRESTWICH,—I have two of yours unanswered: the first is as to whether "Quaternary" would not be a better word than "Post-Pliocene." Most decidedly so, for I hope to see Eocene, Miocene, Pliocene, and all their degrees ere long banished from geological nomenclature. Their introduction was a worse event for geology than even De Beaumont's mountain-systems.

I could not get away on Saturday: an old schoolfellow, wife, and children came here.

The Antiquity of Man question, in respect of which Owen now has his say, is doomed to be damaged by bad evidence and worse reasoning. I have long seen what the fate of the geologist would be from the time that he allied himself with the anthropologist and antiquarian. Falconer and Evans are to us what the two cunning Greeks were who conducted the fatal horse into Troy.

The only thing that can save us is to restrict us to the Silurian system for a year or so.—Believe me, yours ever truly,

ROBERT A. C. GODWIN-AUSTEN.

While Prestwich's researches in the valley of the
Somme had come to so successful an issue, he was ever
watchful of the evidence afforded by the excavations in
Brixham and other caverns, as will be seen by the
following letter :—

J. Prestwich to H. Falconer. [22nd June.]

MY DEAR FALCONER,—I have just received your note. Little
need be said about Brixham Cave, as your Palermo cave will be
the main business of the evening. Still I think some notice
desirable. It is not necessary to give all particulars—a slight
sketch will suffice. The subject is altogether new at the Society.
Ramsay's plan is quite sufficient to give a general idea of the
place, and an abstract of your first report will give all the main
points. I can speak about all the later facts (which are few),
and I have asked Austen to bring his report, and written to
Bristow to ask him for his. I think it important to bring all
forward, as the two cases you have discovered so strongly support
one another.—In haste, yours, &c. J. PRESTWICH.

In the Journal of the Geological Society it is stated
that—

On June 22, 1859, Joseph Prestwich, Esq., F.R.S., gave in a
few words the results of the examination of the Bone-cave at
Brixham in Devonshire.

The cave had been traced along three large galleries, meeting
or intersecting one another at right angles. Numerous bones of
Rhinoceros tichorhinus, *Bos*, *Equus*, *Cervus tarandus*, *Ursus
spelæus*, and *Hyæna* have been found, and several flint-implements have been met with in the cave-earth and gravel beneath.
One in particular was met with immediately beneath a fine
antler of a Reindeer and a bone of the Cave-bear, which were
imbedded in the superficial stalagmite in the middle of the cave.[1]

---

[1] Quart. Journ. Geol. Soc., vol. xvi. p. 189. See also remarks on the
exploration of Brixham Cavern, in Appendix, by Prof. T. G. Bonney,
F.R.S., to the 'Memoir of William Pengelly,' by his Daughter, 1897, pp.
296-300.

H. Falconer to J. Prestwich.

31 SACKVILLE STREET, W., *25th June* 1859.

MY DEAR PRESTWICH,—Many thanks for both your kind notes. I feel exceedingly obliged by the lively interest which you have taken in the Brixham Cave matter throughout. It is your cordial co-operation that has led to so much being effected. If the special results as at present disclosed are not very striking, the indirect consequences have been of great importance in launching the question of the antiquity of human remains in a fair and unprejudiced manner. Much attention will now be directed to the subject everywhere, by inquirers of every shade of belief, and we will arrive at the truth shortly. There is nothing that you have done in the matter in which I would not have joined. . . .

In the Maccagnone cave there was ample work for a pair of collaborateurs for months. I pretend to have done nothing more than *score* the first lines.

Many thanks for Vivian's edition of M'Enery. I have referred to Desnoyer's paper, but can find notice only of bones on the walls, not on the roof of the bone cavern.

We must make an effort to bring out the plates of M'Enery's fossils, &c. If the Palæontographical will not do it, we must set a subscription on foot.—Yours very truly,   H. FALCONER.

J. Prestwich to H. Falconer.   SUFFOLK LANE, *28th June* 1859.

MY DEAR FALCONER,—Thanks for your note. I quite agree with you that it is not the importance and beauty of the specimens that constitute the value of the Brixham Cave. I have constantly heard it objected that we have got but a poor collection of specimens. No doubt Kent's Cave would yield a richer store; but that is a subordinate consideration. The great object effected at Brixham is the complete and thorough examination of our cave, the number of the bones, the relative number of each set and of each animal, their condition, their place, &c., &c. Besides, there are all the sections and valuable physical data obtained, and which could have been obtained by no other means. So that if we cannot show fine specimens, we shall at all events be able to exhibit a yet more valuable, because rarer, array of figures and facts. . . .

You will find a notice by Tournal of bones adhering to the roof in the 2nd vol. 'Bull. Soc. Géol.,' p. 381; and again by Teissier, same vol., pp. 22 and 56. Marcel de Serres also somewhere notices the same fact—I think in a cavern in the Pyrenees. I will try and find out the reference.

On Saturday I was at Erith, where it seems to me the *E. primigenius* and *E. antiquus* occur together. On Sunday I saw only some Tertiary sections.

J. Prestwich to Sir Charles Lyell.　　　　28, 6, 59.

MY DEAR SIR CHARLES,—A main object of our visit to Erith was to see whether the *E. primigenius* and *E. antiquus* occur there in different beds. We found nothing *in situ* to settle the question; but a careful inspection of Mr Spurrell's collection leads me to the belief that no separation can at present be made. The greater number of teeth in Mr Spurrell's collection are of the *E. primigenius*. I saw only two of the *E. antiquus*. In universal character no distinction could be made. Still, the evidence is not complete. The Menchecourt species is, however, decidedly the *E. primigenius;* and then we have the *Cyrena fluminalis.* As to the question you ask me about the Shackle-well Gravel, it is a question I have asked myself the last fifteen years without being able to feel certain about an answer. My opinion long inclined to the belief that the Grays deposit is newer than the Boulder Clay; these other gravels of the Thames valley are consequently of the same recent age. Of late I have not felt so sure. I find the Boulder Clay sweeping down to a very low level in Essex. I find also that many rock specimens I referred to the Boulder Clay may also be referred to the great *Western* Drift, and I am not yet satisfied that I have got the correlation of these two drifts. I hope this summer to be able to work up all my evidence and go through all my collections. I must also again visit a few places in the eastern counties. I shall then begin with the Clay and work upwards, when I hope to find the difficulties which now perplex me disappear as they are handled in right succession. My impression at present is certainly that part of the materials of the Thames valley gravel is derived from the Boulder Clay, *or from a bed of gravel immediately preceding it*—that the Cyrena lived with the Mammoth, and that the *E. antiquus* is not confined to the age of the Bacton Beds. As to the gravel under the Cyrena-bed at Clapton, it contains, I think, almost all the specimens we saw at Victoria Park. Ten years since, I daresay I should have given you more definite answers; but the more I see of the subject, the more I feel involved in its complications. I see some objections to almost every position. . . . —Believe me to be very truly yours,

J. PRESTWICH.

J. Prestwich to H. Falconer.　　　　　　　　　　*2nd July* 1859.

MY DEAR FALCONER,— . . . The points for your inspection are in the first two papers. About the Brixham Cave, have I rightly expressed myself about the Report to the Geological Society, or shall I mention it in any other way? That to you the discovery is due is certain, inasmuch as the cave was started by you and worked in your way; that the weight of your opinion also led us all to consider the matter more serious, and seriously, is also certain. So you are the head and front of the cave, and the leader of this new inquiry, and as such you must allow me to place you. Will you therefore kindly look to these two pages and make such additions, alterations, &c., as you think fit? . . .

I am not sure now that I have said all that I want; but these letters coming in the hours of business, and on a busy Saturday, leave me but little time for consideration. Pray, however, consider me always, &c.,　　　　J. PRESTWICH.

J. Prestwich to Sir Charles Lyell.

2 SUFFOLK LANE, *6th July* 1859.

MY DEAR SIR CHARLES,—You have planned a charming excursion, and I wish I could meet you at Amiens or Rouen; but I doubt whether I shall be able. I shall probably return there later. At present the levels of the different pits are being accurately taken. For these I shall, I believe, be indebted to the Government engineers. Nothing can be done at present in collecting shells at Menchecourt, as the sands in which they

are found are 5 or 6 feet beneath the bottom of the pit, and
are only worked in winter. I had three tranches dug, but they
were not left open. M. Marcotte, a friend of M. de Perthes,
promised to collect for me all he could in the course of the
autumn or winter. There is no Pharmacien there who could
do it.

If you have a trench dug, let it be near where my first
trench was. At the last two I had dug I found nothing of
importance.

Of the sand itself you will find a good heap collected in one
part of the pit, and will find plenty of fresh-water and land
shells; but various shells are very rare. I got a few fragments;
but all my present specimens come from the first trench, so also
the *Cyrena*.

As for the *Cyrena*, here we found it on Saturday week high up
in the section in Simpson's pit at Erith; and you may remember
that Mr Meeson found a *Gryphæa incurva* in the ground quite at
the bottom of his pit at Grays. Was this from the Boulder
Clay? I have never seen one in the Western Drift. As for
these two Drifts, after great work I imagined I had found the
latter superimposed on the former on the top of a hill near
Brandon; whilst last year I found the Boulder Clay in a valley
near St Albans, with the Western Drift capping the hills flank-
ing this valley, and therefore apparently older than the B. Clay.
I must get a third case to serve as umpire.

I think the *Cyrena* existed at the time of the *Elephas primigenius* both at Erith and Menchecourt. Ilford and Grays I am
not certain about; but I have my doubts. The fact is, we have
many places where the *Cyrena* occurs; but unfortunately from
all the elephants having been *E. primigenius* formerly, sufficient
information of the exact fact is now wanting, owing to many
specimens having been overlooked, and not collected, or lost.

When you go to the Norfolk Cliffs, look again at Mundesley.
I have been there three times, and on each occasion came to the
conclusion that the shell- and peat-bed there *was above* the
Boulder Clay. On the last occasion I, however, found *another*
bed of shells *under* the B. Clay.

As for the exact order of succession, it is so complicated
that, as often as I imagined I had detected it, as often have I

been thrown out again.   When I think about it, some 300 or 400
sections and facts flit before me, some tempting me one way and
some another, until I feel fairly bewildered.   In the great coast
sections the matter is clear enough, but when we come inland the
confusion is great.   You have given two or three of the leading
periods in your note, possibly correctly.   I herewith give you
these and some minor ones.   I do not attempt any order, but
give them in round-robin fashion, merely to show you what we
want room for.   I do, however, hope this summer to reduce all
my observations, when I hope all will fall into proper order; and
I am, my dear Sir Charles, yours very truly,   J. PRESTWICH.

Satisfied by the success of his memoir to the Royal
Society, Prestwich addressed a letter to the French
Academy of Sciences urging the significance of M. de
Perthes' discoveries.   The title of this paper was,
" Sur la Découverte d'Instruments en Silex associés à
des Restes de Mammifères d'Espèces perdues dans des
Couches non - remaniées d'une Formation géologique
récente," and it was published in the ' Comptes
Rendus' for 1859.   The effect of this communication
was that his friend M. Albert Gaudry, a distinguished
member of the Institute, visited Abbeville and Amiens
to examine the implements and the flint-bearing beds.
He found worked flints *in situ*, and his researches confirmed M. de Perthes' statements : his report had the
effect in Paris that the paper to the Royal Society had
in England, and a French pilgrimage to the valley of
the Somme began, headed by well-known members of
the Institute, among whom were MM. de Quatrefages,
Lartet, Hébert, and many others.

J. Prestwich to Sir Charles Lyell.   11th August 1859, LONDON.

MY DEAR SIR CHARLES,—I was very glad to receive your
letter and account of your visit to Abbeville and Amiens.

I will answer your questions categorically.   My Cyrena is

nearly perfect. The most important part of the hinge remains, viz., that part showing striations. Morris has seen it, and there can, I think, be little doubt of it. It is about the size of the one from Shacklewell. I found 1 *Purpura lapillus*, 4 *Littorina littorea*, 1 *Buccinum*, 3 *Tellina*, 1 *Cardium*. These shells are scarce and uncertain. On my second visit, although two deep trenches were dug, not one marine specimen was obtained. My first trench went down to the hard conglomerate rock—3 or 4 feet beneath the flints.

I saw Drucat on my last visit and was much interested with the section. M. Boucher de Perthes gave me a flint implement from that locality. . . .

I have often seen the loess, both in France and Belgium, on different levels. A good exhibition of this occurs at St Peter's Mount, Maestricht. I don't believe in the faults.

With regard to the age of the Red Clay Drift with meulières around Paris, I am perfectly satisfied in my own mind that it is *older* than the drift of the valleys with land and fresh-water shells, bones, and granite, and that the valleys were excavated after the spread of the up-level Red Clay Drift.

I missed Chârtres on my last visit to France. I was going there, but waiting for some of my companions from England (who never came), I was detained in Paris until too late in the day. It is a place well worth visiting, as are also the others you name.

I am inclined to think Moulin Quignon older than Menche-court. I would not, however, assert that opinion. So I think St Acheul older than St Roch. This is in physical evidence, but the other evidence is so curious that I must again go over the ground and examine all the collateral facts before venturing at a conclusion. I should not be surprised at all proving of the same age, or nearly so.

I shall certainly go [to] Boves, and will write to M. Pinsard. I also saw one very white flint implement (in M. Boucher de Perthes' collection) with *red clay* adhering to it. It was from St Riquier. I do not remember one (white) with ochre, sand, or earth.

I am going out of town this afternoon for a day or two, and next week I start for Wales, but I doubt whether I shall be at Aberdeen. I shall be very glad, therefore, of a few lines to inform me of the result of your visit to Le Puy, and with thanks for your last long letter, I am, ever truly yours,

J. PRESTWICH.

I enclose you a curious *procès verbal* I have received from M. de Perthes. Please return it to him if you pass through Abbeville.

The following letter from the Rev. Charles Kingsley must have given pleasure to our geologist :—

C. Kingsley to J. Prestwich.

EVERSLEY RECTORY, WINCHFIELD, *August* 26, 1859.

MY DEAR SIR,—I have to thank you for—what I had no right to expect—sending me your pamphlet on the flint arrowheads of Abbeville, &c.

From your conclusion there can be no dissent. I, last of all men, should wish to impugn it from other causes: I have long expected some such discovery. I regret much that I missed Dr Falconer's paper on the Brixham Cave. Perhaps you would kindly tell me where I can obtain it.

You, I am sure, will appreciate the immense importance of your own statement. If corroborated, it must lead to a reconsideration and rearrangement of beliefs, as well as of geologic theories. It seems to me the greatest stride forward which has been made since the Semitic tradition of the six-days' creation was abandoned as untenable.

That religious persons will be angry, and try to crush the truth, you must expect. But I must compliment you on the modesty and tact with which you have at least staved off the evil day, by confining yourself to facts, and building no theories on them. By such a method, sound science will gain a firm root in thinking minds before the ignorant and suspicious public is even aware of its existence.

I must take this opportunity of expressing to you my deep obligations, as to the man who has taught me to find boundless interest and instruction in those barren Bagshot Sands on which I live, and hope to die.—Believe me, ever yours,

C. KINGSLEY.

Ignorant of your address, I send this to Burlington House.

Prestwich, eagerly on the track of any other evidence which might throw light on the antiquity of man, joined Falconer in the autumn of 1859 in an inspection of the ossiferous caves of Gower in Glamorganshire, when they were the guests at Stouthall of their kind friends, Colonel and Mrs Wood. Falconer had visited the caves in 1858 with Colonel Wood, who for a series of years had been engaged in excavations in most of the caves in succession. He had discovered and explored several that were previously unknown, and unreservedly had placed his large collections of fossils at Dr Falconer's disposal. He had been a quiet, persevering worker : the contents of cave after cave had been exhumed at his own charge and without public recognition.

Before joining Falconer for the work in Gower, Prestwich made a geological tour in Wales, extending over several weeks. He was in quest of Drift, Boulder Clay, and ice action, and had in view a personal examination of the slopes of Moel Tryfaen, where shells had been found at a height of 1360 feet underneath a mass of Boulder Clay. Step by step, halting at very many stages, the ground was traversed from Oxford on to St Asaph, where another visit to Cefn Cave [1] was irresistible.

J. Prestwich to H. Falconer.   LLANBERIS, *Septr.* 7/59.

MY DEAR FALCONER,—On receipt of your first note I wrote you a few lines from Ludlow, and hoped they would have reached Bryn Elwy before your departure. I missed you by one day, as I arrived on Friday evening. I was most kindly and hospitably received by your friend Captn. Thomas, who met me at the station—otherwise I should have gone to the inn, as I intended staying but one day, and it happened to be the first week in Sep-

---

[1] Since described by Professor T. M'K. Hughes, F.R.S., Journ. Anthropological Inst., vol. iii. p. 387.

tember. The following morning we drove over to Cefn : the day was fine, and we had a most delightful walk back. The geological interest also I found great. We remained some time in the cave, and I was fortunate enough to find a considerable number of fragments of bones and two nearly perfect teeth. I packed them up as I disinterred them, and have not looked at them since. One, I think, was the tooth of a deer; the other was too much enveloped in its matrix to say what it was.

I left Bryn Elwy on Saturday evening, examined the coast section at Llandudno, and am now here to see the Drift and ice-action around Snowdon. I remain here until Tuesday morning next, then proceed to Carnarvon, Tremadoc, and Cardigan to Swansea, which I hope to reach either on Monday or Tuesday week next, and still, I trust, in time to find you there. Please, however, write me a line per return to this place, to say the latest day to which you will remain at Stouthall, and I will do my best to have a day with you there.—I am, most truly yours,   J. PRESTWICH.

After noting in detail the glacial features of Conway and Capel Curig, he lingered in the neighbourhood of Cwm Glas over the *roches moutonnées* and *blocs perchés*, and gives a striking view in a few touches of the entrance below Cwm Glas. In short, the geology of this particular district fascinated him, and it was with evident reluctance that he tore himself away.

" The sides of Cwm Glas up to the little tarn show traces of rounded and striated rocks. They remind me of the small side glaciers pendent on the mountain-sides between the Glacier des Bois and Montanvert. I could not recognise any terminal moraine. The moraine at the entrance of Cwm seemed to me to be part of the great lateral moraine of the main valley of Llanberis." [1]

[1] It may be interesting to mention that Ramsay's account of "The Old Glaciers of Switzerland and North Wales" was first published in 1859 as one of the chapters in 'Peaks, Passes, and Glaciers,' by members of the Alpine Club. It was reprinted as a separate volume in 1860.

On September 12th he ascended Snowdon, next day proceeding to Carnarvon, and afterwards to Clynnog. Taking a circuitous route, he arrived at Stouthall from Swansea on the 20th. Next day, with the assistance and local knowledge of Colonel Wood, he commenced the joint investigation with Falconer of the caves on the picturesque coast of Gower. To quote the words of Falconer, "Its line of coast stretches from the 'Mumbles' on the E. to the 'Worm's Head' on the W., and with the indentations of Port Eynon, Oxwich, and smaller bays, it presents an iron-bound wall of bold, lofty, and precipitous or scarped cliffs, occasionally exhibiting features of the grandest description."

The best known of the caverns, which are at different heights above the sea, are "Bacon Hole," "Bosco's Den," "Minchin Hole," "Long Hole," and "Raven's Cliff." These all occur in this southern range of cliffs between Worm's Head and the "Mumbles." Nor must "Paviland Cave" be omitted, which was described in 1821 by Dr Buckland, and where the fragmentary skeleton of a woman was found. The bones were stained red; thus the skeleton was known in Gower as "The Red Lady of Paviland." How the poor human form was introduced into this cave, and came to be found in association with tusks and remains of elephant, is a problem that will never be solved. The generally accepted explanation is that the body was brought and laid there for burial.

One of the best-known of the caves is "Spritsail Tor," situated to the west of the Gower Peninsula and facing Carmarthen Bay. It was discovered by quarrymen in 1839, who had cut back into the Carboniferous Limestone. Although of comparatively small size, it yielded a large quantity of fossils. In 1849 it was thoroughly explored by Colonel Wood, who detected a second entrance.

As a whole, the fossil remains from the Gower caves, which varied in each case in numbers and species, were of surpassing interest. Teeth of *Elephas antiquus* and of *E. primigenius*; teeth and bones of *Rhinoceros hemitœchus* and *Rh. tichorhinus*; bones of *Bear* and *Hyœna* were found; but in quantity and in number of species the remains of deer were in the greatest abundance, especially those of the *Cervus Guettardi*.

In a list of fossil bones from " Long Hole" given in a posthumous note to Dr Falconer's 'Ossiferous Caves of Gower,' two species of *Elephas*, two of *Rhinoceros*, two of *Equus*, and four of Deer, &c., are given. Also it is recorded that "flint implements, unquestionably of human manufacture, were found along with these fossil remains, and were sent to me by Colonel Wood. One very fine flint arrow-head was found contiguous to, and at the same depth as, a detached shell of a milk molar of *R. hemitœchus.*"

It was on this joint visit to Gower in 1859 by Falconer and Prestwich that the keen eye of the latter discovered a raised beach in Mewslade Bay, a mile in length, "perched upon the out-cropping edges of the limestone strata of the old cliff, which is but very little changed in the shape of its escarpment since the beach was formed, although still in close proximity to the sea."

He made an attempt to reach " Bosco's Den," but found entrance impossible. The entry in his note-book records that, " descending to the coast after [his examination of Paviland Cave], I found a superb raised beach thickly covered with *angular débris*. The

' head' decreases, but the raised beach continues to nearly opposite the Worm's Head. Then passing round to shore on w. side (Rhôs Sili Bay), the fine bold cliffs are precipitous, with no traces of a raised beach. Passing Rhôs Sili, the shore becomes more shelving, and a mass of *débris* in clay slopes down the hill. Farther on a low cliff commences, apparently Boulder Clay. Farther on a seam of shingle sets in, and in it I found several shells—perfect and broken," &c.

Prestwich returned to town after this interesting exploration of the Gower coast, yet he was again westward as far as Salisbury in the end of October.

One cannot resist giving a quotation from a humorous note of Dr Falconer's; it is dated about a year after his first visit to Abbeville :—

LONDON, 4*th* *Nov.* 1859.

MY DEAR PRESTWICH,—I have a charming letter from M. Boucher de Perthes, full of gratitude to "perfide Albion" for helping him to assured immortality, and giving him a lift when his countrymen of the Institute left him in the gutter. He radiates a benignant smile from his lofty pinnacle on you and me—surpised that the treacherous Leopard should have behaved so well.

M. Boucher de Perthes was by his success incited to pursue his investigations with increased ardour. That bone of contention, "The Moulin Quignon Jaw," had not then come to light, and his happiness and serenity were—for a while—undisturbed.

J. Prestwich to H. Falconer.   2 SUFFOLK LANE, *Novr.* 5, 1859.

MY DEAR FALCONER,—I am very glad to hear of your intention to remain in England this week, as by that I infer you are better able to stand this climate; and I rejoice in the prospect of your overhauling the Brixham Cave spoils. I am quite of your opinion as to sending down the cases to you at Torquay.

I was at Salisbury last week, and saw, in a collection just commenced by a Dr Blackmore, the bone of a bird and part of the jaw of the cave-tiger from Fisherton.

I also have had some very pleasant and kind letters from Boucher de Perthes. I wrote a short time ago to the French Institute respecting his discovery and my visit to the Somme. Have you seen M. Gaudry's paper, the one he read before the Académie des Sciences?˙ He has sent me a copy of it.—Ever truly yours, J. PRESTWICH.

P.S.—As I am going out of town (north) for three or four weeks, I will try to call on you on Monday morning, and will put Gaudry's paper in my pocket. We had a meeting of the Cave Committee on Wednesday. The point for consideration was where we should send the collection to. We considered it desirable to consult the wishes of the Roy. Soc. on this point. I also wanted to know yours.

The following note from Dr Robert Chambers is an evidence of his appreciation of the flints from the valley of the Somme :—

R. Chambers to J. Prestwich.

31 SOMERSET STREET, *Nov.* 12, 1859.

MY DEAR SIR,—I have received your packet containing two of the Amiens flint weapons. I could hardly have supposed you were willing to part with such precious relics of antiquity, and still feel some doubt as to your intentions. Assuming, however, in the meantime that you design me to retain them, I beg leave to thank you for them most earnestly. I shall have great satisfaction in showing them to the large and intelligent audience of the Philosophical Institution in Edinburgh when I give my lectures next month ; and perhaps it will ultimately appear best that I hand them into our National Museum of Antiquities, which already contains examples of such weapons (of ungeological history) collected in more countries than one.—I am, my dear sir, yours very sincerely, R. CHAMBERS.

On December 3rd Prestwich addressed a letter to the 'Athenæum' on "Flint Implements in the Drift," in reply to one through the same channel from Professor Henslow, who at that time objected to our geologist's conclusion that the flint implements of Hoxne were in all probability found as described by Mr Frere—*i.e.*, associated with the remains of the mammoth, and possibly of other extinct animals, in undisturbed beds of the Post-Pliocene age.

J. Prestwich to Sir C. Lyell.   28th December 1859.

My dear Sir Charles,—I think the report of the occurrence of the greater part of the skeleton of a rhinoceros in the "Sable aigu" at Menchecourt is to be depended upon. It is not, however, anywhere referred to that I am aware of, unless by Dr Ravin in the Mem. of the 'Société d'Emulation' of Abbeville. I have the series, but that volume is missing. I am promised it by M. B. de Perthes. Nor do I recollect whether M. B. de Perthes refers to it in his 'Anti[quités] Ante-diluviennes].' I think you have the vol. containing the Menchecourt section, which I sent you before you went to France. It is in the "Sable aigu" that flint implements are said by M. B. de Perthes to have been found, but I do not think the evidence conclusive. Still I think it probable most of the 'haches' M. B. de P. showed from Menchecourt had an opacity and porcelanic aspect which indicated extraction from a light-coloured clayey matrix, and I found that in the lower part of the "Sable aigu" there often is a subordinate seam of whitish clay. Others are stained ochreous, and I found small patches of ochreous gravel in the same position. Others again seemed to me, from the depth noted and their colour, &c., to have come from the loess-like deposit over the "Sable aigu." That the *Cyrena* came from "Sable aigu" I have no doubt. M. Marcotte promised to collect for me during the winter diggings. I shall, however, if possible, run over myself for a few days. It would certainly not be safe to take the hippopotamus of St Roch as of the same set of things. I found no worked flints there, nor had the present workmen ever found any (this, I think, should lessen or remove the suspicion which some have of the St Acheul workmen possibly manufacturing the implements, for if they [fabricated] these why not the St Roch men ?). Still Dr Rigollot mentions them. One of the things poor John Brown[1] did before his death was to spend some four or five days at Hoxne, working out the shells there, taking a load of clay away with him to continue the search at home. He mentions *Cyclas* but no *Cyrena*. I had a visit the other day from man A at Orton, near Peterborough. He still maintained, when I showed him the French specimens of flint implements, that he had found flints like them in the Orton gravel pits, and man B, who accompanied, confirmed it, and observed that he had seen more at the large gravel pits at Water Newton four miles from Orton, and where the gravel is 20 feet deep. I asked him to go over for a day and give me the results.—Ever truly yours,

J. PRESTWICH.

In his recent edition of 'Ancient Stone Implements,' Sir John Evans remarks, "At Overton Longville or Little Orton, two miles S.W. of Peterborough, a spot visited by Sir Joseph Prestwich and myself in search of palæolithic implements, about 1861, some were found a few years ago by the late Dowager Marchioness of Huntly."[2]

[1] John Brown, F.G.S., of Stanway, near Colchester, a zealous worker at the Pleistocene fresh-water deposits of Essex and Suffolk. Born 1779 ; died 1859.

[2] 'Ancient Stone Implements of Great Britian,' 2nd edition, Longmans & Co., 1897.

CHAPTER VI.

1860–1863.

ANTIQUITY OF MAN—FIELD GEOLOGY—
GEOLOGICAL MAPS.

THE subject of the Antiquity of Man now attracted universal attention, and Prestwich, who with Falconer had all along duly estimated the value of the evidence afforded by the English caves, was more eager than ever that the fossil bones exhumed from Brixham Cavern should be accurately determined. They had been sent to the Geological Society in London, but it so happened that as Dr Falconer had selected Torquay this winter as a residence, our geologist wrote early in January, suggesting that the Brixham spoils should be returned to him at Torquay, and this was accordingly done.

There were frequent letters between Sir Charles Lyell and Prestwich at this date :—

J. Prestwich to Sir Charles Lyell.   SUFFOLK LANE, *3rd January* 1860.

MY DEAR SIR CHARLES,—There is no doubt you were wrong originally about Mundesley. I satisfied myself on that point some years since, and have since returned three times to make sure about it before bringing forward my paper on the Crag and

K

beds above it. I worked it out in some detail when I was there, with Mr [the Rev. John] Gunn, and shall be happy to give you any particulars of my section you may require. Seeing its close analogy to Hoxne, I set off to Mundesley again last August, and reached Mr Gunn's. I there, however, heard of a section at Yarmouth which so much interested me and Mr Gunn that we both started for Yarmouth the following morning, leaving Mundesley for a future period. I much wished to examine the bed of gravel, A, under the peaty bed, as there, I think, there might be a possibility of flint·implements occurring. I directed Mr Gunn's attention to this point, and hope he may some day have a successful search. You might also find flints in your bed B, but it would be in A that I should particularly look for them. The *Elephas primigenius* has not been found here, but I believe it to be its position. The *Elephas* teeth at Amiens occur indiscriminately throughout the white gravel just as the flints do, but they are more numerous in the lower part of it. The place of one specimen was shown me some feet above the level of Mr Flower's flint. I wrote two letters to the 'Athenæum' in reply to Prof. Henslow's first letter, but do not think it necessary to write in reply to his letter in the last No. of the 'Athenæum.' I have not drawn up my last notes on Hoxne, but you will find the main points in the 'Athenæum.' I purpose sending them to the Royal Society. I hope, however, to see you to-morrow, and I am, ever truly yours,

J. PRESTWICH.

J. Prestwich to the Same.   SUFFOLK LANE, 14*th January* 1860.

MY DEAR SIR CHARLES,— My collection from Mundesley is very small. Your list I found so good that I did not set to work to collect much from the same bed, but went to new ground. I cannot therefore throw any light upon the occurrence there of the *Paludina marginata.* I am glad you feel some doubts about Grays. I have very strong ones. Hoxne, Mundesley, and Amiens, I should certainly place together, and I believe I mentioned so in my paper before the Royal Society. Another place I named was Copford, which I have not had an opportunity of revisiting, and now poor old John Brown, who knew every inch of that ground, is dead.

You asked me at the last Club dinner to look again at the Supplement you last published. I have done so. I do not quite agree with [S. P.] Woodward's numbers, as I make the species common to the Red and Norwich Crag greater. The difference, however, is not great or important, nor are my own lists sufficiently complete to give a definite answer. The general fact of a refrigeration, &c., I quite agree in; so also that there are more recent specimens in the Norwich Crag. I base my objections rather upon physical grounds and points of geological structure. Annexed is a rough sketch of what I think is the order of sequence. I am ever truly yours,   J. PRESTWICH.

There was less literary production during 1860, yet there was not less industry. The amount of field geology accomplished was extraordinary. Excursions were made to various parts of England—to districts west, south, east, north—and all explored with painstaking care. Frequent journeys were also made to the Somme valley: a flying visit was paid when worked flints had been found in any number. His ever active brain was marshalling the array of facts, and tracing the outlines of the great work which was to be given to the world two or three years later in the form of a memoir on the Geological Age of the Drift Deposits, in which remains of extinct mammalia had been found in association with flint implements. This persistent devotion to his science, however, was never allowed to weaken the affectionate relations which bound him to his family. He was ever the same thoughtful, kind brother.

J. Prestwich to C. Thurburn.   LONDON [31st *March*], 1860.

MY DEAREST KATE,—Very many happy returns of the day. Another year has slipped away, and here is the memorable 1st April and your birthday come round again. How fast time moves seems to me indicated by the growth of these dear dupli-

cates, ending with little Kittie, rather than by any other sign.
The more one becomes acquainted with time, the more slippery
does it appear to be. I know I never seem to have enough of it
between one 12th of March and another, and I doubt not that it
is the same with you between the 1st April and the 31st March.
Yet we all have a few spare, or at all events a few idle or lazy,
hours. To aid in filling up such intervals with what I conceive
to be, and I trust you will find to be, pleasure and profit, and in
the hopes that many long years may afford you many opportunities, accept, my dear sister, not the enclosed microscope but the
microscope of which the key is enclosed, and which I will take
care you find at home on your return. I only wish I could have
presented it personally. It is one of Powell and Lealand's. I
have seen that they have made it with care, and I think you will
find it work easily and well. . . . Dearest Kate, your affectionate brother,   J. PRESTWICH.

A note-book, with sections of gravel-pits on every
alternate page, gives April as the date when Prestwich
again led several of his personal friends to the flint-
bearing districts of Amiens and Abbeville, the party
including Mr Busk, Captain Galton, and Sir John Lubbock. A host of geologists and others followed on the
same errand. Amongst many names may be noted
those of Sir R. Murchison, Professors Andrew C. Ramsay, Rupert Jones, Henslow, Rogers, and Mr Henry
Christy.

While the subject of this Memoir thus went backwards and forwards to the valley of the Somme, generally putting up for the night at his favourite quarters
on the way to or from Paris, at the Hôtel Tête de
Bœuf at Abbeville, or at the Hôtel du Rhin at Amiens,
and tabulating what of interest might have been
revealed by excavations during his absence, he still
continued to send in memoirs to the Geological Society
of London. Two papers are recorded in this year, one

being "Description of the Gravels from Spitzbergen collected by Mr Lamont," and the other, "On the Presence of the London Clay in Norfolk, as proved by a Well-boring at Yarmouth."

No week passed without a geological expedition, if only for the day, and as much field-work was crowded into that one day as was possible.

J. Prestwich to J. Evans.   *Monday, May* 1860.

MY DEAR EVANS,—We start by the 10.15 train for Erith, thence to the Crayford and Perry End brick-pits. Back by train, reaching the Lewisham Station at 2½ P.M., whence to the Lower Tertiary pits of Loam Pit Hill. Morris joins us at the Lewisham Station by train from London. The other men start with me.—Yours most truly,   J. PRESTWICH.

Some idea of the difficulty of access to the Gower caverns may be gained from the letter which, at Falconer's request, Prestwich wrote as an Appendix to the memoir by the former "On the Ossiferous Caves of Gower," communicated to the Geological Society on May 30 and June 13, 1860, and which is here given :—

                               10 KENT TERRACE, *May* 17, 1860.

MY DEAR FALCONER,—I have much pleasure in giving you a few lines respecting the raised beach I met with last autumn to the westward of Paviland Cave in Gower. I find my notes on this subject are not very complete, having taken only a first survey, reserving a fuller examination of the coast until I could obtain access to the caves. You will remember how I was baffled on the last occasion by the state of the tide and the weather. Finding it quite impossible to pass round the foot of the cliff to gain the entrance to Paviland Cave, I proceeded westward along that iron-bound and magnificent frontage of limestone cliffs, ending in Worm's Head, with the intention of examining them at the accessible points, to see whether I could detect any facts bearing upon your very important observations on " Bosco's Den," relating to the connection of marine remains under, and in association with, the wonderful mass of bone *débris* you and Colonel Wood had discovered there. At the distance of about half-a-mile west of Paviland Cave I found a gully, by which I got down to the shore.

I then found in hollows in the cliff, and at an elevation of 10 to 12 feet above the beach, a layer of sand and rolled lime-stone pebbles having all the characters of a beach ; but in the absence of shells, and looking at its small patchy character, no conclusion could be drawn from it alone. The passage at the foot of the cliffs being still impracticable, I had to confine myself for the next mile or two to one or two descents, where I again found traces of what appeared to be a raised beach. Still I was not prepared for the very fine and remarkable exhibition I witnessed, after passing Mewslade, at the bottom of the small bay formed by Thurba Rock and Tears Point, about one mile south of Rhôs Sili. There, perched upon the escarped edges of the grey weathered limestone, is an old beach, raised some 10 to 12 feet above high-tide mark. It is composed of pebbles and fragments of limestones, thinly mixed with a coarse red sand, and in places full of shells and fragments of shells. There are very few species : the *Patella vulgata* is common ; the *Littorina littorea* abounds ; there are a few *Purpura lapillus,* and fragments of *Mytilus;* also pebbles of limestone drilled by boring shells. The whole, which is 3 to 4 feet thick, is agglutinated into a semi-compact mass, and is overlain by a remarkable mass of angular *débris*, from 20 to 30 feet thick in some places. The beach goes back only a few feet, as the limestone hill rises immediately behind. Coastways the raised beach continues almost uninterruptedly, but diminishing in importance for half a mile westward, ending before reaching Tears Point. Its level is persistent throughout. . . .

Taking this in connection with the well - known "raised beach" at the Mumbles, I think it may have an important bearing, in conjunction with your discoveries in those bone caves in Gower, which are situated on the coast between these two points. They are evidently on about the same level, and you have found in them sand and sea-shells under all the bone remains. Should it prove, therefore, that the caves are of this

Raised Beach period, and that the elephant and other remains have been subsequently introduced, we shall arrive at the interesting and curious conclusion that this particular group of mammalia lived after the formation of those beaches—beaches which have always been considered as of very recent origin, as they contain nothing, so far as they have been examined, but the commonest shells of our coasts. At the same time, it is to be observed that they contain but very few species, and that no complete and thorough investigation of them has yet been made. With regard to your suggestion in connection with the two species of elephant, I must confess that I saw nothing in the physical features of the scene, during the somewhat hurried and imperfect view I had of it, to lead me to suppose that the caves, or rather their inhabitants, might be referred to two periods. I should hardly have hazarded this opinion without a further examination of the district; but I give it for what it is worth, and waiting further data.

With respect to the point I had particularly in view, viz., the relation of the Gower caves to the Boulder Clay, I am unable as yet to form a decided opinion. I got the Boulder Clay within a mile of the raised beach, but on *opposite* sides of the point of Rhôs Sili. It spreads from the sea-shore to, as you are aware, the top of the hills. In Rhôs Sili Bay I found intercalated in it, at an elevation almost exactly corresponding to the raised beach on the opposite side of the promontory, a bed of shingle containing several species of recent shells, but not one of the species occurring in the raised beach. Yet the two would appear to be synchronous: the difference might arise from the one being on an exposed and open coast, and the other in a sheltered bay. The subject requires a fuller and more lengthened inquiry.

J. Prestwich to Sir Charles Lyell.   23rd *May* 1860.

MY DEAR SIR CHARLES,—I have been considering some of the questions you propose to me, for the purpose of adding a note to Falconer's paper, which he reads at the next meeting. I hope to finish it to-day or to-morrow, and will send you a copy of it.

The Boulder Clay seems to reach within *two* miles of the

Gower caves and occupies higher ground.   The caves I believe
to be subsequent to that period—in fact [the bones] subsequent
to the raised beaches.   This is a point Falconer will go more fully
into.   I have found a capital raised beach in very close relation to
the caves.   I do not think Devon and Cornwall were submerged
during the Boulder Clay period—yet even here is a difficulty,
for I have in one place a raised beach under land which clearly
is covered in part with B. Clay.   I do not in fact see where the
break is that would ensue upon a very great difference in the
submergence.   Yet I have evidence of shallowing of the sea—
but the subject is so vast and complicated that I should require a
volume rather than a note to say all I should like about it.

  With regard to South Wales more especially, I must return
there, as with the exceptions of Carmarthen and Gower I dwelt
nowhere.   However, on the one important point of the relative
age of the raised beaches of South Wales, Devon, and Cornwall,
I hope we shall be able to decide.   [S. P.] Woodward pronounces
the Menchecourt shell *decidedly Cyrena fluminalis.*—I am, my
dear Sir Charles, very truly yours,   J. PRESTWICH.

H. Falconer to J. Prestwich.

31 SACKVILLE STREET, W., *2nd June* 1860.

MY DEAR PRESTWICH,—You know what a fierce onslaught was
made on me by Lyell and Austen.   I thought the latter was
going to eat me up.   The whole subject will be up again at the
next meeting, when the main brunt of the battle will fall on you.
There is no wavering in the aspect of the mammalian evidence—
it is coming out stronger than ever, as I can show you when you
happen to pass this way.

  But we must be prepared for every aspect, and there is one
point I specially wish to ask you about, namely, the Cefn Cave.
I know all about the contained mammalia, having had the
collection up here.

  But Trimmer, in his paper on the Erratics of the " Norfolk
Areas" (Geol. Proceedings, November 20, 1850, p. 20), states
that "Britain sank as well as rose during that [the Glacial]
period.   These proofs consist in the forest of Happisburgh and
Cromer . . . and in the circumstance that on the western
coast the northern Drift, with its marine remains, has penetrated

into Cefn Cave, and, by its superposition to the deposits containing mammalian remains, testifies, like the buried forest, to the presence of a subaërial surface immediately before the transport of northern blocks."

Now is this correct? You have examined the deposits and found the Boulder Clay near Bryn Elwy.

Does the Boulder Clay penetrate into Cefn and overlie the mammalian deposits? If so, it is a fatal blow to your position in Gower.

Do look into the matter and let me have a line in reply.—Yours very sincerely,   H. FALCONER.

J. Prestwich to H. Falconer.   [*Undated.*]

MY DEAR FALCONER,—I have this morning received your note, and am sorry I missed you in town. I do not feel in the slightest degree uneasy about the difficulties raised by Austen and Sir Charles. Trimmer is mistaken altogether about Cefn Cave.[1] There is plenty of Boulder Clay about the district, but not a bit in the cave. Sand and shells, like your caves, do, however, occur there. I have a note from Mr Horner about extending my note and making a short paper of it, and suggesting a title. The former I accept—the latter will not do. I must see more about the Boulder Clay of Gower before I can venture to say much about it. The raised beach I feel pretty certain about. Still we want the level of the beach at the Mumbles, its position, &c. I shall if possible run over there for a day or two before I return to town. I am now *en route* for Exeter and Plymouth. If you have any suggestion to give me, please drop me [a line] either [on] your return to Barnstaple, or else on Thursday to the P.O., Swansea.—Yours ever truly,

JOSEPH PRESTWICH.

A few extracts from one of the 1860 note-books mention June 1 as the date of a journey to Newbury,

---

[1] More recent observations on the caves in the Vale of Clwyd seem to show that certain of the cave-deposits with Pleistocene mammalia are older than the Boulder Clay of the district. See Dr H. Hicks, Quart. Journ. Geol. Soc., vol. xliv. p. 561, and vol liv. p. 91.

when sections and notes record the most interesting features. Thence he proceeded to Devizes to visit the collection of his friend Mr W. Cunnington. On 3rd June he was at Yeovil and Sherborne. The observations on Wells and Banwell are voluminous, as are likewise those on Weston-super-Mare. Every exhibition of drift that was observed is carefully noted on the route from Exeter to Barnstaple, and again from Exeter to Sidmouth, &c. It was his habit when on a journey to alight at some small station, scan and interpret the geology of its district, and proceed by a later train.

On the way back to Bristol he had been struck at Maiden Newton by traces of flint gravel on the hills. He also observes that "the clay beds seem to have caught the gravel (flint) more than the sandstones and oolites, which are bare. Stop at Bruton station next time."

On this occasion the geological features of Clifton Down and Durdham Down were studied; later on one of many visits was paid to Watford and to a certain gravel-pit at Bushey. A few sentences copied at random from a note-book, or a catalogue of names of places visited, give a totally inadequate idea of the amount of field work accomplished on one geological journey.

A second expedition to the Abbeville district is noticed as having been made this year on July 5, when Mr Prestwich went the round of several gravel-pits, accompanied by M. Boucher de Perthes. Intent on ascertaining the levels at which different flint implements had been found, he sought information from every available source. He emphasised a fact communicated to him by Pierre Halâtre, *jardinier*, Rue de l'Église, Mautort—namely, that "formerly in pits there, and in sand under gravel four to five mètres deep, a great number of shells had been found."

They then proceeded to Amiens—on from one gravel-pit to another, exploring ground where new pits had been opened or fresh excavations made.

His correspondence with Falconer had become very frequent : a community of tastes had drawn them together, and their joint work was a keen pleasure to both.

J. Prestwich to H. Falconer. 2 SUFFOLK LANE, *July* 14, 1860.

MY DEAR FALCONER,—I have felt rather perplexed how to spend my spare fortnight. Inclination attracts me to the pleasant quarters at Irstead and the interesting coast of Norfolk. But I have now visited those cliffs so frequently, and traced every yard of ground between Weybourne and Harwich, that I have come to the conclusion that I had better leave them for some shorter holiday later in the season, and take this fortnight for the York-shire coast, Kirkdale Cave, and Market Weighton, which I have long wanted to visit, and are at present unknown ground to me. I must also leave North and South Wales to a later period of the season.

Since you questioned the fact of the *Elephas antiquus* occur-ring in the forest bed under the Boulder Clay I have not had time to look into the evidence, but my impression is there is some evidence and much indirect testimony to confirm that fact.[1] I hope you and Mr Gunn will look to it closely. Hear above all what Mr Fitch of Norwich has to say on the subject.

Miss Gurney's collection is, I fear, dispersed.[2] You, however, have probably seen it. It was rich in specimens considered to be from under the Boulder Clay. In my own mind I have not a

---

[1] The occurrence is now fully established.

[2] Many of Miss Anna Gurney's fossils are now in the Norwich Museum. See ' Memorials of John Gunn,' 8vo, Norwich, 1891 (edited by H. B. Wood-ward), in which work are numerous references to visits paid by Prestwich to Norfolk.

doubt about the subject, no more than I have that the *E. primi-genius* is above the Boulder Clay and the *E. meridionalis* in the Norwich Crag. Also that the *E. primigenius* and *E. antiquus* are found together in the newer beds at Erith, Ilford, Reading, and some half-dozen other places I could name, have long satisfied me.

If I could have spared time I should have much liked to have gone over some of the coast with you and Mr Gunn. There is a spot between Cromer and Weybourne where I have found bones *in situ*, but there was nothing determinable. A further and longer search was necessary. It was at the base of the cliff.

Along the greater part of the Norfolk cliffs my belief is that the mammalian remains are confined to the beds beneath the Boulder Clay, and that they are not found in the Boulder Clay or in the beds above it, with a few rare exceptions.—Pray make my kind regards to Mr Gunn, and believe me to be, ever truly yours,   JOSEPH PRESTWICH.

Accompanied by Professor Morris, he started on a Yorkshire excursion on the 17th July, and was joined at Blisworth by Mr Samuel Sharp of Northampton. Into this brief excursion, which occupied but a fortnight, many important observations were crowded. Besides the occurrence of "Drift," our geologist was in quest of Boulder Clay, and his pen and pencil were fully engaged. After seeing the Dallington pits they proceeded from Kettering to Rockingham, and then to a close inspection of the cliffs at Bridlington, Filey, and Speeton.

At Scarborough Mr Leckenby's collection was visited, where Prestwich took note of a specimen of *Cyrena consobrina* (*fluminalis*), found in gravel at Hedon, near Hull.

From gravel-pits at Beverley their next point was Market Weighton, where a section is drawn of a large white gravel-pit; thence to Holmehill, Ridgemont, Paul

Cliff, and Hull, at all of which sections are noted, and
especially careful drawings of Kelsey Hill and Kelsey
Hill Pit.　These localities are only a few of those
visited in this memorable fortnight; its work wound
up with sketches of gravel-pits at Water Newton and
at Orton, near Peterborough.

Early in September Prestwich was again out on
field-work.　Several pages of a note-book are covered
with sections near Whitstable and Swale Cliff, which
are succeeded by many pages of sections near Canterbury, following a few sentences of notes.　At Canterbury he was joined by Professor Morris and Dr
Melville.

Late in September a fresh start was made, and many
observations are registered, beginning with Bury St
Edmunds, and through an interesting East Coast district, ending with Hoxne, &c.　The geological work
done was no make-believe.　One biographer has described
what was accomplished in a year as " amazing."　When
it is remembered that field-geology was his holiday
work, it is difficult to understand how so much could
have been crowded into a single year.　It may be
partly accounted for in that his City partner released
him as much as was possible, but chiefly in that, wherever he turned his steps, whether for business or pleasure, he was always geologising.　The contents of the
sixty note-books—the entries, alas ! in several, faint by
the lapse of time—would form at least one bulky printed
volume.　A chronicle of the Life of Joseph Prestwich,
to be faithful, should trace his progress step by step,
and record those innumerable journeyings made year
after year, from cliff to cliff, from section to section,
when, to use his own expression in speaking of the
eastern counties, he knew every yard of ground.　The

number of these geological journeys is simply bewildering, especially as debatable points were visited over and over again.[1]

A letter from Sir Charles Lyell[2] to the Rev. W. S. Symonds, dated October 1, 1860, contains a reference to Prestwich's work :—

My idea of going to South Wales, and taking your district on my way, and getting the benefit of your co-operation, was dependent on some progress having first been made by Prestwich, Falconer, and Colonel Wood in regard to the age of the South Wales caves, with not only *Elephas primigenius*, *Rhinoceros tichorhinus*, but also some of them with the other elephants and rhinoceroses (*E. antiquus* and *R. leptorhinus*, now called by Falconer *R. hemitœchus*), the age of these relatively to the glaciers, glaciation, and submergence of Northern Wales, and the deposition of the northern Drift.

Again, on October 2nd, a geological excursion is reported to Hertford, when sections of a new cutting at Hatfield, with those of gravel-pits at various points, at Collier's End and near Puckeridge, are given.

The following letter is addressed to Dr Falconer, who was about to spend the winter on the Riviera :—

J. Prestwich to H. Falconer.   10 KENT TERRACE, *14th Oct.* 1860.

MY DEAR FALCONER,—I am very sorry I missed you on the last two occasions I called at Sackville Street. However, you can have no difficulty about Amiens. The pits are near at hand and easily accessible. I hope M. Pinsard may be at Amiens to show you the collections. The one you should first see is not the town collection near the Hôtel de Ville, but a small collection in

---

[1] An account of some of these journeys is given in "Memoranda, chiefly on the Drift Deposits in various parts of England and Wales: being Extracts from the Note-books and other MSS. of the late Sir Joseph Prestwich," printed in the Geological Magazine, Decade iv. vol. v. pp. 404-417, 1898.

[2] Life and Letters of Sir Charles Lyell, vol. ii. p. 358.

the Salle at the Jardin des Plantes, at the N.W. corner of
the town.　You will there find a good series of the fossil bones
from St Roch.　If you cannot meet with our M. Pinsard, try to
see M. Garnier at the Bibliothèque, or M. Ferguson, *fils.*

It was M. Pinsard who lent me the elephant's tooth from St
Acheul, and to whom the uncut tooth of the rhinoceros from
Boves belongs.　I should much [like] to have a few lines from
you after your visit to Amiens, with your opinion of the pits
and the bones.

Field-geology for this year was by no means at an
end.　Wells-upon-Sea is the locality where he was at
work on 28th October; a description of its marshes
within the sea-wall being followed by pages of sections
of the railway-cuttings near Walsingham.　Next day
he was at Irstead Rectory, with his old friend the Rev.
John Gunn, who, with the Rev. S. W. King (of Sax-
lingham, near Norwich), joined in a visit to Bacton.
After Happisburgh and Mundesley, Norwich was visited
on the way back to London.

Before starting on a tour to the west, a working
expedition was made to Brentwood with Professor
Morris.

The long western journey began on the 9th November
with a section at Froxfield, four miles from Hungerford.
Two days later, Prestwich was at Frome, sketching
as usual, and in pursuit of the tusk of an elephant,
which had been found at Fairwood, three miles from
Frome, in making the railway.　Langport occupied one
day, and Exeter was reached on the 16th.　From Truro
he proceeded to St Agnes Bay, where, although there
was no evidence of any raised beach, a deposit of sand
and clay spread at the eastern base of St Agnes Hill,
and also over its western shoulder, attracted his
attention.　From Penzance he went on to Falmouth,

where he was rewarded by the exhibition of a fine raised beach, of which several sketches were drawn; thence to Bideford, Sidmouth, &c., in search of gravel-pits and Drift. Axminster was reached on the 25th, whence visits to Colyton, Seaton, and Axmouth brought this western journey to a close.

In those short November days our geologist must have worked from sunrise to sunset.

J. Prestwich to H. Falconer.   LONDON, *7th December* 1860.

MY DEAR FALCONER,—I was much obliged by and interested in your letter giving me the account of your visit to Amiens, with the results of your inspection of the fossil bones. I made the extracts you allowed me to do, and then handed the letter to your brother. I much wish, however, not only to have your remarks for my own perusal, but I should much like to give them in the appendix to my paper, as their palæontological bearing is so important. I do not, however, feel at liberty to do so before consulting you and showing you what I should wish to print—this, not only for your permission, but also in case you wish to make any alteration.

With regard to the *happement à la langue*, I am not inclined to attach very much importance to it. I find it varies much in specimens from the same deposit. Much depends upon the nature of the bed and its facility of percolation by water.

The lower level and greater accumulation of water, and the loose gravel of St Roch, would, I think, lead generally to a more rapid decomposition of the bones than at St Acheul, especially in such beds of the latter place which contain any iron. There is also a great difference between bones or teeth which occur in sand and in chalk rubble: the latter are much less robbed of their original materials, the matrix of carbonate of lime robbing the water of its carbonic acid before reaching the bones.

With regard to the theoretical views, I must discuss them with you hereafter. I may here merely mention that I think the lower gravel as well as the sand above it to be of fluviatile origin, and not of very tumultuous origin, for in it there are at places seams of sand similar in composition, *and containing the same fresh-water shells* as the sand above. The top brick-earth and gravel I feel disposed to attribute to some more active and powerful agency. I think, with you, that St Roch and St Acheul cannot be separated by material interval. (The hippopotamus tusks from the former place adhere strongly to the tongue.) M. Pinsard has sent me the levels of St Acheul. I hope you find your winter quarters pleasant and suitable, and hoping shortly to hear from you, I am, my dear Falconer, very truly yours, J. PRESTWICH.

I have just returned from a month's journey in the West.

J. Prestwich to H. Falconer. LONDON, 27th December 1860.

MY DEAR FALCONER,—I wrote you a short time since to ask your permission to give an abstract or extract of your last letter to me, referring to the elephant remains at St Acheul and St Roch. I enclosed also a copy of that portion of your letter which bears on the subject. I could either give your information in the form of a short paragraph in the Appendix, or, as the revise is still in my hands, I could add the *E. antiquus* to the list of St Acheul organic remains, with a note stating it was on your authority: probably this would be the better way, as it would be more certain to be seen. I wait, however, your sanction before taking either step. As I expect I shall shortly have to give in the last revise, would you be so kind as to oblige me with an answer at your early convenience?

I understand that remains of the hippopotamus have been found this autumn at St Acheul. I have not yet been able to see the specimen, which is in Mylne's possession.

Boucher de Perthes writes me word that he has now found several specimens of the *Cyrena consobrina* at Menchecourt. He also asks whether you are in town, and [says] that he was looking for a visit from you this fall.

We have had several hard Scotch papers this session, and with a further store in reserve. Nothing yet bearing upon the superficial deposits.

The weather here has been very severe for the season. My thermometer marked 9° at 8 A.M. on Christmas day. I trust you are enjoying a mild and pleasant winter, &c. . . .

L

J. Prestwich to J. Evans.   LONDON, *5th Janry.* 1861.

MY DEAR EVANS,—I have this instant seen four flint imple-ments of the true race.   One specimen is identical with one of my best lance-head shaped specimens from Amiens; a second has the point broken and is rolled; a third is stained brown and is also worn; whilst the fourth is a good honest *Tertiary flint pebble* about the size of a goose egg, one half chipped into a point, and the other end retaining its pebble form.   They were brought me by a Mr Leech, who found them on the *shore* at the bottom of the cliffs between Herne Bay and the Reculvers.   The cliffs are there capped by gravel, but he could not get at it.

He is going down again, and will look for more and for the deposit of them.—I am ever truly yours,   J. PRESTWICH.

The first excursion in 1861 was apparently that on February 23rd : "With Evans to Strood, Herne Bay, and Reculvers."   Mr Leech joined them at Faversham, when they proceeded to Whitstable—a frequent resort. The two friends were both successful in finding flint implements on the expedition to the Reculvers, and Mr Evans was rewarded by the discovery of one at Swalecliffe.

The Easter trip is briefly mentioned : "*27th March.* To Newhaven and Dieppe with Captain Galton." [1]

The same system of work was carried out—numerous sections drawn, with explanations and notes ; the shingle, gravel, and angular flint-rubble examined. "Out of Eu and on the right is a large pit of loess— no shells.   Ascending the hill of Canbles, we found the sides fringed with some seven or eight terraces, and the top capped with Tertiaries (*Cyrena, Ostrea*, &c.), sand, and clay."   Précy and Creil were also visited.

J. Prestwich to Sir C. Lyell.   *April* 9, 1861.

MY DEAR SIR CHARLES, — Thanks for the account of your

---

[1] Afterwards Sir Douglas Galton, K.C.B.

Photo by Dickinson, London.

SIR DOUGLAS GALTON, K.C.B.

Abbeville proceedings.   The implement question is, I think,
now as clear there as at Amiens.   On my first visit I myself
got *three* knives or flakes from the flint-bed under the *Sable
Aigre*.   On my last visit the workmen procured four more for
me from the same bed, and you now have obtained five more.   You
say you reached the Chalk.   Did you meet with the bed of subangular gravel immediately over it ?   I just reached it, but did
not traverse it.   It is the lowest bed which you saw at the Porte
Marcadé.

With regard to Mautort, there can, I think, be little doubt
of the occurrence of marine shells.   At Ducastel's pit a little
boy, hearing my inquiry, said, " Oh yes, I have seen (using the
common name for *Littorina littorea*, which I forget) " come out
of the bottom of the pit."

The pits you saw at Maneil were those which I visited.   Were
the men at work when you were there ?

The pit at Epagne is on the hill on the road to the pits at St
Gilles.

I still have my doubts about the shells at Drucat.   One fragment was a mere hollow piece of white flint.   The sands are
bent in all the pipes there, but I did not clearly see the connection between the indentation where the flint was found with any
pipe at present exposed.   I have a rude white implement from
the upper beds.   I have been all the way up the valley from
Abbeville to St Riquier.   It is full of brick-earth, but no gravel
till at St Riquier—and that very angular and earthy.   I also
went to Ouen, but the pits there are now filled up.   They were
in the valley near the brook, and three to four inches deep.—
Ever truly yours,   J. PRESTWICH.

The following letter is of special interest : it announces the discovery of flint implements in the very
spot indicated by the two friends :—

J. Evans to J. Prestwich.   NASH MILLS, *April* 18, 1861.

MY DEAR PRESTWICH,—Jubilate !   Wyatt has found the flint
implements we have so long been looking for at Bedford.   I enclose his letter and sketch, which please return, and am writing
to him that I hope to be at Bedford at 10.30 on Saturday, if it

will suit him to meet me. Can you come? I am in a state of disgust at finding that we have a long-standing engagement to dinner on Saturday, *the 26th*. It is to meet a bishop with a beard, which in this shaving diocese of Rochester is a rare privilege, and under all circumstance cannot be neglected. If you *cannot* come any other Saturday, you must come all the same that day, and arrange for Monday being spent somewhere "in the Drift": but if you can go to Bedford this Saturday, perhaps Miss Prestwich would meet you here on our return and arrange to spend a few days. You can go backwards and forwards to Suffolk Lane just as well from here as from Kent Terrace, and sleeping in the country will do you good. I don't wonder at Wyatt being half crazy at his discovery. It is most wonderful and *satisfactory*. We must go down and have a regular day there without delay. Excuse this hurried and distracted letter. Ever yours,   JOHN EVANS.

J. Prestwich to J. Evans.   LONDON, *Thursday.*

MY DEAR EVANS,—I also had a note from Wyatt, and rejoiced to hear of his discovery. Two other notes (to Sir C. Lyell and Mr Horner) turned up at the Council yesterday. Sir Charles proposed going down as soon [as] possible. I told him of my visit to you on Sunday week, and fixed to meet him at Bedford on the following Monday. I might alter the day, but, after the long postponement, I think it had better stand, notwithstanding the Bishop. If I am down early on Saturday I can find plenty of amusement and occupation in your library. Besides there are the children, and I have no doubt Master Norman will feel himself fully equal to receive his papa's guest. So I come on the understanding that it makes no difference in your and Mrs Evans's proceedings. In fact, consider me in the nursery for the evening.

I have asked Wyatt to have a pit opened for our visit, and I am ever truly yours,   JOS. PRESTWICH.

This discovery of flint implements in the Bedford Gravel was of great importance. In the year 1858 Prestwich had known of the occurrence of remains of

elephant and other extinct mammalia in the railway
cuttings there, and when visiting it with Evans, after
their return from Abbeville in 1859, they fixed on Bedford as a likely place to yield implements—Mr Evans on
a later visit directing Mr Wyatt to turn his particular
attention to the Biddenham pit, where the two well-
formed flint implements were actually found. This
discovery, following on the recognition of flint implements in the valley of the Somme, was corroborative
and irresistible evidence in support of the theory of the
geological age which Prestwich assigned to primitive
man. The prediction of the two enthusiasts having
been so literally fulfilled, was a well-earned triumph
for both.

Sir Charles Lyell, in a letter[1] to Sir C. Bunbury,
dated 26th April 1861, mentions this visit : " I am laid
up for a day or two after an excursion to Bedford with
Prestwich and Evans to see a section where a Mr
Wyatt, editor of the Bedford provincial newspaper, has
just found two hatchets of the true Amiens and Hoxne
type. They occurred in a gravel pit at Beddingham
[Biddenham], which I visited more than thirty years
ago."

In June our geologist was alone when working out
the district round Shelford and Cardington.

According to a foreign note-book, he was at Chârtres
on the 26th July, examining the remains of *Elephas*,
Rhinoceros, *Hyæna*, and *Cervus* in M. Boisvilette's
collection, also a species of *Hippopotamus* which he
emphasises as being distinct from *H. major*. An
elaborate section is given of Le Mans. High-level
gravel is noted near Caen, and " Drift " in a cutting
at Bayeux. From Charenton he went to St Sauveur,

<hr />

[1] Life and Letters of Sir Charles Lyell, vol. ii. p. 344.

thence by St Lou to Cherbourg, and on by rail to Paris, where several days were spent in viewing the collections in the École des Mines and in the Jardin des Plantes.

This French excursion was one of close work. The heights at which gravel and other " Drift " were found are recorded, and the composition of these in each locality is carefully noted. He was preparing for an important paper on the geological age of the Drift deposits, which was read next year at the Royal Society.

The letter which follows was probably written at this date :—

J. Prestwich to H. Falconer.   KENT TERRACE, *Saturday* [1861].

MY DEAR FALCONER,—City business drove yesterday morning's work out of my head for the rest of the day.

On my return at night I looked over my Grays specimens, and now send you the results of Heer's examination. I hope next winter to clear up some of the points of doubt, and add to the list before publication. Of the Mundesley woods, cones, &c., the only specimens that could be determined were, as I told you, *Pinus abies*—common ; *Pinus sylvestris*—rarer—together with a seed vessel. . . .

PLANTS—GRAYS.

Quercus robur, var. *sessiliflora ? Hedera Helix. Vaccinium myrtillus ? ? ? Pteris aquilina ? ? Alnus ? Cyperus ? Fagus ? ? Rubus. Populus. Equisetum* and *Phragmites.*

This is very good so far.

In September he was at work at Highbury with his friend Mr Alfred Tylor.

J. Prestwich to Sir Charles Lyall.   *Sept.* 16, 1861.

MY DEAR SIR CHARLES,—You will find the best account of Trimmer's Moel Tryfaen case in his paper " On the Drift of the Cambrian Chain." He mentions only two species of shells, the

Fusus Bamffius and *Fusus antiquus.* On this evidence alone, the question of age could hardly be decided. In Derbyshire I have got marine shells at a level, I imagine, of at least 700 feet above the sea.

Of the extent of the old glaciers in Switzerland there can be little doubt, and I am of your opinion that the Neuchâtel block was transported by glacier action. With regard to the extent of subsidence during the Glacial period, that period lasted so long and witnessed so many changes that I hardly know how I should fix it. If, however, you take, as you propose, the whole period, then I should be disposed to leave very little of Scotland, Wales, or England above water. Without going very fully into the question, your map seems to give a fairly correct approximation.

I was at Wycombe yesterday, and discovered another Elephant and Cyclas bed near Princes Risborough. I have sent on your note to Ramsay, and I am very truly yours, J. PRESTWICH.

The three papers from his pen published during this season were evidently founded in part upon observations made in the early spring, and also upon his researches in previous years. The first on the list, "On some New Facts in Relation to the Section of the Cliff at Mundesley, Norfolk," appeared in the 'Geologist,' vol. iv. pp. 68-71. Mundesley had been a favourite haunt.

The second, which came out in the Geological Society's Journal, was entitled: "Notes on some further Discoveries of Flint Implements in Beds of Post-Pliocene Gravel and Clay; with a few Suggestions for Search elsewhere." The materials for this paper were doubtless obtained from his researches in Suffolk, at Bury St Edmunds and Icklingham; in Kent, between the Reculvers and Herne Bay, and at Swalecliffe near Whitstable, which he had visited again and again in the hope of finding flint implements. At last John Evans was fortunate enough to discover on the shore an oval-shaped implement identical in form with those so common at Abbeville. A long list of localities is given where, by diligent search, flints fashioned by the hand of man are likely to be found.

The third paper, also published in the Geological Society's Journal, is "On the Occurrence of *Cyrena fluminalis*, together with Marine Shells of Recent Species, in Beds of Sand and Gravel over Beds of Boulder - clay, near Hull; with an Account of some Borings and Well-sections in the same District." This memoir doubtless embodied his observations when on the Yorkshire tour in the preceding year.

A note of thanks from Mr Ruskin for a copy of the Flint Implement paper is expressed in quaint terms :—

DENMARK HILL, *6th January* 1862.

MY DEAR SIR,—Returning on the last day of last year from Switzerland, I find on my table your most interesting account of the flint implements of the French Tertiaries, inscribed, "With the author's compliments." Pray accept my best thanks. I wish we were all reduced to "flint implements" once more — and could only fight with arrow-heads — and hadn't chemistry enough to poison them.—Most truly yours,   J. RUSKIN.

The geological memoir which was read at the Royal Society this year, and published in 1864, was one in which its author widely generalised, and was entitled : "Theoretical Considerations on the Conditions under which the (Drift) Deposits containing the Remains of Extinct Mammalia and Flint Implements were accumulated, and on their Geological Age. On the Loess of the Valleys of the South of England, and of the Somme and the Seine."

The following letter apparently refers to this Memoir :—

Friday
(March 21 1862)

My dear Evans,

My paper at the Royal is to come on on Thursday next. Will you dine with me on Tuesday at $5\frac{1}{2}$ to meet Lubbock & talk over Easter art. Ever yours,

Wm. Crooknull

J. Prestwich to H. Falconer.　　　　　KENT TERRACE [*undated*].

MY DEAR FALCONER,—Thanks for your friendly criticism. I am, however, going to contest some of this. First, with regard to river floods.

There is no doubt but that the peculiar position of the Siberian and North American rivers is one condition in the case, but it is not the only one. There is not the same damming up by ice, but still the floods in rivers such as the Kama and the Volga, which flow from north to south, are also annual and considerable. (See Pallas's Voyages, vol. vii. pp. 39, 210; vol. i. p. 296.)

So again in Lapland the rivers with a southern flow are subject to very considerable spring floods. Wrangell also speaks of the floods in Southern Russia as well as Murchison (his ' Russia '). They both mention that whole districts are flooded, and the river valleys converted into great lakes. The majority of these rivers have a southern flow. In more northern regions, Richardson and Simpson speak of the small local floods caused by the melting of the snows, quite independent of the great rivers. As I mentioned yesterday, I conceive the effect of a severe winter must be to store up the rainfall and restrict its delivery to a short period in the spring—whence increased river discharges and floods.

Now with regard to the hippopotamus I give its tusk-teeth legitimate use, but still I am not disposed to give up the cold winter and its cold-climate associates. It is certainly found with the reindeer, and I am inclined to believe that the gravel at Hurley Bottom with the hippopotamus, and that at Taplow with the musk-ox, are synchronous. I do not suppose the cold to have been so extreme as at the Terrace Gravel period, and if there were rapids in places on the old rivers at such parts, there might have been open water all the winter. Otters are found frequenting such rapids in the severe climate of North America, and in rivers which at other places are frozen all the winter.

R. A. C. Godwin-Austen to J. Prestwich.

CHILWORTH, *March* 30 [1862].

DEAR PRESTWICH,—Thursday evening last places me under the obligation of saying how much I congratulate you on your

last paper. I am glad that you took the subject in hand, for I
fancied that others, if not poaching on your land, were at least
establishing "squatter rights" on what you had left unoccupied.
It was with feelings akin to wonder that as the paper proceeded
I found that you had become a Glacialist, but for a long time I
fancied that you were putting such conditions in a hypothetical
form only, and that the *coup de grâce* was at last to be dealt out.
I congratulate you on this.

We have heard of thee

                                               "zeal
         Which young and ardent converts feel" ;

and on thinking over the matter since, I am still of opinion that
you will do better not to have recourse to so low a mean winter
temperature as you have named.

There is a difficulty in the river theory, in placing the terrace
gravel of St Acheul with that at Menchecourt, unless you suppose that all at that place belongs to the second or lower valley
gravel. I do not see any objection to this, but I know that such
was not your notion at one time. Hooker was mightily taken
with the speculation as to the ice-hatchets, but I must confess
that I do not like it. As perhaps this offspring may be a
favourite, I will not ask you to discard it, but I think that if
you mentioned it in a footnote it would be enough.

I would examine into the question of the *Dreissena polymorpha*.
I have no doubt but that the shell will turn out to be a *D.
Brardii* washed out from the upper Paris Basin beds, where
it is often most abundant. In the Mainz basin it is washed into
the alluvia of the Rhine.—Yours ever truly,

                                    Robert Godwin-Austen.

The first note-book entry for 1862 is, "Easter Excursion, 17th April: J. Evans, J. Lubbock, J. P.

"*Route.*—St Valery, Abbeville, Beauvais, Rouen,
Nantes, Poissy, Paris, Creil, Amiens; back on Monday
morning the 28th inst."

Although only one geological memoir proceeded from
his pen in this year, there was another publication

which, in its exhaustiveness, is quite as remarkable. He was one of the jurors for the International Exhibition for 1862, and was requested to draw up the report on wines, &c., of different countries. It was published in the form of a booklet, and is written with the concise clearness which characterises all his work. As one who knew him throughout life observed, " Everything that he did was done in the best possible way."

J. Prestwich to Sir Charles Lyell.　　　KENT TERRACE [1862].

MY DEAR SIR CHARLES,— . . . I have been much engaged during the last two months at the Exhibition (as a juror in Class III. section C), and have done but little geology. I have been down at Hertford, and took the opportunity of looking again at parts of the valley of the Lea. The high-level Gravels are tolerably well shown, and are of considerable extent. The lower-level gravels are more obscure—neither contain shells, but both elephant and rhinoceros have recently been found in the latter. The Boulder Clay is just now well shown in a small pit near Woodhall Park (Abel Smith's). It is full of pebbles and small boulders of hard chalk, many of them scratched.

Next week I am going to the North, taking Stamford, Retford, Gainsborough, Hull, Malton, and other places on my way to Richmond. Thence by Stainmoor to Kendal. Then to Blackpool, Preston, and Manchester, back by the 1st August. I call on Mr Wood at Richmond, and Mr Binney meets me at Kendal or Blackpool. I shall be glad to hear by bearer how you are, and I am, dear Sir Charles, yours very truly, 　J. PRESTWICH.

This year, to judge from the evidence of note-books, was as notable for the amount of field geology as its predecessor. Early in June, "With J. E. to Wolverton, a neighbourhood where certain gravel-pits proved of special interest." July 12th was the date on which Mr Prestwich started on a tour in the northern counties, when a visit was made to Settle and the Victoria Cave, and where he found his way again to Cefn and Llangollen. During the first week in August he was in the eastern counties, working from pit to pit.

J. Prestwich to J. Evans.   LONDON, *7th August* [1862].

MY DEAR EVANS,—I hope to go to Auvergne next week early. I shall spend a day in Paris. When Daubrée was here he expressed a great wish to get a copy of your paper. I don't know which. He said he saw it at Babbage's. Can I take a copy over for him?

I have had a very pleasant excursion north. I was a day at Settle, and saw the Victoria and other caves, and the collection of British and Roman antiquities of Mr Jackson. I also spent a day at Salop and Wroxeter. I have since been to Colchester and Saffron Walden. I there saw at the enclosed address a so-called British coin, but it appeared to me to be too fresh and sharp, and the metal too undecided. The device was all right.

A fortnight's tour in Auvergne, beginning on the 12th August, was one of keen enjoyment, the volcanic character of the ground traversed being of special interest. Towards its close our geologist summarised in a sentence :—

The general features of this excursion so far are the undisturbed position of the scoria, the slight decomposition of the lava, the great decomposition of the granite and gneiss, and the considerable decomposition of the trachytes, and the absence of drift.

J. Prestwich to J. Evans.   LONDON, *22nd September* 1862.

MY DEAR EVANS,—You deserve your excellent sight from the excellent use to which you apply it. I fancy I can do pretty well in a state of rest, but for geology in motion none equal you. It is truly progressive geology. I am glad you have traced the source of the gravel. I am quite ready for the hunt. Shall it be direct, or from Cambridge? Orton should be visited again.

It is the same bed no doubt.   What a pleasant excursion you are
taking.   You and Mrs Evans must enjoy it much.   When at
Torquay, visit Hope's Nose and see the raised beach (if you have
time).   First, however, see Brixham and *adjacent* caves.   Mr
Pengelly, to whom make my kind regards, is, I understand, at
Torquay, and will give you any information.   As you pass up
the valley between Axminster and Chard, look at the gravels.
See also the gravels on cliff between Dawlish and Star Cross.   I
hope to [be] at Cambridge from the Saturday to the Monday
evening.—Ever truly yours,   J. PRESTWICH.

September and October were full of short geological
expeditions made from town, first, in examining well-
sections at Reigate and other localities, later on at
Erith and Ilford (both of which places had been visited
a score of times) in quest of elephants' teeth and other
fossil remains.

The following letter shows the cordial relations existing between Prestwich and the officers of the Geological Survey, and their appreciation of the accuracy of
his work :—

J. Prestwich to H. Falconer.   10 KENT TERRACE.

MY DEAR FALCONER,—You asked me the other evening to let
you know what I had contributed to the new geological map.[1]
The case stands thus : Thirty years ago I commenced exploring
the neighbourhood of London, and, seeing there was no map, I
laid down the boundaries of all the beds at the same time that I
worked out their superposition.   Wishing to make the work
complete, and with a view to publication, I worked hard at it for
some 15 to 20 years.   Just, however, as completed, the Survey
came up with me, and Sir H. De la Beche asked me for the use of
my maps, which I gave him ; and which I have since continued

---

[1] This probably referred to the Greenough Geological Map published by
the Geological Society, new editions of which were largely based not only
on the work of the Geological Survey, but on that of Prestwich, to whom
the Geological Survey was greatly indebted.

to give to Ramsay as required. Whether I shall do anything further with them I know not.

When the new map was commenced, I gave Mr Best my rough MS. maps, and from them he reduced all the London Basin district, with the exception of the portion adjacent to and west of Newbury. The Eastern counties I had not so accurately surveyed, and therefore only laid them down from my note-book and recollection.

I send you some of my working maps that you may judge of the extent of work, which, though long and laborious, was to me for many years a source of great pleasure, recreation, and health.

I have received your parcel, which I shall have much pleasure in taking to M. Lartet, and I am, ever truly yours,

J. PRESTWICH.

P.S.—I have not always kept to the same colours. I commenced the Chalk in pink after Buckland, but ended in having it uncoloured, as also the marsh lands. The Gault and Upper Greensand count for nothing, being [on] a more general plan to match the boundary of the Chalk and Tertiary outliers. The North Down Crag I have also only put in red outlines.

In his address to the Geological Society in 1865, Mr W. J. Hamilton referred to the publication of a new edition of the Greenough Geological Map of England and Wales, mentioning the name of Mr Prestwich among "the most active contributors to this work." He states that "Mr J. Prestwich has supplied the geological data for the Tertiaries round London and in Kent, and the Bagshot series in Surrey and part of Berkshire, from his own MS. notes on the 1-inch Ordnance maps, at which he had worked from 1835 to 1855. From the Newbury district to the Isle of Thanet and Harwich the new map adopts Mr Prestwich's divisions and outlines as far as could be done with the imperfect topography of the original plates. Mr Prestwich also undertook to put in the Chalk, Crag, and Drift areas in Norfolk and Suffolk, and adopted the division of only two Crags, a conclusion at which he had arrived after some years' labour, but which he had not laid down on any previously published map." [1]

The Geological Survey has at all times been indebted to various geologists, who, labouring out of pure love of the science, have made maps and recorded sections which have been generously placed at the service of the Institution. De la Beche himself gave the results of many years' private work in the south-west of England as the basis on which the Geological Survey was founded. Godwin-Austen gave effectual help in Devonshire, William Sanders in Somerset and Gloucestershire, William E. Logan in South Wales, and later on Prestwich largely aided the field-staff by allowing copies to be made of his Tertiary work in the western portions of the London Basin.

On the 3rd March 1863 Prestwich had the honour of being specially admitted into the Athenæum Club by the Committee, who have power to elect annually nine men who have gained distinction in science, literature, or art, or in the public service.

The following letter gives the date when the structure of the Ouse Valley was made out :—

J. Prestwich to H. Falconer.

GEOLOGICAL SOCIETY, SOMERSET HOUSE, *Tuesday.*

MY DEAR FALCONER,—I have just seen Evans. We go to Peterborough, March, and Oundle at 9 A.M. on Saturday next, returning at 8.15 P.M. on Monday. We shall not go to Bedford.

Should you go, you will easily find Mr Jas. Wyatt. He is, or was, the editor of a paper, and resides at the other end of the town, near a church. There are a few specimens also in the museum ; and a man of the name of Read has the original haul

---

[1] Quart. Journ. Geol. Soc., vol. xxi. p. lvi.

taken from the railway-cuttings, which first drew Evans and me there after my return from St Acheul. I see by my note-books that I first made out the structure of the Ouse Valley at Bedford in 1854. . . .

The Easter excursion is thus mentioned: "7th March 1863.—To Peterborough with Evans and Lubbock." They geologised at Peterborough, March, Essendine, Oundle, and Orton, &c.

The publication by Lyell in 1863 of his 'Antiquity of Man' brought prominently before the general public the geological evidences of the great age of the stone implements. Lyell was naturally regarded as the judge who would better than any other geologist sum up the evidence, and place it clearly and intelligibly before those who had no special scientific knowledge. So successful was his great book that soon a second edition was called for; and a third edition was issued before the end of the year, two months later. It was unfortunate, however, that his treatment of the history of the subject was in important respects so meagre that the labours of the original investigators were not made manifest. Dr Falconer drew attention to this in the pages of the 'Athenæum' (April 14, 1863), and, writing with the authorisation of his friend Prestwich, he pointed out how important it was to state clearly how, and by whom, the antiquity of man was established; whereas Lyell had mentioned certain conclusions as if they were original results arrived at by himself, and had failed in many cases to indicate the sources whence his information was derived.

In his reply, Lyell contended that he could not give a full history of the various views, and that all his readers wanted was to learn from him, in as few words as possible, what his own conclusions were, after reading what others had written, and after examining himself the clearest sections to which he could get access. A letter from Prestwich (dated April 20) was published in a later number of the 'Athenæum,' wherein the writer pointed out that Lyell was addressing a scientific as well as a popular public, and that it was not so much a question of frequent as of accurate reference to the authorities who had established the antiquity of man.

This correspondence was at the time naturally painful to all concerned. If we turn to the fourth edition of the 'Antiquity of Man,' published in 1873, we find that the author completely recast the chapter relating to Brixham Cavern and Kent's Hole, and that the history of research both among cavern and river deposits was as fully told as the original workers could desire. Prestwich and Falconer had been the pioneers in the inquiry throughout, and were the patient investigators of the evidence.

CHAPTER VII.

1863–1870.

HITHERTO the excavations in the valley of the Somme
had yielded a rich harvest of worked flint implements,
yet no vestiges of man himself had ever come to light.
But on the 9th April 1863 a startling announcement
was made by M. Boucher de Perthes in the 'Abbevillois,' the local paper of that date. In this he asserted
that a workman had found a "human jaw" with flint
haches in the *Couche noire* of the gravel-pit of Moulin
Quignon. In a letter of the 14th, from the late Dr
W. B. Carpenter, F.R.S., which appeared in the 'Athenæum' of the 18th, he remarked: "I may add that
the gravel-bed of Moulin Quignon is about 100 feet
above the present level of the river, and therefore
corresponds in position with the upper Gravels of St
Acheul, not with the lower Gravels of Menchecourt, so
that if we accept the conclusions of Mr Prestwich as to
the relative ages of these Gravels, this human jaw was
buried in the deepest, and therefore the oldest, portion
of the earliest of those fluviatile deposits."

But the authenticity of the jaw, which M. Boucher
de Perthes firmly believed to be of the same age as the
accepted palæolithic implements, was generally questioned in face of his assertion of having extricated it
with his own hands on the 28th of March 1863. The
announcement, as we have said, had been made early
in April, and two days later Evans and Prestwich were
at Abbeville, Falconer following on the 14th, when the
evidence was most minutely examined and sifted.
Naturally the most lively interest was shown in the
subject on both sides of the Channel. Falconer at first
had been inclined to believe in the remote age of the
jaw, but the "deliberate scrutiny" of the materials
which he carried away from Abbeville compelled him
eventually to alter his opinion.

M. de Quatrefages, the eminent naturalist, was also
on the spot, and carried the jaw back with him to
Paris, while M. de Perthes confided to Falconer a
detached molar from the jaw, which he took to London
for examination. Here it was submitted to his two
friends, Mr George Busk, F.R.S., and Mr (Sir John)
Tomes, F.R.S., both of whom were practised anthropologists. They proceeded to saw up the detached
molar from Moulin Quignon, and the question was soon
settled. To quote Falconer's words,—it proved to be
quite recent; the section was white, glistening, full of
gelatine, and fresh-looking. There was an end of the
case. First, the flint hatchets were pronounced by
highly competent experts (Evans and Prestwich) to be
spurious; secondly, the reputed fossil jaw showed no
character different from those that may be met with in
the contents of a London churchyard.

M. de Quatrefages, like the majority of his French
confrères, persisted in the jaw being a genuine fossil,

and at first seemed to think that any doubt of its authority was a reflection on the honour of France.

"The French *savants*, the more they went into the case, were more convinced of the soundness of their conclusions; while their English opponents, the more they weighed the evidence before them, were the more strengthened in their doubts."

To settle the question definitely, it was agreed that a conference between the English *savants* and their French brethren should take place, and that for this purpose the former should proceed to Paris. As is evident from his note on the occasion, Falconer wrote with boyish glee at the prospect of a good fight :—

H. Falconer to J. Prestwich.　　　　　　　　　　*5th May* 1863.

MY DEAR PRESTWICH,—Make your arrangements instanter.

Dr Carpenter has called on me with a formal *cartel* from Quatrefages, challenging me, you, and Evans to go over to Paris, and to do battle about the Moulin Quignon human jaw.

I have written to Lartet, accepting.

Carpenter as "avvocato di Diavolo," *i.e.*, pro, and I, con, start by the mail train of Friday next, 8th, for Paris.

Either *you* or *Evans* must come. He *cannot*—you can. Get ready, oh Gravel Sifter! and send me anyhow all your forged Moulin Quignon *hâches*.

Try and get Alfred Tylor to deliver up his one.

The term "gravel sifter" was applied to Prestwich in a humorous and satirical caricature of a scientific controversy, entitled "Report of a sad case, recently tried before the Lord Mayor, Owen *versus* Huxley, in which will be found fully given the merits of the great recent Bone Case."

This was attributed to Dr Pycroft of Exeter, and it was printed anonymously in April 1863. It was reprinted, except the last paragraph, in 'Public Opinion' for May of the same year.

In the course of the case the following conversation is supposed to take place :—

The Lord Mayor here asked whether either party were known to the police?

Policeman X. Huxley, your Worship, I take to be a young hand, but very vicious; but Owen I have seen before. He got into trouble with an old bone-man, called Mantell, who never could be off complaining as Owen prigged his bones. People did say that the old man never got over it, and Owen worrited him to death; but I don't think it was so bad as that. Hears as Owen takes the chair at a crib in Bloomsbury. I don't think it be a harmonic meeting altogether. And Huxley hangs out in Jermyn Street.

Lord Mayor. Do you know any of their associates?

Policeman X. I have heard that Hooker, who travels in the green and vegetable line, pats Huxley on the back a good deal; and Lyell, the resurrectionist, and some others, who keep dark at present, are pals of Huxley's.

Lord Mayor. Lyell, Lyell; surely I have heard that name before.

Policeman X. Very like you may, your Worship; there's a fight getting up between him and Falconer, the old bone-man, with Prestwich, the gravel-sifter, for backer.

J. Prestwich to M. Edouard Lartet.　　　　LONDON, *5th May* 1863.

MY DEAR SIR,—I much wish I could accompany Dr Falconer to Paris to assist and aid at this curious inquiry respecting the Abbeville jaw, which promises to be one of the *causes célèbres* in science. When Mr Evans and I called on our excellent friend M. Boucher de Perthes early in the morning of Monday the 13th of April, M. de Perthes at once showed us the jaw, together with the flint implements he had found with it. About the jaw I will say nothing more, as we were not competent witnesses as to its peculiarities, and as to its fossil condition we had no opportunities of examining.

We were, however, both at once struck with the peculiar form of all the flint implements, with the sharpness of their angles, and with their peculiar soiling. We, however, reserved our opinion and went to look at the pit. Unfortunately a fall of the gravel had taken place, and the section was covered up so that we could only see one end of it. That there was a black band was evident, and one fact struck me in favour of the probable authenticity of the specimens, which was, that heretofore all the specimens of the flint implements had been obtained from the ochreous gravel, and it seemed to me that if ignorant workmen wished to imitate the real specimens, they would rather have adopted the usual matrix than have sought one which was exceptional. As we were walking to St Gilles from Moulin Quignon, one of the men took two specimens from his pocket and gave them to me. These were both from an ochreous or ferruginous matrix, and it seemed at once evident to us that they were both false. I therefore took the opportunity to wash one at the first cottage we came to. All the soil came off immediately, and left the flint quite fresh and clean and sharp. This further evidence satisfied us both then that some imposition was practised, and immediately we got back to Abbeville I at once told M. Boucher de Perthes of our doubts and suspicions about the workmen. He did not see it in the same light that we did, even after he had himself washed one of the specimens. We were unable to stop longer to follow up the inquiry, and I only much regret that M. de Perthes did not mention in a sufficiently pointed manner our doubts to Dr Falconer and M. Quatrefages, as it might have led to a stricter examination of the flints on the spot and more reserve on the part of my friend. It was only in fact after washing and close inspection that the nature either of the jaw or of the flints could be determined. They were all so much soiled, and that seemingly with intent. The reasons why I doubt the genuineness of the flints are these:—

1. Their shape upon a type *different* (only slightly) from all others previously found at Abbeville or Amiens.

2. The *sharpness of all their angles*, whereas all the specimens I had previously seen from Moulin Quignon showed *more wear than the specimens from any other locality* except La Porte Mercadé.

3. The entire absence of *staining and discolorisation*, except such slight effect as might be produced by a few days' contact with the matrix, whereas I had never before seen one specimen out of six (if so much) but what were much *stained and permanently discoloured*, usually *brown*, at times with traces of *black*.

4. The absence of all *dendritic markings*, and of any portion, however small, of the *matrix adhering*. Such absence is most unusual.

5. The great number of the specimens. I had been before some six or eight times to Moulin Quignon, and have never been present at the discovery of a single specimen, nor had the workmen any to offer me.

6. The evident soiling of all the specimens as though they had been put in gravel and then water thrown over them, or as if they had been taken in the hand and rubbed with wet gravel and sand. In fact, on two specimens I have seen distinct streaks produced by the passing of gritty particles over a wet surface and of adhering matrix.

These are my chief reasons; on the other hand, I must admit that I have seen two specimens which have the appearance I assign to the false ones, and which yet show on one side a certain amount of wear. Some few specimens also are so close to the genuine forms that it is most difficult to distinguish; and further, Mr Antonio Brady, who has just returned from Abbeville, and who has been in the habit of visiting the gravel-pits around London, has been to Moulin Quignon and carefully examined the section, and seems satisfied of the genuineness of the discovery.

I have now given you the "pros and cons" respecting the flint implements and of this remarkable case. I am still satisfied that there is imposition in some, if not the greater part, of the flint implements, and that of course throws a doubt in my mind on the whole affair. The ultimate conclusions must, however, depend upon a close examination and analysis of the jaw, and in the able hands in which the matter now rests I have no doubt the truth will be elicited. I much regret to hear how much our difference of opinion affects M. Boucher de Perthes, and nothing would please me better than he should be able either to substantiate this case or be the first to prove another.—Believe me to be, my dear sir, truly yours,　　　　　　　　　　　J. Prestwich.

J. Prestwich to J. Evans.   LONDON, *Saturday* [1863].

MY DEAR EVANS,—I have a letter of twelve pages with a supplement of two from Boucher de Perthes. Dr Falconer, Carpenter, and Busk went to Paris last night. I have a letter from Lartet this morning. He much wishes you and me to go over: I have just decided to do so, and am off by this mail train tonight. If you have anything to say, or if you come, you will find me at the Hôtel de Tours. Will Friday next suit you as well as Wednesday to meet Dr Torrell? I shall write to him from Paris. I hope to be back on Tuesday, but it is uncertain.—Ever truly yours,   J. PRESTWICH.

J. Prestwich to H. Falconer.   LONDON, *9th May* 1863.

MY DEAR FALCONER,—I have arranged to run over to Paris, and shall start by mail train to-night. As M. Quatrefages could not attend a meeting to-day, in consequence of his lecture, until after 4½, I suppose there will not be much done to-day, and that I shall not be much after time if I present myself to-morrow morning. I propose stopping at the Hôtel de Tours, and will call at M. Lartet's between 10½ and 11. I feel the case to be one in which the good understanding with our French friends is so much concerned that I feel as you do, most anxious to discuss in a personal and amicable interview all points of difference, and have therefore arranged to play truant from the City for two or three days.

I shall bring over a few more specimens with me, together with various gravels and some fragments of bone. *Au revoir.*— Yours ever truly,   JOS. PRESTWICH.

Pray thank M. Lartet for his kind letter to me received to-day, and which has considerably influenced my decision.

The English deputation consisted of Messrs Prestwich, Falconer, Busk, and Carpenter, while the French members consisted chiefly of members of the Institute, —MM. de Quatrefages, Edouard Lartet the palæontologist, Desnoyers the geologist, and Delesse, professor of geology, with Milne-Edwards the zoologist as their president. Other distinguished naturalists joined in the investigation, as, for example, M. Albert Gaudry (our geologist's old and valued friend), M. A. Milne-Edwards, and the Abbé Bourgeois. Mr John Evans, who, as we have seen, had taken the keenest interest in the inquiry from the time the asserted discovery had been made, was prevented by other engagements from joining at this stage.

Three meetings of the Commission were held in Paris early in May 1863, the proceedings being conducted with great solemnity. Each member present, whether French or English, had been led to recognise the value of M. de Perthes' discovery of flint implements in the valley gravels of the Somme, by the persuasive power of one of their number, who perhaps was the most silent though not the least thoughtful in that remarkable assemblage. It was Prestwich who had won them all to a belief in those old worked flint implements. Nor was his influence the least among his fellow-members of the Conference.

Unable to agree, they adjourned to Abbeville, where the members were reinforced by the presence of M. de Perthes, with that also of several eminent *savants*, such as MM. Hébert, de Vibraye, &c. The sitting was prolonged far into the night at the quaint old Tête de Bœuf. They separated at 2 A.M., only to reassemble a few hours later for the summing up. The *procès verbaux* of each meeting had been voluminous and minute, but the evidence was so perplexing that there was only unanimity on the first clause, namely, "The jaw in question was not fraudulently introduced into the gravel-pit of Moulin Quignon : it had existed previously in the spot where M. Boucher de Perthes

found it on the 28th March 1863." Thus the proceedings of this *cause célèbre* came to a close.

The result of the conference was a bitter disappointment to M. de Perthes, since his English friends,
although acknowledging the fact of the human jaw
having been truly found as he described, yet refused to
admit that it belonged to a remote antiquity. His
letters subsequently to Prestwich and Falconer were
more than pathetic. To the latter he wrote, "*Vous
m'avez tué!*" Still he had achieved a great work :
he had obtained public and full recognition of his flint
hâches as the tools and weapons of primitive man.
"Besides, he had the support among the members of
the Commission who were his distinguished countrymen,
and might well have been content to leave the age of
the famous human jaw as it rested in the minds of his
English friends—in doubt."

It had been painful to Prestwich and Falconer to
differ in opinion from their French *confrères* as to the
remote age of the jaw, but the latter were conscious that
their English brethren were loyal, and actuated solely
by their convictions, and by anxiety to arrive at the
truth. If we except the natural disappointment of
M. Boucher de Perthes, the two sections (the French
and English) separated with the same old feeling
of friendship and esteem, and with a perfect understanding between both parties.

J. Prestwich to H. Falconer.   ABBEVILLE, 13th *May* 1863.

MY DEAR FALCONER,—I seem scarcely to have had time to
have a word with you the last few days. It is, I must confess,
with surprise I find myself at the conclusion to which we have
arrived. The case is a remarkable one, and apart from a few
impatient words, has, I think, been most fairly and friendly

conducted. It is with pain, however, I have watched its effects
on you the last two days. For my own part, I am truly glad
the difference has been so speedily arranged and the mistake
corrected. I must take some blame to myself for expressing an
opinion in default of not having better studied the section. To
you there attaches nought but the most honourable straight-
forwardness. . . . We are just off to Boulogne. My kind
regards to M. Lartet.

In another note to Falconer of the 20th May, he
wrote, "I am glad to hear matters have passed off
so well in Paris. Don't you go and fraternise with
Elie de Beaumont. You see I am losing all reverence
for high authorities."

There was a humorous side to the deliberations over
the human jaw :—

R. A. C. Godwin-Austen to J. Prestwich.

CHILWORTH, *May* 21 [1863].

MY DEAR PRESTWICH,—Strange that whilst mine of yesterday
was on its way to you, a copy of the 'Abbevillois' should be on
its way here, in answer to my doubts.

I recognised the pen of M. B. de Perthes, but has it all passed
off as he narrates ? If so, it must have been an interesting sight.
I can picture the procession *se rendant chez M. de Perthes pour
lui [faire] leurs félicitations.*

Milne-Edwards.	Quatrefages.
Lartet.	Delesse.

Vibraye.
(Here come the three English heretics.)

Hébert.	Desnoyers.
L'Abbé Bourgeois.	Garrigou.
Gaudry.	Delanoue.

A strong rearguard, for fear Falconer should bolt.

Here in England we must have a day : the Royal, Geological, and
Anthropological Societies must muster in the quadrangle of

Burlington House, a fire must be kindled, and into it must you, and Falconer, and Lyell, and Tylor cast in all that you have written against B. de P. and his gravel-diggers.

On the same day you shall be limited to such a dinner as Galton shall order for you at the Athenæum. — Being yours truly, ROBERT A. C. GODWIN-AUSTEN.

J. Prestwich to H. Falconer. 2 SUFFOLK LANE, 25th *May* 1863.

MY DEAR FALCONER,—I was not anxious to write to the 'Athenæum,' and as your short notice appeared last week, I think I had better say nothing. . . . I might then have said a few words about the beds, but should have been silent about the jaw. This, in fact, will be very much the subject of my paper to the Geological Society. I wish to confine myself strictly to the geological evidence, as the important question of the age of the beds has again been raised by Elie de Beaumont. The two points are independent—don't let us mix them. We were at Bedford yesterday. I wish you could have been with us. I had no intention of going when I went to Nash Mills on Saturday. Mr Wyatt was from home: I, however, called on my acquaintance Read, and found his collection from the railway-cutting still unsold. I made a bid for it, and have obtained possession. It contains some capital specimens. One remarkably fine tusk-tooth of hippopotamus. Several teeth of the same and of rhinoceros, deer, elephant, felis, &c. Also 2 small tusks of hipp. Would you kindly look at this collection? I should much like to give a corrected list of the Bedford mammalia in my notice of the Bedford beds forming part of my paper now before the Royal Society. I am sorry to find that neither Christy nor Busk can dine with us to-day.—Ever yours, J. PRESTWICH.

As might be expected, a paper on the subject from Prestwich was read at the Geological Society, entitled, "On the Section at Moulin Quignon, Abbeville, and on the Peculiar Character of some of the Flint Implements recently discovered there." The following letter refers to it :—

J. Prestwich to H. Falconer.   2 SUFFOLK LANE, *29th May.*

MY DEAR FALCONER,—I send you the title of my paper. I have ascertained that the 3rd and 4th papers do not come on. So I hope you will be able to bring on your notice about the jaw, which I now think you were right in wishing to have on the same evening as my paper, especially as there is but one more meeting after the 3rd June. The 1st part of my paper on the Geological question I shall send in to-morrow, but the 2nd part on the Flints I must reserve till Tuesday, after our return from Abbeville, when I hope the question of their authenticity or forgery will be finally settled by the further opinion of Evans, Flower, Lubbock, and possibly Austen.

As the matter now stands, Evans considers, as you, that there is some inexplicable mystery about the matter which he cannot explain. This, however, is a question of fact respecting which I hope he will be able to satisfy himself one way or the other on this visit. Not so the jaw, about which I can well understand your reserve, though I do not share it. There is the same mystery, whilst unfortunately there are not the same means to investigate it. As the section has been worked so many feet back, I do not see how now it can ever be solved without the discovery of another jaw or human bone in the same position, or, if there has been fraud, by the confession of the culprit. I send you Delesse's letter, which please return.

A note-book entry after the conference records :—

30*th May* 1863.—3rd visit to Abbeville with Evans, Lubbock, and Wickham Flower. Dr F. Garrigou of Toulouse met us at Abbeville.

31*st*, morning, to l'Hôpital Champ de Mars and Moulin Quignon. One flint implement found by us *in talus*, seemingly just fallen from black-band. . . .

Out to Mesnières by Mautort and Moyenville.

A letter on " The Human Jaw of Abbeville," which appeared in the 'Athenæum' of June 13th, was from

Prestwich's pen.   The following note bears reference
to it :—

From John Evans to J. Prestwich.

NASH MILLS, HEMEL HEMPSTEAD, *June* 17, 1863.

MY DEAR PRESTWICH,—I got back to London this morning,
having left Belfast yesterday and spent the day in Dublin. I
had to get down here by midday or I would have called, as I
should like to have had a chat with you about two letters I have
seen to-day—yours to the 'Athenæum,' and one to me from
Keeping. I think yours "judicious," and at the same time
"suggestive." It gives one rather the impression of a palimp-
sest MS., in which beneath the modern writing one can discern
the traces of an earlier and more valuable document. However,
I quite agree with your standing up for your French and *absent*
friends, and admire your audacity in calling my deliberate expression of opinion after holding my tongue so patiently, "thinking aloud." Also aren't the finger and brush marks just like
sand scratches? *Mes yeux!* as Quatrefages would say. . . .

J. Prestwich to H. Falconer.   2 SUFFOLK LANE, 19th *June* 1863.

MY DEAR FALCONER,—Pray think over what I talked to you
about yesterday. Remember that Delesse particularly asked to
have any errata or omissions pointed out to him for correction,
I presume before publishing in France. How much better that
the version so corrected should be published there and here, than
that a wrong version should appear, subject to comments and
corrections which would be unnecessary and superfluous, if, in
conformity with Delesse's wish, the opportunity be given him to
correct if he saw occasion. I do not in fact see how, without
offence, publication can take place without previous communication. I should feel aggrieved if I were in Delesse's place. You
have known my opinion all along about these corrections, and I
think you have seen Delesse's letters both to Dr C. and to me.
I told Delesse I saw little to alter, and that agreeably with your
request I had returned you the *Procès Verbaux* to complete your
examination of them. Any notes or corrections beyond my own
remarks I of course did not touch upon, presuming that each

member would see to his own.　I foresee trouble enough with the difference of opinion on the main question, but I should be very sorry to see other causes of differences with the French members introduced.　I wish to *have no share or part whatsoever* in the contemplated publication.　As I told Delesse, I had little to alter or comment upon.　My opinions are fairly represented, and subsequent events I have recorded as far as I wish to record them in the 'Athenæum' and at the Geological Society.　With you it is different.　You wish, if I understand rightly, to show that your protest implied more than the *P. V.* gives, and you amplify your reasons.　At what time do you meet on Sunday morning?　I will try to be present, altho' my head and hands are full of other matters at present, as my partnership here shortly expires, and the question of renewal is just now under discussion.　I had some idea of going to the Scotts at Walton. If I don't, I will make a point of calling on you on Sunday morning.—And I am ever truly yours,　　JOS. PRESTWICH.

J. Prestwich to H. Falconer.　　2 SUFFOLK LANE, 24th June 1863.

MY DEAR FALCONER,—Thanks for your note and enclosure. I know Lexden, near Colchester, very well.　I have visited it several times, both alone and with John Brown.　The fossils are not found in a bed of true peat, but in a carbonaceous bed a foot thick, [such] as occurs occasionally at Grays, but more especially like the Mundesley bed.　It is overlaid by loess. . . .

On the 18th July Prestwich was again out on a geological tour, beginning with Whitchurch and including eighteen different localities, ending with Portland Bill, &c.　Later on he was at Thame, and on September 6th he was working out the district round Grayshot, near Haslemere, and Reigate.

J. Prestwich to J. Evans.　　LONDON, 11th Sept. 1863.

MY DEAR EVANS,— . . . I am thinking of running down to Newmarket to-morrow evening, and back on Monday morning.　*I must revise*, if possible, my sections of Bedford, Icklingham, Herne Bay, and the Waveney Valley for my Philosophical Transactions paper, and I do not now see what time I can get except my old plan of Saturday night to Monday, and making each a separate excursion. I must also try for two days at Amiens.

I shall be glad and curious to hear what you saw and what you did at Icklingham. Can you give me a few lines by the morning's post, or have you not been there, and will you go?

September 15th was the date of this visit to Bedford ; on the 19th he was at Herne Bay, and on the 26th at Icklingham.

Early in October he was measuring the heights round Harleston, while on the 25th he was back in the valley of the Somme, ascertaining the levels and dimensions of the beds round Amiens and St Acheul. This expedition was at least the fourth to the Amiens district during the year.

The first notice of a geological expedition in 1864 was to " Fareham—Red Lion, with Evans, 14th February 1864." In describing the coast at The Hook, he observes: "Gravel rises from the sea-level, and continues without break to highest part of the cliffs—30 feet high. Here on the beach, midway, J. Evans found a flint implement of the St Acheul type—worn, but not stained."

During the spring, one of the Friday-evening lectures was given by Prestwich at the Royal Institution, its subject being, " On the Quaternary Flint Implements of Abbeville, Amiens, Hoxne, &c.: their Geological Position and History."

The following letters are of interest :—

J. Prestwich to J. Evans.   69 MARK LANE, LONDON, *6th May* 1864.

MY DEAR EVANS,—I don't think you have ever been to the Isle of Sheppey. What say you to Sittingbourne and the Island, back mid-day on Monday? Or else Walton and Clacton? I will fix, however, definitely, this evening; and if you can call to-morrow at Kent Terrace, or write me here, to say when you will call, I will give final instructions.

To the Same.　　　　　　　　　　　LONDON, *20th June* 1864.

MY DEAR EVANS,—My sister and I are going to Rickmans-worth this morning to look at the house you name. I have, however, just bought eleven acres of land at Shoreham in the valley of the Dart. The sale came off on Friday afternoon, and the situation is so charming, and the opportunity so rare, that I sent down Mr Ellis to bid for me. The drawbacks are that there is not a drop of water, and scarcely an inch of soil on the ground. It is a bare piece of chalk-down with a topknot of wood.

Late in August he was at Walton-on-the-Naze, where, as he remained several days with his sister Civil, there was leisure to sketch sections and to visit locali-ties within reach, such as Clacton, &c., where elephant remains had been found.

"*Grays, Sept.* 1864.—With Austen and Tylor."

The above brief entry precedes minute descriptions of thirty-three localities.

"*Sept.* 17, 1864.—To Horsham and Petworth," where he was at work on the new line of railway; then on to Chichester and Bognor.

While thus in vague and general terms indicating the unswerving devotion to his favourite science—how he availed himself of every possible opportunity for its prosecution, and how it absorbed so large a portion of his daily life—it must not be forgotten that the social side of his life was a very full and active one. As years went on the affectionate relations with his family never relaxed. No week passed without at least one happy little family meeting, either at one of his sisters' houses or his own. He was not only a member of the Geologi-cal Society Club, as previously noted, but also of the

N

Philosophical Club, one of the two dining-clubs composed of Fellows of the Royal Society, and he very frequently dined out with friends. His Christmas and New Year family gatherings were invariably a success, when his house seemed to have developed wonderful expanding capacities.

The delightful entertainments given each Christmas for the young nephews and nieces, when there was also a muster of little cousins, were the occasions when our geologist, surrounded by the children, was in his very element. It was his custom to provide himself with a bag of new silver "pennies" for distribution among the little ones, to whom no party was ever equal to Uncle Joseph's.

One paper was published in the 'Geological Magazine' for this year—"The Brick-earth with Elephant Remains at Ilford."

The following letter from Sir Roderick I. Murchison refers to Prestwich's appointment as a member of the Royal Water Commission :—

1st December 1864.

MY DEAR PRESTWICH,—On Monday last the Duke of Buckingham explained to me his views respecting the water-supply of the Metropolis, as set forth in the paper enclosed, and asked me to recommend the person best qualified as a geologist to form one of the new Royal Commission, of which, at the Duke's suggestion, the Government has approved.

I hope you may be able to join this body, and if you abandon the Jerusalem search, you may perhaps do so.

At all events, I consider this question of the water-supply more pressing and more serious than that of the coal-supply; and knowing your capacity to aid such a very important material enterprise, I felt bound to mention you as the person best qualified for the task.—Yours sincerely,   ROD. I. MURCHISON.

You will, of course, send your answer direct to the Duke of Buckingham and Chandos, Council Office.

Another memoir was read at the Royal Society, "On some further Evidence bearing on the Excavation of the Valley of the Somme by River-Action, as exhibited in a Section at Drucat, near Abbeville."

The death of Hugh Falconer, which took place on 31st January 1865, was a severe blow to Prestwich, who to the end of his life did not cease to lament the loss of this friend. They had been on terms of close intimacy almost from the date of Falconer's return from the East, some ten years before ; they had joined hand in hand in attacking difficult geological questions ; and they had made plans for joint work in the future— plans, alas ! never to be realised. One of the last notes dictated by Falconer, when unable to hold a pen, was addressed to Joseph Prestwich, requesting him to take charge of the interests of a case which concerned a mutual friend, for whom he had suggested the award of the proceeds of the Wollaston Fund. "I would have seen you to-day if I could, but they would not let you come up," were among the last words dictated by Hugh Falconer.

In subsequent years, Prestwich was often heard to exclaim when handling undetermined specimens of fossil bones, "What work we should have done together if he only had been spared !" There was no naturalist who possessed Hugh Falconer's vast palæontological and botanical knowledge combined (botany had been his profession), no one more ready of access or more willing to co-operate and impart that knowledge. His boyish mirth and racy originality made him a brilliant com-panion, while underlying all the glee and laughter-provoking sallies there was the deeply affectionate and genial nature which drew Joseph Prestwich as with a magnet.

The Easter excursion, dating 14th April, was made to Antwerp *viâ* Harwich, when the three friends who accompanied Prestwich were Captain Douglas Galton, Mr J. Gwyn-Jeffreys, and Mr Godwin-Austen.

To judge from the ground traversed, this expedition to Belgium must have been of great interest. Our geologist, as usual, was in search of Drift and Loess, and intent on tracing the features of the Gravel deposits, in which remains of elephants and other extinct mammalia had been found, the observations of his friends being quoted and interwoven in his voluminous notes. When at Liége they saw the Schmerling Collection ; and Prestwich noted " the Engis skull very fresh-looking, so also some of the bear remains. The Engis Cave worked out."

They were joined at Louvain by M. Van Beneden, and at Brussels by M. Nyst. Amongst other places visited were Maestricht, the Engis Cave, Dinant, the Grotte du Frontal, Namur, Mons, Spiennes, &c. It must have been hard work to crowd so much practical geology into a ten days' tour. To make the most of their time, the journey from Marsières to Lille and Calais was by night train. One day was devoted to an examination of Sangatte Cliff, to which Prestwich returned alone on the 24th. He was keenly interested in the geology of the coast between Calais and Sangatte, and in going back to the ground wished to satisfy himself on points which to his mind had not been perfectly clear. He was desirous of ascertaining the composition of the Raised Beach at Sangatte —the relative proportion of angular chert, pieces of rolled red granite, lydian stones, and pebbles of sandstone, &c.

How many visits were made to the Calais coast ?

Shall we say twelve? Twice twelve would be within the number!

J. Prestwich to J. Evans. LONDON, *5th August* 1865.

MY DEAR EVANS,—You must have had a delightful excursion. I long to hear the details. I see Dupont has sent in a preliminary report about the caves. I and other members of our Easter party abstained from any communication on the subject until Dupont and Van Beneden had made theirs. Do you know when the final one will be, as I shall then have a short notice to give of our visit? I see Dupont has modified some of the views he held when we saw him. Thanks for your Archæopteryx paper. As the 'Reader' has taken it up, you will, I expect, have a battle to fight. . . .

A paper of general interest, evidently embodying the observations on his Easter trip, was read to and published by the Geological Society, entitled, "Additional Observations on the Raised Beach at Sangatte with Reference to the Date of the English Channel, and the Presence of Loess in the Cliff Section."

The next entry in a note-book for this year is, "Aldborough, 20th August 1865. By Snape Bridge and Tunstall to the Oyster Inn at Butley, with J. Evans and M. Gaudry, &c."

The object of this expedition was the inspection of various crag-pits in the neighbourhood, and the amassing of further materials for his series of Crag Memoirs.

Weymouth and its geology engaged his attention in October; and Blackdown Hill, near Dorchester, with its great beds of flint, and quartzose gravel, and transported blocks, was a source of special interest.

The last expedition for this year was apparently that made "to Thetford with John Evans and Wickham

Flower." Before walking to Brandon by the river valley, they were refreshed by the sight of eight fine flint implements belonging to Mr Bartlett.

It was in 1865 that Prestwich was awarded one of the Royal Medals of the Royal Society, in recognition of his original researches on the valley-deposits yielding flint implements and weapons of early man.

J. Prestwich to Sir Rod. I. Murchison.

69 MARK LANE, LONDON, 3rd *Novr.* 1865.

MY DEAR SIR RODERICK,—Very many thanks for your great kindness in bringing me forward for the medal of the Royal Society, and for the very kind and friendly terms in which you have announced to me the award of the Council. I am not usually ambitious of public honours, but I feel deeply sensible in this case of so honourable a distinction, and especially do I value it as a mark of the kind interest of my friends, and amongst them of one so distinguished as yourself.

With many thanks, believe me to be, my dear Sir Roderick, most truly yours,   JOS. PRESTWICH.

This year was not so notable for field-work crowded into it as for a step he took which, though apparently insignificant, had a great influence on his life. During several years he had been living and working at the highest pressure—pressure so severe that it could not go on. It had told on his health ; and, conscious of the strain, he felt that a measure of rest was imperative : the difficulty was to tear himself from London friends and from the Societies. A happy compromise was made. A country cottage as a summer home for him and his sister Civil was first thought of; but as one to suit was not easily found, Prestwich decided to build on the few acres of chalk down which had happened to be for sale, overlooking the valley

DARENT-HULME.

Photo by C. Essenhigh Corke, Sevenoaks.

of the Darent, and just above the picturesque village
of Shoreham, amid its hop-gardens. Fascinated by
the views from this hill, he had bought the land off-
hand in the summer of 1864, and now set about planting and building.

Most men would have shrunk from erecting a house
upon a high position which was bare of trees and
without water; but the old habit of mind prevailed,
and difficulties were nowhere. It may be remarked
that ultimately the bleak chalk down was converted
into an ideal garden. The first step towards building
was to find an accessible water-supply, for although
the Darent was in sight,—

> " The still Darenth, in whose waters cleane
> Ten thousand fishes play and decke his pleasant streame,"—

yet it was far down in the valley, shining and gleaming
in its tranquil winding course, just as in the day when
Spenser sang its praise.

So confident was Prestwich in respect of water-
supply, that he at once engaged an old well-digger
to sink a well 168 feet deep. The boring proceeded,
but when a depth of 166 feet was reached, the two
workmen went to the city and sought an interview
with their employer, whom they found at his desk.
They explained that there was no sign of water, and
that in their opinion it was useless to bore to a greater
depth. " Go on," was the quiet rejoinder. " You will
come upon water to-morrow. You are within two feet
of it."

Next day it proved exactly as Prestwich had foretold; and ever after, among many of the denizens of
the valley, he had the reputation—much to his amusement—of not being quite " canny." He knew the

exact level of the springs in the valley, and that the well-diggers must touch water when they reached that depth.

The laying out of the ground and planting were carried out according to his own plans, those of a professional landscape gardener who had been called in not being approved. An Arctic plantation crowned the highest point, and a clump of berberis where the soil was most surly; a sophora and a lavender walk were marked off, but taking precedence of all, the only level strip of ground was transformed into an acacia walk. This straight formal path, bordered by tuft-headed acacias, was to remind him of a garden in his beloved France. It may be added that these little acacias have had a hard struggle for existence: they found the chalk an unfriendly soil, and have had to be replaced from time to time.

When the foundation of the house was laid, it was characteristic of our geologist that he invited a little festive gathering of relatives to share in the proceedings and rejoice with him. The building was an interest and a recreation, and it is not surprising that it was destined to illustrate geology within and without. Tertiary flints faced the outer walls, while the coigns and mullions were of white Paris stone. Within, the mantel-shelves throughout were to demonstrate the use of English marbles. As a matter of course, the decorations were geological. The graceful fronds and foliage of the Coal-measures were to be adapted for cornice ornament, while extinct animals, which had flourished in this country in bygone ages, were stencilled in panels on the dining-room ceiling, and were not grotesque.

It was in this year (1866) that Prestwich was ap-

THE DINING-ROOM, DARENT-HULME.

pointed a member of the Royal Coal Commission, of
which he became a prominent worker. He contributed
two of the sub-reports,—one, "On the Quantity of
Unwrought Coal in the Coal-Fields of Somerset," and
the other, "On the Probability of finding Coal under
the Newer Formations of the South of England." These
were written in 1866, and printed in 1871.

In reply to an inquiry about water-supply on a
farm near Ruddington, four pages of a letter are written
to his young niece Sarah Scott,[1] dated 21st May 1866,
and describing the process for freeing hard water from
carbonate of lime. He then proceeds:—

But I suspect the hardness of your house-water arises not
from carbonate of lime, but from the presence of sulphate of
lime (plaster rock), which is much worse and more difficult to
get rid of. Boiling will do something. The best thing to do
is, however, to add carbonate of soda to the water, and then boil
it, when a considerable sediment will be thrown down. Test
with reddened litmus paper to see that no free alkali remains.
One or other of these processes will, I trust, my dear Sarah, save
your complexion and Alice's hands. If they do not succeed,
write me again at once. It is a great bore you have not got
a garden—apply forthwith for a cottage allotment. I should
much like to see your quarters: I hope you will send up a
sketch of them. If you have nothing better to do, write very
often to your affectionate uncle,   J. PRESTWICH.

There is a spice of fun in the suggestion of a cottage allotment: the farm had been taken by a nephew
of independent means as an interesting experiment.

In 1866 Dr Henry Woodward, our chief authority
on fossil crustacea, published a particular account of
several forms allied to the living king-crabs (*Limulus*),
which had been described by Prestwich in his early

---

[1] Wife of Mr O'Neill, British Consul at Rouen.

researches on the coal-field of Coalbrook Dale. For
the two species of *Limulus* then recorded by Prestwich
Dr Woodward proposed the new genus *Prestwichia*, as

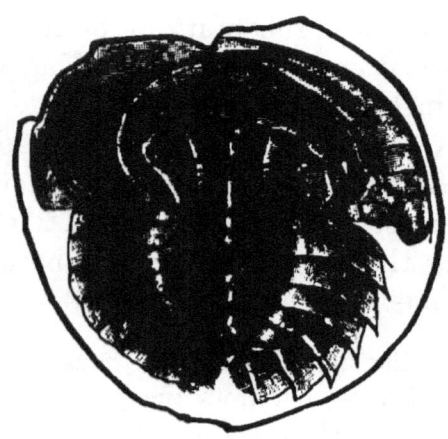

Prestwichia (*Limulus*) *rotundata*, Prestw.

it was necessary to separate the old forms of *Xiphosura*
from those now living.[1]

Prestwich was now serving on two Royal Commissions, his practical knowledge of each subject
rendering him a valuable member of both. The only
leisure for superintending his planting and building
was snatched on Saturdays, when by the earliest
train on dark winter mornings he and his sister
Civil made their way to Shoreham to watch each
step of progress. But before the end of December
the shadow of death darkened his home, and he
was overtaken by the greatest calamity which had
yet befallen him. This was the death, after a
short illness, of his sister Civil, which took place on
the 27th December. She had been his devoted companion during the last ten years of her life. This loss

[1] Quart. Journ. Geol. Soc., vol. xxiii. p. 32.

is made known in a few lines to his friend John Evans :—

10 KENT TERRACE, 27th Dec. 1866.

MY DEAR EVANS,—I have lost the best of sisters. She passed away this morning tranquilly and without pain. I feel the loss is to me irreparable. She was my object in life, and so good, gentle, and affectionate. I feel assured of your sympathy. With kind regards to Mrs Evans, I am, your affectionate and distressed friend,   J. PRESTWICH.

His kind sister Emily took the vacant place : she arranged to remain and make a home for him, and soon the weekly visits to Shoreham were resumed. Happily, he was as usual overwhelmed with work, and in the spring he led a little band of his old companions out on a geological expedition.

Easter Excursion, April 1867.—J. P., Godwin-Austen, Gwyn-Jeffreys, and Captain Galton; joined at Plymouth by Spence Bate.

This expedition was an examination of the Bovey Tracey district. The age of its interesting Lignite beds had, until Professor Heer's determination of the plant remains, been an unsettled question among geologists. The accuracy of his opinion that the group of the Bovey Lignites belonged to the Lower Miocene period has, however, been questioned by Mr J. Starkie Gardner,[1] the leading authority on Tertiary Flora, who considers the Bovey Tracey fossil plants to be of the same age as those found at Bournemouth, and therefore to belong to the Bagshot Series.

Prestwich's object was not so much to explore the Lignite beds as to examine the geological structure of

[1] British Eocene Flora, Monographs of the Palæontographical Society, vol. xxiii. (1879), p. 19.

Bovey Tracey and the surrounding district,—to trace every exhibition of Gravel, ascertaining its constituents and the various heights of its occurrence above the river. His notes are suggestive and of much interest, but we give only one brief extract : [1]—

Beyond Bovey Tracey the rocks are bare ; but descending to the river at Woolford Bridge, we found ledges of a Gravel terrace fringing the valley at a height of about 25 feet above the river. It contained largish blocks of rolled granite, no scratched pebbles, and is about 4 to 6 feet thick. At one place it is overlaid by imperfect loess and angular *débris*. ·

To judge from one early morning's start, the little band of geologists was indeed enthusiastic—" Saturday by rail to St Austell, at 3 A.M."

An interchange of letters with Sir Charles Lyell took place this year, in reference to the foundations of St Paul's Cathedral.

Sir C. Lyell to J. Prestwich.

73 HARLEY STREET, LONDON, 12*th June* 1867.

DEAR PRESTWICH,—I have been requested by the Dean of St Paul's to read a page in Wren's 'Parentalia' (p. 285), in which he mentions the strata or layers of earth one above another through which they dug when they made the foundation of St Paul's.

It is said that the old church had stood on very close and hard pot-earth, which was about six feet thick, but thinning to four feet towards the south. Below this they found nothing but dry sand ; and still lower, water and sand mixed with periwinkles and other sea-shells. These were about the level of low-water mark. They continued boring till they came to hard clay. In conclusion, it is said, " by these shells it was evident the sea had been where now the hill is on which St Paul's stands."

---

[1] Further notes have been printed in the Geological Magazine, Decade iv. vol. v. p. 414.

I remember some years ago somebody showing me a section which was dug in our time at St Paul's, and my notion is that the strata belonged to the Plastic Clay and sands below the London Clay. Can you tell me whether this is the case, and whether anything has been printed on the subject? I suppose Wren would call any fossil marine univalves, periwinkles.

Milman also asks me what the pot-earth is. I suppose, as he says that the Romans made pottery of it, that it may be an argillaceous bed of the Plastic Clay series? Wren says that, viewed by a microscope when dissolved in water, this pot-earth was impalpable fine sand which would vitrify with fire.

As Milman leaves town in a few days, I should be very glad of an early reply. Excuse so much trouble, and believe me, ever truly yours,   CHAS. LYELL.

J. Prestwich to Sir Charles Lyell.

10 KENT TERRACE, 14*th June* 1867.

DEAR SIR CHARLES, — I know of no account of the strata beneath St Paul's besides that given by Wren. Some time ago I went carefully into the matter, and the conclusion I came to was that the beds he described were all Drift beds.

In the 1st place, the London Clay under St Paul's must be about 140 to 150 feet thick, and in it no bed of sand occurs about the level of low-water mark. Secondly, if the L. C. had been traversed, the sand-bed beneath it would at that time (whatever may now be the case) have been found full of water. If by "hard beach" had been meant any of the conglomerate beds of the Woolwich Series, "sand" and not "natural hard clay" would most probably have been found under it. It is true that the words "periwinkles and other marine shells" might naturally enough have been applied to the fossil *Paludina lenta*, the *Pectunculus*, &c., of those beds, or might apply to some fossils of the London Clay, especially the masses of univalves occasionally found in the blocks of *Septaria*; but the other reasons are, I think, too strong against the description referring to the Tertiary strata.

On the other hand, "pot-earth," 6 feet thick, and thinning off to 4 feet, and containing fine sand, applies very well to the top brick-earth; under this comes dry sand (the upper part of the sand and gravel is always dry); then the lower part of the sand and gravel, in which the water is held up by the London Clay, and in which all the old pump springs of London occur, is all in order. In this part of the series, Unios, Cyclas, Limnea, &c., might occur, and it would not be surprising that Wren should have described them as he did, as the occurrence of a like deposit in the gravel at Clapton or Hackney was described in some of the newspapers in nearly similar terms, only about six years since. Certainly the depth would not be about the level of low-water mark, as the ground at St Paul's is 40 feet above the Thames, and the depth to the London Clay cannot be more than 20 to 25 feet, but it might have been considered that "about" would give the measure near enough.

By "hard beach" I think compact subangular gravel must be meant. Beneath this, "natural hard clay" applies perfectly to the London Clay. Pray excuse this rather hurried scrawl, and believe me to be truly yours,   J. PRESTWICH.

There is no record of published papers for this year, but this is accounted for by the fact of his having thrown himself with his usual zeal into the requirements of the Royal Water Commission. Every spare hour was devoted to the delineation of maps, in order to show the available sources of water-supply. He was also elaborating the first of his series of Crag memoirs ; and although he had explored the Eastern counties times without count, he went again and again into Norfolk during this year to investigate some special point, or to obtain some fresh piece of evidence.

The Saturdays at Shoreham had become an institution, and the garden an unending interest—each shrub, each tree, being planted under his own immediate superintendence. These weekly visits to the garden and frequent geological excursions were more than ever needed for the restoration of his health, which had become impaired by continued high pressure. His kind physician, Dr Owen Rees, declared that he was suffering from "nothing but overwork." If the subjects on which he was engaged could be passed under review, we should only wonder that he had not altogether incapacitated himself. The Reports for the two Royal Commissions were imperative, so that his own personal work had for a time to be set aside. He had been eagerly amassing and arranging materials for his memoirs on the Crag; besides which the Brixham Cave Committee had passed a resolution that Mr Prestwich should draw up the General Report for the Royal Society, so that all the special reports were one by one handed over to him.

Letters to his attached friend, Mr William Colchester of Ipswich,[1] refer to his forthcoming Crag memoir :—

J. Prestwich to W. Colchester.

69 MARK LANE, LONDON, 23rd January 1868.

MY DEAR COLCHESTER,—My long-in-hand paper on the Crag is coming on at the Geological [Society] on Febry. 26th. Although my sections are numerous, I find I want some exact levels. Do you know of any youth at Woodbridge or Ipswich who could run a line of level from the river at Sutton, passing over the top of the hill at your farm (and by the old Coralline Crag coprolite pit), then by the Bullock-yard pit to the Crag pit at Shottisham —a day's work for 20s. to 30s. ?

I think I must also run down again myself to see it done and to visit a coprolite pit I have heard of near Orford, and which I suspect to be in the Coralline Crag. My friend Jeffreys, the distinguished conchologist, proposes to accompany me. Are you disposed to join us ? It will be for a three-days' run—camping out at Bawdsey and Orford. I shall want to spend an evening also at Woodbridge to see Mr Whincopp. No fixed time yet. With kind regards to Mrs Colchester and family, I am, very truly yours,　　　　　　　　　　　　　　JOS. PRESTWICH.

---

[1] William Colchester, born July 21, 1813 ; died November 15, 1898.

J. Prestwich to the Same.

MY DEAR COLCHESTER, — Mr J. Gwyn - Jeffreys and I have decided to leave town (Water Commission permitting) on the evening of Monday the 10th. We shall go to Wickham Station, and next day make a round of the Orford district. We shall get to Woodbridge at night, and pass Wednesday at Sutton, returning in the evening to see Mr Whincopp's collection. Thursday we shall pass at Bawdsey Cliff.

Join us if you can and if agreeable. As I may want to trespass at Sutton, can you oblige me with a line to anybody there? Will you allow me also to dig a hole or holes in your ground? We shall leave on Thursday evening.—In haste, I am, very truly yours, JOS. PRESTWICH.

The first two of his memoirs on the Crag were published this year in abstract by the Geological Society, the full text not appearing until 1871. He also wrote a Report for the Metropolitan Board of Works, "On Boring Operations at Crossness."

The preparation of the water - maps did not altogether absorb his leisure, since early in May we read of his being again at Walton-on-Naze, working on sections doubtless with a view to the completion of the third of the series of Crag memoirs. The same object led him to Saxmundham, where, in Mr E. Cavell's collection, he noted "one beautiful tooth of Mastodon with Coralline Crag in hollows." Numerous Crag localities were explored.

During Easter, Prestwich was again at Amiens and St Acheul, examining the pits to ascertain whether any new features had been disclosed. Before returning to England he made a list of shells in M. de Vibraye's collection from Pontlevois.

In early summer he was geologising with his friend Evans in the neighbourhood of Nash Mills, the interesting home of the latter, which is practically a museum crowded with archæological and antiquarian riches, and where our geologist was a frequent guest. He notes, " June 7, 1868. To Kings Langley, thence with J. E. to Colney Street."

In July Devizes and Frome were the centres for exploration, and in August Professor Morris accompanied him to another old haunt—Grays Thurrock, the attraction there being a new section, of which several sketches are given, and in which he discriminates that " these gravels seem derived direct from the high-level gravels, and are not like those in adjoining pits."

But the field work for this year was not yet over, as in October he was hard at work in the coal-field of Bristol and Radstock, with the geology of which he was well acquainted.

Early in January 1869 the final move was made to the house at Shoreham, which was called " Darent-Hulme "—Hulme being in remembrance of the old family place in Lancashire. Instead of merely a cottage for summer sojourn, it was henceforward to be Prestwich's home, the bulky collections of fossils, minerals, and flint implements filling every available corner. The season was midwinter, but he was eager to be on the spot, ready to watch the first promise of spring. Terrace walks had been cut on the steep chalk slope, and other paths devised, which were concealed from one another by intercepting shrubberies. The pyramid and cordon fruit-trees came from the nursery-gardens near Paris, and indoors as well as out-of-doors there were numerous reminders of France.

On January 15 Prestwich was elected a member of the American Philosophical Society, an honour which he greatly prized.

The two companions who joined him at Easter are mentioned thus: "March 26, 1869. Galton and Smyth," [1] with both of whom he was on terms of closest friendship.

From Paris they made a delightful tour to Cœuvres, and at Soissons M. Watelet accompanied them in their rounds. From Rheims they proceeded to Epernay, and thence to Rilly. Although plant remains of the *Calcaire Grossier* had been noted, and lignite beds at Avize were of special interest, still it is evident that the object of this excursion was to note the localities in which "Drift" could be traced. Later in summer he was again in Belgium, while in August the district round Petersfield was explored in pursuit of "Drift"; and for the same object nineteen other localities were inspected on a brief ten days' tour. The following letter refers to this expedition, and to the meeting of the British Association at Exeter :—

J. Prestwich to J. Evans.   LONDON, 31st *August* 1869.

MY DEAR EVANS,—I returned from Belgium here yesterday, and was preparing for a start to Suffolk to-day. I, however, last night saw occasion to alter my plans, and am off this evening to look at one or two points I have omitted to see, regarding the spread of the gravels between Petersfield and Winchester. I shall take the opportunity to run on to Southampton and Romsey to see the flint implements and gravels there. Can you give me the *exact* spots ?—the bearing in inches and from the nearest church on ordnance map, or still better, if you are yourself disposed to run over the ground again. I shall go to Shaftesbury, and possibly farther. At present letters will find me to-morrow (Wednesday), P. O., Petersfield. On Thursday morning I shall

---

[1] Warington W. Smyth, at one time Mining Geologist to the Geological Survey, Professor of Mining at the Royal School of Mines, and Crown Inspector of Mines ; knighted in 1887. Born 1817 ; died 1890.

Photo by C. Essenhigh Corke, Sevenoaks.

Sᴉʀ WARINGTON W. SMYTH, F.R.S.

be at Bishop's Waltham. On Thursday evening at Southampton. On Friday morning at Romsey. On Saturday morning at Cranborne (?). You seem to have a good meeting at Exeter.—Believe me to be truly yours,　　Jos. PRESTWICH.

During this season the maps for the Royal Water Commission were completed and handed in. Prestwich in after years was heard to say that they had cost him two years of hard work. But as the colouring of these maps for publication was considered too costly, they were relegated to the Stationery Office, where (such was his belief) they have been lying ever since. The subject was one to which he rarely alluded, but when he did so, it was to express his intention to request some friend to ask a question in Parliament as to the fate of his maps. Somehow this was never done.

In the following letter Sir Roderick Murchison writes in generous terms as to our geologist's work on the Royal Coal Commission :—

Sir R. I. Murchison to J. Prestwich.

16 BELGRAVE SQUARE, 21st October 1869.

MY DEAR PRESTWICH,—In the little exordium and brief summary with which I commence the Report on the labours of the Committee D of the Coal Commission, it is my wish to conclude the references I make to geological labours in England to strengthen our case, by a citation of the general result of your labours in the district which you undertook to examine. Your own report *in extenso* will necessarily follow.

But *ad interim* a few words of honest praise from your admirer and old friend can do nothing but good, and it will gratify me to have your assent for the insertion in my preamble of the accompanying paragraph.—Yours sincerely,　　ROD. I. MURCHISON.

" Even in respect to the well-known coal-fields, parts

of which are covered by various deposits, and wherein coal exists at greater depths than those of the present workings, I am bound specially to record my admiration of the researches of one of my colleagues. In his examination of the Bristol and Gloucester coal-basin, this distinguished geologist, Mr Joseph Prestwich, has shown on large maps and elaborate sections, the results of much close work, that in this tract alone there remains untouched an amount of coal which, if worked to a maximum depth of 2000 feet (a depth now reached in some coal-pits), will last during a period of 850 years at the present rate of consumption!

"The evidences on which this cheering estimate are founded are given by Mr Prestwich himself in his Special Report as one of the Royal Commissioners."

J. Prestwich to Sir Rod. I. Murchison.

SHOREHAM, *nr.* SEVENOAKS, *24th Oct.* 1869.

MY DEAR SIR RODERICK,—Many thanks for your kind note and friendly proposal to notice my work in the Bristol coalfield. I can assure you I very much value the approval of so old and valued a friend, and my early leader in geology. I have no alteration to suggest in your paragraph except " Somersetshire " for " Bristol," and instead of " will last during a period of 850 years at the present [rate] of consumption," it should be, "would suffice for the consumption of the district now supplied by that coal-field for a period of 850 years at the present rate of consumption," for my estimates referred only to the local supply and consumption. — Believe me to be, my dear Sir Roderick, yours truly and obliged,   JOS. PRESTWICH.

Professor Huxley's term of office as President of the Geological Society being about to expire, the choice fell upon Prestwich as his successor.

T. H. Huxley to J. Prestwich.　　　JERMYN STREET, *Dec.* 16, 1869.

MY DEAR PRESTWICH,—Many thanks for your letter. Your consent to become President for the next period will give as unfeigned satisfaction to the whole body of the Society as it does to me and your other personal friends. I have looked upon the affair as settled since our last talk, and a very great relief it has been to my mind.

There is no doubt public dinner and speaking (and indeed all public speaking) is nervous work. I funk horribly, though I never get the credit for it. But it is like swimming—the worst of it is in the first plunge, and after you have taken your header it is not so bad (just like matrimony, by the way, only don't be so mean as to go and tell a certain lady I said so, because I want to stand well in her books).

Of course you may command me in all ways in which I can possibly be of use. But as one of the chiefs of the Society, and personally and scientifically popular with the whole body, you start with an immense advantage over me, and will find no difficulties before you.

We will now consider this business generally settled, and I shall speak of it officially.—Ever yours very sincerely,

T. H. HUXLEY.

A few days before his marriage Mr Prestwich, on the Anniversary Meeting of the Geological Society, assumed the Presidency on his friend Professor Huxley vacating the chair. The Anniversary dinner was enlivened by a humorous speech from the retiring President, who twitted his successor in office on having forsaken the geological exploration of the Holy Land for the holy estate of matrimony. This allusion referred to the fact of Prestwich having assented to the request of the Committee of the Palestine Exploration Fund to go out as geologist to the Holy Land. Somehow public interest in the subject lagged, and the projected expedition was not for some years organised.[1]

The following letter refers to this Anniversary dinner :—

J. Prestwich to Sir Rod. I. Murchison.

SHOREHAM, *near* SEVENOAKS, *Feb.* 20, 1870.

MY DEAR SIR RODERICK,—I have to thank you very much and very sincerely for the kind and handsome and only too flattering way in which you spoke of my geological work on Friday. One of the pleasantest recollections of my life was that to which you alluded, when I, quite as a young man—almost in fact a boy —met you on your own ground, was taken by you by the hand, encouraged to persevere, and instructed how to proceed.

I shall always remember with sincere gratitude the effect that encouragement and kindly sympathy had on me — a kindness which has been continued and repeated on many subsequent occasions, and of which I am truly and deeply sensible.

I alluded in my speech to old leadership in the early days of the Society that was much more active than now. I well recollect the admiration I felt for your work, and the respect I felt for your opinion, and I know there are still many points in theoretical geology on which our opinions still show strong alliances.

I feel extremely thankful everything went off so well the other evening, and there again I feel much indebted to the support of kind and valued friends, in the first rank of whom I hope you will always allow me to consider you. And I am, my dear Sir Roderick, most sincerely yours,   JOS. PRESTWICH.

Sir R. I. Murchison to J. Prestwich.

16 BELGRAVE SQUARE, *Feb.* 21, 1870.

MY DEAR PRESTWICH,—I am glad to find that you were gratified with the manner in which I proposed your health at our anniversary.

---

[1] The survey of Western Palestine was eventually undertaken by Prof. E. Hull, F.R.S., and his Report was published in 1886.

I spoke from the warmest feelings of my heart, and I rejoiced that my expressions were so cordially cheered by the assembly.

So much reliance do I place on your judgment and fairness, that if it should be considered desirable to have a good record as to truths of geology prepared under the title of a '*Geological Bible*,' you should be the man I would select to bring out such a work.

Mr [Charles] Falconer has invited me to your wedding and the *déjeuner*, which has much pleased me, and I shall certainly be present to wish you all joy and happiness.—Ever yours sincerely,

ROD. I. MURCHISON.

CHAPTER VIII.

1870–1874.

MARRIAGE—VISIT TO PARIS—ITALY—RETIREMENT FROM
THE CITY—AIX-LES-BAINS—PROFESSORSHIP OF
GEOLOGY AT OXFORD.

On the 26th February 1870 Mr Prestwich's marriage
took place at St Marylebone Church, London, with
Grace Anne, eldest daughter of James Milne, Esq., J.P.,
Findhorn, Morayshire, and widow of George M'Call,
Esq., Glasgow. She was the niece of his lamented
friend Hugh Falconer, at whose house they had met.

Before proceeding to Italy, Mr and Mrs Prestwich
spent a short time in Paris, taking a thorough holiday.
Several of Molière's plays were then on the stage, and
as our geologist had a keen appreciation of good French
acting, frequent visits were paid to the Théâtre Français, and also to the Opéra Comique. With boyish
zest he viewed the popular sights in Paris, and it
would have astonished the members of the Geological
Society not a little could they have seen their grave
President standing with his wife on a bench in the
thick of the voluble French crowd, straining and eager
for a good view of the procession of the *Bœuf Gras*. It
was a reminder of schoolboy days.

Among the old friends of whom they had a glimpse were M. Edouard and Madame Lartet, also M. Hébert and M. Desnoyers—both of geological fame. There was also one who had shown very great kindness to Mrs Prestwich in former years, and whose individuality and originality were so strongly marked that her name cannot be mentioned without a brief comment. This was Madame Mohl, author of ' Madame Récamier and the History of Society in France.' She was the wife of Jules Mohl, the eminent Oriental scholar ; and, although by birth an Englishwoman, she had for a long series of years presided over one of the most brilliant salons in Paris. Men who were foremost in science, in literature, and in political life were *habitués* of Madame Mohl's salon, where they came in contact with men and women who had risen to fame as dramatists or artists. Rank and fortune were themselves in her estimation of no account : only individual merit or personal distinction gave the *entrée* to her drawing-room, with the exception that to her own and her husband's old friends—whether distinguished or not—a warm welcome always greeted them.

Mr and Mrs Prestwich called at an early hour in the Rue du Bac, and were received by Madame Mohl in the traditional dressing-gown and in curl papers, the latter of varied and brilliant hues—red, green, and blue circulars being utilised for this purpose. She made no apology for receiving a countryman—a complete stranger—in this costume, and did not seem to consider that any apology was needed. Her attractive niece, Miss Mohl, who afterwards became Madame Helmholtz, was by her side, busily occupied with her painting. The use of the curl papers was one of Madame Mohl's small economies which amused her friends, who knew of her acts of noble generosity and benevolence.

The quaint, gifted little woman at once plunged into conversation with Mr Prestwich, getting with direct questions at the very pith of the subjects discussed, and becoming so much engrossed as to appear unconscious that any one else was present. Her vivacity and sagacity and inexpressible charm of manner exercised a magnetic attraction for all who came in contact with her. She made use of her talents in brightening the lives of others, and there are many still surviving who hold dear the memory of Mary Mohl.

Mentone was the point aimed at after Paris, and where Prestwich made an inspection of the Baussi Raussi Caves in the red limestone cliffs to the east of the town. He ascertained their position and general features, clambering up to the high - road through groves of oranges and lemons. The human skeleton in the cave of " La Berma du Cavillon " had not then been discovered by M. Rivière—not until 1872.

Mr Matthew Moggridge (who was spending the winter at Mentone on account of his invalid son) was our geologist's guide to the most interesting points. In one locality (not named) he showed to Prestwich "a bed of sandy clay abounding in fossils (sub-Apennine?), worked for bricks at base of hills half a mile from sea. The red earth and angular fragments spread over it and over the valley to the sea. This red earth was still more apparent in other valleys, and could be traced 400 to 500 feet high. No more traces of raised beaches."

Mr Moggridge also pointed out a fresh - water fountain at sea near the cliffs to the east of Mentone, its subterranean course not having then been

traced. He accompanied the tourists as far as Bor-
dighera, whence two days' drive along the coast of the
Riviera del Ponente, with its succession of beautiful
bays and rocky headlands, brought them to Savona.

This was the birthplace of Chiabrera the poet. The
inscription which he wrote for his tomb, to be seen in
the church of San Giacomo, is as follows :—

> " Amico, io vivendo, cercava conforto
>   Nel Monte Parnasso,
>   Tu, meglio consigliato, cercarlo
>   Nel Monte Calvario."

The travellers could not, as they wished, read this
epitaph for themselves: they were only in time for
their train to Genoa, where a short stay sufficed for
Prestwich to see the Museum and to call on the Mar-
chese Giacomo Doria, as he was eager to press on for
an exploration of the caverns in the islets at the
entrance of the Gulf of Spezzia. The route lay along
the comparatively less known Riviera del Levante, on
through the magnificent scenery of the hills of Varese.
Leaving the railway at Chiavari, the journey was continued in a light carriage to Spezzia, with a halt at
Borghetto to enable Prestwich to visit the cave of
Cassana, where he found no fossils, but satisfied himself as to the physical features. The expedition to this
inland cave he made on foot with a desperate-looking
character for a guide, and when his stipulated absence
of a couple of hours was lengthened to several, and the
shades of evening began to fall, the anxiety of his wife,
who waited at Borghetto, was very real. He had
called on the " superiore " of the district, who had conducted him to other caverns in an adjoining valley.
Spezzia was reached in moonlight.

Next day was chiefly spent in a boat on the Gulf of Spezzia, our geologist being desirous of seeing the Grotta dei Colombi, situated high in the steep sea-cliff of the island of Palmaria. The two excellent boatmen took an interest in his proceedings, and urged that they should row as far as the islet of Tinetto, which lay beyond Palmaria, and where they reported a sea-cave full of living natural-history objects. But suddenly a *burrasco* struck them, and with it breakers, which prevented any attempt at landing. Seeing that Palmaria was also impossible, Mr Prestwich directed the boatmen to row nearly opposite to the Grotta dei Colombi, and as near to it as possible, eagerly pointing out its position, but the Italian sailors regretfully answered that they dared not proceed farther. Heading round, they did their utmost to reach Porto Venere on the mainland for shelter, where there was a detention of several hours. This picturesque spot had been a nest of pirates before it became a stronghold of the Genoese Republic : it also had its cave, called the Grotta di Arpaia, more recently known as the Grotta di Byron, but the sea was running high and it could not be entered. The cliff in which it is situated abounded in fossils, which the Porto Venere boys called the *frutta di mare*. The detention was not lost time : the heights and vestiges of buildings were well worth a visit, the arches of the ruined church showing bands of black and white marble intact. As the day wore on the wind fell, and the two travellers, re-entering the boat, were at last landed at Palmaria, where Prestwich had a ramble over the cliff and as near a view as possible of the stratum in which is situated the fossiliferous Grotta dei Colombi.

In the row back to Spezzia a fountain of fresh water

was clearly visible at a distance, from the circle made by it in the salt water. The water, which was tasted in passing, was brackish, but the boatmen asserted that a few feet below the surface it could be drawn up perfectly fresh. Shelley's house was pointed out—a white house on a hill of olives above the village of San Lorenzo and close to Lerici. Two or three boat-loads of convicts, who had been at work at the arsenal, crossed our course on their way back to their prison. The golden sunset was glorious, and each incident in the day had been like a bit of romance.

By a hill-path through olive grounds and vineyards, and about a mile from Spezzia, another cave was explored, named La Bocca Lupara. Most picturesque in itself and in situation, a fringe of maiden-hair and other delicate ferns draped the low entrance, and overhung the little stream which flowed out from it—this stream making exit and entrance rather difficult. Several peasants, attracted to the spot by the appearance of strangers, were employed to burn straw so as to show its dimensions. These twisted blazing torches had a weird effect, and their stifling smoke necessitated a stay for one and all of brief duration. A block of rock had fallen, obstructing the corner in the cave where fossil bones had been found.

Very soon Prestwich was across Italy and on the Adriatic shore, examining the structure of the grand headland of Ancona. The writer has a vivid recollection of the mode in which his observations were made, and of the unpleasant sensations in a skiff on a chopping sea, and of her outspoken protests lest it should be driven against the wave-washed cliff.

One of the most enjoyable excursions on this Italian tour was that made from Rome to the Lake of Albano

and Monte Cavo.   Prestwich, with his wife and her
sister, joined M. de Verneuil at Albano, the last
accompanied by the Archbishop of Rheims and Signor
Mantovani of Rome.   Dr Landriot, who was tall and
slight, with great refinement of expression, was young
in years to hold so high a place in the Roman Catholic
Church.   He had been noted for his scientific tastes,
and to him it was an evident enjoyment to be able once
more to indulge in his old love for geology.

An order being given for good donkeys for the party,
the people of the Albergo replied that the best had all
been taken by American excursionists who had gone on
before.   A sorry lot of animals was brought together.
The writer, who was allotted the largest, headed the
cavalcade with the Archbishop, who was mounted on
an absurdly small donkey, which his robe completely
covered, the feet of the animal only showing beneath
it.   With his enormous hat, and long inflated robe, he
presented a very ludicrous appearance, and conscious of
this, he laughed until the tears came, the others joining.   The animal which the writer rode began to
develop a will of its own, therefore one of the donkey
guides was requested to hold the bridle while its
rider got off.   " Keep quiet, Signora," was the ad-
monition *sotto voce*, " keep your seat ; yours is the only
one that has not been down."

The little animals, however, clambered like goats up
the steep crater-like walls, above which rose Monte
Cavo.   Prestwich on foot was soon far ahead of the
party, intent on pondering upon the story to be read
in that marvellous landscape.   What added to the
general enjoyment was the cloudless sunshine, the
perfect placidity of the crater lake, the first fresh
foliage of spring which clothed its walls, and the

masses of the lovely blue *Anemone stellata,* starring the
delicate undergrowth.

Several shorter excursions were made from Rome,
including those to Monte Mario, to the Campagna, &c.
Prestwich made the acquaintance of Professor Ponzi,
and, in the Museum of the University of Rome, he
noted remains of three species of elephant—all from
Ponte Molle. It was a pleasure to him also to have
personal intercourse with the courtly Monsignor Castra-
cane, who had written on *Diatomaceæ,* and who was
as enthusiastic as ever on his special subject.

As may be supposed, the Bay of Naples and its
neighbourhood were of surpassing interest. Baiæ and
its classical shores fascinated him, and the time was
only too short for exploring the ground a little way
inland. The pillars of the Temple of Jupiter Serapis,
immortalised by Lyell's pen, were duly inspected. An
elaborate section in a note-book, now dimmed by time,
was taken from a point one mile east of Pozzuoli ; and
another page gives a section at the end of a street in
Pompeii, and one of the theatre at Herculaneum. A
visit was also made to the entrancing shore of Amalfi.
With his friends M. de Verneuil and Sir Archibald
Geikie, he ascended the Anio, and on the 8th of April
with the latter he made the ascent of Vesuvius, remaining the night at the Observatory. Next day
they descended from Somma.

Before leaving Naples, Prestwich had an interview
with the aged Mrs Somerville, who was then living
with two daughters in a flat on the Chiatamone.
She was alone when he called with his wife, the latter
having had the privilege of knowing the authoress
during Dr Somerville's lifetime in the home at Florence.
They were received with the old cordial welcome, it

giving her evident pleasure to see Mr Prestwich, who was only known to her by reputation. Her quaint Scotch accent and the remarkably soft voice were unchanged, and the simple natural manner was as of old. Perhaps she had become a shade more grave, still there was the same serenity, the same unquenchable thirst for knowledge, and the same trenchant questions. Her mental powers were keen and clear as ever, and the penetrating grey eyes, which had not lost their shining light, were turned full upon the speaker with rapt attention. Vesuvius and volcanoes were discussed by Mrs Somerville and our geologist, her room —flooded with sunshine — admitting a view of the mountain and the beautiful bay.

Mary Somerville was then verging upon ninety, while Joseph Prestwich had just completed his fifty-eighth year. What a picture the two made ! An Ary Scheffer would have done justice to it. Hers was a glorious old age. Her last work, which was published in the preceding year, was on 'Molecular and Microscopic Science,' appearing just three years before her death. For a motto she chose as most appropriate, " Deus magnus in magnis, maximus in minimis."

Lingering in Italy and leaving it with regret, Mr and Mrs Prestwich travelled direct to Paris, crossing Mont Cenis by the temporary Fell Railway, which wound in serpentine course over the mountain. They reached home in time for the outburst of the early summer, for the blossoming of the may, the lilacs, and laburnums. During their absence Emily Prestwich had remained at Darent-Hulme, her brother, before going abroad, having confided to her the care of the Brixham Cave papers. His one injunction in case of fire had been, " Whatever happens to the house, save the Brixham Cave papers."

Accordingly, his sister retired to rest, with the parcel of manuscripts on a sofa at the foot of her bed, and she was heartily glad to hand it safely back to him.

The home life, apparently so quiet, was a busy one. Besides our geologist's daily journey to the City, there were frequent demands upon his time, owing to his official position as President of the Geological Society. The most important paper during this year from his pen was one sent in to this Society, " On the Crag of Norfolk and Associated Beds." Among minor notices he edited a MS., " On Earthquakes," written by his kinsman, Sir John Prestwich, about the year 1798. It is curious as a record of the crude notions on volcanic phenomena prevalent so near to our own time. But the engrossing interest was the elaboration of the third and last of his series of Crag Memoirs, " On the Norwich Crag and Westleton Beds," which was to appear the following year.

For the completion of this memoir several weeks were spent at Lowestoft in the autumn, whence expeditions were made again to many familiar localities on the coast, including Corton and Kessingland ; repeated visits to pits near Norwich, and visits also to Bacton, Wangford, Southwold, Pakefield, Easton Bavent, &c., &c. Thirty-eight different localities were explored in this East Coast excursion, and forty-nine sections noted. He was intent on observing every trace of Westleton Shingle, and on ascertaining the origin of the boulders occurring in this district in the Boulder Clay. The discovery of a specimen of gneiss in the upper Boulder Clay near Kessingland has not been forgotten. Its weight was beyond the power of any ordinary mortal to carry, but aided by his sister-in-law, with immense effort it was moved, or rather dragged,

two miles to Lowestoft.   He never alluded to this
exploit without a smile.   No day passed without some
point visited—some special work accomplished.   And
thus it was wherever he turned his footsteps.

A note from Sir Roderick Murchison shows that,
although debarred by failing health from sharing in
public functions, the heart of the old chief was with
his geological brethren on their anniversary :—

Sir R. I. Murchison to J. Prestwich.

16 BELGRAVE SQUARE, 13*th February* 1871.

MY DEAR PRESTWICH,—Although shut out from personal par-
ticipation in the affairs of the Geological Society, I cannot allow
the approaching anniversary to pass by without assuring you
that I take as lively an interest as ever in the advancement of
our favourite science.   I rejoice above all that the Society is now
under your guidance, and it has of course given me great satisfaction, as Director-General of the Geological Survey, to observe
that you have given the Wollaston Medal this year to my distinguished associate, Professor Ramsay.—Yours ever sincerely,

ROD. I. MURCHISON.

If we except two sub-reports to the Royal Coal
Commission, the only publications in 1871 were his
Presidential Address and the memoir on "The Nor-
wich Crag and Westleton Beds."

The subject chosen for his address to the Geological
Society was "Deep Sea Life and its Relations to
Geology."   In this interesting essay he reviewed,
among others, the researches of Edward Forbes,
Spratt, Wallich, Carpenter, Gwyn-Jeffreys, Wyville
Thomson, &c., giving lists of temperatures at depths in
the Atlantic and Pacific.   He touched upon the circulation of cold under-currents in the great oceans, and
the influence of submarine temperatures on pelagic life.

He demonstrated how continental Europe, with much of its western sea-bed, "was subject to successive changes of level, giving rise to a series of Eocene, Miocene, and Pliocene strata, with their diversified and varying faunas." His treatment of the subject gauged the knowledge up to date, and was very suggestive. The study of the circulation of polar and ocean currents had always had a special attraction for him.

Instead of a refreshing Easter excursion, there was persistent home with city work at high pressure. The result was indisposition, and peremptory medical orders for change and rest.

J. Prestwich to J. Evans.　　　St Leonards-on-Sea, *9th May* 1871.

My dear Evans,—I thought of you all on Friday, and have heard from Jeffreys of what a pleasant and large party you had.

I at last got permission to leave town on Saturday. We arrived here yesterday in most beautiful weather, took an early dinner with Bowerbank, and settled down here in the evening. I like none of these seaside places, but since the 26th February 1870 I feel right anywhere. I hope also to polish off the Brixham Cave and Coal Report No. 2. We may be here for a fortnight. To-day winter seems to have come back again. It is wet and cold. I am, however, I am happy to say, decidedly better, and hope to be at my posts again at Somerset House and the City at the end of the fortnight. I shall be glad to hear that Kaup is elected to-morrow, and, believe me, ever truly yours,　　　Jos. Prestwich.

The quiet of Darent-Hulme was enlivened by frequent visits from relations, and by the welcome sight of busy geological friends, whose stay was usually limited from Saturday until an early train on Monday. The walk on Sunday afternoon was often out high upon the down, whence far-reaching views were a

delight to the eye. Can they ever be forgotten ? On
the opposite side of the Darent valley was the steep
chalk slope, presenting an unbroken face southward until it abutted on the wide fertile Vale of
Holmesdale, when its trend was suddenly to the east.
There was a glimpse of the plateaux on the heights
with their capping of red clay with flints—a soil which
is transforming the district into one great fruit-garden.
Wellhill with its Tertiary flints made an attractive
walk for active geologists, who, by skirting hop-
gardens, gained the steep path which led up through
rich fruit-fields to the summit ; while those more rest-
fully disposed reclined on the grassy down and scanned
the far distance in the north-east, where perchance
they might detect the smoke of an ocean liner on her
way down the Thames, and, when atmospheric conditions were very favourable, had also a glimpse of the
faint hazy outline of the Essex shore beyond.

" O tempo passato, perche non ritorni ? "

One of the most frequent guests was Professor John
Morris, the palæontologist, so well known as the author
of the ' Catalogue of British Fossils,' a book necessary
for every practical geologist. He had worked with
Prestwich in-doors and out-of-doors, and was perfectly
happy day after day in the library, consulting or making extracts from books. He seemed to prefer wet
weather, or any weather that made going out undesir-
able, so that he should not be disturbed, unless that
his host proposed some little excursion : then he was
all alacrity, ready to accompany, observe, and enjoy.
Few possessed such an amount of knowledge—knowledge that was many-sided — and withal he was so
modest and simple. Professor Morris knew the pro-

perties of plants, and was conversant with habits of beasts and birds and creeping things : an expert chemist, he was unconsciously a teacher — "a born teacher," as Canon Bonney, in an interesting notice, describes him—ever ready, when appealed to by the uninstructed, to explain the why and wherefore of common things. When ordered out for health's sake, he was to be found in the garden tracing earth-worms and mole-hills, or with his host he walked backwards and forwards discussing the marvellous mechanism and adaptation of natural objects, perhaps speculating on the formation of dew.

The following note was an acknowledgment to Sir Roderick Murchison of his last public address. The veteran several months previously had been struck by paralysis, and had partially recovered, but this address to the Royal Geographical Society was felt to be a farewell to public life.[1]

J. Prestwich to Sir R. I. Murchison.

SHOREHAM, *near* SEVENOAKS, *9th June* '71.

MY DEAR SIR RODERICK,—I am much obliged by the copy of your Address, and still more pleased at the evidence it affords of your continued mental activity, notwithstanding the severe illness you have undergone.

I cannot tell you how much I, in common with all your geological friends, rejoice at your recovery, and at the same time how much we have missed you at our Council and [evening] meetings.

Believe me to be, my dear Sir Roderick, very sincerely yours,
JOS. PRESTWICH.

Early in August Prestwich attended the meeting of the British Association in Edinburgh, where perhaps he was less attracted by papers in the various Sections

---

[1] Murchison died in the eightieth year of his age, on October 22, 1871.

than by the geology in the immediate neighbourhood
of the beautiful northern city.

He made a longer stay at St Andrews with his wife's
family, when the coast north and south of the picturesque old university town was explored.   Here also he
made the acquaintance of Professor Heddle the miner-
alogist, whose recent death has been so much deplored.
His search was for traces of drift, raised beaches, and
ice-action, and Professor Heddle's local knowledge was
most generously placed at his disposal.   He also paid
a visit to the famous locality of Dura Den, observing
the fine cliffs of soft, yellow, Old Red Sandstone, and
noting that " the fishes occurred in a single bed at the
base."

Prestwich returned to Darent - Hulme with, as
usual, many fresh observations and ascertained facts,
each briefly entered in a sentence or two, with its distinct section.   He was ever eager to work up the unpublished notes of all his excursions, but they were
accumulating year by year, and, alas! when would
there be time?   Each day he went backwards and
forwards to Mark Lane, and in addition to long hours
in the City, nearly four were spent in the journey out
and home.   At the end of the day he was refreshed
by a walk in the garden, yet was little able to throw
himself into the elaboration of those geological theories
which were his delight to demonstrate.   The wear and
tear of these daily journeyings, early and late, did
not tell injuriously on his health,—on the contrary,
those drives through the lovely woods to Chelsfield
Station were beneficial; but he begrudged the time
abstracted from his geology.   He found that there
was actually less leisure for writing than when living
in town amid its many interruptions, and he became

restlessly anxious as he thought of the mass of unpublished material, and especially of the delay in bringing out his Report on Brixham Cave. The writing of
this Report had been again and again interrupted by
illness, and had become a great anxiety. All work,
except two or three slight papers, had been set aside
for the Sub-Reports and Maps of the two Royal
Commissions, the subjects of both of which were
especially his own. The fact was that his health
being no longer vigorous, the city work alone taxed
his energies.

He was not a letter-writer, yet had a large correspondence — notes in reply to frequent inquiries on
geological and allied subjects being dashed off with
incredible speed. Still, in spite of the resultant fatigue
after a full day, he was persistent in snatching every
hour, or rather every minute, for his geology. He
made a point of making himself acquainted with the
leading articles in the 'Times,' but otherwise his reading was entirely geological literature. He felt what
his true vocation was and adhered to it, and with that
tenacity of purpose which was so strong a feature in
his character he refrained from opening other books.

"Why, you read nothing but geology—your very
soul is steeped in geology," was a remark made to
him when he would not look at a book which had
made a sensation. His reply was a smile and an
affirmative nod. But in repeated attacks of sciatica,
which his kind physician altogether attributed to over-
work, and when ordered to read nothing but novels,
the patient was entirely submissive, and so anxious
to get rid of his malady that he read novels only,
and that very earnestly, in a manner peculiar to himself. There was no skipping — he read every word.

As soon as he was well the novels were discarded and his geological books resumed.

He indulged, however, in one passion, and that was transplanting : perhaps the open-air exercise it necessitated prevented a complete breakdown. A garden-book was kept, in which he had during summer entered every shrub and tree to be moved into a better position at the proper season. Consequently, in November the whole garden seemed to be in motion. With the exception of a few which succumbed, the result was generally good, as when a tree changed place it was into a trench with improved soil, and so with holes for the shrubs. Thus they made more vigorous and rapid growth. He liked to give surprises, and used to introduce his wife to some clump of foliage, which without her knowledge had been rearranged with larger plants, and mischievously ask whether she had not noticed the great start they had made during the year !

The Sundays were such happy days, and really a rest—they never seemed long enough. He was rarely absent from Morning Service, leaving guests who were not disposed to go to church to take care of themselves. When fluctuating health prevented his attendance at church, he always liked to read aloud the Morning Service (or greater part of it) verse about with his wife, one of them repeating the responses.

Certain Sundays can never be forgotten : one in particular, some two years later, stands apart in the writer's memory. Mr David Forbes the metallurgist (brother of Edward Forbes) had promised to bring down his charming young Polish wife for the day, but as they did not arrive at the appointed time, it was supposed that the steady rain had prevented them. Between two and three o'clock, however, a mud-bespattered cab drove up to the door, bringing Mr and Mrs Forbes, who had been carried past the junction at Swanley on to Meopham, whence they had come over the many miles of Chalk plateau and down the steep escarpment to the Darent valley. There was no room, alas! for them for the night, as the house was full, so they had to return to town. Not long after the gentle Vanda Forbes was called away from her husband and little children. He did not recover from the shock, and the words of the late Dr P. Martin Duncan, the writer of the Biographical Notice of David Forbes, to the Geological Society, are of deep pathos: " He was wounded in spirit by the loss of his wife, who was singularly adapted to his tone of mind."

The address which Prestwich gave to the Geological Society at the Anniversary Meeting in 1872, the second year of his Presidency, was on subjects of which he was master. It was in two portions : the first, " Our Springs and Water Supply," and the second half on " Our Coals and Coal Supply."

An Easter excursion was planned by him, as shown in the following letter ; but, as it proved, he was unable to join, and this particular expedition to the Boulogne district was therefore postponed.

J. Prestwich to J. Evans.

LONDON, 19th *March* 1872.

MY DEAR EVANS,—If I go to Boulogne my plans are as follows. We make that place our headquarters and visit—

1. Wissant and the coast on one side to Blanc Nez, and the other to Gris Nez.
2. La Marquise, with the Oolites, Mountain Limestone, Coal-Measures, and Devonian rocks of the neighbourhood.
3. The hills beyond Ferques, Guisnes (and its springs), and the Chalk hills around.

4. The coast on the other side of the Basin, and the Dunes beyond.

5. Rue and Étables, and the banks of the Canche for Gravel beds.

6. Samer (Lower Greensand) and some outliers of Tertiaries on the Chalk hills beyond.

7. Some deep valleys among the Chalk between Boulogne and Pol, in which the Palæozoic rocks show on their floor.

We shall get a few Drift beds on various levels, and, I hope, traces of raised beaches. . We may look also for flint implements in the valleys of the Canche or Authie. We will talk the matter over to-morrow. . . .

Instead of the chosen Boulogne route, his friends selected another district, when it is evident from the annexed letter, in which the subject of this Memoir drafted out a plan for their guidance, that his thoughts were regretfully with them.

J. Prestwich to J. Evans.   London, *29th March* 1872.

My dear Evans,—Yesterday it blew a gale and rained incessantly; to-day we have the rain without the wind. This, however, is a sorry consolation to me, and very sad work, I fear, for you and Galton.[1] Gosselet of Lille has kindly offered to meet us at Boulogne and accompany us on a proposed excursion, which I still hope may come off later in the season. If the weather continues so bad, go to Paris and luxuriate in the museums and theatres there under cover. Weather permitting, go to Beauvais, where you have—

1. A valuable local museum.

2. A magnificent fragment of a cathedral.

3. Loess and valley Drift one mile south of the town.

4. A fine fossiliferous exhibition of the *Calcaire grossier*, and of all the beds, in fact, between the Chalk and the *Calcaire lacustre supérieur;* also the "*Diluvium*" of the French at Chaumont, about five or six miles distant.

---

[1] Sir Douglas Galton, K.C.B., born 1822 ; died 10th March 1899.

5. The Neocomian, Greensands, Wealden, Portland Beds, and Kimmeridge in the Pays de Bray.
6. Le Château de Gisors. Thence across to Compiègne, where you have—
  (1) A very rich locality for the shells, "*Lits Coquilliers*," in a small valley just beyond Pierrefonds.
  (2) The fine Château de Pierrefonds. Again, on the main line, just above Anvers or Angers, there is on the right bank of the Oise, near the top of the hill, a site noted for its Quaternary mammalian remains.

With kind regards to all who may be with you, and wishing you well through and soon out of this weather, I am sincerely yours,   J. PRESTWICH.

Remember me to MM. Pinsard and Garnier if you see them. My wife sympathises more with Mrs Evans than with you—I don't.

In March a review appeared from his pen in 'Nature' on the magnificent work of his old friend M. Belgrand, on '*La Seine: le Bassin Parisien aux Ages anté-historiques.*'

A very pleasant friendship which he made while on the Royal Coal Commission was with its secretary, Mr J. F. Campbell, the accomplished author of 'Frost and Fire.'

J. F. Campbell to J. Prestwich.

NIDDRY LODGE, KENSINGTON, *8th May* 1872.

DEAR PRESTWICH,—I have not had the grace to thank you for your Address, but I have been much obliged and instructed thereby. When you happen to be in these regions come and geologise in my garden. It is on the Clay under the Gravel, well on the top of which some Company has made waterworks and a tower. You will easily find your way by the tower, and if the waterworks burst, you will return to the Thames faster than you came up this hill.—I am, yours very truly,   J. F. CAMPBELL.

Curiously enough, this was a locality, near the old Kensington gravel-pits, to which Prestwich many years before had often paid visits, and sometimes in company with Professor Morris.

At last, to his infinite relief, and that of his friend Pengelly, the Brixham Cave Report was sent in to the Royal Society. It was read in abstract in May, and was published in the Royal Society Proceedings for 1872, the full text appearing in the 'Philosophical Transactions' for 1873. The exploration of the cave had been completed in 1859, but largely owing to the sad death of Dr Falconer, the full report was unfortunately postponed. In the end the animal remains were described by Mr George Busk, and the worked flints by Sir John Evans.

A short paper on a raised beach at Portsdown Hill, near Portsmouth, was published in the 'Geological Journal'; and Prestwich also found time for a magazine article (on popular lines) on the probable extension of coal-measures in the south-east of England, which appeared in 'Popular Science Review.'

The event which signalised this year, and which had a marked influence on his subsequent career, was his retirement, after forty years of City life, from business and Mark Lane. This step was not taken without long and anxious deliberation, but when his mind was once made up there was prompt action. He never regretted this step, and often remarked the mistake was that he had not retired several years sooner. Owing to this, a reduction in the home establishment became necessary, but could such a consideration ever be weighed in the balance with leisure for the work to which he had dedicated his life!

His character and integrity were recognised in the

City, and his wife was never more proud of him,
never more deeply touched, than when told that the
firm who had purchased his business property had
simply taken it over on his word.   In later years his
eyes glistened when reverting to his early life, and to
the great kindness which he had received from City
friends.

The hard-earned leisure was won, yet with it no respite from close intellectual work, which was to him as
a second nature.   Deprived of it, he would have been
bereft of his greatest happiness; and now he sat down
to grapple with manuscripts, with papers begun on
various questions, all geological, and with the vast
quantity of material amassed during a long course of
years.   Perhaps the garden was then of greater service
as a distraction than at any other time.   The trees and
shrubs, being in an early stage of growth, were in need
of fostering care; and the interest and occupation of
this wiled him from his desk, and from hours spent in
tabulating his observations on Clays or Gravels, and in
deciphering the history which they reveal.

For the first time since moving to Darent - Hulme,
he was able to turn his attention to the collections,
which were found to have outgrown the space assigned
to them.   A room originally intended for the library
was lined with cabinets, some of them reaching to the
ceiling, and with every drawer filled.   Cases of rock
specimens and fossil bones had to be left unopened in
a cellar for lack of space.   Prestwich first limited his
task of arrangement to the contents of cabinets in the
library itself, which contained the specimens of Drift.
A folio-book written to his dictation gives the very
numerous localities where he had examined Drift and
the component parts of each gravel, a work exten-

sively used during the preparation of later papers on
the Westleton Beds and more recent deposits.

His connection with City life had been severed on the
1st of August, and on the 12th September he started
for Boulogne with his two friends, Mr Godwin-Austen
and Mr H. B. Mackeson of Hythe, both of whom have,
alas! since passed over to the majority.   Never losing
sight of special points he had in view, the route was a
part of the programme planned for the Easter excursion, which, owing to the state of his health at the
time, he had been unable to join.   The notes and sections of this Boulogne expedition are voluminous.   The
three friends proceeded to Cape Gris Nez by Vimereux,
Ambleteuse, and Andrecelles, and a careful analysis is
given of the subangular gravel near Wissant.

"Between Wissant and Cape Blanc Nez we found
Dunes, but under them in places cropped out the Lower
Greensand (Sandgate and Folkestone Beds), capped
by angular white Drift, same as that which overlies
the raised beach at Sangatte; but no beach occurred
here."

This angular Drift at Wissant did not extend far
inland, but near Equihen he found the strata covered
by a greater thickness of flint Drift.   In short, he was
noting every trace of Drift and Loess, and there are
forty-five pages of notes and sections on this one expedition.   M. Rigaux of Boulogne informed him " that
the fragments of elephant's tusk, and tooth of rhinoceros, were found in the railway-cutting through the
Kimmeridge Clay between Boulogne and Wimille, at a
height of about 60 m., and in a pocket of Drift."

Wimille was visited with M. Rigaux just a year later,
when another of the many expeditions to the Boulonnais was made.

The last letter which we find addressed to Sir Charles
Lyell is one expressing sympathy on the death of the
beloved Lady Lyell.

J. Prestwich to Sir Charles Lyell.   *17th May* 1873.

MY DEAR SIR CHARLES,—I am very much obliged to you for
the copy of the last edition of the 'Antiquity of Man,' which I
have not yet had the opportunity of reading, but which I feel
sure I shall find well posted up to the day.

My wife will have already conveyed to you through Mrs Lyell
our very sincere sympathy in your sad and unexpected bereave-
ment. We both felt and shared greatly in your irreparable loss,
a feeling I am sure in which all who knew her must participate,
for I believe no one could ever have inspired a more general feeling amongst all, of true regard and affection. With our united
kind regards and best wishes for your own health, believe me to
be sincerely yours,   J. PRESTWICH.

Towards the end of May 1873, Mr and Mrs Prestwich hurried to Aix-les-Bains, on account of the illness
of the youngest sister of the latter, whom happily they
found convalescent. The journey was one of interest
(which was the case with every journey) : it was, however, with keen pleasure that our geologist recognised
the long plateau of Drift Gravel after passing Dijon,
and about 40 to 60 feet " or may be less " above the
level of the river, planted with vines and extending
for several miles.

Aix was a centre whence the surrounding neighbourhood was explored, beginning with the hill above it
leading to Mouxy. As a matter of course, our geologist
was interested in the various weapons, tools, &c., dredged
up from the Lac du Bourget, but much more so in the
natural phenomena and features of the district. M.
Perrin, *libraire* at Chambéry, accompanied him to its

Museum, where he made a list of the fossils of the
"*Alluvions Anciennes*" of Sonnax. M. Pillet guided
him to the section at La Boisse, near Chambéry, and
also kindly accompanied him by train to Viviers,
whence they visited the Lignite Beds of Sonnax.

One of the most delightful drives out of Aix was
made to a small underground lake some ten kilometres
distant. Situated on the side rather near the foot of a
mountain, the entrance to it, which resembled that of a
low cave, was reached through fields sloping downwards
from it. After à little delay two or three peasants
were found to act as guides, and they carried lights
showing the long low passage which widened as the
explorers penetrated farther underground, and where
they were able to stand upright. It felt unworld-like
and uncanny when the spacious cavity was reached,
and its size was shrouded in the darkness of night.
The water was perfectly still, and the lights shone on
it and its strand of fine white sand, which showed no
sign of ripple-mark. How weird it all looked !

Prestwich took in all the conditions at a glance, and
was speedily satisfied. After a brief halt, he and his
companion turned to leave, and keeping close to the
light-bearers, picked their steps, or rather crept slowly
through the long slippery channel out to the open air.
An agreeable incident in the day was luncheon afterwards at the homely *auberge*. Several workmen
trooped in to the kitchen, the only room for dinner.
Always courteous, the Englishman, speaking their language like one of themselves, was treated by them with
the most marked respect—with a consideration equal
to his own.

It was in 1873 that a stay was made at Weymouth,
which was one of great enjoyment. The season was at

its best, Mr and Mrs Prestwich being there during
August and part of September, occupying rooms near
those of other members of the family, with whom joint
excursions were made. The isle of Portland and the
Chesil Beach were the chief attractions. It cannot be
averred that visits were paid to them every day, as
there were long expeditions to Dorchester, Maiden
Castle, and Blackdown, near Portisham (the geology
of this hill of gravel being a special object), and separate days to Osmington, Preston, Lulworth, Abbotsbury, &c., also to Fleet and Upway. But on every
day *possible*, Prestwich was off by steamboat or by
road with hammer and bag, to Portland and the Chesil
Beach. In the expedition to Maiden Castle and Blackdown his old friend Mr Edward Cunnington accompanied the party, Prestwich breathlessly busy in collecting, from various levels, specimens from the gravel
of rolled and subangular flints, and of quartz, slate, and
other pebbles. He was much interested in finding on
the road to Dorchester a long hill on the right capped
with precisely the same gravel as at Blackdown, but
about 300 to 400 feet lower in level. Mr E. Cunnington also joined one of the excursions to Abbotsbury,
when, besides the geology, an inspection was made of
the swannery and the decoy.

Prestwich paid one visit to Portland with Mr J. C.
Mansel-Pleydell,[1] the Rev. Osmond Fisher,[2] and Captain
Galton — the last - named being his guest. He con-
ducted these three friends to the Admiralty Quarries
—Captain Clifton, the Governor of the Convict Prison,

---

[1] President of the Dorset Natural History Society. Author of works
on the Natural History of Dorset.

[2] Author of 'Physics of the Earth's Crust,' and many geological and
mathematical papers.

being especially kind, and affording every facility for seeing the stone - beds and specimens obtained from them.

The sojourn at Weymouth would have been delightful to every one but for the anxiety of our geologist's visits to Portland Bill. In 1863 he had noted a fragment of the old raised beach there overhanging a sheer precipice, with the wild conflict of waters below. Although never foolhardy, the risk in reaching this vestige of beach was so great that, after the first visit, he made a promise never to climb to this perilous point without the help of either the lighthouse-keeper or a quarryman. The existence of this fragment of beach was important, and no piece of geological evidence was ever more thoroughly sifted.

J. Prestwich to J. C. Mansel-Pleydell.

WEYMOUTH, *25th August* 1873.

MY DEAR MR MANSEL-PLEYDELL,—Thanks for the names of species. I am glad you enjoyed your excursion here, and shall be glad to join you in another one. I cannot, however, yet fix a day for Swanage, nor am sure yet that I shall have time to spare, as I want to work out Portland fully. I was at the Bill again on Saturday. There are clear indications of the Middle and Upper Purbecks having existed there; while I think it also clear that the movement of elevation which has raised Portland into its present conspicuous position is of late Quaternary date.[1] You will find me here until the 3rd September, &c., &c.

At Lulworth he wished to examine the coast in the direction of the White Nore, and for that purpose engaged a tradesman's cart, the only obtainable vehicle;

---

[1] This view of the age of the Weymouth anticline is not generally accepted. See Hudleston, 'Proc. Geol. Assoc.,' vol. xi. p. liii.; and A. Strahan, 'Quart. Journ. Geol. Soc.,' vol. li. p. 549, and 'Geology of the Isle of Purbeck and Weymouth,' 1898, pp. 200, 229.

but after a mile and a half found the roadway impassable. Our geologist, however, had full occupation at Lulworth. The day was one of fervent heat, and the tiny *Acarus*—that pest of a Chalk district—was seen to cluster in large red blotches on the face of an unfortunate donkey.

Next to the Bill of Portland, the Chesil Bank absorbed his time and attention. Day after day he stood on its ridge watching the sweep of the eddying currents : sometimes when a grand sea had risen and the waves swept high up, sending their spray right over the Bank ; sometimes in a calm, when on one occasion there was an enormous haul inshore of mackerel. In storm or calm, in rain or sunshine, as he stood on the ridge listening to the scour and friction of the pebbles, or speculating silently on the direction of the currents, his tall figure was a familiar object to the fishermen of the Chesil Beach.

In a letter of this date to Mr Evans, he remarks that he had never enjoyed any stay at the seaside so much as this visit to Weymouth.

Towards the end of September he was again at work in the Boulonnais—a district which had already received many visits, and was destined to receive yet more. On this occasion he was accompanied by his old friend Mr Colchester, determinedly carrying out the programme which he had planned for an Easter excursion a year and a half before. Again he was searching the district for traces of Drift and for Loess, gleaning materials for those wide generalisations which were to be embodied in subsequent papers. Much of the ground traversed in the year preceding was further worked over. M. Rigaux of Boulogne accompanied the friends to several localities.

Usually an early morning's start was made after a slight breakfast, with the understanding that he would return to dinner at seven, or at latest eight, o'clock; yet often nine had struck before he appeared—tired, yet very happy after a good day's work. On being questioned, a confession was made that lunch had consisted of the most meagre fare—perhaps a crust of bread with wine at some little roadside inn. The equanimity of the landlady would have been disturbed by the unwonted late and early hours, but for the presence of a faithful old servant who had been nearly thirty years in the service of our geologist, and who made all the domestic machinery work smoothly.

October was well advanced before his return home, where, although now his own master, work at high pressure was resumed. Early in the year he had contributed articles to the 'Manchester Guardian,' two of which were on "Coal and our Coal Supply"; and although ostensibly reviews of Professor E. Hull's work 'On the Coalfields of Great Britain,' and of the Coal Commission Reports (including the General Report and Sub-Reports), they were practically essays on a subject on which he was well qualified to give an opinion. In August a notice of Professor E. Hull's 'Building Stones' also appeared in the 'Manchester Guardian,' while in December he was the author of an article on Sir Wyville Thomson's 'Depths of the Sea.'

His energies were now centred on the elaboration of a paper on Deep Sea Temperatures, upon which, with infinite care and trouble, he had been at work for some time. His reading hitherto, as we have observed, except during attacks of illness, had been purely geological: now it included voyages to Polar regions, Arctic and Antarctic. This paper was, in fact, a treatise on oceanic circulation in relation to certain geological questions. He had theories to bring forward which he had long thought out, and in support of these he had collected and reduced all the observations made, from 1749 to 1868, at great depths. The conditions which these observations proved were discussed, and "the sections of bathymetrical isotherms which extend from Pole to Pole gave results which, in the Pacific especially, were quite new." Besides those of inland seas, 548 observations were recorded in the Northern hemisphere and 522 in the Southern. A valuable adjunct was the map of these deep - sea temperature soundings, with the observations marked in figures. It is not too much to say that the preparation of this memoir, more especially the compilation of the tables of submarine temperatures, cost him more real toil than any other of his numerous geological writings.

Letters from the numerous authorities whom he consulted on the subject of temperatures at depths are of great interest. For the Mediterranean temperatures he was indebted to his old friend Admiral Spratt,[1] who supplied him with the soundings made when he was at the head of the survey in the Mediterranean. Sir Edward Belcher sent him voluminous notes, as did likewise Captain Pullen, R.N. Admiral Bedford stated that the temperatures recorded by him from soundings were all his own and his officers' personal observations. In one of Sir Edward Sabine's letters an interesting account is given of his work in taking soundings while

---

[1] Author of 'Travels and Researches in Crete,' and joint author with Edward Forbes of a paper 'On the Geology of a part of Eubœa and Bœotia'; also of a work, 'Travels in Lycia,' &c.

on the North Sea and Arctic voyages of the Griper; while Dr Hooker furnished the details of evidence obtained on the voyages of the Erebus and Terror in Antarctic regions.

The materials and references for any memoir on which he happened to be engaged were carried to London in winter, a great part of which was spent with his wife at 21 Park Crescent, the hospitable home of Mr Charles Falconer, the uncle of Mrs Prestwich. This house was always open to them, and a lengthened winter visit was regarded as a matter of course.

The date on which a paper was read at the Institution of Civil Engineers, " On the Geological Conditions affecting the Construction of a Tunnel between England and France," was December 1873. It appeared in the Proceedings of the Institution for 1874. Prestwich's knowledge of the strata on both English and French coasts made the writing an easy task. The map, sections, and soundings are given with the utmost clearness and completeness, and the reading of his paper gave rise to an animated discussion, which was resumed at the next meeting, and was continued throughout the evening, several leading engineers as well as geologists taking part.

After reviewing other strata through which a tunnel _might_ be possible, Prestwich, in summing up, remarked that " the great mass of the Palæozoic rocks, so protected by impermeable overlying strata, is of such great dimensions, and so compact, and holds its range so independently of the more irregular range of the Secondary strata, that it offers the conditions most favourable for the secure construction of a submarine tunnel; and that such strata can be worked in safety, and for considerable distances, under great bodies of water, has been proved at Whitehaven and Mons. But, on the other hand, the depth of these old rocks below the surface is very great, and they are much more dense and harder than the overlying formations."

The following letter, in acknowledgment of a copy of the Brixham Cave Report, from Colonel Wood of Stouthall, himself the explorer of so many caves, reveals his affection for the lamented Hugh Falconer :—

Colonel E. R. Wood to J. Prestwich.

STOUTHALL, SWANSEA, 23rd *March* 1874.

MY DEAR MR PRESTWICH,—I hasten to thank you for having kindly sent me your Report on the Brixham Cave. I shall peruse it with very great pleasure. The descriptive arrangement is admirable, and detail clear and intelligible.

My interest in this branch of geology is not keen now; indeed I almost felt a distaste for the subject after the death of my dear friend Hugh Falconer: he was so associated with the pleasures which I experienced in the pursuit of the subject, and so encouraged and assisted me by his kind instructions, that when he was taken from us I found a void which I have never been able to overcome. Our acquaintance was but a short one, but he had greatly endeared himself to me, and I loved him sincerely.

I send you a flint implement for your collection, but I am sorry to say that it tells no tale. It was picked up by a workman on the coast near Long Hole, when engaged in cutting a pathway for bringing the *débris* of a wreck to the top of the cliff. It seems to me a capital typical specimen of its kind, very perfect in its proportions for so small a flint.

Mrs Wood desires me to send her best love to Mrs Prestwich, to whom also I offer my best regards. With our united kind regards to you, believe me, always yours sincerely,

E. R. WOOD.

Instead of accompanying a party abroad in the following Easter, Prestwich turned his steps north-

ward, intent on working out some special points, and
after two days of solitary exploration of the hills
between Skipton and Lotherdale, as usual in quest
of "Drift," on the 2nd April he joined Professor Boyd
Dawkins and Mr R. H. Tiddeman of the Geological
Survey, at the New Inn, Clapham, in the West Riding
of Yorkshire, which was made their headquarters. He
had visited the Victoria Cave at Settle, at least once
before, but the first day's work was a re-examination
of it and of two small caves near. The Cave at Ingleborough was also explored. On this interesting excursion Prestwich was busily engaged with his two
companions in noting every occurrence of boulders, of
Boulder Clay, or traces of Drift or of ice-action, in the
districts of Selside, Long Preston, Whalley, and Hol-
combe, &c.

Early in May his great paper on "Deep Sea
Temperatures" was handed in to the Royal Society.
It was read on the 18th June, a week later than the
date on which another of his papers was read at the
Geological Society, entitled "Notes on the Phenomena
of the Quaternary Period in the Isle of Portland
and around Weymouth." Into this latter were woven
many of the observations made during his sojourn at
Weymouth (see p. 242).

During this year also, a translation into French of
his memoirs on the Crag—'La Structure des Couches
du Crag'—was published by M. Michel Mourlon,
Docteur-ès-Sciences at Brussels.

But 1874 was a year memorable in the life of Joseph
Prestwich,—the one in which he agreed to become
the successor of the deeply regretted Professor John
Phillips, and to fill the Chair of Geology at Oxford.

CHAPTER IX.

1874–1878.

OXFORD—FIELD GEOLOGY IN ENGLAND, FRANCE, WALES, AND SCOTLAND.

Mr Prestwich was not a candidate for the vacant Professorship at Oxford, and the intimation that the Chair of Geology was about to be offered to him came as a great surprise. It was so unexpected that he had actually given testimonials to two of the candidates. An official position in the old University was very tempting, yet there was one element of anxiety, and that was his uncertain health. Dr Owen Rees, his medical adviser and the friend of his boyhood, on being consulted, gave an encouraging opinion. Accordingly a prompt acceptance was sent to the letter, dated 23rd June 1874, from the late Dr Liddell,[1] Dean of Christ Church, who at the time was Vice-Chancellor of the University, and in right of his office made the offer of the appointment. The terms in which the Dean wrote were thought only too complimentary by our geologist. The writer cannot withhold a brief extract :—

"I am fully sensible that the University will derive

[1] The Very Reverend Henry George Liddell, born February 6, 1811 ; died January 18, 1898.

more honour from having a person so eminent as yourself among her Professors than she can bestow on you
by receiving you into their numbers."

These words from the Dean foreshadowed the welcome with which he and Mrs Liddell received the new
Professor and his wife. Their constant kindness led to
a warm mutual friendship, which was greatly prized,
and which throughout a thirteen years' residence never
faltered nor varied.

Professor Prestwich was the recipient of a number of
congratulatory letters, all expressive of the pleasure
which this appointment gave. A telegram was put
into his hands on the evening of the 1st July, dated
from the "Scientific Club," with hearty congratulations. It bore the signatures of "Ansted, Rupert
Jones, Dallas, Wallace, Woodward, Seeley, Lobley,
Davies, Morris, Green, Hudleston, and Marshall Hall."
This evidence of affectionate interest from the friends
he valued gave him the keenest pleasure.

A note from Professor Owen is dated 8th July
1874 :—

MY DEAR PROFESSOR,—Let me first congratulate Oxford on
your acceptance of its Professorship of Geology. When I first
heard of the probability, I thought it too good news to be true.
Next accept my best thanks for your prompt transmission of the
vertebra of *Ceteosaurus Oxoniensis*, Phillips. It has arrived in perfect safety, and I trust you will receive it in as good condition
when the lithograph is finished.—Believe me, most truly yours,
                                        RICHARD OWEN.

The new Professor lost no time in securing a house
at Oxford, where he and Mrs Prestwich were received
with the most hospitable kindness by Dr [1] and by Mrs

---

[1] Now Sir Henry D. Acland, Bart.

Hills & Saunders, Oxford.

Acland of saintly memory. The house taken was that at the corner of Holywell and Broad Street, its recommendation being that it was within two doors of Dr and Mrs Acland. When the wife of our Professor expressed regret at their not having succeeded to the pretty Museum villa which had been occupied by Professor Phillips, instead of confessing to disappointment, he declared (and he was so true) that he much preferred *not* having the Museum residence—that it would be selfishness to hold two such good houses as it and Darent-Hulme.

Just before this (June 26th), he had had the pleasure of receiving the members of the Geologists' Association at Darent-Hulme, when their excursion happened to include Well Hill and the ground in the near neighbourhood.[1] Breaking up the party into two sections, the one half made way for the other, so that all were rested and refreshed. The sun shone out brilliantly, the picturesque highlands of Kent looked their best, and the day—at least for the entertainers—was a very happy one.

Preparations for Oxford had to be made so as to be in residence there during the October term. Prestwich was about to begin a new life and altogether new work, yet although unaccustomed to lecture to students, he was conscious that the Professorial duties would be altogether congenial, and he began without delay to shape out the course of instruction for his class. This girding himself for the duties of the Oxford chair did not, however, interfere with further geological observations which he had in view.

Ilfracombe in North Devon was the centre, in August, whence explorations were made along that

[1] See Proc. Geol. Assoc., vol. iv. p. 155.

wild rock-bound coast. The first was to Croyde Point, where the consolidated sands were noted, and also the rarity of shells. At Westward Ho he came upon the raised beach "immediately covered by the Head," and traced the raised beach at places near to Morte Point. At Morte Bay he descended to the shore with his sister-in-law, when they found great difficulty in clambering back from the rising tide. Little wonder that wreckage lay scattered near to those awful rocks with their knife-life edges. The chief interest, however, was at Baggy Point, where he was busied in securing specimens of sand, &c., from fragments of the raised beach and "Head." A search was made on the hills near Berrynarbor for the Drift mentioned in the "Guide," but he could find no trace of it. Bideford, Barnstaple, and Clovelly were visited—in short, every part of the north-west coast of Devon at all accessible was carefully examined.

From Lynton and Lynmouth a long drive skirting Exmoor took the Professor and his wife down to the comfortable little inn on the shore of Porlock Bay, the former searching at low tide for vestiges of the submerged forest. On the way to church next day by the shore-path outside Lord Lovelace's grounds, the two tourists were struck by the extraordinary luxuriance of the shrubs, in especial by the marvellous colouring of the arbutus, all testifying to the mildness of the climate.

Minehead was the next halting-place, whence the coast was examined backward toward Porlock : inland excursions were also made, including a day at Dunster and its neighbourhood. The greatest attraction, however, was the shore at Watchet, where the gypsum beds in the New Red Marl and the Rhætic Beds and

Lower Lias are so clearly exhibited. His intense enjoyment of this out-of-door work was infectious, even
for those to whom the record of the rocks was as a
sealed book.

When the date drew near for the move to Oxford,
Prestwich had to face the prospect of leaving his home
and that garden so entirely his own. He arranged with
his wife that they should leave it only after nightfall,
and this continued to be their practice in subsequent
years when quitting Darent-Hulme at the end of the
long vacation. It was less of a pang to say good-bye
to it in the dark.

Their reception at Oxford was the kindest, and not
from the science side only, but from all sides. They
soon came under the spell of the ancient home of
learning, and perceived that there was a subtle essence
in its mental atmosphere which made it somewhat
different from any other. They felt the fascination
of the place, and were sensible of their privilege.
Shortly after his arrival, the new Professor of Geology
had the honour of being elected a member of Christ
Church College. He had also the distinction of being
chosen one of "*The* Club"—a private dining club which
consisted of twelve members (several of whom were
Heads of colleges), who in term met once a fortnight
at dinner in rotation at each other's houses : only a
Royal command was allowed to interfere with this
engagement. A larger dining club was the "Ashmolean," whose members were chiefly men of science,
and who also did our geologist the honour of adding
him to their number.

He likewise had a cordial invitation from Mr Ruskin
to co-operate with him in a series of social gatherings
for the discussion of University interests, but his time

was so fully occupied that he was quite unable to join.

J. Ruskin to J. Prestwich.

CORPUS CHRISTI COLLEGE, OXFORD, *7th Novr.* '74.

DEAR PROFESSOR PRESTWICH,—I very earnestly petition you, if it be at all in your disposition of days possible, to honour me by dining with me at Corpus next Thursday. It is the beginning of a series of quiet meetings which I hope may take place weekly in my rooms : any Masters of the University coming who care to talk with each other, over the coffee, of matters at present doubtful in our University work and prospects.

It seems to me that, not prolonged to fatigue and conducted on the comfortable after-dinner principles, such discussion may every now and then elicit things (otherwise not determinable) with security up to a certain point.

Dinner will always be at seven punctually. Coffee at half-past eight, when any chance visitor who wishes to join in the talk will come in. Talk to finish in *formality* at ten. Subject for a beginning on Thursday next : What is a University ? The subjects will always be *questions*, and *some* kind of answer will be set down in memory of the evening, as agreed to by such and such guests. The records, of course, always private. Please join us. I want you so much, and am always faithfully yours,

J. RUSKIN.

The University Museum was a daily resort, or rather it should be said the working day was spent there. With the old energy he sought to make himself acquainted with the geological collections, and to complete their arrangement. His Inaugural Lecture, "On the Past and Future of Geology," was very well received, the audience increased by friends from a distance. After reviewing the strides that had been made in geological science, and indicating how much still remained to be accomplished, he summed up with a profession of the faith which had been his from boyhood—"the belief of great purpose and all - wise design."

On this subject the following letter is interesting :—

R. Mallet to J. Prestwich.

ENMORE, THE GROVE, CLAPHAM ROAD, S.W., *29th March* 1875.

MY DEAR SIR,—Let me thank you for a copy of your Inaugural Address, which has been read to me, and from which I have derived great pleasure and instruction. You have touched on none but important and broad questions, and dealt with them ably and well.

The time has fully come for us to clear our ideas as to those shifty old shibboleths of the past generation, Uniformitarianism and Paroxysmalism, and it delights me much to find you presenting a courageous front towards their correction.

I wish much you could devote a share of your powers to the clear unprejudiced statement and discussion of *all* the evidence for and against the notion of a glacial epoch and the limits of ice-action at any period. People talk about "the glacial period" much as an older world did about "the golden age" or the millennium, and without a thought as to whether there be or be not evidence of the existence of any one of the three.

To me the admission presents immense physical and mechanical difficulties, against which Palæontological evidences seem weak and dubious. And the alleged evidences from grooved and scratched rocks, I believe, can be accounted for by other than glacial action.

Do you not rather overrate the toughness of the inner surface of the globe's crust ?

A section to true scale across the Pacific Ocean would not be a trough, but an *umbo* covered by a varying but always relatively thin stratum of water—a *saucer*, not a *basin*, as I have called it elsewhere (Fourth Report, Earthquakes).

The superior inequalities, however great, will rapidly tend to lessen as we pass farther inwards, and thus the nucleus tends to a perfect spheroid, with increase of depth.

May I venture to add another remark ? — you seem to continue to attach to Hopkins's precession notions and to Sir W.

Thomson's rigidity theory a degree of authority and truth to nature to which, as it seems to me, neither are entitled, and both which, brought forward without expression of doubt, if not of discredit, are likely to exercise a retarding effect on geological true progress. Both seem to me striking examples of what Huxley has so happily styled "putting peas-cods into the mathematical mill and expecting to obtain good wholesome flour."—With much esteem, sincerely yours,   R. MALLET.

On the 2nd of February 1875 Prestwich read a paper at the Institution of Civil Engineers, which created almost as lively an interest as his Channel Tunnel paper, the discussions on it occupying portions of three evenings, and in which engineers, geologists, and naval men took part, among the latter his old friend Admiral Spratt, who had been the associate of Edward Forbes in researches in the Mediterranean. It was entitled, "On the Origin of the Chesil Bank, and on the Relation of the existing Beaches to past Geological Changes independent of the present Coast Action."

It was only on a special occasion such as this that our Professor absented himself from Oxford during term. By the end of it the strain of work, added to many hospitable social engagements, told upon his health, and he was ordered by Dr Acland to the south coast to recruit. After geologising round Eastbourne, at Pevensey and St Leonards, following the same skilled advice, a move was made to Hayling Island. At that early season there were no visitors, so that Professor and Mrs Prestwich had the hotel at South Hayling all to themselves, and the restful week spent there was ever a most happy reminiscence. The sea air worked like a charm, and as on arrival a glimpse had been had of numerous scattered boulders, there was

constant occupation. On the strip of common front-
ing the hotel there were three of about a quarter to
half a ton in weight, one being of fine white granite,
and the other two of sandstone; while within the distance of a mile thirty boulders were counted — of
granite, sandstone, diorite, &c. The circuit of the
island was made in a pony carriage, which was generally laden with chips hammered off from the transported blocks, and carried away for examination.
Fragments of Portland fossil wood were reported to
him, and as a matter of course the thin spread of
gravel on the south shore was traced and inspected:
a saltern then in use was an easy walk from the
hotel. The whole place felt so remote and out of
the world, yet there was the constant sight of sail
off Spithead. The apple - trees, so plentiful in the
island, had burst out in blossom in the continued
sunshine, and in the memory of the survivor Hayling Island will ever be associated with a daily search
for boulders amid clouds of apple-blossom.

On the first stage of the way back to Oxford the
drive from Havant to Fareham over Portsdown Hill,
keeping close to the fortifications, was magnificent.
Putting up at the "Red Lion" at Fareham, Hill
Head and Stubbington Cliff were explored, where at
both places the Professor lost no time in collecting
old rock pebbles and subangular fragments of quartz,
granite, &c. Another expedition was made to the
fort on the top of Wallington Hill to inspect the
capping of fine subangular gravel, three to four feet
thick.

The Saturday excursions for his students in the
summer term out from Oxford were always popular,
and by no means restricted to his class. There was

R

often a sprinkling of graduates, and always a certain number of ladies. No pains were spared to make his lectures and the instruction in the field perfectly clear, and it was a duty with him to explore any new ground before leading the class to inspect it. Oxford indeed was a splendid centre.

On the 20th of May, in a letter to Mr Evans, he remarked: "I am still busy here lecturing and examining. We were out, thirty-two of us, last Saturday at Yarnton, and disinterred a mammoth's tusk. To-day we go to Fawler and Stonesfield."

One of the most popular expeditions and one of the most instructive was to the top of Shotover Hill with its capping of ironsands. The several strata forming the hill were clearly seen one above another in ascending to the summit, where those whose walking powers enabled them to proceed as far as Wheatley were able to distinguish the outcrop of several of the strata on the farther side of the hill. Enslow Bridge, so rich in fossils of the Great Oolite, was another favourite excursion, as was also Kirtlington and its fossils in the Forest Marble. The neighbourhood of Cumnor was likewise a frequent resort, and many busy hours were spent in its pits hunting for corals and other specimens in the Coral Rag, and always with success. In short, no ground within reasonable reach of Oxford that could serve as an object-lesson remained unvisited.

The new Professor was determined to make himself of use to the University, and without delay took up the question of a better water-supply for Oxford: some of the best-remembered days were those spent in exploring the distant hills in search of springs of sufficient volume to be utilised for the purpose. On this particular quest he was rarely accompanied by his students:

for these long distances he went out with only one companion.

He threw himself with zest into the Oxford life, enjoying it to the utmost. He was not a speaker in Convocation, yet never failed to be present among the group of Natural Science men, to record his vote when any science measure was under discussion. Delightful intimacies grew out of almost daily intercourse. Foremost among his Oxford friends were Dr and Mrs Acland; many evenings were spent under their roof, when (as was so often the case) they had a houseful of interesting guests. He had a great regard for his brother Professors at the Museum, two of whom indeed were his old personal friends, Dr Odling, the Waynflete Professor of Chemistry, and Professor Clifton, who had the chair of Experimental Philosophy.

Outside the Museum staff there was the Rev. Charles Pritchard,[1] whose friendship was of many years' standing, and who gave him a hearty welcome. In short, the position of our geologist at the old University was peculiarly happy.

Two of the friends with whom he was much in contact in the early years of his professorship were Dr Rolleston,[2] the brilliant speaker, and Professor Henry J. S. Smith,[3] the mathematician, who succeeded Professor Phillips as curator of the University Museum. If he did not possess Dr Rolleston's rare gift of oratory, he had nevertheless that almost as rare power of persuasive speech. With inimitable tact Professor Henry Smith

[1] Savilian Professor of Astronomy, born 29th February 1808; died 28th May 1893.

[2] George Rolleston, Linacre Professor of Physiology, born 30th July 1829; died 16th June 1881.

[3] Henry John Stephen Smith, Savilian Professor of Geometry, born 2nd November 1826; died 9th February 1883.

struck in when discussions waxed warm, pouring "oil on the troubled waters." These two remarkable men had vied with each other in holding out the hand of fellowship to Prestwich. Alas! the powerful pleadings with which Dr Rolleston was wont to electrify Convocation on behalf of some liberal measure, and the "golden speech," as it has been fitly termed, of the genial Professor Henry Smith, have long been silent. Jowett, in his 'Recollections of Professor Smith,' observes, "He may be regarded as one of the most remarkable persons of his time."

Outside the Professoriate, Joseph Prestwich had gained so many friends that the difficulty is to enumerate them. One of these was the Rev. Dr Cradock, the Principal of Brasenose, who, during several years, presided at the geological class lectures: the kindness shown by him and Mrs Cradock was constant until the end. At their pleasant luncheon-parties the new Professor and his wife were frequent guests. When after adjournment to the drawing-room it was the practice of the sprightly little hostess to insist on any man of note present writing an epigram, or sonnet, or something original, in her book of autographs, our geologist finally succeeded in satisfying her with a quotation. Mrs Cradock invariably wore black, and as her slight figure was draped in black lace which was thrown over her cap and fell enveloping her shoulders, the appearance of the kind little hostess was unconventional and highly picturesque. She had a rose-garden at the end of Holywell which gave much pleasure to her friends; but each year, as the season of roses drew near, our Professor hurried home so as to be in time for his own beautiful roses, which flourished in the sunshine, on that high chalk hill overlooking the Darent valley.

At the beginning of the long vacation, and back at Darent-Hulme, he was almost speechless with pleasure, going from shrub to shrub and from tree to tree, to ascertain what havoc had been done by winter frosts, and to contemplate the growth made during his absence. The young Gingko trees, *Salisburia adiantifolia*, were among the first to be inspected. He had always been eager to nurture them into vigour, but it must be confessed that their growth was stunted and the slowest. Other delicate trees of which he took special care were the *Cryptomeria elegans*, whose feathery foliage was beginning to recover its proper tone and throw off the russet-brown of winter. Then there were the pines in all their varieties—the "Austrians," which flourished everywhere, and those from more sunny climates, such as *Pinus Laricio*, *P. excelsa*, *P. pinea*, *P. Pinaster*, &c., and the dark green *P. nobilis*,—one or two of them, if the frosts had been severe, making new leaders. Prestwich's residence at Oxford gave some respite to these young trees, as there was less transplanting : still, every season a certain number were marked for removal into other positions—all carefully indicated. No garden ever afforded keener enjoyment. No one realised more than he the truth of the words of Douglas Jerrold, that " a garden is a beautiful book, writ by the finger of God : every flower and every leaf is a letter. You have only to learn—and he is a poor dunce that cannot, if he will, do that,—to learn them and join them, and then to go on reading and reading, and you will find yourself carried away from the earth by the beautiful story you are going through."

A letter with his views on the origin of the Drift and its relation to the submergence of the land will be read with interest. In it reference is made to a visit paid to the Rev. W. S. Symonds at Pendock Rectory.

J. Prestwich to Rev. W. S. Symonds.   OXFORD, 16th *July* 1875.

MY DEAR MR SYMONDS,—You asked me to give you some idea of what my views were of the Drift phenomena you so kindly guided me to on Monday and Tuesday last.

I told you on the spot what generally they were, and I have little to add to the conclusions I then came to. In case, however, I did not clearly express myself, and to avail myself of the use of diagrams, I will now briefly state my views, so far as I can at present form them. To commence with the last section, which is a very instructive one, I think we there have the only instance I saw in the Malverns of old river action—of the same age probably as the great river drifts of the Severn and Avon, but of a more torrential and mountain-stream character. The stream in its floods carried down the bodies of the drowned animals and transported large quantities of gravel, while on the breaking up of the winter frosts the side-ice of the stream took up and carried down angular blocks of the rocks higher up. We thus have mixed together rolled and rounded gravel and sand, and perfectly angular blocks, together with detached and fragmentary bones of mammalia. This gravel is overlain by a drift of angular local *débris* derived from the Wenlock rocks on the ridge above. See Section No. 1, which shows the probable relation of the different points.

Section No. 2 shows the probable relation of the gravel to the valley and old river. There may be more than one terrace.

The other mammalian deposits had clearly no relation to old rivers, for the two chief ones were on the eastern slope of the Malverns at places where the ridge was continuous and no streams or valleys debouched. From the limited localisation and great abundance of the bones, it would seem that the carcasses of many animals may have been drifted to those spots; and, in the absence of evidence of river-action, we must suppose them to have been drowned by the encroachment of the sea on the land. Now this may have taken place at the time of the northern drift, and the deposit of sea-shells in the Severn valley; but, from the character of the animals, it may have been of later date, and the only evidence of the possible submergence of the land at that later period is the angular "landwash" which subtends the base of all your hills.

It is true that that angular *débris* might have been formed by land-ice and snow; but, besides the reasons I have given in my

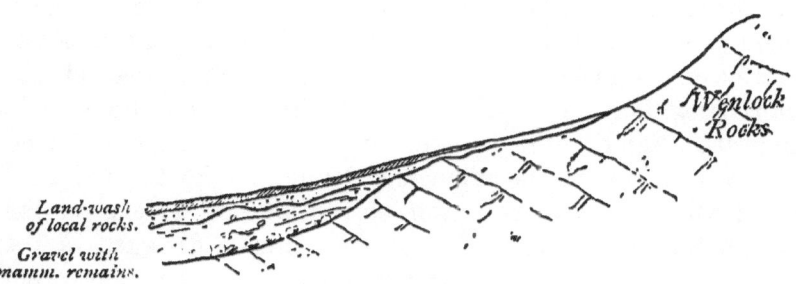

Land-wash of local rocks.

Gravel with mamm. remains.

1. Section near Clencher's Mill, Malvern.

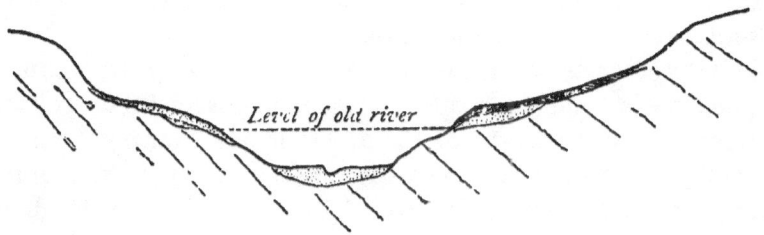

Level of old river

2. Theoretical Section across Valley at Clencher's Mill.

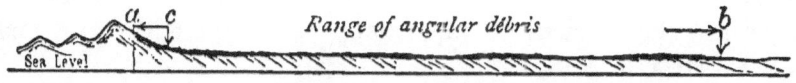

Range of angular débris

Sea Level

3. Section of the Malverns and adjacent Plain on the East (nearly true scale for height and distance).

Portland paper for adopting the sea view, I would point out, in the case of the Malverns, the great distance to which, relatively to the height, it extends from the base of the hill.

Section No. 3 will show you this on a true scale of height and distance. It seems to me that no bank of snow on the slope of the Malverns could have propelled the *débris* the distance *a b* in an *open plain*. It might have extended to *c* or a little beyond, but scarcely more.

I do not think the cause adequate to the effect.   For this, and
the reasons I have given elsewhere, I am inclined to consider the
angular drift of the West and South of England all referable to
the cause I named in my Portland paper, viz., the submergence
of the land, and its emergence in a comparatively short period of
time—like that which might, for example, accompany a series of
earthquake movements.   This would give a considerable transporting power, but a transport neither of sufficient distance nor
of sufficient duration to produce much, or any, wear of the
materials which we might expect to find in and under this
(landwash), namely, the remains of the land animals and land
shells which lived on the submerged land.   I take the red mud
deposit with its heaped collection of bones to be evidence of the
slowly advancing waters, and of the animals drowned in the
plains; while the angular *débris* is evidence of the more rapid
emergence and off-flow of the waters, carrying down the slopes
of the hills, and for some distance into the plains and valleys, the
loose *débris* of the submerged hills.

This hypothesis seems to me to explain the greater number
of phenomena, and to keep a reasonably harmonious relation
between the several sets of them.   It is one I have not arrived
at hastily.   It has, in fact, been the result of many years' observations.   Still I am not at all wedded to it, and if it can be shown
that ice and snow or any other causes are more likely to have
been the agents which have operated that remarkable series of
changes of which you have so interesting an example in the
Severn Valley, I shall be most happy to adopt a theory which
seems better or truer.

I now have to thank you for two very pleasant days which I
enjoyed much, though to my regret I found out that my walking
powers are not what they were; and with the kind regards of Mrs
Prestwich and myself to Mrs Symonds, believe me to be very
truly yours,   J. PRESTWICH.

During the first few years at Oxford, Prestwich's
time was absorbed by the preparation of his lectures
and by work connected with the collections at the
Museum; and, having no scientific assistant, he found

the Museum work heavy and fatiguing. In 1876 he brought out a useful pamphlet, 'On the Geological Conditions affecting the Water-Supply to Houses and Towns, with Special Reference to the Needs of Oxford.'

About this time also he read a paper to the Ashmolean Society, in which he drew attention to an artesian well of mineral water at St Clement's, a suburb of Oxford,—its nearest allies among English waters being those of Cheltenham and Leamington. The existence of this well had been known to Dr Buckland, who in 1835 had given notice of it to the Geological Society; afterwards it had dropped into oblivion. Prestwich expressed his opinion that the water of St Clement's had its origin in the New Red Sandstone, consequently that the Coal Measures might not be far below—a point to him of great interest.

Frequent visits at Christmas were made to the Manor House at Old Eastbourne, which Mr and Mrs Russell Scott tenanted for several years. The latter gave her two guests the frequent use of the carriage, when they were out as long as daylight lasted, and when the amount of country traversed was startling to the coachman, who had then been fifty years in Mr Scott's service. When out, on one long day, several miles from Eastbourne, and when directed by the Professor to drive up a steep chalk slope by a sort of rough track, the old coachman turned round and said gravely, and with due respect—" Sir, I would do a great deal for you, Mr Prestwich, but I could not take my horses up there."

Then the faithful servant glanced again at the supposed road, and at its utter impracticability, and burst into such a fit of laughter that the two occupants of the carriage could not help joining heartily with him.

Our Professor had wanted to see what was the capping of that impossible hill.

As he was advised to keep away from Darent-Hulme in winter, so that he should not have the temptation to stand about transplanting trees, a week of the Christmas vacation was generally spent at Eastbourne for several successive years, and the remainder with his wife's family at Park Crescent, where he was within reach of many old friends.

In the early spring of 1876 another break was made in the family circle by the death, after a brief illness, of Edward Prestwich, the only brother of our geologist. He had returned from India a few years before in shattered health. It was sad that the telegram which arrived at Oxford announcing his alarming illness came too late for his brother (who hurried to town) to find him in life.

A short Easter trip with Mr Warington Smyth to the Boulonnais, where they were joined by Mr J. Evans, was very enjoyable and of much geological interest. Extracts from two letters show how vigorously their work was prosecuted :—

To his Wife.   BOULOGNE, *April 23rd,* 7 A.M.

We returned late last night, and to my regret I missed the post. I therefore write a few lines this morning, knowing not where we may find rest for letter-writing before night, or where we may sleep. We had a beautiful summer's morning yesterday, and drove by Le Wast to Hardinghen, where we met Gosselet and his class. After visiting the coal-pits, we proceeded to Haut Baur and Ferques. There we were caught at about 4 in a most violent thunderstorm, so that we had to shut up and drive back in all haste to Marquise, where we left Gosselet and afterwards returned to Boulogne, none the worse for the storm, but the delay and loss of sections.

This morning we purpose driving to Dœsvres, Brunembert, and Lottinghen, thence per rail to St Omer, and then probably to Lillers—returning to-morrow night here.

To his Wife.   BOULOGNE, *Friday,* 8 P.M.

We have just returned from our Bethune and Lillers excursion, which has been highly successful. We accomplished all we went to see, and have suffered no inconveniences. We started early yesterday and drove to Dœsvres ; thence to Mennenville, to call on the *curé* there, an archæologist, and rather a stout opponent of the Republic. Thence to Brunembert to see the Wealden iron-ores, and then to the station at Lottinghen to catch the train for St Omer and Bethune, where we arrived at 6. We stopt at an old Spanish-built hotel—had a very fair dinner at 7, good rooms and coffee in the morning, and our bill was 7 francs each—that, by the bye, included a bottle of margaux at 5 francs. . . . This morning we started at 5 A.M. and drove to Pernes—another unspoilt place, our *déjeuner* there costing us 1.50 each. We there saw the sections we wanted, and then proceeded to Auchy-au-bois, where we introduced ourselves to the engineer—an excellent fellow, who gave us all the particulars, and they were extremely curious. He wanted and pressed us to stop to lunch, but time did not allow. We made ourselves perfectly acquainted with this, the most western, prolongation of the North of France coal-field, and with some geological phenomena cf great interest. He offered to send us on to Lillers per coal railway-engine, but as we had already experienced a mile of this travelling we declined, and managed to drive to Lillers just in time to catch the train. To-morrow we start at 7 for Guines and Belinghen, but shall return early. I am also looking forward now to travel home.

He generally returned from an Easter excursion refreshed and invigorated.

In a letter of 6th March 1877, Captain Petrie, the courteous Secretary of the Victoria Institute and editor of its journal, requested Prestwich to authorise the publication of a sentence quoted by the Rev. Professor Pritchard in a communication to the Institute, namely, " My brother Professor of Geology tells me the geology of the Bible is not the geology of nature." To this Joseph Prestwich made reply :—

J. Prestwich to F. Petrie. OXFORD, *7th March* 1877.

SIR,—I am obliged by your courtesy in submitting to me before publication the words I am reported to have used in conversation with my friend and colleague the Professor of Astronomy. There must be some misunderstanding on the part of Professor Pritchard in attributing the words to me, as the association of the Bible and geology is one I never make, holding the two to be perfectly distinct and to be studied independently. I accept the truths concerning our moral and spiritual nature from the Bible, but in all that concerns physical nature I look to Nature herself for an explanation.

I therefore always avoid controversy on a subject where the terms are not equal, and which do not, I think, at present admit of discussion. Wishing to adhere to this rule, kindly avoid bringing my name forward in the matter, and I am, sir, yours faithfully,

J. PRESTWICH.

I have just seen Professor Pritchard, who will write to you. In the general sense of my friend's remarks I quite agree.

In an article in 'Nature' (May 3, 1877), on " Deep Well-Borings in London," Professor Judd, F.R.S., refers to our geologist's work—'The Water-Bearing Strata around London, &c.'—as

A masterpiece of minute observations and close and accurate reasoning. . . . After a most elaborate study of the nature and relations of the various strata which crop out all around the London Basin, and of the disturbances to which they have been subjected since their deposition, Mr Prestwich ventured on a bold *prediction*—namely, that the Chalk beneath London would be found to have a thickness of 650 feet, the Upper Greensand of 40 feet, and the Gault of 150 feet.—*Op. cit.*, p. 142.

At the time when this announcement was made, no well in London had been sunk to a greater depth than 300 feet in the Chalk; but now we can appeal to no less than four deep borings in the Metropolis, which afford the most convincing proof of the reliability of the data, and the accuracy of the reasoning by which Mr Prestwich arrived at his interesting result. . . . It will be admitted on all hands that the agreement between the estimated and proved results is marvellously close.

Further investigations for a better water-supply for Oxford led our Professor far afield. A long expedition in quest of perennial springs was to the Cotteswolds, approached from Bourton-on-the-Water. On one other he ventured to take his class—namely, to the remote village of East Hendred, nestling in a depression of the chalk-hills, several miles above Wantage. From the railway at Didcot a brake carried about a dozen of the party, the others proceeding on foot. On the return journey, when on the summit of the bare down (the driver of the brake having left the road and having begun to go at a foot's pace down the uneven, grassy slope), the party was overtaken by a terrific thunderstorm. The undergraduates had just begun to troop down in the direction of the fine spring issuing at the foot of the hills, and which had been the sight reserved for them on their homeward road, when the rain fell as if from a waterspout. Coats and umbrellas were never carried. Our Professor pulled off his overcoat, throwing it to the first man overtaken. The only course was to make for Didcot, and, pressing on at their hardest pace, it was happily reached just in time for the train for Oxford. Fortunately none of the students caught cold, as the trusty Caudell[1] ascertained by inquiring at the several colleges next morning. It was an experiment never repeated.

While touching on this subject, it may be mentioned that a few years later (1882) Professor Tyndall wrote to say that he was about to build a rural retreat on Hind Head, 800 feet above the sea. After explaining that it would be necessary to bore to a great depth for water, he ·proceeded to say : "If by any geological magic you could help us to obtain water on cheaper terms than the sinking of a [deep] well; and if, by the magic of kindness, you could be induced to communicate to us the secret, we should be greatly obliged."

Just at this time there was frequent correspondence with the Rev. Osmond Fisher on cosmical questions.

J. Prestwich to Rev. O. Fisher.

SHOREHAM, *near* SEVENOAKS, 12*th July* 1877.

MY DEAR FISHER,—You judge rightly that we are here, but, I am sorry to say, only in part enjoyment of my country residence. . . .

The glacial action was so general in Europe, Asia, and America —and we have reason to believe also in the southern hemisphere—that I cannot but attribute it to some cosmical phenomena, and consider that the earth lost more heat absolutely in equal periods to what it did before or since. You, however, raise a question I had not considered before, and which I will reflect over. I am sorry to hear you are so poorly. As soon as I am better, I hope you will come and take a few days' change here.

Professor and Mrs Prestwich always found the kindest of friends and neighbours at Shoreham Vicar-

[1] Henry Caudell, the faithful museum servant of the late Professor Phillips, and subsequently of Professor Prestwich.

age in the Rev. J. and Mrs Lovett Cameron — the parents of Commander Verney Lovett Cameron, the distinguished African traveller and pioneer, who had lately returned from his wonderful walk across the Dark Continent. He was one of the first explorers of Africa, and always foretold its great future.

A very pleasant trip was a driving tour with Mr and Mrs Evans. The start was made from Bletchley on the 31st July, Mr Evans's carriage having been sent on in advance. The route was through Buckingham, skirting Stowe and other fine country seats, on to Towcester, whence next day they proceeded to Daventry. The ostensible object of this tour was health and recreation, yet it was combined with well-planned geological purpose. A richly wooded and undulating country without water was traversed, until they crossed the Avon before arriving at Warwick. Each day had furnished pits as well as spreads of gravel for the two geologists, who, however, joined their wives in a visit to the museum and also to the historic castle — a monument of ancient splendour preserved in habitable order.

One of the finest views seen in leaving Warwick was the sweep of the Avon round the base of Guy's Cliff, where, by the side of the river, our Professor detected a valley terrace eight feet above it. Both geologists were delighted with Kenilworth, which, in contrast with Warwick, is the ancient castle in ruins. Coventry, with its great churches and ribbon factories, had a visit; yet their keenest interest was in gravel-pits on the road to Atherstone, and in the large boulders passed in approaching Stoke Golding. Market Bosworth was selected for the Sunday's rest: it was full of memories for Mr Evans, being his father's resting-place and that of several of his kindred. The drive through the Moira coal-district showed no evidence of its being a mining country, except for the chimney-stalks standing in the greenest of fields.

The two geologists being desirous of a clear day for exploration of the upper Trent Valley, a stay of two nights was made at Ashby-de-la-Zouch. They inspected the ruined castle of Scott's 'Ivanhoe,' as well as the "Tournament Ground"; yet it was with keener zest that next morning, in spite of rain, they started on a drive of many miles through the greenest of green valleys, where they found pits to please them, with exhibitions of "Drifts" of varied character.

From Ashby-de-la-Zouch the route was through what remained of Charnwood Forest—the scenery on its borders most striking from the dark slate-rocks which protruded, piled up in ridges and pillars on the hills. The culminating interest of this tour was, however, in the granite quarries of Mount Sorrel: it was with difficulty that Prestwich could be persuaded to leave them. After a hurried glimpse of quarries of blue slates at a little distance off, their road took the party close to Bradgate Castle, the early home of Lady Jane Grey — a ruin standing in the park, with a picturesque surrounding of gnarled and knotted old oak-trees. Grooby Castle had also a brief visit. But for two of the party the ruin was not the attraction: they had heard of a certain pit close to it, and also of a syenite quarry. A five miles' drive took the tourists to Leicester, where the carriage was exchanged for the railway, and late in the evening they reached Nash Mills.

The excursion had been altogether delightful: our Professor had got rid of sciatica, and had made voluminous notes of pits and Drift and boulders. The great granite quarries of Mount Sorrel alone were more than enough to repay a journey to the north.

Folkestone, which was familiar ground, was a resort in the autumn—one excursion being made to Dover and Walmer, where, it can be affirmed, he knew every bend and cliff of that coast. The same may be said of Margate and Ramsgate, where a day was spent, and where another careful survey was made.

Early in October he was accompanied to Maidstone by the Rev. Osmond Fisher, whence they made an inspection of the pits and brickfield near Aylesford. Prestwich next paid a flying visit to Hitchin, in order to examine a certain clay-pit on Messrs Ransome's ground, and of which he as usual sketched a section.

He had been repeatedly urged by an aged relative— a cousin of his family—to take up the baronetcy, and it was at this time he again decided to have his claim to it sifted. The following letter was addressed to a young barrister, his nephew by marriage :—

J. Prestwich to H. B. Tomkins.

SHOREHAM, *near* SEVENOAKS, *8th October* 1877.

MY DEAR HENRY,—I hear you have been devoting much time and attention to the family genealogies. My own, as you are probably aware, is somewhat intricate, and involves the holding of a baronetcy. This I have never thought fit to take up, from considerations of position, incompleteness of evidence, and expense. I should now feel disposed to take it up if the evidence could be complete without too much expense. My old friend Mr Flower the solicitor had the papers in his hands for some time, but his death interrupted his friendly investigation.

What I should like now to do would be, if you have the leisure and inclination to undertake such a work, to place it in your hands as a professional matter. It may give you a little occupation till you are more fully engaged in your ordinary law business. As I have said, the evidence is incomplete, but it was, I believe, at one time complete or nearly so, but many of the important documents were lost in a pocket-book of which my father was robbed many years ago. His cousin, Sir John Prestwich, took up the title, but did not enter it. It is his papers chiefly that we have, and as he or his father was descended from, I believe, a junior brother, his collection is more complete in that direction than my father's. All the papers, however, such as they are, I have, and I can place them in your hands to look at and see what could be made of them. As your Aunt Emily is here, I will ask her to take up the tin box with her to South Street, and if your mother could kindly call for it some day she is driving past, I should be much obliged. The books we have at Oxford, where we should be glad to see you at any time; and I am, your affecte. uncle,

JOSEPH PRESTWICH.

I enclose a copy of the best table I was able to make out many years since.

The death of Mr H. B. Tomkins took place before he had completed his search among the old family papers and registers, and no other steps were taken.

The following letter gives the route for an Easter excursion, which was afterwards modified:—

J. Prestwich to J. Evans.   OXFORD, 17th March.

MY DEAR EVANS,—I have not yet quite planned the route, but as well as I can make out the points we should visit, it will be about this:—

Paris to *Montluçon.* Miocene, Granite, and Coal-Measures.
Ahun and *Lamaraix-les-Mines.* Coal-Measures in a Granite basin. Kaolin works. Valley Drift. Deep valley cut through Gneiss and Granite to
Aubusson. Thence, if there is a road, across the Corrèze to
Ussel. Crystalline rocks. By rail (?) to

Tulle and *Brives*, and then a short visit to some pits in the valleys of the Vezère and Dordogne.

Then *Toulouse, St Gaudens, Tarbes, Pau, Bayonne, Biarritz, St Jean de Luz*, and *Irun* for caves and coast-sections.

When planned, I must write to L. Lartet and Raulin. I hope to see you on Wednesday. . . .

You see I omit Limoges and keep farther east. My wife says I am not to be allowed to go unless you are of the party. She has just been looking at the map, and condemns somewhat strongly the Central France portion—hills, mountains, precipices, frost, and snow; but approves of the South of France part. I tell her we can report of the country when we come back.

J. Prestwich to Rev. O. Fisher.   OXFORD, 17th *March* 1878.

MY DEAR FISHER,—You encourage me to ask you any geological question involving mathematical investigation. There is one I have been considering, and which you have already closely touched upon. Is it possible that earthquake waves can be transmitted by a crust so rigid as that which Sir W. Thomson [1] would establish? In those cases where trees wave from side to side, and we have other evidences of a rolling motion of the crust, it seems to me impossible that a mere vibration of the shock is sufficient. Such vibration may be transmitted, but it seems to me hardly in that form and to such distances.

What think you on mathematical grounds? Are you going to pay Oxford a visit this term? I have yet two weeks of lectures on Tertiary and Quaternary Strata. Next term I commence excursions, and lecture on the ground to be visited. If you can join in any of them it will give me much pleasure. Mrs Prestwich desires her kind regards, and hoping you and your boys are all well, I am, sincerely yours,

JOS. PRESTWICH.

J. Prestwich to Rev. O. Fisher.   OXFORD, 28th *March* [1878].

MY DEAR FISHER,—Thanks for your note and explanations. I can quite understand the propagation of a wave in a given

---

[1] Now Lord Kelvin.

direction through or along a rigid and at the same time an elastic body like steel, provided it has the form of a plate moving in or on media not of sufficient resistance to interfere materially with the play of the plate, as it would be with the crust of the earth, with the atmosphere on one side and a fluid nucleus on the other. But I cannot understand the transmission of a rolling motion and the production of great transverse fissures without the actual movement, as you would have in the shaking of a carpet, of the whole mass of the crust affected by the disturbance.   ·

Admitting that Sir William Thomson's investigations established great rigidity as a whole, it still appears to me that there must be fluid remnants at no great depth, although the central nucleus as well as the outer crust are solidified. I certainly understand from Mallet's description, and the account of others, that although the movement or shock is vertical in places, that in others it is one from side to side.

No hypothesis, it seems to me, meets all the conditions of geological phenomena so well (or if it meets [them] all) as that of the original fluidity of the globe, and I would think that none meets the present condition of volcanic and earthquake disturbances so well as that the solidification is not yet thoroughly complete, though the remaining quantity of fluid matter is not such as to interfere with the rigidity required by Sir W. T. to answer his determined conditions. This, in fact, is very much the hypothesis of Mr Hopkins, but I should hesitate to accept the thickness he assigns to the external crust. I would refer earthquakes to that cause which has ever been affecting the crust of the earth—the incessant readjustment to a contracting nucleus, however small that contraction may have become.

I saw Hughes[1] yesterday, and heard of the Barnwell discovery. I hope he will accompany Evans and myself this Easter to some of the French caves. I am sorry to hear your armchair has such a hold of you, but trust it will become less fixed as summer advances; and with our united kind regards, I am, sincerely yours,   JOS. PRESTWICH.

---

[1] Woodwardian Professor of Geology, Cambridge.

The following letter gives the itinerary for the Easter excursion; it was only slightly altered on the return journey to Paris:—

J. Prestwich to J. Evans.　　　　　OXFORD, *28th March* 1878.

MY DEAR EVANS,—M. Massénat will do as well as M. Lavallant for Brives. What was the place you had in view in the neighbourhood of Poitiers? The caves on the Charente, between Civray and Charroux, seem to me of considerable interest. See M. de Longuemar's 'Rapport sur une Exploration méthodique des Grottes du Chaffaud'; also the 1869 'Congrès International d'Anthropologie,' Copenhagen, pp. 128-134.

I would therefore propose to take the 9.30 A.M. train on the 14th April from Paris to Civray, and the omnibus at once to Charroux, where a M. Brouillet has a collection.

15. Work our way along the Charente to Civray: sleep there, and take the 9.14 A.M. train to Dax.

16. Proceed by the 11.25 A.M. train to Bayonne.

17. Bayonne and neighbourhood.

18. Coast from Biarritz to St Jean de Luz, &c., on to Irun or San Sebastian.

19. Coast-section, and return to Bayonne.

20. 5.50 A.M. train to Toulouse, stopping one day at some place to be settled on *en route*.

22 and 23. Toulouse and neighbourhood.

24. 5 A.M. train to Brives, and spend the day there. You know, I suppose, the few papers on this district.

25 and 26. Brives to Tarascon, and thence along the Vezère by Martignac to Le Bugue and Les Eyzies.

27. Périgueux and some other place, and on to Limoges.

28. 10 A.M. train to Paris.

29. Return to London, or if the 3 train would do for our return there, we might have a day to spare for Paris or elsewhere. I find I must leave out the Creuse and the Corrèze. Our route south of Bayonne must also depend on information we receive there. You can discuss this plan with Hughes on Sunday, and next week I hope to meet you at the Geological.—Ever sincerely yours,　　　　　J. PRESTWICH.

Prestwich had invited his old friend Mr George Busk,[1] the distinguished surgeon and anthropologist, to be one of the party :—

G. Busk to J. Prestwich.   32 HARLEY STREET, *March* 28, 1878.

MY DEAR PRESTWICH,—I have taken two or three days to think the matter over, and though sorely tempted, feel that it will be better that I should not attempt to join your party at Easter. The party and the route are equally tempting, and I should have been much delighted to visit Toulouse. . . . I am above measure delighted, however, to find that you are so well as to induce Mrs Prestwich to allow you to go. Pray give her our kindest regards. Believe me, yours very truly,   GEO. BUSK.

Before starting on this Easter trip, Prestwich was made a livery-man of the City of London, having been elected a member of the Turners' Company.

On the 8th of April a letter was received from the General Secretary of the British Association (Captain Douglas Galton) requesting Prestwich to allow himself to be put in nomination for the office of President of the British Association Meeting for 1879. He was much gratified, yet felt it his duty to decline the honour. He was living at far too high pressure, and decided to accept no office nor duties which would abstract time from his own science.

A few days later he set out for Bordeaux, Toulouse, &c., with " Evans, Galton, and Hughes, Smyth joining for three days at Bayonne." An extract is given from a letter to his wife from Paris, to which he travelled with Professor Hughes :—

We arrived here in due course, and by 7.30 we were comfortably at dinner in the Corazza Café in the Palais Royal. Evans

---

[1] George Busk, born 1807 ; died 1886.

and Galton arrived this morning, and we have been out the whole of the day, having returned just in time for these few lines. The weather is lovely—cloudless and warm—the chestnut trees green with young leaf. We have seen Hamy, Quatrefages, and Hébert, who has invited us to dinner on Sunday fortnight. We called also on Gaudry, but only found Madame at home. Daubrée I hope to see to-morrow—Emily also. Paris is more beautiful than ever—little traces now of the war. The Hôtel de Ville is, however, still to be rebuilt. How I wish you were here with me. We are now off to Champeaux and then to the Vaude-ville or the Variétés.

Again to his wife on leaving Paris, 14th April :—

Just one line as we are starting. . . . We were out the whole of the day, visiting Gaudry, Hébert, Daubrée, &c., and found it difficult to get away from them and from Paris. The weather continues lovely, and we leave at 8.45 this morning. M. Longue-mar wishes us to stop three hours at Poitiers, so we are doing so, and reach Civray at the same hour, 6.20. You cannot now hear from me till Wednesday.

To his Wife. BAYONNE, *20th April.*

After all we are going to San Sebastian. We are now just starting for St Jean de Luz, and thence on to Irun and San Sebas-tian. We return here on Sunday night to proceed by early train to Caresse, Lourdes, and Toulouse, which we shall reach on Tuesday and remain at till Thursday, or rather Friday morning. The weather is again lovely. Yesterday we had a most delight-ful day in one of the beautiful valleys in the Pyrenees with M. Detroyat and Le Marquis de Folin. The latter is Mr Jeffreys' friend and a capital fellow. They are most hospitable and kind. In fact, we find it difficult to get away. Yesterday, while at Itzatzou, a carriage passed with a friend of one of our compan-ions, who invited us all to proceed and spend the night and next day with him in the very heart of the Pyrenees. We met with at this little village an excellent geologist—a Dr Guidu—who acted as our guide, and showed us a fine collection of the rocks of the Pyrenees. We are fully occupied and out all day long, but it suits me perfectly, and I am quite well and enjoying myself immensely. My only wish that you were with me.

To the Same.   LOURDES, 23rd *April* 1878.

Since writing to you from Bayonne we have been to La Guetanz, thence along the cliffs to St Jean de Luz, and by carriage to Hendaye. On this walk I witnessed one of the most singular tempests I ever experienced. The morning was hot and sultry in the extreme—not a breath of air, so hot that even I had to put up my umbrella. At Guetanz we went at 1 to the hotel to breakfast, or rather lunch. Suddenly the sky clouded over, the wind rose, and in fifteen minutes it was blowing a hurricane as though it would blow the house down. It lasted two hours and then partly ceased, when we continued our route. The sea was a mass of foam and running very high. At a distance of a mile from shore we saw a boat full of people, whose position we thought extremely dangerous. In fact, after watching it for ten minutes we walked on, but on looking there again we could see nothing of the unfortunate boat. The next day we heard that almost every village along the coast had lost boats which had gone out and were caught by the suddenness of the gale. We heard of 50 lives having been lost. The high road was blocked by fallen trees. I hope this gale did not reach our coasts.

On Sunday morning we drove over from Hendaye to San Sebastian—got there to breakfast, and then went to high mass at the large church. The music was a full orchestral band. I called on a M. Brunet, who insisted on accompanying us to the coast and to the various sections in the neighbourhood. There was not, however, much to see. After dinner at an excellent hotel, where, however, the *cuisine* was entirely French, we returned to Bayonne, which we reached at 10.15 P.M. We found the commandant and M. Detroyat waiting our arrival, and the latter offered to accompany us to-day—an offer which we gladly accepted. Starting at 5.45, we stopped at Peyrehorade, and then hired to visit *"la grotte de Sordes"* and some implement-bearing beds on the top of a hill above Caresse.

The weather at starting was very wet, but it cleared up and

we have had a fine day. At 3 we came on to this place, stopping
half an hour at Pau, which gave us time to see the Terrace and
Castle. . . . I must confess that I am disappointed with the
scenery. There are places of great beauty, such as Cambo and
Itzatzou, and this, but the rest of the scenery we passed through,
were it not for the distant Pyrenees, is somewhat tame and
monotonous. This place is in a beautiful situation. After
dinner we strolled down to the *Grotte Miraculeuse*. It was like
going through a fair—solicited on all sides to buy photographs,
wax candles, rosaries, medals, &c. . . . To-morrow we see the
other (ossiferous) *grottes*, and then proceed to Lannemezean and
Toulouse, which I hope to reach at 9.20 P.M., and there to find
letters from you.

To his Wife.   TOULOUSE, 24*th April* 1878.

   On arriving here last night we found L. Lartet waiting for us.
He has been out with us all day, and we have arranged to go
this evening at 5.50 to Foix in the Pyrenees. So I have only
time to write a very few lines. We return here to-morrow
morning—stop here Friday, and proceed early on Saturday to
Brives. After that it is uncertain where we stop, unless at Périgueux. So please write to P. R., Paris. Madame Lartet inquired
particularly after all—Uncle Charles and sisters—and hopes to
see you here some day. . . .

   The Lartets are full of recollections of your dear Uncle Hugh.

   The party travelled home *viâ* Paris, and the Professor reached Oxford at the given date to begin his
summer-class excursions. At the end of term, on the
22nd June, he set out on a journey of exploration to the
Gower Coast and St David's. Two or three days were
spent at Gloucester, where he was joined by Mr W. C.
Lucy in examining the gravel which caps some of the
hills in various directions in the neighbourhood, and in
ascertaining its component parts.

   From Swansea he proceeded by the Gower coast to
Rhôs Sili in a day of fervent heat, which added greatly

to the fatigue, there being no shelter. Still, as he had come upon evidence of a raised beach on the hill between Full Bay and Rhôs Sili, and of a large bed of Drift, he would not hear of fatigue or exhaustion. When hour after hour had passed, and his wife urged that the heat was hardly endurable, and that although there was "water, water everywhere, yet not a drop to drink," he only applied himself harder to work, with the old answer, "Now or never," and climbing up the beach as if on springs, set to dig out specimens of it and of the Drift to carry to Oxford. His exertions in that fierce glow seemed superhuman.

They reached Rhôs Sili when the shades of even had gathered, the horse almost as exhausted as the two tourists. Entering the lodging engaged, Mrs Prestwich's first petition was for water or something to quench their thirst. "Please, some soda water, and *quick!*"

To the puzzled landlady, it was explained with a gesture that it was water that fizzed up.

"Ah, ma'am, you will be meaning pop?"

"Yes, pop, but please *quick, quick!*"

The landlady hereupon sent to the "Ship" for "pop," but owing to the heat it had all been sold out.

"We shall be so thankful to have something to eat—we have had no dinner."

"Dinner, ma'am—and what have you brought?"

"Nothing, we have brought nothing."

"Every one brings their victuals here, ma'am."

It was a poor look-out, no meat in the village and one egg in the cottage! The worthy landlady did her best; tea and eggs were forthcoming, but as it proved afterwards, two days upon this fare did not suit our geologist to work upon, while making very unusual

exertion. Yet the scarcity of food, or rather the ab-
stention from food that he could not eat, did not
trouble him in the very least, though it did trouble
his companion. He was so absorbed and delighted
with the Drift and the fragments of a raised beach,
that he only thought of the details of the day being
entered in a note-book.

Next morning they called on the Rev. Ponsonby
and Mrs Lucas, to whom they had a letter of introduction, the former the brother of the late Lady
Gardner Wilkinson. They had heard of a gentleman
and lady passing the night in the village, and had been
compassionating them on account of the unprecedented
heat. When Professor Prestwich expressed his intention to send his wife across country in the waggonette,
while he himself should walk along the shore north of
Rhôs Sili Bay, so as to examine the coast, Mr Lucas
most kindly volunteered to accompany him. The long
walk with its traces of old beach was one of surpassing
interest to the geologist, who also came upon vestiges
of Drift, but it caused Mr Lucas a serious illness. The
heat was so great that they could not sit down to rest
on the glowing sands, and many weeks passed before
Mr Lucas recovered.

Prestwich prophesied a future for Rhôs Sili and its
stretch of beautiful sands,—that one day it would become a great sea-side resort. He found traces of
raised beach at Burry Holmes, Spritsail Point, and at
the station next beyond Llanelly.

The drive from Haverfordwest to St David's was a
comparative rest, but at the end of a week of severe
climbing up and down the old rocks on the rugged
coast of St David's, to Porthclais, Caerbuddy, Porth-
lisky, not forgetting a day at Whitesand Bay, he was

struck down by an attack of sciatica. The kind
doctor at St David's advised immediate return to
Oxford, with the halt of a night at Neath. The
first part of the journey was a terrible experience.
The invalid had been assisted out and lifted up beside the driver of a waggonette, his wife behind with
their light luggage. When about five miles from St
David's, with nearly twelve to be traversed before
reaching Haverfordwest, and on a bare exposed road
beyond reach of aid or shelter, a violent thunderstorm
burst. When at its height—the lightning vivid, and
the rain falling in such force that it penetrated the
leather bags — the Professor called out to the driver
to stop, that his leg must be moved—that his position
was insupportable! What a moment! And what a
journey! Mercifully, the storm was not of long
duration, and the last few miles to the railway at
Haverfordwest were got over without further incident.

After a fortnight's rest at Oxford, Prestwich was
able to accompany Professor Morris to Wantage, and
also to drive with him and Mr Hudleston to examine
the summit of Brill Hill, which had always been of
special interest. In the end of July a long day was
spent at Ewelme, the object being to see the fine spring
which rises at the base of the Chilterns, issuing at the
foot of a slope in the garden of the Manor House, which
is situated at the north end of the village. On being
told that all the members of the squire's family were
absent, the Professor, followed by his wife, went down
through the garden, and they on their knees were
rejoicingly laving up the pure water from its source,
when they were startled by a voice. The trespassers
scrambled to their feet, and made apologies to a young
man, apparently one of the family, who was much

amused : he begged of Professor Prestwich to continue
his researches, and hurried away.

It was not the geology only of such places as
Dorchester, Shillingford, and Wallingford, which were
explored on the way to Ewelme, that made the visit to
it memorable. The history of several of the localities
appealed powerfully to the imagination, most of all that
of the old-world village of Ewelme itself. A pathetic
human interest pervades its very atmosphere, and its
group of ancient buildings. The church, grammar-
school, and especially its picturesque old alms-house,
could not be dissociated in one's mind from the tragic
end of the ill-fated Duke of Suffolk, their unhappy
founder.

The excursion, however, which stands out amongst all
other excursions, was that made in the autumn of 1878
to Glen Roy and the Parallel Roads of Lochaber.
Prestwich had long been desirous of seeing these famous
" terraces " for himself, and he now planned a journey
to the north, which should include also a search along
the western and south-western shores of Scotland for
raised beaches, boulders, and Drift.

After a couple of days with relatives at Stirling,
when every hour was utilised in reading off the features of the district, the two tourists proceeded to Tyn-
drum and on by coach through Glencoe to Ballachulish
on Loch Leven. Heavy rain compelled them to take inside seats in the Glencoe coach : fortunately, however,
they had the *coupé*, so that views were had of the wild
Highland country. At Inveroran, where horses were
changed, they had a pleasant meeting with Mr Herbert
Spencer, who had been waiting there several days for
rain which was needed for fishing. The downpour
had resolved itself into fitful showers, and the storm

clouds which had veiled the mountains were uplifted as they entered the never-to-be-forgotten Pass of Glencoe. Gradually a glorious sunset lighted and touched the mountain summits and outlines with a beauty indescribable. The scene was solemn and awe-inspiring, and the travellers sat in silence, almost over-powered by its grandeur. That sunset upon the rugged towering cliffs, apart from the tragic memories of the Glen, would alone have been well worth a thousand miles of travel.

The day following being Sunday, Professor and Mrs Prestwich accompanied the Rev. Dr Story from the Ballachulish Hotel to Glencoe, where the rev. gentleman conducted the service of the Church of Scotland. The deep reverence of that small congregation was very impressive ; and as all joined with fervour in singing from the Scottish metrical version of the Psalms to their own plaintive melodies, one could not but remember that this remnant of the clan represented the few descendants of the MacDonalds who escaped the cruel massacre.

In a long afternoon walk on the seaward shore, Prestwich was charmed with the scenery, the evidence of a raised beach, ice-action, and geology in general. One large boulder on the Loch Leven shore was pointed out to him next morning as St Peter's stone, and he was well satisfied with the display of polished stones and *roches moutonnées*. The morning was spent in the slate quarries of Glencoe, and a brief visit was made to a newly opened granite quarry. Rain fell heavily as they left Fort William and got out in the wild tract skirting Ben Nevis, but by the time Roy Bridge was reached it had cleared, so that there was a fine view in the evening light of the mountains patched with snow.

Mr Mackintosh of the comfortable inn of Bridge of
Roy suggested Loch Laggan for the first excursion
in case of rain : it involved little walking, and the road
was excellent. Starting in a light dogcart, the travellers had only gone a few miles when the clouds
vanished, the mists fled from the mountains, and in
driving in bright sunshine up through the romantic
Glen Spean, they felt as if transported into fairyland.
Branching off from the grand road of the Spean valley
was one to the right leading to Loch Treig, which
Prestwich was eager to visit. He had noted the mounds
of moraine crossing the valley through which the Treig
had cut a passage. An hour's halt at the lonely and
silent Loch Treig, treeless, and enclosed by high hills
literally covered with heather, enabled him to climb
the heights of its western shore, which he found glaciated to 400 or 500 feet or more above the Loch. Re-
gaining the main road, he was absorbed in the drive
to Loch Laggan in observing all around the exhibition
of ice action. " On north side of Spean Valley, thence
to Moy, met with enormous accumulation of moraine
blocks, which became less and less mixed with gravel
in ascending, while the bare rocks everywhere showed
striation." They put up at a refreshment house,
originally built by Mr Ansdell, R.A., near which, feed-
ing on grassy knolls, were to be seen specimens of the
" ewie wi' the crookit horn," made familiar by his
paintings : a walk of a mile and the low bleak shore of
Loch Laggan was reached. The drive back to Roy
Bridge was taken leisurely. From time to time Professor Prestwich alighted to measure the direction of
the striæ on the rocks by the roadside.

On August 14th, in glorious weather, the object of
the journey to Scotland was achieved, and a visit paid

to Glen Roy and its Parallel Roads.   At an early hour
Bohuntine was passed, and when some way up the
Glen the Professor and his companion alighted to climb
the upper side of Bohuntine Hill, whence there was a
good view of the "terraces."   The Roy or Red Glen
had been well named.   The air in that blazing August
sun was scented by miles of heather in bloom which
carpeted the hills, and which mingled its perfume with
the sweet wild gale in the lower slopes.   Within a
mile or so of the head of the Glen they ascended to
the two higher "Parallel Roads," and following them
round to Glen Turret, descended to the entrance to
Glen Gluoy.   A little volume might be filled with
sketches and details of this ever-to-be-remembered visit
to Glen Roy.   The tourists found themselves again in
fairyland, and to Professor Prestwich the day was one
of keenest geological interest.

A week's sojourn at Bridge of Roy was employed in
daily exploration of the hills nearest to those of Glen
Roy and of the accessory glens.   Brilliant weather
added to the intense enjoyment, and until the end of
the week there had not been a shower.

After a morning spent in climbing the hills, whence
they descended over the pass to Boheenie, a romantic
road by the left bank of the Roy brought them back to
the Inn.   In the afternoon they started for Glen Larig,
driving as far as Spean Inn, and then up on the
opposite bank of the Spean nearly to Insch.   Finding
at a hovel called Achnafraschoille a tall young High-
lander to act as a guide, they trod on through the long
heather, Glen Larig seeming always to recede.   When
nearing its entrance, and about three miles from where
the dogcart had been left, rain began to fall heavily.
Our Professor, however, determined to press on with

Macdonald, his wife agreeing to wait by a boulder. But the rain was persistent, dark mists closed round, obscuring any view of the glen, and when he returned with the guide it was with disappointment that he had not found the "Parallel Road," which ends in Glen Larig, more clearly exhibited. Still the walk in the heavy rain through the long wet heather was more than compensated for by the geological features he had been able to see of Glen Larig Leacan, and of the remarkable ravine at its entrance.

Roy Bridge was left with regret and in a steady downpour, but mine host had found a close carriage for the travellers, who followed the road to the Falls of Mucomir, near to which the Spean enters Loch Lochy. In spite of rain, geological observations were made. It was seen that all the low islands thence from Loch Linnhe to Oban, including Lismore, are strongly glaciated, from their summit down to the water's edge. Oban was reached in the evening, and early next day they crossed the ferry to the island of Kerrera, rain unluckily beginning to fall before they stepped from the boat, and increasing as they followed the cartway by the shore, whence they went steadily on in search of raised beaches. After ascending high ground in face of wind and rain, they came down to the ruins of Castle Gulin, a Danish fortress where Alexander II. of Scotland died in 1249. Here they were besieged by a herd of Highland cattle, and might have been detained about ten minutes (which under the conditions seemed a time interminable), when the herd suddenly moved off down to better pasture near the shore, and the excursionists gladly made their escape up the steep track which they had previously descended.

The next day's geologising was on the mainland,

T

when a visit was made to the large quarry of coarse
black slate with the great Old Red conglomerate in
apparent juxtaposition, just outside the town.   The
Professor had previously detected traces of the 10-feet
raised beach on the south end of Kerrera : now in Oban
he noted that "a fine example of the 40-feet raised
beach is exposed at the back of the United Presby-
terian Church and of Victoria Place."   The 10-feet
raised beach on the north side of the Great Western
Hotel was examined.   In short, his notes of Dun-
staffnage and of the geology round Oban are voluminous.   But he had not done with Kerrera, and before
leaving the district another day was spent in going
over the northern coast of the island, when only slight
traces of the 10-feet beach were met with.

The journey to Inverary by the Pass of Brander and
Dalmally supplied abundant material for geological
notes, as did in especial the entrance to Glen Orchy
with its hummocks of moraine.   The observations on
the route from Inverary to Lochgoilhead are on the
distribution of boulders and glacial drift, the glacial
gravel on the side of Loch Long, and on the glaciation
of the rocks on the side of Loch Goil.   Detention at
Greenock station was the occasion for exploration of a
railway-cutting through moraine matter.   The shelving
shores of Largs afforded no clear section, but two miles
inland a grass-grown cliff was noted, and beyond Fairlie
a range of inland cliffs.   The evidence at Ardrossan
was negative.   Here Mr Herbert Spencer happened to
enter their railway-carriage, continuing his journey
southwards, while Professor and Mrs Prestwich alighted
at Ayr.   With what infinite patience and thoroughness
the coast was explored on to Girvan and thence on to
Stranraer !   The quest for raised beaches was a suc-

cessful one, as shown from his numerous sections and notes. A night spent at Stranraer enabled him to examine the shores of Loch Ryan, well known from the researches of the late J. Carrick Moore. "The best sections are on the east side of the loch, which shows a range of inland cliffs." Descrying one northward, they drove back through the town, and a mile or two off the Professor had the satisfaction of finding a fine section with traces of two raised beaches.

In the same patient painstaking journey from Stranraer to Wigtown he was impressed by the evidence of widespread glaciation, and that a great ice-sheet must have covered and slid over this part of Galloway, leaving the rocks polished and striated. The route to Dumfries, from the high bleak rocky district down by a gradual descent into a pastoral country, and thence among rich corn-fields diversified by wood and stream, was of much interest.

The Sunday at Carlisle was one of grateful rest, as after morning service at the Cathedral rain interfered with any walk until the evening, when it cleared, and they were able from the bridge to have a view of the grand sweep of the river and its banks.

During the driving tour of the previous year certain pits near Loughborough had been unvisited, therefore Prestwich had planned the homeward journey so as to include the stay of a night there. Travelling by the then new portion of the Midland line through a beautiful hill country, he attributed the greenness of the grass in the Vale of Eden to the soil of the New Red Sandstone. Ingleborough Hill having been passed, and also the village of Settle, he was able to point out the position in the cliffs of the Victoria Cave, and after a run of some miles they glided through the manufacturing districts of Leeds and Sheffield on to Nottingham. Here an hour was agreeably spent in driving from point to point, the most interesting of all being the mass of New Red Sandstone on which the castle is built.

Next morning he was off betimes to the brick-pits, which were a mile or more from Loughborough, returning at mid-day laden with bags of gravel and packets of specimens, having come upon Drift. Through a bricklayer he had heard of another gravel-pit, and started off on a new quest, for which there was just time before getting into the train for Oxford.

Already the country of Lochaber and the " Parallel Roads " loomed like a beautiful vision in the dim distance. But this never-to-be-forgotten excursion was followed at once by illness—the manifest result of over-fatigue—of over-work. Happily he had reached his home, where he had the best medical care and skill.

The following letter was addressed to his friend the day after arrival in Oxford :—

J. Prestwich to J. Evans.   OXFORD, 29*th August* 1878.

MY DEAR EVANS,—We have just returned from Scotland, having visited Stirling, Glencoe, Ballachulish, Glen Spean, Glen Roy, Oban, Inverary, Largs, Ayr, Stranraer, and Wigtown, and stopt last Tuesday on our way back at Loughborough, to look again at the pits unvisited last year, and which interest me much in connection with my old heresy—a diluvial theory, and a theory which I think I shall now venture to revive before the Royal Society, if they will listen to it. As soon as I get rid of a slight attack of lumbago, which is on me to-day, we shall, I hope, go for a few days to Paris. I suppose there is no chance of your being there yet ?

Afterwards, if time allow, we shall return to S. Wales to look again at the glacial and diluvial phenomena there.

It proved to be an attack of sciatica in its acute form, and Prestwich was compelled to instruct his wife to write to Paris to explain his inability to be present at any of the International Geological or Anthropological Congresses, as notice had been given of his intention to be there. In the official reply which she received from M. Gaudry, a member of the Institute, occur these words, "*Nous aurions été heureux de voir parmi nous Mr Prestwich, qui est un de nos maîtres les plus illustres.*"

His spirit was indomitable. Only two months had elapsed since he had been struck down by illness at St David's, and yet he had planned to return there this same year to complete his unfinished work! Early in October he had, however, so far recovered that, contrary to the expectation of his two doctors, he was able to go to Eastbourne for change. One day was spent in taking stock of what interested him in the Museum; but his delight with return of health was to be out of doors, and, the season being fine, his time was devoted to drives (not without geologising) along the familiar coast. As his observations were made under (for him) luxurious conditions, this visit to Mr and Mrs Russell Scott was inspiriting and health-giving. Sections of Birling Gap cover several pages of a note-book; and as Mr Godwin-Austen chanced to be at Eastbourne at the time, the two old friends were able to go together to several sections.

J. Prestwich to J. Evans.   Oxford, 23rd October 1878.

My dear Evans,—I received the enclosed in London, but my doctor here will not hear of my geologising at present. I have written accordingly to M. Prarond asking how long the section is to remain open, to send me a small sketch, and to purchase a series of specimens.

If you, however, could run over, it would be still better.

I enclose you M. Prarond's pamphlet, which, please, return at your leisure. There are also some discoveries making near Cambridge which I should have liked to have seen, but cannot. I had just begun my visit to Eastbourne when I met Austen. How are Arthur[1] and his wife? and have they started for their foreign home? My wife joins me in kind regards to Mrs Evans, and I am sincerely yours,   ·   JOSEPH PRESTWICH.

J. Prestwich to R. A. C. Godwin-Austen.

OXFORD, *27th October* 1878.

MY DEAR AUSTEN,—Your inquiry, which I had intended to have answered from London, quite escaped me.

Your map hardly takes in the Kentish Town well. I have marked its near whereabouts with an X. It is 3 miles N. of Meux's well. I have several specimens of the Kentish Town Old Red at Shoreham, and a few here. Shall you be here and see them, or shall I send them to you?

I do not attach much guidance to the 35° dip. The folds in the strata may, as they do near Dinant and through the Ardennes, bring in the same strata over and over again. It is *north* of the great folds and disturbance of the Devonian that the Carboniferous strata come in in Belgium and Northern France, and I am inclined, therefore, to place them anywhere N. of London. The Old Red of K. T. corresponds with the Old Red of France and with some beds I have seen near Mons; that at Meux's, with beds I saw at Pernes, near Lillers.

On thinking over the section we saw at the gas-works, I believe the grey clay under the Flint Drift and over the Gault must belong to the base of Chalk or U. G. S. [Upper Greensand], . . . or the U. G. S. may be wanting.

I am, however, not satisfied, and must return to the first pit we went to, where they are digging clay. I think the elephant,

---

[1] Mr Arthur J. Evans, keeper of the Ashmolean Museum, Oxford; author of 'Through Bosnia and the Herzegovina on Foot,' 'Illyrian Letters,' &c.

&c., remains occur in the Flint Drift—as they do at Eastbourne, only there it is thicker. Still, I understand Dr Ward to say they were 17 feet deep at the Victoria Inn. I was only sorry our excursions were so short.

J. Prestwich to J. Evans.   OXFORD, 29*th November* 1878.

MY DEAR EVANS,—I am very sorry I shall not be amongst you to-morrow. I did not bear in mind when we formed an engagement (a dinner-party at home) for to-morrow, that you and Spottiswoode were the elected Grand Officers of the [Royal] Society, or I should have tried to be present, although Saturday is an awkward day—the Sunday trains being slow, few, and inconvenient. I shall be thinking of you to-morrow. Please tell Spottiswoode of my regret, and believe me to be ever sincerely yours,   J. PRESTWICH.

Rolleston gave us a paper on a Tenby Cave at the Ashmolean, and I understand that Max Müller will give a paper on "Iron"—I suppose in relation to the Bronze Period—after Christmas.

A paper published in the 'Journal of the Geological Society' in 1878, touching on the range of the Palæozoic rocks under London, was of general interest. Its title is a long one: "On the Section of Messrs Meux & Co.'s Artesian Well in the Tottenham Court Road, with Notices of the Well at Crossness and of another at Shoreham, Kent; and on the Probable Range of the Lower Greensand and Palæozoic Rocks under London."

CHAPTER X.

1878–1888.

PRESIDENT OF THE *RÉUNION EXTRAORDINAIRE* OF THE FRENCH
GEOLOGICAL SOCIETY AT BOULOGNE——TEXT-BOOK ON 'GEOLOGY'
——PRESIDENT OF THE INTERNATIONAL GEOLOGICAL CONGRESS.

AMONG public questions in which Professor Prestwich
took a keen interest was the best locality for a deep
boring in the south of England, in order to ascertain
the trend of the Coal-Measures. The following letter
refers to this subject :—

J. Prestwich to R. A. C. Godwin-Austen.

21 PARK CRESCENT, 1*st January* 1879.

MY DEAR AUSTEN,—The fossils I give on the authority of
Etheridge. I felt they were not characteristic species of the
L. Greensand; but then, as the Upper Greensand and Gault
were both traversed, there remained only one other member of
the Cretaceous series to which such fossils could be referred.

With regard to the important question of another boring, of
which you speak, I hope and trust that not only one but that
several will be made. But this is a bad time for the attempt,
on account of the general financial depression, and because so
many coal-pits have been opened within the last three or four
years, that some hardly pay to work at the present price of
coal. I do not, however, know what Major Beaumont is doing.

He was to see what could be done by some of the City people. I hope to be at the next meeting of the Society, and will hear what Ramsay and others say.

I, however, do not think with you that the line between Meux's and Kentish Town is the best place for a trial. These Devonian strata roll so much that I should give them a wide berth. Kentish Town may be the central axis, and the coal strata lie a few miles north of it. This new well of the New River Co. will throw some light on the subject. Mrs Prestwich joins me in kind regards and best wishes for the New Year to you and yours; and I am, ever sincerely yours,

JOSEPH PRESTWICH.

A final effort was made for the publication of his Water Maps, as shown in the annexed letter, but his application was unsuccessful.

J. Prestwich to the Duke of Richmond and Gordon.

OXFORD, *6th May* 1879.

MY LORD DUKE,—May I be allowed to recall to your recollection the circumstance of my having drawn up, at the wish of the other members of the Water Commission, on which I had the honour to serve under you, a hydro-geological map of the Thames Basin for the purpose of showing the extent of the permeable and impermeable strata and the position of all the principal springs. To these were added contour lines laid down by the late Sir H. James to mark the height of the springs and of the rivers in the different parts of their course. This map was accompanied by a plate of sections showing the dimensions of the underground reservoirs furnishing the springs, which, with the direct flow of the rainfall from off the impermeable strata, gives the total quantities of water available for the supply of London and other towns in the Thames Basin.

The map and sections were engraved, and, as I understood, the necessary number of copies was actually struck off, but owing to some cause, of which I believe the cost of colouring was one, they were never completed and put into circulation, with the exception of the single copy furnished to each member of the Commission, including, I presume, yourself.

As I am reminded by the action taken by the Society of Arts at the instigation of H.R.H. the Prince of Wales last year, and again about to be resumed this year, of the renewed interest in the question of a national water-supply, I should feel it a very great favour if you could obtain the sanction, on the part of the Treasury or the Stationery Office, to the publication and issue of this map and plate of sections. They were prepared with considerable care, and would, I have reason to hope, be of some public service in the inquiry now about to be instituted respecting the supply of towns and villages generally, but more especially having reference to those in the Thames valley. Much of the information they contain is not otherwise accessible, and it seems a pity that, if an available stock of uncoloured copies exists in the Stationery Office, it should not be utilised. I should trust that the extra expense of colouring would be more than covered by the sale to the public.

I have to apologise for troubling you upon a matter which would have been of the past, but for the renewal of the inquiry above alluded to, and the importance of which was so readily admitted by Lord Beaconsfield when the subject was lately brought before him. I beg to enclose a few of the papers issued by the Society to show their line of inquiry; and I am, my Lord Duke, with much respect, yours faithfully,

JOSEPH PRESTWICH,
Professor of Geology in the University of Oxford.

Although not published until 1880, his memoir " On the Origin of the Parallel Roads of Lochaber and their Bearing on other Phenomena of the Glacial Period" was read before the Royal Society in 1879. The next three letters refer to this paper.

J. Prestwich to J. Evans.   OXFORD, *2nd May* 1879.

MY DEAR EVANS,—I omitted to explain a rather important point in your objections last night. You referred to the probability of winter-ice and snow throwing down *débris* into the *water.* This I quite admit in my paper, and refer the upper 2 to 3 feet of the road to this origin; but that they were entirely formed in this way is scarcely possible, because—

1. The talus was too temporary.
2. There is no wear.
3. No cliff talus.
4. No difference in the slopes.
5. And the waved line of the roads is incompatible with shore-origin in the first place.

How could a shore-line be 10 to 12 feet above the water-level in one case, and 8 to 10 feet below it in another? If a sub-aerial talus caused the difference, the roads would suffer interruption in their level, which they don't. I must make this clear in my paper. . . . I am sincerely yours,

JOSEPH PRESTWICH.

J. Prestwich to the Same.   OXFORD, 12*th May* 1879.

MY DEAR EVANS,—With regard to what you say in your last note as to why the terraces may now be uneven—

1. If the rise in the land had not been uniform. Yes; but all the terraces would then have had the same curve, whereas *each terrace* has its own curve.
2. If some parts of the shore had slipped. There are no traces of this.
3. The difficulty of conceiving a slip on so large a scale. I see no limit except the absence of similar favourable conditions. So long as they obtain, so far would the terraces extend. The more I think of it, the more inevitable does the slip appear.

The whole mass of detritus being saturated, and being at an angle greater than the angle of repose of the detritus in a saturated condition, would at once slip when set in motion. But the outflow of water gradually lessening, the fall would be gradually checked.

Then again the detritus gradually left dry would, as it drained by degrees, acquire a higher angle of repose owing to the circumstance of the water draining from it in innumerable rills. With the loss of water the angle of repose would become greater. . . .

This morning I by chance opened the vol. of Min. Proceed. Inst. C. E., just received, vol. lv. for 1878-79. In it, at p. 339 you will find a paper on "Slips in Clay Soils." . . . A very close approach to my theoretical diagram. I really see no other explanation, and see only an inevitable consequence.

J. F. Campbell to J. Prestwich.

NIDDRY LODGE, KENSINGTON, LONDON, W., 7*th May* 1879.

MY DEAR PRESTWICH,—Somebody once quoted St Paul to a German, who said, " Oh yes, I know. He was a very clever man, Paulus, but I do not agree with Paulus." I have the greatest respect for your opinions as your former Secretary in the Coals and otherwise, but I am hopelessly convinced that the Lochaber roads are ancient sea margins.

Darwin was so convinced till somebody assured him that there are no such beaches on the side of the watershed. There are, as I have assured you, but you do not believe. I have a paper from a man about British Columbia which goes in for American submergence equal to the European submergence for which I have gone in. But my last paper will probably be my last sent to the Geological Society, and I shall die disagreeing with you, an authority, and with pundits generally who go in for Glacial periods. Thanks for the paper. Unless you ask for it I will keep it with my own on the same subject. I am, yours very truly,   J. F. CAMPBELL.

The following note from Charles Darwin, although of later date, is inserted here, being also on the subject of the Lochaber Parallel Roads :—

C. Darwin to J. Prestwich.

DOWN, BECKENHAM, KENT, 3*rd Jany.* 1880.

MY DEAR PROF. PRESTWICH,—You are perfectly right. As soon as I read Mr Jamieson's article on the Parallel Roads I gave up the ghost with more sighs and groans than on almost any other occasion in my life. Believe me, yours very sincerely,

CHARLES DARWIN.

Oxford term over, Prestwich, avoiding the gaieties
of Commemoration, set out again for St David's, his
wife (with great misgivings as to the effect of over-
fatigue) accompanying him. The first stage was
Newnham-on-Severn, the expedition from there being
to Garden Cliff—a classical spot where, although only
slight traces of Northern Drift could be seen on its
summit, the section was very fine, being New Red
Marl banded with sage-green layers. The fields on
the same level, or a little higher, showed Drift pebbles.
A portion of the drive to the Forest of Dean was
through rich apple and damson orchards.

Tenby and the choice geological specimens in its
Museum were of much interest. Wet and stormy
weather did not interfere with a visit to the caves
of Great and Little Hoyle, which Prestwich saw under
the guidance of Mr E. Laws — Black Rock quarry,
also near Tenby, and in which a fissure had yielded
mammalian remains, being explored at the same time.
He had intended to cross to Caldy Island to examine
the site where hippopotamus and other fossil bones
had been exhumed, but, to the relief of his companion,
the continuance of very rough weather and high seas
made this expedition impossible. It was only on being
assured that landing on Caldy Island could not be
effected that a visit to it was most unwillingly given up.
Good-bye was said to Mr Laws near Lamphey Station,
the travellers proceeding by Manorbeer and Pembroke
to Haverfordwest—thankful in a chilly evening to find
a close carriage waiting them from St David's.

Whitesand Bay first engaged Prestwich's attention,
and detailed sketches of it were made at different
points, including a general section which included the
Lingula Flags. On the way back to St David's he

had sight of a conglomerate of the Cambrian rocks in
position at Porth Seli, and again visited the Pebidian
and Dimetian quarries. Caerbuddy formed a separate
expedition on foot, where the grand massing of the
older rocks was very striking. The cliff-road back
was severe walking : walls had to be climbed when
they stood in the way, and the geologist on one
height found he had the best view by stepping along
the top of a stone dyke, his companion following at
his heels. A walk from Caerfai, another beautiful
rocky inlet, was accomplished with difficulty across
fields and stiles to the Nuns' Chapel and the Nuns'
Well, situated in the most picturesquely wild and
secluded position near the rugged shore. The magnificent coast scenery of St David's more than compensated for its bleak and treeless inland district.
Near the entrance to Porth Clais harbour the Professor, much to his satisfaction, traced a raised beach
which farther westward became thicker. It overhung a
cliff where the dark rocks looked awfully grand, several
of them with edges upturned like so many knives.

With every energy intent on his science, he still
found time at St David's for inspection of the cathedral.
Planted on low ground, or rather in a hollow, its site
confirmed the idea of having been chosen as a safe-
guard from the raids of the wild sea-rovers, as from
its position it might escape their notice. A cathedral
service was always a delight, and at St David's, as
elsewhere, he was not absent from morning service.
A close inspection of the venerable building and its
exquisite Norman clerestory was reserved for next
morning, when, with the appreciation of an artist, he
again lingered over the beautiful ruins of the bishop's
palace.

Taking leave of the kind hostess of the City Hotel,
they set out for Fishguard, making two or three hours'
stay at Abereiddy Bay in order to see its slate quarries.
The blackness of its beach was most curious, it being
composed of fragments of black slate, this tint being
probably due, our geologist supposed, to the mass of
decomposed organic matter from the myriads of grap-
tolites. The turned-back edges or " terminal curva-
ture" of the slate rocks, and their fractures and crump-
ling, interested him greatly.

Goodwick and Dinas Bays were diligently explored,
and, after a night at Newport, the Precelly Hills were
crossed, the two tourists proceeding to Narberth, one
of them thankful to have reached the region of railways without misadventure.

The following extract from a note-book describes his
visit to Gilfach quarries :—

25th June 1879.—From Narberth drove out to Gilfach and
called on Mr Shields, who showed me the quarries whence the
trilobites in the Tenby Museum came. It is at the foot of the
hill, near the brook in the N.-E. corner of his grounds. It is
a very remarkable section. The strata are vertical, and thin
seams of limestone alternate with slate, the limestone being more
or less decomposed into a brown earth with stony fragments and
fossils. The edges of the strata look like upright rafters worn
and soiled at the edges, and the section has all the regularity
of a wooden paling. The surfaces of the strata are at right
angles to this, and show on their surface an extraordinary pro-
fusion of trilobites (*Asaphus tyrannus* of large size and others),
most of them quite perfect and not at all distorted.

J. Prestwich to J. Evans.　　　　　SHOREHAM, 15th *August* 1879.

MY DEAR EVANS,— . . . I have not been up to town since our
return, but expect to be there next week, lumbago (of which I
have a slight attack) permitting. I had a visit from De Koninck

a short time since, but beyond that I have seen none of my geological friends. We have, however, had a house full of the Scott children, who have just left us.

Should you see Daubrée, Hébert, or other of our French friends at Sheffield, please tell them how happy I should be to see them here. . . . —Ever sincerely yours, J. PRESTWICH.

Soon after his return home, it is significant that Dr Owen Rees summarily forbade all work, and prescribed novels to be the only reading until the middle of October. Perhaps it was in conformity with this advice that a visit was paid to Paris in September. Professor and Mrs Prestwich had only been there a few days when they were recalled by the illness of Mr Charles Falconer.

The following letter has reference to this and to the discovery of palæolithic flint implements in the neighbourhood of Ightham, Kent.

J. Prestwich to J. Evans.   SHOREHAM, *near* SEVENOAKS, 10*th Oct.* 1879.

MY DEAR EVANS,—I am happy to say that Mr Falconer is somewhat better. We have therefore returned to Shoreham preparatory to packing up for Oxford. My wife, however, will go up to town every other day, and is yet unwilling to make any engagement. If, however, you will have me by myself, I would run down some day between (including) Wednesday the 23rd and Monday the 27th inst. My lectures begin on the 28th.

Weather permitting, I should like also to give a couple of days to Fisher's pit at Barrington and Skertchly's pits at Brandon, if that time would suit you. Is there any chance of our seeing you here? A Mr Harrison at Ightham has been doing some good work, and has collected numerous flint implements and one British gold coin. I am thinking of going over to see him next week.—Ever sincerely yours, J. PRESTWICH.

The illness of Charles Falconer, the best and kindest of relatives, was not a protracted one. He lingered on for a time, but passed away before the close of the year.

To turn to the life at Oxford. Prestwich's appointment had been at a fortunate time, when science was no longer looked upon with disfavour, when the heavings and heartburnings of the Tractarian movement had died away or quieted down, and when—perhaps to his own surprise—the great-souled Benjamin Jowett reigned at Balliol. Among movements indicative of broader views and a widened outlook was the establishment in the two old Universities of Halls of Residence or Colleges for Women. Cambridge had led the way with " Girton " and " Newnham," Oxford following later in 1879 (amid misgivings at such an innovation) with the foundation of " Lady Margaret Hall," which was almost immediately succeeded by that of " Somerville Hall." The result of the admirable management and irreproachable conduct of the women-students at Oxford has been, that passive resistance has gradually been withdrawn, and a generous appreciation is felt to have taken its place. From small beginnings these two Halls have become a signal success, while one or two others on a smaller scale have been found to supply an acknowledged want. It was only natural that Prestwich's sympathies should go out to " Somerville Hall," now " Somerville College," whose doors from the beginning had been thrown wide open to bid welcome among others to women students of varied race and creed, who, like their English sisters, hungered for the bread of knowledge.

Easter fell early, and a trip to the south coast was organised by Professor Prestwich, on which he was accompanied by Mr John Evans, Mr Warington Smyth, and Professor T. M'Kenny Hughes. But, alas!

no sooner had they reached Christchurch than he was
overtaken by illness. His friend Evans took him back
to town in an invalid carriage, where at Park Crescent
he was nursed with devoted care by his sisters-in-law,
until able at Oxford to rejoin his wife, who had been
detained there by her own illness.

J. Prestwich to J. Evans.   OXFORD, 27*th April.*

MY DEAR EVANS,—Dr Acland has put a stop to my going to
town this week, so, much to my regret, I shall miss both the
Geol[ogical] meeting and the Royal Society Soirée. Please express
my regrets to Spottiswoode at my absence from the latter. . . .
I am sorry also to miss Hulke's paper and the Council. . . . I
am very glad to see that Dr Rae is amongst the chosen 15.[1] . . .

A more detailed account of the position of the strata
in which a new species of Iguanodon had been discovered in a brick-pit in the Kimmeridge Clay at Cumnor Hurst, near Oxford, and named by Mr Hulke,
Iguanodon Prestwichii, was read in April to the
Geological Society. In May of the previous year
Prestwich had sent a brief announcement of this discovery, with "Notice also of a very Fossiliferous Band
of the Shotover Sands," to the 'Geological Magazine.'
Early in May the death of his brother-in-law, Mr
Russell Scott, was a real sorrow. In a letter to a frequent correspondent he expresses a deep sense of his
loss, and that Russell Scott "was one of the best and
kindest of husbands and of friends." He was the last
of his three brothers-in-law, who had all shown him
sincere affection, the close intimacy with Mr Russell
Scott having endured almost half a century. It has
often occurred to us that much of that happiness in the

---

[1] Fifteen names of candidates selected for election into the Royal Society.

circle of near relatives was due to our geologist's perfect regard for the feelings of others. He always testified respect for any one who acted up to his or her convictions, inculcating by his example the practice of that perfect " law of liberty." For instance, the Prestwich family belonged to the Church of England, to which he was strongly attached, yet the fact that one sister became a Unitarian and another a Roman Catholic never weakened the lifelong warm fraternal affection.

No summer passed without some members of the family staying at Darent-Hulme, and one of his greatest pleasures was having the little Russell Scotts. Among letters of this date we come upon a note to the eldest, then a little girl :—

To his grand-niece, Isabella Prestwich Scott. Oxford, 26th May 1880.

My dear little Isabel,—Had you known your great-grandmamma Prestwich, I am sure you would have loved her very much, for she was very good and kind to everybody, and she would, I am sure, have been very fond of you, because you are a very good little girl. When your great-grandmamma was young she had a very pretty Geneva watch, and I do not think I can do better than to give you this watch in remembrance of her, and for the love of your affecte. uncle,

JOSEPH PRESTWICH.

A visit at his country home from geological friends was ever looked forward to with eagerness. He delighted in their society, and at the end of each Long Vacation it was a frequent theme of regret that there had not been time to invite and welcome many wished-for guests. Those summer days seemed to pass like a flash. He often remarked that the glimpses of Professor and Mrs Judd, of the Rev. Professor and Mrs Wiltshire,

and of numerous other friends, were all too rare.   The
fact of Professor and Mrs H. G. Seeley being for several
years at Sevenoaks, and thus within easy reach, was
a great pleasure.   Now and then American friends
came, and had a warm welcome.   The lamented Professor Asa Gray and Mrs Gray paid a short visit,
when Dr and Mrs Carpenter were the guests to meet
them.   On another occasion Professor and Mrs Joseph
Le Conte, who were strangers, stayed a night, when,
as was remarked to our Professor, it was a case of
entertaining angels unawares.   He kept up a correspondence with the late Professor J. D. Dana; in
short, he had many honoured friends in America.

Short excursions were made during the summer of
1880 within easy distance from Darent-Hulme: one
trip being with Mr Spurrell to pits at Crayford; another, to Brasted and to railway cuttings close to
Combe Bank, the residence of his friend Mr William
Spottiswoode.   But he was intent on amassing further
evidence in support of his theory of a widespread submergence, and for that purpose set out early in August
on a tour in the Channel Islands, accompanied by his
wife and her youngest sister.   A day or two at Lyme
Regis enabled him to acquire the fine collection of
Lias fossils, presented by Mrs Philpot to the Oxford
Museum; and as Mr Etheridge chanced to be at the
same hotel, the old friends had a pleasant time
together.

Perhaps no geology was more carefully worked out
by Prestwich than that of Guernsey and Jersey.   Day
by day the circuit of the coast of Guernsey was followed, the search for raised beaches being continued
next morning from the point arrived at on the previous
evening.   The northern half of the island was first

ROBERT ETHERIDGE, F.R.S.

taken. Owing to a storm of wind and rain, an attempt to drive across at low tide to Lihou Island was unsuccessful. Prestwich, however, utilised the time by sketching a roadside quarry inland, when the driver did his best to hold an umbrella over him. After one wild gust the umbrella continued to shake in a very odd manner, when the occupants of the carriage saw that the driver was so much overcome by suppressed laughter that he could not hold it steadily. The enthusiasm that impelled the tall elderly gentleman to stand in a gale of wind and rain, drawing the rocks as if his life depended on it, must have been a puzzle. The visit to Lihou was eventually made, the raised beach on its sea-front, and not its manufactory of iodine, being the attraction.

The precipitous character of much of the Jersey coast prevented the same unbroken line of research round it. Wherever possible, a careful examination was made coastwise and inland; and evidences of raised beaches at different levels were in sufficient number to reward the explorer.

After a night at Avranches and one at Coutances, the coast round Cherbourg on to near Cape la Hague was the subject of the same quest.

The next halting-place was the familiar ground of Alum Bay, which, it might be supposed, Prestwich knew pretty well by heart, yet along coasts made up of such soft strata changes are constantly in progress, and eight pages of his note-book give new sections of Headon Hill, and also of Totlands and of Colwell Bays. The drive along the coast was by the little-used military road from Freshwater to Black Gang Chine, his interest centring in that well-known spot, classical to geologists—Brook Bay. As a matter of course, sections were sketched of it and of Brook Cliff, likewise of Brixton Cliff.

The annexed letter explains in his own words the object of his journey to the Channel Islands :—

J. Prestwich to J. Evans.   Shoreham, Sevenoaks, 24*th August* 1880.

My dear Evans,— . . . We returned from the Channel Islands and France on Saturday night last, all the better for our trip, and with evidence which satisfies me with respect to the diluvial origin of a portion of the Drift which I have so long suspected, but hesitated to bring forward without the further proof I went to the Channel Islands to obtain. I have now no longer any doubt about it; and, as I should much like to have a discussion of the subject on the occasion of Ramsay's being President, British Association, I have written to Sorby (not knowing who the Secretaries are) to ask whether I am too late, and offering to have a paper and sections ready by Monday if they can give me room on that day. I think I shall be able to show that a deluge spread over part of England and much (if not all) Europe in late Quaternary times, and that it destroyed palæolithic man (in part). It approaches, in fact, singularly near to the tradition of the Noachian deluge. This is between ourselves.

Not expecting to go to Swansea, I have kept none of the papers giving particulars of sections, &c. Could you kindly send me any such lists to-morrow ? I fear, from what you say, that you will have left Swansea before we arrive on Saturday. I would have gone to-day, but have my paper and sections to get ready, and we are a little done up by a somewhat rapid journey. . . . You have a delightful journey before you in Spain and south of France.—Hoping that you and Mrs Evans will enjoy it much, and with our united kind regards, I am, sincerely yours,   Joseph Prestwich.

The main paper I reserve for the Royal Society. I shall now merely give the chief results, so as to obtain a discussion of the subject.

Another letter of the same date with the same information gives, however, a glimpse of his home life :—

J. Prestwich to I. C. Scott.   SHOREHAM, *24th Aug.* 1880.

DEAREST ISABELLA,—We returned here on Saturday night last, after a very pleasant and successful trip to the Channel Islands and Normandy. Here we intended to remain till the October term; but having obtained in the Channel Islands the evidence I required respecting my diluvial theory, we are going to Swansea to bring it before the Brit. Assoc., of which my old friend Ramsay is Pres. this year. I think I am now in a position to show that the south of England, France, and probably the greater part of Europe, have been submerged during the early human period, and that palæolithic man was thereby destroyed (in great part). It revives in a curious way the tradition of the Noachian deluge. I have long had cause to suspect this, but hesitated even to mention so unexpected a result until I was sure of the facts I obtained in the Channel Islands. After my return from Swansea I may possibly go to the meeting of the Geol. Soc. of France at Boulogne. There is one thing I regret in all this, which is, it postpones the arrival of the many visitors we looked forward to in Aug. and Septr. I suppose Russell and Jessie are back—where are they now? Are they all well and you too? I shall look forward to see you and them about the middle of Septr. I the more hope this as I fear we shall hardly be able to visit Eastbourne. Grace sends her best love to all, and I am, dearest Isabella, your affect. brother,

JOSEPH PRESTWICH.

Professor and Mrs Prestwich with Louisa Milne reached Swansea in the middle of the meeting of the British Association, and were the guests of Sir Hussey [1] and Lady Vivian. Our geologist read two papers in Section C, both very brief, both raising new questions and pointing to important conclusions in support of his Submergence theory. The first was

[1] Afterwards Lord Vivian.

"On a Raised Beach in Rhôs Sili Bay, Gower"; the second was entitled, "On the Geological Evidence of the Temporary Submergence of the South-west of Europe during the early Human Period."

September was chiefly spent at Boulogne-sur-Mer, where the French Geological Society held a *Réunion extraordinaire.* On Prestwich's arrival he was paid the honour of being elected President for the occasion by his French brethren, and with pleasure he filled the chair at their meetings and took part in several excursions. He himself at the sitting of the 13th Sept. communicated a paper "Sur la Plage Soulèvée de Sangatte," which was published in the 'Bulletin Soc. Géol. de France' for that year.

Pleasant visits were paid in October, one being to Mr and Mrs Godwin-Austen at Shalford, and as usual a day or two at Nash Mills on the way to Oxford. The work of the term—lectures and Museum collections—proceeded as usual, but the illness at Easter had left its effects, and exposure to cold had to be avoided. Our geologist happened to be President of the Ashmolean Society; and, as it devolved on him to take the chair at its evening meetings, the following note was dictated by the most thoughtful kindness. It was from Dr Rolleston just before he went abroad on account of failing health, and the presiding at the 'Ashmolean' on behalf of his friend was almost his last appearance in public. He returned to Oxford in the summer, just in time to die in his own home.

G. Rolleston to J. Prestwich.   Oxford, 20*th* November 1880.

My dear Prestwich,— . . . I entreat you not to come out on Monday night unless Acland explicitly encourages you to do so. I will bring—

1. A skeleton of Iguana;
2. Marsh's big book on Tooth-bearing Birds;
and will talk as much or as little as the occasion may demand.
Yours very truly,　　　　　　　GEORGE ROLLESTON.

P.S.—It is the boar's head dinner at Merton to-day, but there are bores enough outside that college, so I don't ask you to go there.

A note to Mr Harrison urges a search for fossil bones as well as for implements.

J. Prestwich to B. Harrison.　　　　OXFORD, *9th Feb.* 1881.

DEAR SIR,— . . . I am glad to hear of your further finds, and to learn that you have been more successful than I was two or three years ago in finding flint implements in the high-level Gravel. The cutting we examined was the one at the station. We had not, however, much time to give to the search. The position is very analogous to the flint-bearing high-level Gravel at Salisbury, and bears some analogy to the Reculver Gravels. In neither of these places have bones been found. You will of course, however, look out for them as well as for implements when the new cuttings are made. I hope to be at Shoreham in the summer; and I am, yours truly,　　JOSEPH PRESTWICH.

Prestwich was deeply affected by the intelligence of the death of Dr Rolleston, which followed him a few days after arrival at Darent-Hulme. In writing to Mr Colchester on the 21st June, he observed, "The death of poor Rolleston has indeed been a blow and shock to us all. He was the ornament and power of the University on its science side. I have known very few men who were his equal."

Sir John Lubbock being President of the British Association at York in 1881, Professor Prestwich made a point of being present at the meeting, when he contributed three Papers—namely : " Some Observations on the Causes of Volcanic Action ; " " On the Strata between the Chillesford Beds and the Lower Boulder Clay : The Mundesley and Westleton Beds ; " and, " On the Extension into Essex, Middlesex, and other Inland Counties of the Mundesley and Westleton Beds, in Relation to the Age of certain Hill Gravels and of some of the Valleys of the South of England."

The hotel at York in which Prestwich and his wife stayed held several friends besides Mr and Mrs Evans, so that the meeting was remembered as one of much social enjoyment.

J. Prestwich to J. Evans.   SHOREHAM, 22*nd September* 1881.

MY DEAR EVANS,—I went after all to Suffolk on Tuesday, calling at Harlton for Fisher. Thanks for your maps which I found there. It is well you did not come, for we had a very wet day. We saw, however, Culford brick pit and Warren Hill. I returned last night none the worse for the trip. We found nothing except a flake on Warren Hill. I am glad, however, to see the position of things at Culford, and I think it is a case for further inquiry. The Spottiswoodes dine with us to-morrow, and possibly Lubbock. . . .

In the Chronicle of St Edward's School, Summertown, Oxford, a letter to the Warden from Professor Prestwich, dated 12th December, was inserted, giving an account of the section exposed in digging the foundations for the new buildings through the old river gravel. The interest of this section was the discovery in it of the bivalve shell *Cyrena* (or *Corbicula*) *fluminalis*, now extinct in Europe, and which is only found in the Nile and in some rivers of Central

Asia. It was the most abundant shell in the St Edward's section, of all sizes, and double, proving that it lived and flourished here at the period in question. A specimen of it had previously been discovered by Mr R. H. Tiddeman, F.G.S., of the Geological Survey, who found it " when an undergraduate in some gravel close to and not far above the level of the Cherwell on the left bank."

To the February number of the 'Geological Magazine' for the following year, a notice of the occurrence of the *Cyrena fluminalis* in the Upper Thames Valley was communicated by Prestwich. In short, his pen was never idle : it was busiest when he was precluded from joining in, or remaining out, on long geological excursions. He wrote a small but very complete Index Guide to the Geological Collections in the Oxford University Museum, which was published by the Clarendon Press in 1881.

After repeated visits to Upton and Chilton he read a paper to the Geological Society in May, " On a peculiar Bed of Angular Drift on the Lower - chalk high Plain between Upton and Chilton." This deposit was of special interest, and several members of his class were introduced to it.

As years stole on the love of our geologist for little children, and his delight in their innocent prattle, did not lessen. His appearance among them was the signal for a rush, when, with one consent, they all took possession of him. If a shy little girl choked back her sobs on being led into the room among strangers, smiles took the place of tears when the master of the house held out his arms to her. About this date one of the little Russell Scotts—not two years old—had stayed on at Darent-Hulme with her nurse, who, one day, just as dinner was over, sent down a message to say that the child was exceedingly naughty and would not go to sleep, crying herself almost into fits for her "Uncle Jovis." The moment he entered the room the sobbing ceased ; and sitting down beside her, he held the little hand in his, until in a few minutes she fell fast asleep.

There was another gathering of friends at the South-ampton meeting of the British Association in 1882, when Mr (Sir) W. Siemens, for whom Prestwich had a great regard, filled the post of President. Joint rooms were shared with Mr and Mrs Evans ; but, alas ! this pleasant time has its sad memories. The brightest of the party was Mr Evans's talented and beloved daughter Alice, and Mr William Minet, whose wife she was soon to become, was one of the number. His happiness was short-lived. Alice Minet—Alice with the beautiful mind—is enshrined in the memory of those who loved her. She had been a special favourite with the Professsor from her childhood—or rather, it should be said, from her infancy.

Two papers were read by Prestwich at Southamp-ton,—the first, "On Drift Phenomena of Hampshire: 1. Boulders, Hayling Island. 2. Chert *débris* in the Hampshire Gravel. 3. Elephant Bed, Freshwater Gate." The second was also an important memoir, being "On the Equivalents in England of the *Sables de Bracheux*, and on the Southern Limits of the Thanet Sands."

J. Prestwich to B. Harrison.   SHOREHAM, *6th Oct.* [1882].

SIR,—I am much obliged to you for the offer of the flint imple-ments from Hadlow, which I should value as having foreseen the probability of the discovery. Should you go there again or obtain permission to dig the Gravel, you will be most likely to find both flint implements and mammalian remains at or near the base of the Gravel.

An event occurred early in the following year that affected him deeply, and which threw all Oxford into mourning. This was the death of Professor Henry Smith, one of the first mathematicians of his time, who in debate swayed the destinies of the University, and was to so many the beloved friend. His sister, Eleanor E. Smith, who was considerably his senior, shared his home and watched over him in his last illness. She was quite as remarkable among women as " Henry Smith " was among his fellow-men. With masculine powers of mind she had great tenderness of heart, and was the guiding spirit of almost all the large charities in the place. Both brother and sister possessed a delightful touch of Irish humour, with not a little originality. It was a privilege to count them both as dear friends.

J. Prestwich to J. Evans.   OXFORD, *January* 1883.

MY DEAR EVANS,—We are all dreadfully upset here. We have lost our dear and valued friend Henry Smith. Our party to-morrow is consequently postponed. . . . The loss will throw a gloom over the place. I hope your visit will be postponed, and that we may have the pleasure of receiving you and Mrs Evans as we could wish. . . .

The same year Professor Prestwich sustained another great loss. Mr William Spottiswoode, who had so recently filled the office of President of the Royal Society, succumbed after a rather lingering illness. He and Mrs Spottiswoode were the kindest of neighbours, and the blank caused by his death has never been filled. Among the interesting guests whom Mr Spottiswoode delighted to gather round him at Combe Bank, none seemed equal to the host himself. In the touching tribute to his memory by Professor Huxley, in a Notice to the Royal Society, no words were ever more appropriate: "He always seemed to me the embodiment of that exquisite ideal of a true gentleman which Geoffrey Chaucer drew five hundred years ago :—

> " '. . . He lovede chyvalrye,
> Trouthe and honour, fredom and curtesie.
>
> . . . .
>
> And though that he was worthy he was wys,
> And of his port as meke as is a mayde.
> He never yit no vilonye ne sayde
> In al his lyf unto no maner wight.
> He was a verray perfight gentil knight.' "

In the mournful assemblage round his grave in Westminster Abbey, none were more conscious of the loss to the world of science, and of their own personal loss, than the two sorrowing neighbours from Darent-Hulme.

Among relics carefully kept, we come upon a little pencil note which had been passed on to our geologist from Professor Huxley at his first council meeting as President of the Royal Society, with the words—"I have just nominated you a Vice-President. Will you be so kind as to serve?" An affirmative nod was the reply.

Prestwich had for many years entertained the idea of publishing a treatise on Geology, and at last his dream was about to be realised, as in February 1884 he signed an agreement with the Clarendon Press, in which he engaged to write a text-book on Geology in two volumes. This was undertaken at a fitting time: there had been many warnings that the burden of

years would no longer allow him to share with his
fellow-geologists in active field-work; he had the experience of a long life, and the mass of unpublished
material was overwhelming.   With the prospect of
speedy publication, he at once wrote to his friend of
many years, the late Professor Jules Marcou of Cambridge, Mass.,[1] for permission to make use of his map
of the world.

OXFORD, 15th February 1884.

MY DEAR M. MARCOU,—Many thanks for the several Science
papers, [by] yourself and your son, that you have sent me, and
especially for your paper on the geology of California, recently
read. This paper interests me much, both with reference to
your account of the Glacial and Quaternary deposits, and with
reference to what you say about the age of the granite of the
Sierra Nevada. I was under the impression that the Jurassic
age of that granite had been well established, as it has been
generally received, but I see you give good reasons for ques-
tioning the conclusions. In fact, in writing on that subject a
short time since for a sort of text-book on Geology I have had
in hand for a long time past, I accepted the conclusion, and have
reasoned accordingly. This I must modify. In this work I also
am giving a *small* geological map of the world, reduced from
your large map, with a few additions, and proper acknowledgment to you. As I shall be shortly putting it into the hands
of the artist, I should be very glad to know if you are bringing
out another edition, or if you have made any additions to that
capital piece of work that I could, with your permission, avail
myself of. I hope to have the pleasure of sending you a copy
of the first vol. of my work about the end of this year.   I
get on but slowly, as I have to contend carefully against the
extreme Uniformitarian views which prevail in this country.
I trust you keep well. Mrs Prestwich desires her kind regards,
and I am, my dear Marcou, sincerely yours,

JOSEPH PRESTWICH.

---

[1] Jules Marcou, born 1824; died April 18, 1898.

To the Same.　　OXFORD, *4th April* 1884.

MY DEAR M. MARCOU,—I am very much obliged to you for your kind offer to assist in the preparation of the reduction of your map of the world. I shall value such assistance very highly. Owing to the illness of Professor Bartholomew Price[1] of the Clarendon Press, I have not been able yet to put it in hand, but hope to do so shortly. I shall follow as close as possible your grouping, but, with respect to colours, I think it will be better to conform as far as possible with the colours proposed by the International Congress. I also have another work in hand for the Royal Society—viz., a list of all the underground temperature observations from 1740 to this date, with their systematic arrangement and reduction. I am nearly at the end of it, but it has given me a good deal to do. This is preliminary to a paper on "Volcanic Action," of which I think I sent you a short abstract a year or two ago. I am very glad also to hear that you continue so well occupied, and have on hand a work on the important subject of the Primordial rocks. But, above all, I hope to see another edition of your large map.

I sincerely trust that the illness in your family, mentioned in your last note, may not be prolonged, and that Mme. Marcou and your son may soon be restored to health. And with our united kind regards, I am sincerely yours,

　　　　　　　　　　　　　　JOSEPH PRESTWICH.

His advice in regard to water - supply had already been acted upon with benefit to Oxford, and the only publication traceable from his pen during this year is a 'Letter on the Water-Supply' to the Vice-Chancellor, in the form of a pamphlet of twelve pages. In this is pointed out the steps to be taken for a supply safe from contamination,—three springs being indicated as the best for drinking purposes, which, with the growing needs of the University, it might be

---

[1] The Rev. Bartholomew Price, Sedleian Professor of Natural Philosophy; subsequently Master of Pembroke College, Oxford; born in 1818, died December 29, 1898.

desirable to utilise in the future. One of these was the spring at the foot of the chalk hills between East Hendred and Wantage, which was not likely to pass out of the remembrance of those who had shared in a particular class excursion.

The following note to his friend John Evans refers to a tour in France :—

DARENT-HULME, *2nd September.*

My thoughts were much with you last week, and greatly did I regret I could not be present in person. A few years since I should never have hesitated to draw 10 days on time. But since I have turned 70 I awake to its value and importance, and until I have finished the work I have had so many years in hand I feel reluctant to turn aside, however tempting the occasion may be. . . .

As years glided on, rarely one passed, alas! which was unmarked by the loss of a friend. In a letter, dated January 1885, addressed to Mr Evans, Prestwich records the death of Mr J. Gwyn Jeffreys, the conchologist, who had been his companion in geological excursions, and with whom he had so many interests in common. " The death of our dear old friend Jeffreys was a great shock to us. How dreadfully sudden it was! We called on Sunday, but too late to see him." Only on the previous Friday evening Mr Gwyn Jeffreys had listened to a lecture at the Royal Institution by his distinguished son-in-law, the late Professor Moseley.

Hilary term in 1885 was heavily weighted. In addition to the regular work, there was the steady preparation of 'Geology,' and no fewer than three papers in hand for the Royal Society. One of these, which represented a vast amount of research, was sent in on the 24th January. Its title was, " On Underground

X

Temperatures, with Observations on the Conductivity of Rocks, on the Thermal Effects of Saturation and Imbibition, and on a Special Source of Heat in Mountain Ranges." Two days later Joseph Prestwich received telegrams from Paris from two members of the Institute (M. Albert Gaudry being one) to inform him of his election into the Academy of Sciences as a Corresponding Member in the Section of Mineralogy. Not one of the many honours which he received was more prized, or gave greater pleasure than this. This pleasure was shared by his friends, and among the congratulatory notes, that from the late Dr W. B. Carpenter, F.R.S., may be cited :—

LONDON, *3rd February* 1885.

MY DEAR PRESTWICH,—Pray accept the hearty congratulations of Mrs Carpenter and myself on your election as Corresponding Member of the Institute of France,—an honour which you have nobly earned by your long and distinguished services to geological science. It is a great pleasure to me to see so many of my old and valued friends receiving—in one way or another—that recognition of life-long labours which carries the sense of their value to many who were previously unaware of it. And this becomes the more gratifying when — as has been preeminently the case with yourself—the work has been purely for its own sake, without the least regard to personal interest or public applause. May you long continue to set so good an example to the generation that is now rising into our places.

I was very sorry to miss seeing you when you were last in town. I had a great many committees and other engagements; and, hoping to meet you at the Royal Society, I did not take any special step to find you.—With kindest regards to Mrs Prestwich, believe me, always yours faithfully,

WILLM. B. CARPENTER.

Another letter to the Vice - Chancellor, " On the Oxford Water-Supply," was published in February:

it gave the chemical analyses of the various samples of river and other waters by leading analysts. His investigations had been again of use to the University. The next memoir, sent to the Royal Society in the end of March, was "On the Agency of Water in Volcanic Eruptions, with some Observations on the Thickness of the Earth's Crust from a Geological Point of View, and on the Primary Cause of Volcanic Action." This was published in 1886. The hypothesis put forward was an interesting one to geologists.

A stay at Weston-super-Mare early in April was refreshing—its main purpose being the acquisition of material, in the study of raised beaches, for his projected Submergence paper. But the weather after a fortnight became unseasonably cold, and the sojourn there was not prolonged.

The origin or segregation of flint was a subject to which he gave much thought; but the experiments which he was carrying on in the Oxford Museum, in a series of jars of fresh and of sea water, were extended over too short a term of years to yield definite or satisfactory results. These experiments were begun in 1882, with pure precipitated chalk dissolved in dilute hydrochloric acid, and the results are recorded at intervals in a book in his handwriting. Pieces of sponge, or small cup-sponges, empty shells and fragments of wood, &c., had been added to the contents of the jars, half of which contained sea-water, the other half fresh-water. An entry dated 24th June 1884 registers "Sponge rendered brittle—requires examination for silica." In the same MS. book of notes we find a series of experiments registered on "Aylesford sand with Woolwich flint pebble moistened with a solution of soluble silica."

J. Prestwich to J. Evans.   WESTON-SUPER-MARE, *9th April* 1885.

I have sent in my Volcano paper to the Royal Society. It
has been a heavy piece of work, having been in hand some time
before the York meeting; but I did not care to finish it until
I had completed my paper on Underground Temperatures, so as
to have a surer rate of increase of temperature with depth. . . .
I could be up at its reading any day this month, but the 16th or
the 23rd would suit me best. . . .

The third paper was sent in early in June, and was
entitled "Regional Metamorphism." The amount of
work accomplished during this first half of 1885 was
enormous. Happily, several years before, Sir Henry
Acland had peremptorily limited his dining out to
twice a - week, so that five out of the seven were
restful evenings at home, which he preferred to all
others. But the passing of these Memoirs through
the press—more especially the Tables of Underground
Temperatures—was arduous, added to all the duties
of his chair—and those were very faithfully fulfilled.

Allusion is made in the following letter to the dis-
coveries of implements on the Chalk plateau. The
"friends in Kent" working in this direction were Mr
Harrison at Ightham, Mr De Barri Crawshay in the
Sevenoaks district, and Mr A. Montgomerie Bell at
Limpsfield.

J. Prestwich to J. Evans.   OXFORD, *15th June* 1885.

You will see by the enclosed that our friends in Kent are
working successfully. I hope we shall be able to look them
up this summer. We leave to-morrow for Park Crescent, and
on Friday or Saturday proceed to Shoreham. I am glad to say
that two days ago I despatched the proofs of my two Royal
Society papers. I have now only the reset tables of the Underground Temperatures to see to, and can then devote myself

uninterruptedly to Vol. II., nearly half of which is now in type. I am well and about again now, but fear my hand-writing is not improving, to judge from what our friend M. Cornet tells me this morning : "Trois jours m'ont été nécessaire pour lire et bien comprendre votre lettre du 9me à cause de l'imperfection de l'écriture." . . .

The excursions during this long vacation were very numerous ; yet they were all confined to those within the day from Darent-Hulme to the ground where flint implements had been found, Mr Harrison frequently joining. He accompanied Professor Prestwich to the Powder Mills, near Green Street Green, to which reference is made in the letter of 17th November.

J. Prestwich to B. Harrison.　　　　DARENT-HULME, *5th August* 1885.

DEAR SIR,—I suppose you refer to Vol. IV. of the Geological Mem. by Mr Whitaker. I shall have pleasure in lending it to you. I have recently discovered two new terraces of river drift at 250 and 350 feet in this valley. They may be worth a search on your part. Both are close to Eynsford. I could show you the exact spot on a map. Have you been again to Green Street Green ? and have you got more of the curious siliceous rock of which you left me a specimen ? I must go there some day. Please give me the exact name of house or farm where the well is.

To the Same.　　　　　　OXFORD, *17th November* 1885.

DEAR SIR,—I wrote to Messrs Isler & Co. for a section of the well at the Powder Mills. This they sent me, but as it seemed to me insufficient, I wrote for further particulars and specimens. The rock they sent was the ordinary green-coated flint from the top of the chalk. I then sent a specimen of the siliceous stone, and I enclose their reply received this morning.

I fear there has been some mistake. We saw none of the rock at the Mills, and we got no confirmation of its having been found there.

I fear the rock may have been carted to the spot to mend the road.   Vessels are constantly arriving in the Thames in ballast, which often comes in usefully for road-mending.   It is common to find rocks from China and Japan on the London roads.   When you are next at Green Street Green can you make some inquiries about it of roadmakers or others ? . . .

An estimate of his paper on " Regional Metamorphism " is given by an eminent American geologist in the following letter :—

Prof. Joseph le Conte to J. Prestwich.

BERKELEY, CAL., 18*th November* 1885.

MY DEAR SIR,—I need not tell you how deeply interested I have been in your paper on metamorphism.   I had already read au abstract of it in ' Nature' for July 3rd, but am very glad to have a fuller copy.   I have long believed that crushing is an important source of the heat of metamorphism, and have spoken of it in that connection in my 'Elements of Geology,' under Metamorphic Rocks and under Volcanos and the source of their heat. But I have never, I believe, given it sufficient prominence, and I am glad that you have now done [so], especially that you have brought forward positive evidence in the case of the St Gothard Tunnel.

I have also noted with great interest your views of the sources of volcanic water and of volcanic force.   I have no doubt that the violent explosions of many volcanos are due to superficial water, but even in the quietest eruptions, as in Hawaiian volcanos, there seems to be considerable water in the lavas.   Let me draw your attention without comment to Dutton's memoir on the Hawaiian Islands, Fourth Annual Report of United States Geological Survey (the page I cannot now refer to), where he gives reason for thinking that water is intimately incorporated with igneous magmas, not as vapour vesicles but as a sort of hydrate, and does not separate in vesicles until the lava is about to solidify.   So that lava after running 40 miles, and therefore after many days' exposure to atmospheric pressure only, still solidifies as a light sponge: the separation may be compared to the spitting of silver in the act of solidification.

I was in camp last summer two months with Captain Dutton on the great lava field of Northern California and Oregon. These immense lava floods are a strong confirmation of your views. These surely have never been erupted by elastic force of vapour, but have been squeezed out.

The rocks of this coast are puzzling to the last degree. The gradations from unchanged sediments through various degrees of metamorphism to Plutonics is in many places complete and over wide areas. Thanking you again for your pamphlet, and hoping soon to reciprocate, I remain, yours faithfully,

JOSEPH LE CONTE.

Although Professor Prestwich was not present in person at the next Annual Meeting of the Geological Society, his thoughts were with his brother geologists. A note addressed to his friend Evans is dated 22nd February 1886.

I am glad to hear that the Anniversary Meeting went off so well. Your joke was excellent. It would have taken me a week to elaborate a joke on so solemn a subject as the foliation of schists. . . .

It was a trial to him to have been absent. Mr Evans was in the habit of occasionally announcing geological facts to his friend Prestwich in rhyme, especially when the latter was a prisoner to the house from indisposition, and the promotion at this Anniversary Meeting of their common friend Professor Judd, F.R.S., from the post of Secretary to that of President, was told in the following lines :—

" The plant will follow on the seed ;
The blossom follows on the bud :
The Secretary—good at need—
Blossoms as President in Judd."

A couple of notes to his little grand - niece show how perfectly he understood what would interest and please children, and how completely he could withdraw his thoughts from "underground temperatures," "volcanoes," and "regional metamorphism" :—

OXFORD, *3rd May* 1886.

MY DEAR LITTLE GRACIE,—I am very glad to see that you can write and spell so well. It is very nice for you all to have gardens of your own. When I go to Shoreham I must see that some flowers are sown in your garden there. When will you come and see your gardens? Will you come when the strawberries are ripe or when the gooseberries are ripe—there will be lots of them,—or will you come later when the pears and apples are ripe or when the peaches and grapes are ripe? We have no tame rabbits at Shoreham, but we have lots of wild ones, and you may have all you can catch. So I hope you will come as soon as papa and mamma can spare you, and bring brothers and sisters with you. Aunt Grace sends her love, and I am, gentle little Gracie, your affectionate uncle,

JOSEPH PRESTWICH.

A little before this date, 'Geology, Chemical and Physical,' Vol. I., had appeared. The following note from the great statesman over whom, to the grief of his country, the grave has so recently closed, was the beginning, through Sir Henry Acland, of the interchange of occasional letters :—

W. E. Gladstone to J. Prestwich.

HAWARDEN CASTLE, CHESTER, *6th June* 1886.

DEAR SIR,—I am exceedingly obliged by the gift of your volume, and I earnestly hope ere long to profit much by an examination of it. Sir Henry Acland has recently bestowed upon me more than one kindness, and none of them was more useful or more appreciated than the acquaintance he enabled me, by your permission, to make with a portion of your researches. I remain, dear sir, faithfully yours,   W. E. GLADSTONE.

Mr Evans, when on a visit to Christchurch (14th June 1886), was unsuccessful in finding flint implements on the coast, and was compelled to buy. A rhyme ended a letter to his invalid friend :—

The annexed receipt may be of use to you. I hope you are better. With kindest regards, yours sincerely, JOHN EVANS.

HOW TO OBTAIN FLINT IMPLEMENTS AT HORDLE.

"Geologists who go to Hordle,
   Hoping flint implements to find,
Need now no longer walk and dawdle,
   Searching the shore in rain and wind.

A surer way that saves all travel,
   And all fatigue to leg or eye,
And gets flint hatchets from the gravel,
   Just like those sought for, is—to buy!"

An excursion about this date with his usual companion was made to the Isle of Sheppey, its main object being the inspection of the London Clay cliffs at Warden Point and a search at their base for fossils. The drive from Sheerness by Minster, and keeping as near as possible to the range of east coast cliffs, was a relief in that sultry summer day after the close atmosphere of railway stations. The plan had been to put up at Warden and scramble over the cliff down to the beach at Warden Point. But before reaching it, our Professor descried something amiss with the landscape. He knew the ground so well that there could be no mistake in his bearings. Entering a cottage, an inquiry was made as to what had become of the customhouse "look-out," and of the churchyard, in the corner of which the little building stood, and all of which he remembered as being situated in the rear of the cottage.

"Gone, sir," was the reply. "They are all gone."

The woman then explained that some years before, during a dark night, they had all without any warning slipped down into the sea. Previous to this occurrence a field had intervened between the churchyard and the edge of the cliff, but owing to the encroachments of the sea the field disappeared, also the churchyard with its contents, and the church was then pulled down, being considered unsafe. As we looked down a height of nearly 165 feet, a talus stretching out at the base was to be seen on the beach, the fallen fragments composed of soil, of London Clay, and of what else we dared not conjecture. Our geologist, however, was not deterred from descending some 20 or 30 feet, so as to examine the recently exposed section. There was no danger of falling down that awful clay cliff, but the sun which beat upon it was sickening, and his companion, who remained helpless on the summit, made an inward resolution—as had been often made before—never to encourage excursions on cliffs beyond the reach of aid,—of a strong arm to help in case of need.

Professor Lapworth, in an appreciative letter acknowledging the first volume of 'Geology,' also remarks :—

C. Lapworth to J. Prestwich.

MASON COLLEGE, BIRMINGHAM, *Oct.* 21, 1886.

DEAR PROFESSOR PRESTWICH,— . . . I have read, too, your paper on "Underground Temperatures," with wonder and admiration at the great mass of material you have collected upon the subject, and the clear and convincing way in which it is laid before the reader. This is certain to be one of your future classic papers of reference.

In the matter of the "agency of water in volcanic eruptions," I see at present little chance of escape from your conclusions. I read the paper on the subject with exceeding pleasure, as your conclusions appear to me so practically identical with what I have been, broadly speaking, teaching my students for years—at any rate as regards causes; the *modus operandi* I have never seen so clearly suggested as in your paper. That the earth-skin or super-crust crushed up in mountain ranges is comparatively thin, has always seemed to be demonstrated by the facts of geology, and that the explosions and volcanic actions must be due to the downward passage (or lateral) of surface (or sea) waters almost equally clear. I am, sincerely yours,

CHARLES LAPWORTH.

Although Sir Henry Acland had limited dining out to twice a week, the fatigue of Oxford society, which Prestwich so dearly enjoyed, became more than he felt able for. There were besides so many other social functions—breakfasts sometimes began the day, and there seemed to be always luncheon engagements. There were the pleasant parties at Balliol (and what Oxford parties were not pleasant?), when Jowett made the most delightful of hosts. Two little notes in his clear microscopic writing are before us, each giving an invitation for either of two evenings—one to meet Mr and Mrs William Spottiswoode, the other to meet Browning, &c. Alas! host and guests have all passed away.

It is notable that Prestwich, who was so quiet in general society, should have exercised to such a degree the magnetic power of attraction. Was it the instinct of brotherliness which was so strong within him that made itself felt, or was it the charm of his simple and sincere manner acting as a loadstone? If not a talker, he was always an interested and intent listener, and the flash of merriment that lit up his features when a good story was told testified to his thorough appreciation of it. It seemed to one who knew him intimately that prolonged conversation, even on his own special subjects, was a fatigue : an over-active brain taxed his energies, so that at the end of the ever arduous day he was capable of enjoying evening society only in a restful fashion. Yet his personality was so marked that in no crowd, in no company, could Joseph Prestwich pass unnoticed.

Residence in Oxford had been such a happy time that year after year the decision as to his resignation of the Professorship had been postponed, so reluctant was he to sever his connection with the University and leave the Oxford friends. In taking the appointment he had hoped to hold it for a few years—perhaps as many as five,—but the fascination of the Old University held him, and the five years had run on to thirteen. On the score of years alone, for he was now 74, he felt that the time had arrived for him to take the step, and as he thought of his unpublished notes, remarked with sadness, "There is so much to be done and so little time to do it." In sending in his resignation he expressed a hope to be allowed to retain the Professorship until the end of the year, and that he might have the work of the last term done by deputy, so that Vol. II. of his ' Geology ' should be published while he was still Professor. His wishes were met in the kindest way, and he pressed forward with his book, resolving to stay during the long vacation in order to finish it, and then to retire to his dear home among the hills of Kent. (Mr W. W. Watts, M.A., acted for a time as Deputy-Professor after Prestwich had retired.)

J. Prestwich to J. Evans.   OXFORD, 31*st March* 1887.

MY DEAR EVANS,—Many thanks for your letter. I am glad you agree with me in the step I have taken. I think also it is

better for a younger man with more push and with the newer
petrological ideas to take the chair, especially as geology is now
to take its place amongst the subjects for examinations in
Science Honours. Although we shall miss you in Oxford I hope
we shall see more of you in London. . . . I had a note a few
days since from Mr F. Latchmore of Hitchin, telling me he had
found bones of birds in the brick-pit. This is very interesting.
He sent me spec[imens], which I shall take to London. I also
had a note from Mr Prigg of Bury, telling me he had found implements at *all* levels as in Kent.

In writing the last (Glacial) chapter of Vol. II., I became more
convinced than ever of the mistake of Croll, and of the risk of
his lead to geologists. On the questions of geological or rather
glacial time I am becoming more heretical than ever. I do not
like to broach it abruptly in Vol. II., so shall probably send a
short paper to the Geological Society to ventilate the subject
beforehand. I am satisfied that if, instead of Croll's 1000, we
were to take 100, we should be nearer the mark, if not beyond
it. Still Croll's is a most attractive and valuable work. . . .

The paper alluded to was a very important memoir
read in May to the Geological Society, its title being
"Considerations on the Date, Duration, and Conditions
of the Glacial Period, with Reference to the Antiquity
of Man." The author dwelt on the light thrown on the
duration of the Glacial Period by recent observations
on the movements of Greenland ice ; and the reading of
this paper gave rise to an animated discussion. His
views are expressed in the following letter to the friend
who shared his thoughts :—

J. Prestwich to J. Evans.　　　　　　OXFORD, 13*th May* 1887.

I don't know whether you remember when we were working
at the Somme Valley that my first impressions were that the St
Acheul beds were of glacial times, and that the excavation of
the valley was the work of post-glacial times. In working up

the last chapter of Vol. II., I had occasion to go over the whole question again, with the advantage of some remarkable Greenland observations by the Danes, and all my old heresies revived so strongly that I then and there converted a chapter into a paper, which I have just sent to the Geological Society. I feel more than ever that it is impossible to work on Uniformitarian lines. They cramp and narrow us, and inevitably lead to wrong conclusions. It is true that they are the right and correct basis to work upon, but the conditions of past times were so different from those of the present day that it is impossible to reason correctly upon them. Let them be taken as the *known* quantity, but the *unknown* quantities must just as surely be taken into account if we are to arrive at a just conclusion. Of course we can only do this in most cases approximately. After another careful overhaul I have made up my mind on the matter, and cannot find that there are grounds for extending the Glacial Period beyond 15,000 to 20,000 years, and the post-glacial period from 8,000 to 10,000 or 12,000, while I would carry man back to pre-glacial or rather mid-glacial times. The evidence in the Eastern counties and in the caves of Wales and the North, though not strong enough in any single instance, furnishes as a whole good corroborative testimony. My paper is not a long one, but will serve to put my views on record, and to ventilate the subject. It will of course meet with much opposition, as Croll's views, which are so attractive, have been so generally accepted of late. I shall be glad also to see if I should have occasion to change or modify my views, and to do that before I publish Vol. II.

We are expecting the Lubbocks to-morrow to stay with us over Sunday. He is to lecture on Savages. My wife joins me in kindest regards to Mrs Evans. . . .

In another note to Mr Evans, the following passage occurs :—

OXFORD, *May* 19*th* [1887].

The first thing, however, is, I think, to get rid of a rigid theory which fixes dates and consequences not in accordance with geological facts, and to find some possible clue to the duration of the glacial period. This has been the main object of my paper.

To the Same.   OXFORD, 27*th May*.

The main point of my paper was, I think, missed the other night. It was not the question whether long or short time was required for the Pleistocene phenomena, but whether the now known ice-conditions of Greenland did not warrant some material change from the Alpine data of Croll and others. With our united kind regards, I am, sincerely yours,

JOSEPH PRESTWICH.

J. Prestwich to Professor Jules Marcou.   OXFORD, 15*th Sept.* 1887.

MY DEAR MARCOU,—In reply to your inquiry, I am glad to say I can report favourably of myself as to health. It is on the score of years that I resign the Professorship here and retire to my old home at Shoreham, where I shall be more at leisure to work up the notes of the past years relating to the Quaternary and Glacial Period.

I should have taken this step a year or two ago, but that I wished to finish Vol. II. of my 'Geology' before I left. This I hope to do by the end of the year, until which time I hold the chair and have my work done by deputy. I had no conception the work would have taken so long. It is now more than 10 years since I undertook it.

The Taconic question much perplexed me, not knowing the ground. I have devoted a short space to it, and I hope I have given a fair *résumé*. You will see. It was very pleasant to have news of you, though I wish you could have given a better report of yourself. I am glad, however, to find you are busy with good geological work, and do hope you will be present with us next year to take part in the Geological Congress. I have just sent you a short paper on the Glacial question, which will, I expect, provoke discussion. Mrs Prestwich desires her kind regards, and I am, sincerely yours,   JOSEPH PRESTWICH.

The final move from Oxford was made in the end of September, Professor I. Bayley Balfour,[1] F.R.S.,

---

[1] Then Professor of Botany in Oxford, now Professor of Botany in the University of Edinburgh, eminent for his knowledge of the fossil flora of successive epochs.

having most kindly undertaken to give the Geological Class lectures for the last term of the year.

J. Prestwich to Rev. O. Fisher.   OXFORD, 26*th Novbr.* 1887.

MY DEAR FISHER,—Thanks for the paper announcing your conversion to Inter-Glacial Man. With such a lead it is quite possible I may follow, and I am the more anxious to see the ground. Such a discovery will throw quite a new light on the subject. I see also by the Brit. Assoc. report that Skertchly makes out a good case, inasmuch as the overlie of the Boulder Clay in the several sections he gives is sufficient and distinct. Still I reserve my opinion till I see the ground, although I am quite prepared to accept the conclusion.[1]

In a letter to Mr Evans, dated 2nd December, he remarks :—

Owing to a delay with the map, Vol. II. will, I regret to say, not be out till middle of January. . . . I have had some very kind letters from Judd, Bonney, Blanford, and Topley, asking me to accept the Presidency of the Geological Congress. I would much rather work in quiet as an ordinary member, and others would, I know, make much better Presidents. I don't like to decline, yet don't care to accept. So I ask my old friend's and counsellor's advice. . . .

The honourable post so kindly urged upon Prestwich was accepted, and, as it proved, the meeting of the International Geological Congress in London in the following September was a signal success.

The close occupation of seeing the proofs of Vol. II. of 'Geology' through the press did not prevent the production of another important paper to the Geological Society, which was read on 21st December and pub-

---

[1] The evidence still wanted is the finding of an undoubted palæolithic implement in the brick-earth or other deposit, beneath an undisturbed mass of the chalky Boulder Clay ; and later observations render such a discovery improbable.

lished early in the following year, entitled, "Further Observations on the Correlation of the Eocene Strata in England, Belgium, and the North of France."

The publication in January 1888 of Vol. II. of 'Geology' was a great satisfaction and relief, as it set its author free to turn to his notes and collections of rocks, fossils, and worked flints. His interest in Mr Harrison's discoveries of rude flint implements on the high plateaus of the surrounding Kentish hills was not less keen, but the season rendered it impossible for him to explore at the time their different localities. Several winter months were spent at 21 Park Crescent with his sisters-in-law, where note-books were studied and digested, and weighty papers planned.

C. Pritchard [1] *to J. Prestwich.*

UNIVERSITY OBSERVATORY, OXFORD, 22*nd Febry*. 1888.

MY DEAR PRESTWICH,—Your grand vol. arrived here at 9 A.M., and by 10.10 was cut open to the very Index.

It creates many thoughts.

1st. Thanks for the kind remembrance, carrying me back many days amid old reminiscences of some half century wellnigh. How heartily I congratulate you on finishing the work of your life as you have done.

I congratulate you also on the fair fame and pleasant memory you leave behind you here. You may leave this earth thankful for your career as one who has left the world (or will have left) wiser for your work therein. God be thanked, say I, for you.

I am glad to see that our Press has done itself justice, and has been liberal in the getting up of your great work.

How many old faces I recognised in the plates and woodcuts —many of them handled, too, by me, but not studied as I could desire.

I delight to find you put a reasonable interpretation on the

---

[1] Rev. Charles Pritchard, F.R.S., Savilian Professor of Astronomy at Oxford; born Feb. 29, 1808; died May 28, 1893.

forces of nature—some of them surely were once *more intense* than now. But that you know.

The next generation of geologists may have something to say about meteoric formations, and the consequence of the conflict of the brickbats—if they ever did collide.

. . . You and Phillips have left the memories of *pleasant* ways of act and thought, and I hope your successor will clothe his outward being in your mantles. I am still working on: it may be that I may be permitted to leave a record of work behind me that may endure among the stars.

I hope you and your wife are in the enjoyment of pleasant rest: rest you have earned. Again sending you my hearty thanks for these two noble books—adornment and instruction and full of old memories—I am, yours gratefully,

C. PRITCHARD.

Pray assure your wife that we often think and speak of her—how kindly I need not say.   C. P.

The following acknowledgment of the second volume of 'Geology,' from Professor H. Alleyne Nicholson,[1] is expressed in the warmest terms :—

H. Alleyne Nicholson to J. Prestwich.

UNIVERSITY, ABERDEEN, *Feb.* 23, 1888.

DEAR PROFESSOR PRESTWICH,—Pray accept my warmest thanks for the present of Vol. II. of your admirable treatise on Geology. I shall value it on the one hand as a personal gift, and on the other hand for its great intrinsic value. I have studied the first volume of your great work with the utmost interest and profit. I do not know of any treatise, in any language, in which there is to be found such a masterly exposition of such vital geological questions as internal temperature, vulcanicity, mountain-making, and the like. I do not doubt that I shall derive at least equal profit from the second volume. With renewed thanks and kind regards, I am, yours very sincerely,

H. ALLEYNE NICHOLSON.

----

[1] H. A. Nicholson, born Sept. 11, 1844 ; died Jan. 19, 1899.

W. Colchester to J. Prestwich.

BURWELL, CAMBRIDGE, 25*th Feb.* 1888.

MY DEAR PRESTWICH,—On my return home last evening I found your very acceptable and most *generous present* of the second volume of your 'Geology.' I value it as the lifelong labour of a lifelong friend. As I turned over its pages last evening, how many pleasing recollections flashed on the memory! Thank you most heartily. The whole get-up of the work is most elaborate, map and all. How delighted Mrs Prestwich must be that you have been able to embody your knowledge in this publication without injury to your health! I was afraid at one time the work would prove beyond your strength. I begin to find the strain of threescore and fifteen years tells; but I am wonderfully well, and set this east wind at defiance— and we get it here in its bleakest form. . . .

When the crows have picked up the dirt, I have planned many a raid into the flint-knife pits. How I should like to have the company of you and Mrs Prestwich and Evans to do the district! I am settled here now for the rest of my life, and there is a most serene-looking churchyard at the other end of the vicarage. Before that time comes I should like to see you and Mrs Prestwich here. Alas! there is no Crag, but we have other interesting deposits. With kindest regards to you all and Mrs Prestwich, I remain, dear Prestwich, your obliged and faithful friend,   W. COLCHESTER.

Our village consists of a great number of peasant proprietors, many of whom inherit their land with heavy charges upon it, and, now that all agricultural produce is so reduced in value, their lot does not favourably impress me with the three acres and a cow system.

I stumbled the other day on the grave at Wicken of the Protector's widow — buried there on her return from banishment! My wife is a Cromwell, and we had plenty of food for meditation on the mutability of human affairs by that grave.

Prestwich's name was announced in the list of recipients of the Hon. D.C.L. degree to be conferred at Oxford during the Encænia. The following letter, which explains the cause of his absence then, was addressed to Mrs Prestwich by their dear and honoured friend, the late Dr Liddell, then Dean of Christ Church College.

OXFORD, 24th *June* 1888.

DEAR MRS PRESTWICH,—Sir H. Acland sent me the enclosed to be delivered to your good husband on the occasion of his honorary degree. I tore it open without thinking, and have neglected to send it on. But you, at all events, will be glad to read what our friend says of one whom he truly loves and honours, and whom to have brought into connection with the University I reckon not the least honour of my Vice-Chancellorship. I deeply regret that his state of health prevents his accepting in person the last acknowledgment of his services which it was in our power to give.

Remember me to him most kindly, and believe me to be, ever yours most sincerely,   H. G. LIDDELL.

Mrs Liddell joins in all affectionate remembrances to him and yourself.

J. Prestwich to Professor Jules Marcou.

DARENT-HULME, 28th *July* 1888.

MY DEAR PROF. MARCOU,—Many thanks for your kind letter and suggestion respecting the map, &c., of which I shall most gladly avail myself in case of a second edition. I did not go into the historical part of the glacial theory, as the subject was too large for the space at my command. The small scale of the Glacial map renders the colours somewhat indistinct, but I will see to the points you name.

I am also very much obliged to you for two papers. The one on American Geological Classification is of particular interest and use to me. The Classification of the Cambrian and Silurian rocks will be one of the main subjects for discussion at the Congress, and will no doubt involve a full discussion of the Taconic rocks. I do not think that the English geologists have formed any foregone conclusion about them. They seem to me to require a special local knowledge. It will be a very large meeting: above 400 names are now down. I am only very sorry that you cannot be present. I was prevented by a sharp attack of illness from going to Oxford to receive my D.C.L. degree; but I am getting about again now, though not yet up to much. Mrs Prestwich desires her kind regards; and trusting you are fairly well, I am, dear Professor, sincerely yours,

JOSEPH PRESTWICH.

Minute instructions had been sent to Mr Harrison to examine, among other localities, the Tertiary pebble-beds at Crowslands, and the Drift clays at Terry's Lodge, on the road between St Clere and the Maidstone high road. Late in August Mr Harrison was requested to meet him at Wrotham station, whence they were to drive to Malling, and to the pits at Leybourne mentioned by Mr Topley, and "possibly to Trotters-cliff." The ground in the neighbourhood, although already familiar, was again patiently explored with at least a twofold object—namely, for the occurrence of Drift and of palæolithic plateau implements. Here it may be observed that in the many journeys to London, as often as practicable, our Professor drove to a different station from which to travel, and not to that nearest home, so as to have a view of the ground that led to it. During one summer Westerham and its heights (some twelve miles distant) were visited five times—not to speak of repeated journeys there in other years.

Now, however, a sudden stop was put to both in-door and outdoor geology by the arrival of a telegram with the tidings of the death of his sister Kate (Mrs Thurburn). During their long life there never had been a cloud between them. His affectionate heart was wrung by this sorrow, and at once he set off with his wife to Brighton, there to look on the face of his dear sister for the last time. For several days he had no heart for work, and it was well that the nearness of the date of the International Geological Congress compelled him to make the necessary preparations.

The idea of an International Geological Congress had originated in America. The first had been held in Paris in 1878, the second at Bologna in 1881, and the third in Berlin in 1885; the fourth congress met in London in the rooms of the London University at Burlington House, on the evening of the 17th September 1888, when Professor Prestwich delivered the Presidential Address in French. An old geologist in congratulating him remarked that he spoke much better in French than in English! The Address treated of the unification of geological terms over the world, and of an agreement as to colours used in maps. It indicated the questions to be considered—"the classification of the Cambrian and Silurian formations, the relations between the Carboniferous and the Permian, between the Rhætic and the Jurassic, and between the Tertiary and the Quaternary. Among the new questions which would be brought before the London Congress was, above all, the fundamental question of crystalline schists, &c., . . ." The assemblage was larger than that of any of the three preceding congresses: upwards of 300 members attended in London, representing twenty-one different countries—from Norway, from Peru and Mexico, and even from the Argentine Republic—in short, from all quarters of the globe. The personal intercourse with many of the distinguished American geologists present, was to the President ever a most happy reminiscence. Amongst them were Professors Marsh from Yale College and Claypole from Akron, Professors G. K. Gilbert and C. D. Walcott from Washington, G. H. Williams from Baltimore, H. S. Williams from Ithaca, N.Y.,—but it seems invidious to instance names.

Among French members were M. Gaudry, the old and valued friend; Professors de Lapparent, C. Barrois, Gosselet, all men of world-wide fame; and, among others, Prince Roland Bonaparte and the Marquis de Saporta. Italy's list was headed by Professor Capellini, Rector of Bologna University, and the intimate friend of thirty years' standing. Germany sent a number of notable members, including such names as Von Richthofen, Beyrich, Zirkel, and Von Zittel. Among geologists from Austria-Hungary were such well-known names as Stur, Neumayr, and Szabo; Belgium contributed a group of attached fellow-workers — Mourlon, Dewalque, Renard, Rutot, Van den Broeck, &c.; whilst Holland also sent members. Among thirteen from Russia were the distinguished names of Pavlow and Nikitin. The two Professors Stefanescu represented Roumania; members from Spain were present, and Colonel Delgado and Señor Choffat from Portugal. Dr Otto Torell travelled from Sweden, and there was a muster of brother-geologists from Switzerland, among them Professors Renevier, Heim, and Mayer-Eymer. Steenstrup represented Denmark; Bulgaria also sent its member. Geologists from India, Canada, Australia, and New Zealand swelled the assemblage, all of them men who had made their mark, such as Oldham, Sterry Hunt, &c. It is hardly necessary to add that all parts of Great Britain and Ireland contributed representatives. The two General Secretaries were the lamented friend Mr J. W. Hulke, F.R.S., and Mr W. Topley, F.R.S., another friend who has likewise joined the majority, while the energetic Treasurer was Mr F. W. Rudler, F.G.S. Objects of great interest received from geologists all over Europe, mainly illustrative of questions to be discussed before the Congress, were exhibited, the President sending his collection of Coalbrookdale fossils; and also a series of types of flint implements from the River Drifts of France and England. The Organising Committee had done its work very efficiently : there were many voluntary assistants, so that with such an assemblage and the indefatigable exertions of the secretaries, the Congress could scarcely have failed to be a brilliant success. The sun, which does not always show in London, shone out during the daily sittings; and it was only when bands of the members headed by active British geologists were scattered in different parts of the country — in the Isle of Wight, North Wales, Yorkshire, &c.—that the weather broke, and gave proof to foreigners of the vicissitudes of an English climate.

The pleasure of meeting so many fellow - workers at the Congress in London had been very great, and instead of returning to Darent - Hulme fagged and tired, Professor Prestwich found himself actually refreshed and invigorated. He came home with renewed zest for field work, forgetful that he bore the burden of years. Owing, however, to the lateness of the season, further explorations were peremptorily forbidden, and we find numerous notes to Mr Harrison, his enthusiastic *aide*, with detailed instructions for him to examine certain localities, and to observe special points in his walks.

Before the close of the year Prestwich received the degree of Hon. D.C.L. in Convocation at Oxford, when he and his wife were the guests of their valued friends Professor and Mrs Bartholomew Price. As was so often the case, Nash Mills was their hospitable half - way house, where a couple of days were spent prior to that very gratifying visit to Oxford.

CHAPTER XI.

1888–1895.

PLATEAU IMPLEMENTS OF KENT — LETTERS ON POST - GLACIAL SUBMERGENCE — CORRESPONDING MEMBER OF THE ROYAL ACADEMY OF THE LINCEI — VICE - PRESIDENT OF THE GEOLOGICAL SOCIETY OF FRANCE.

DURING the summer of 1888 the tusk of a mammoth, 6 feet long, had been found in a trench dug for drainage works in the village of Shoreham, 30 feet above the Darent, and a piece of this tusk about one foot long reached Prestwich. A brief announcement of this discovery appeared from his pen in the 'Geological Magazine' for March 1889. Two months later, his paper "On the Occurrence of Palæolithic Flint Implements in the Neighbourhood of Ightham, Kent; their Distribution and Probable Age," expressed his views to the Geological Society. In this memoir, which is one of extreme interest, he gave an account of Mr Harrison's discoveries of high-level Drift in the Ightham district, and of palæolithic flint implements at all levels up to 600 feet. He noticed also the collection of palæolithic implements made by Mr De Barri Crawshay from the adjoining Sevenoaks district, and that by Mr A. Montgomerie Bell of Limpsfield from the head of the Darent Valley. The author assigned these rude works of early man to a period long anterior to the valley‑gravels formed under the present river *régime*, and considered that they might prove even to belong to an early stage of the Glacial or Pre‑Glacial period. The paper, which was illustrated by a map of the Drift Beds around Ightham, and also by a series of flint implements from the hill‑drift of unmistakable human workmanship, was well received.

The increasing load of years had not diminished his enthusiasm, and Prestwich never ceased to take a keen interest in the geological features around his Kentish home. Writing to Mr William Topley (20th May 1889), he invites him to spend a day at Otford and Westerham, in order to examine two considerable patches of gravel which, until the railway was made, escaped notice. With Mr Topley he directed an excursion of the Geologists' Association, on the 1st June 1889, to Ightham,[1] for its members to examine its Gravel Beds and those in the surrounding district, and from which Mr Harrison had made his large collection of flint implements. Again, on 13th July, he and Mr Topley conducted another excursion of the Geologists' Association to Limpsfield (Surrey).[2] To quote Mr Topley's report, "This excursion was intended to supplement that to Ightham on June 1st, and to give an opportunity of examining Gravels at the western end of the Darent Valley, partly within that valley, partly on the watershed between the Darent and the Medway." The inspection of the very interesting collection of flint implements made by Mr A. Montgomerie Bell from the Limpsfield gravels was also one of the objects of the excursion.

[1] Proc. Geol. Assoc., vol. xi. p. lxvi.   [2] Ibid., p. lxxxii.

Prestwich was on very affectionate terms with Dr Gustave Plarr, the eminent mathematician, who left Strasburg during the siege, and thenceforward made England his home. Madame Plarr had been an old and valued friend of the Prestwich family, and was nearly connected by marriage.

J. Prestwich to G. Plarr.

DARENT-HULME, SHOREHAM, SEVENOAKS, 24*th June* 1889.

MY DEAR GUSTAVE,—I am glad we shall have the pleasure of seeing you on the 6th July. I will then endeavour (if time permit) to answer your query respecting the Chalk escarpment. I would not attempt it in a letter, for a volume would hardly suffice for the conflicting opinions and evidence. I may, however, say that Lyell's theory of sea action and sea cliffs is now generally abandoned.[1] You will find a *chapter* on the subject in Ramsay's 'Physical Geology and Geography,' if you have the book. With our united kind regards to all your party, I am, sincerely yours, JOSEPH PRESTWICH.

The short geological expeditions during the summer gave the greatest pleasure to Professor Prestwich, whose health with vigilant care had improved, and who seemed to have drifted out of the condition which had led to frequent and serious illnesses during a series of years. The following note from the skilful physician whom he had once or twice consulted may not be out of place :—

Sir Andrew Clark to J. Prestwich.

16 CAVENDISH SQUARE, 26*th Oct.* 1889.

DEAR PROFESSOR PRESTWICH,—I have received the copy which you have been pleased to send me of your work on 'Geology,' and I return you my grateful thanks for this valuable and welcome expression of your consideration.

---

[1] Lyell himself abandoned this theory in his 'Student's Elements of Geology,' 1871, p. 81.

I regard it as one of the great privileges to which my profession has admitted me, that I have had the opportunity of ministering, even in small degree, to the health and comfort of one whose life and work have secured for him universal and deep respect. With renewed thanks, yours faithfully,

AND. CLARK.

The age of the plateau implements constantly occupied the attention of Prestwich.

J. Prestwich to B. Harrison.　　　DARENT-HULME, 21*st Sept.* [1889 or '90].

DEAR SIR,—There is still some doubt about the relative position of the Drift, of chert fragments, flints, and implements, to the "Red Clay with Flints." There is some reason to suppose the former is the older. On the other hand, I have never seen such a Drift under the Red Clay. It may be that the clay wraps round, but generally it seems to pass under; or do the implements, &c., belong to the Red Clay? To assist this point I want an excavation at Bower Lane. The Lenham Beds are certainly under the Red Clay. . . .

Although not published until the following year, Parts I. and II. of the memoir on the " Westleton Beds" were read to the Geological Society in 1889. Their title was, " On the Relation of the Westleton Beds, or Pebbly Sands of Suffolk, to those of Norfolk, and on their Extension inland; with some Observations on the Period of the Final Elevation and Denudation of the Weald and of the Thames Valley, &c." It was acknowledged that no one was so well fitted as Prestwich to deal with the question of the correlation of the Drifts of the eastern counties with those of the Thames Basin and southern counties; and it was admitted that no strata furnish problems more difficult of solution. Part III. of the memoir, which embraced a very wide range, was read in February 1890, and was entitled, " On the Relation of the Westleton Shingle to other Pre - Glacial Drifts in the Thames Basin, and on a Southern Drift, with Observations on the Final Elevation and Initial Subaerial Denudation of the Weald, and on the Genesis of the Thames." These three great papers were well illustrated, and they summed up the observations of many years. It was an untold satisfaction to their author to see them put on record in the pages of the Journal of the Geological Society.

J. Prestwich to J. Evans.

DARENT-HULME, SHOREHAM, 16th *December* [1889].

MY DEAR EVANS,—I was looking forward to meet you on Wednesday next, when I have a paper coming on; but I shall be unable to be present, I am sorry to say. This changeable weather does not suit me, though I have not much to complain of. This paper embraces some of my earliest notes (1842-7), when the Gt. Eastern Railway was made. I wish I could have published them long ago; but many things intervened, and the subject was an intricate and extended one. It has taken me some months to go over my old notes and put the paper in ship-shape. It has not lost by waiting, though I have lost some things in matters of priority. . . .

J. Prestwich to Sir A. Geikie.

DARENT-HULME, SHOREHAM, 18th *Decbr.* [1889].

MY DEAR GEIKIE,—I am very sorry not to be at Burlington House this evening, when my paper is to be read. This paper is in great part the result of observations made many years ago, and which I should have made public long ago but for the pressure of business when in the City, which only left me time for nightwork, and [of] University work and 'Geology' when at Oxford. I have now commenced looking up my old notes and papers, and hope yet to give many of the interesting sections exposed when the Gt. Eastern and other railways were made. All I cannot hope to give, but I have told Whitaker, if they can be of any use to him in future editions of maps or memoirs, they are quite at his service as soon as I have put them in a little order.[1] Many of those are at present merely in the form of rough notes, intelligible only to myself. The delay in bringing them out has been a loss and vexation to me. With my wife's and my best Xmas and New Year's wishes to you and yours, I am, sincerely yours,   JOSEPH PRESTWICH.

J. Prestwich to J. Evans.   DARENT-HULME, 10*th April* 1890.

MY DEAR EVANS,—I regret deeply the loss of my old friend Hébert. . . . Paris will not seem to me the same without him. It must have been about the year 1836 that we first became known to one another, and I never passed through Paris without seeing him. At first we had many differences, and his vigorous, hearty, and good-tempered discussions were a great pleasure to me. His robust frame led me to hope that his would have been a longer life.

J. Prestwich to G. Plarr.

DARENT-HULME, SHOREHAM, SEVENOAKS, 6*th June* 1890.

MY DEAR GUSTAVE,—Many thanks for the copy of your papers, though I regret to say they are sealed books to me. Pebbles of white quartz are originally derived from veins in the metamorphic rocks by marine action. They may occur in any formation, and are common in many. A few are found in the Lower Greensand; many in the Millstone Grit. Those in the Westleton Beds may come from the rocks of Ardennes, or from some of the sedimentary rocks of Belgium. The Westleton pebbles are rarely larger than a marble.

Mrs Prestwich joins me in kind regards to Mme. Plarr; and I am, yours sincerely,   JOSEPH PRESTWICH.

With the advent of summer several short visits were

---

[1] The notes and papers here referred to, as well as many field-maps, have now been presented to the Geological Survey Office in Jermyn Street, London.

made, when the Professor displayed as much energy
and activity as if he had received a new lease of life.
A stay at Brighton, as guests of Mr and Mrs Willett,
was an enjoyable time, as much geology as possible
being fitted into two or three days. When out near
Newhaven it was a pleasure to others to witness the
keen interest and precision with which his quick eye
detected traces of low inland cliffs, showing the limit
of the former wider range of the river. A few days
were spent also at Broomfield, near Stockport, with
his sister, Mrs Russell Scott, when the sight of a new
district lured him to keep on the move — early and
late.

J. Prestwich to J. Evans.

DARENT-HULME, SHOREHAM, 1*st November* 1890.

MY DEAR EVANS,—Time is slipping on, and still finds us here.
I have, in fact, not been to London, it seems to me, for months.
The Geological Session will, however, soon be beginning, and I
hope to meet at some of the meetings. When do you leave for
the South? I have done little field-work this summer, owing to
the long-continued wet weather. My allies have, however, been
busy. Mr Harrison has not left a ridge unexplored, and has
now discovered some fifteen localities, ranging from 450' to 750'
above O. D., for implements of the Ash type; and Mr Crawshay
has found some eight or nine others ranging from 470' to 860',
also one of the Hill type near Green Street Green. I need not
say, if you have leisure, how much pleasure it would give us to see
you down here on a little visit. We shall be glad to hear how
you all are; and with our united kind and affectionate regards, I
am, ever sincerely yours,   JOSEPH PRESTWICH.

We were grieved to hear of Mrs Busk's death. We valued
her greatly.

The following letter to the Rev. R. Ashington Bullen

has reference to Mr and Mrs H. Bingham Mildmay's absence from Shoreham Place for a term of years:—

J. Prestwich to R. A. Bullen.　　　DARENT-HULME, *28th Novr.* 1890.

MY DEAR MR BULLEN,—In case I should not be present at the meeting to-morrow, I write to mention that I would have proposed a short address somewhat in the enclosed terms, or modified, as it may be thought suitable, to Mr Mildmay. But the best proof of the esteem and regard in which we hold Mr and Mrs Mildmay will be by carrying on, as far as lies in our power, the many acts of kindness and charity to our poorer neighbours of which they have hitherto taken charge. Their benevolence we can probably hardly expect to equal, but we may do something to mitigate the loss. I shall be most happy to join in any suitable scheme that may be proposed. With respect to the schools which have been so well conducted, I should regret to see any essential change made; but if we are not prepared to carry them on on the voluntary system, I presume the same work could be carried on under the School Board system. These are the chief points which occur to me. There are others, but they will all require further consideration. You may reckon on my assistance; and believe me to be, dear Mr Bullen, yours very sincerely,　　　JOSEPH PRESTWICH.

The next letter refers to a paper which, in January 1891, he read to the Geological Society.

J. Prestwich to Sir A. Geikie.　　　21 PARK CRESCENT, *20th Jany.* [1891].

MY DEAR GEIKIE,—Very many thanks for your kind letter. We came up to town during a break in the weather just before Christmas, but I have not been out since. I am, however, better now, and with this pleasant change I will, providing it continues, be with you to-morrow. I am glad you can put my paper first, as some friends coming from the country may have to leave early, and I may possibly have to do the same. My paper, as you will see, opens some wide questions, and I should be glad to benefit by any criticisms that the discussion may give rise to. I am coming round, as you will see, to breaks in the Glacial period.

The title of the paper was, "On the Age, Formation, and Successive Drift - stages of the Valley of the Darent; with Remarks on the Palæolithic Implements of the District, and on the Origin of its Chalk Escarpment." The sections and map of the Darent basin illustrating this paper were, as usual, of the clearest, telling their story at a glance.

J. Prestwich to J. Evans.
21 Park Crescent, 14*th February* 1891.

My dear Evans,—You have been much in our minds, and we thought of what a pleasant time you [were having] in Sicily and Greece; but I understand you did not escape the bad weather we had here, although with you it was rain, while with us it was snow. My paper was read at the meeting before the last, and I gave my final views about the age of the plateau specimens. Having given the geological evidence, I think it will be well now to give the anthropological side of the question, with a good series of illustrations in the style of Pl. II. in your 'Stone Implements.' I have spoken to [E. B.] Tylor about it, and will see about arranging specimens for the Anthropological Institute.

I hope you will have something to tell me about the Sicilian caves. I fear, though, that you had little time for geology. Much hoping to see you soon. . . .

To the Same.
London, 27*th March* [1891].

My dear Evans,— . . . I fear you are having very unpleasant weather for your visit to the South Coast. If you have time and opportunity, I wish you would look again to see whether you can find any better arguments than have yet been adduced in support of an old Solent river.[1] I wish I could go over the ground again myself with you. I am glad to say I am now down-stairs again, and have just finished the proofs of my Darent Valley paper. . . .

---

[1] Prestwich's observations on "The Solent River" were printed in the Geological Magazine for 1898, p. 349.

To the Same.   DARENT-HULME, 22*nd April* 1891.

MY DEAR EVANS,—Having done with the geological question
of the Chalk plateau implements, I am taking up the anthropological side, and getting up a paper for the Institute, for which
Mr Peek[1] tells me they can give me the 23rd June. I am now
going over the 700 (?) specimens of Harrison's to sort the types
and select for exhibition. I wish you could see them. I feel
satisfied that their rude and elementary characters corroborate
the geological age to which I have assigned them. I fear you
are spoilt by the beauty of your own collections, and are unwilling to admit the relationship of these poor cousins. To me
it cannot be denied, though I admit it is often difficult to recognise their work. I am getting about again, though I keep much
at home and indoors. . . .

The paper in which he laid his views before the
Anthropological Institute was published some seven
months later in its Journal, in February 1892, being
entitled, "On the Primitive Characters of the Flint
Implements of the Chalk Plateau of Kent, with reference to the Question of their Glacial or Pre-Glacial
Age. With Notes by Messrs B. Harrison and De Barri
Crawshay." The reading of this paper gave rise to a
certain amount of discussion and much adverse criticism
—a novel experience for the author. Several of the
audience questioned the fact of the rude flint implements
exhibited being worked, and asserted their belief in
these chipped flints being only natural forms. This
opposition did not in the least shake Prestwich in his
opinion. It seemed to revive the incredulity which he
had to face when, more than thirty years before, he
made public his convictions as to the genuine character
of the implements discovered in the valley of the Somme
by M. Boucher de Perthes, and which up to that time

[1] Now Sir Cuthbert E. Peek, Bart.

the world of science had scouted. In his previous paper on palæolithic flint implements, read before the Geological Society in 1889, he had recorded their occurrence in about forty places in the neighbourhood of Ightham, Kent. Sir John Evans, our leading authority on the flint and stone weapons of primitive man, refers to this paper in the second edition, recently issued, of his magnificent work.[1] He remarks :—

Since that paper was published, Mr Harrison, aided by Mr de B. Crawshay, has extended his researches, with the result that many more implements have been found at high elevations to the north of the escarpment of the Chalk. These discoveries enabled Sir Joseph Prestwich in another paper, " On the Age, Formation, and Successive Drift - stages of the Valley of the Darent, and on the Origin of its Chalk Escarpment," still further to extend his interesting speculations. It is true that he accepts as being of human manufacture flints with bruised and battered edges which I and some others venture to regard as owing their shape to purely natural causes. But, fortunately, this does not invalidate his arguments, as in most cases where the so-called " Plateau types " have been found, more or less well-finished palæolithic implements of recognised form, though much abraded and deeply stained, have also been discovered. The evidence of such witnesses is not impaired by calling in that of others of more doubtful character.

To the last Prestwich persistently maintained his belief in the rude plateau implements as being the handiwork of man, and not mere natural flints. He insisted that they admitted of classification into three distinct groups, illustrating the different uses for which they were designed. To speak generally, the first group included flat flint flakes, with their edges

[1] On the Ancient Stone Implements of Great Britain : Longmans & Co., 1897.

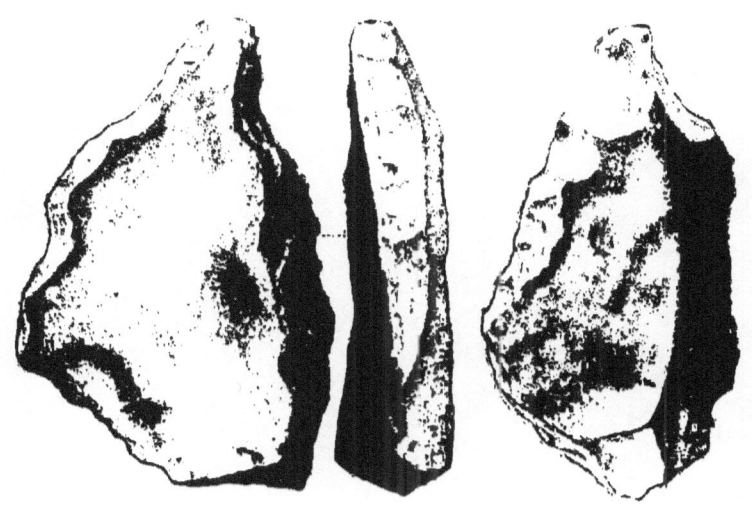

GROUP I.

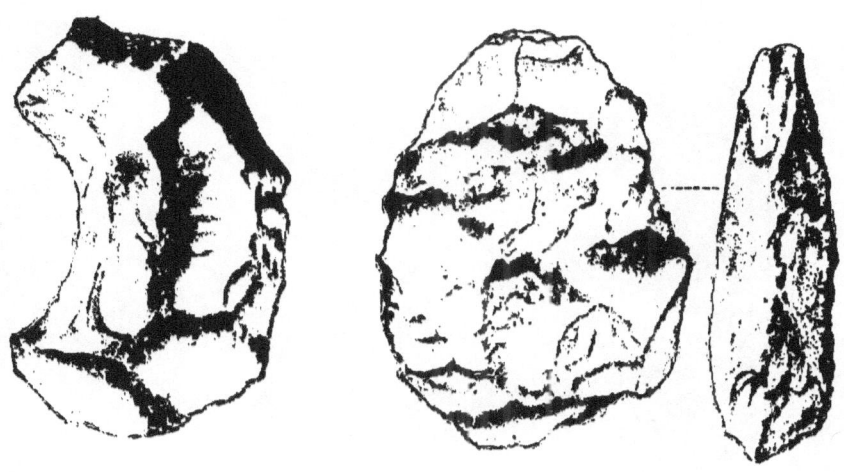

GROUP II.   GROUP III.

PLATEAU IMPLEMENTS.

notched or chipped, the larger fitted to break bones or other hard substances. The second consisted chiefly of scrapers of varied types—square, crescent or beak-shaped, or double. The plateau implements of the third group were more rare, and closely resembled forms common in the valley — such as those of Abbeville and St Acheul. Although Sir John Evans could not agree in this classification, and considered many of the rude types only natural forms, the difference of opinion between the two friends never made any difference in the brotherly footing on which, during so many years, they stood to each other, and to which they both held fast to the end.

It may here be mentioned that Dr H. P. Blackmore, F.G.S., has obtained a number of rude "Eolithic" implements, from the plateau gravel of Alderbury Hill, near Salisbury, and his testimony (given in the sequel) in favour of their use by man is of great value.[1] Many examples may be seen in the famous Blackmore Museum at Salisbury.

From the series of plateau flints described in Prestwich's paper, read before the Anthropological Institute, we give a plate illustrating specimens from each of the three above-mentioned groups. Although isolated types of these rude flint implements often fail to carry conviction, it is otherwise when a series with identical chippings and markings are grouped together : then the design and guiding hand of man to shape them are evident. In no case has this been so clearly shown as in the interesting paper recently published by M. A. Thieullen,[2] in which numerous specimens of each type

---

[1] See also Quart. Journ. Geol. Soc., vol. liv. p. 297.

[2] Les véritables Instruments usuels de l'Age de la Pierre. Par A. Thieullen : Société d'Anthropologie de Paris, 1897.

are ranged side by side, showing the close resemblance of many to the plateau implements, and thus telling their own tale.

It is usual to regard old age as the season of rest from labour. Yet, although in his eightieth year, Joseph Prestwich was now, with undiminished mental vigour, preparing to continue his series of papers, Glacial and Post-Glacial. Never were the declining years of life more . thoroughly enjoyed. In a note written in May of this year, he remarks, "I am revelling in the unwonted leisure for my own work." At intervals during the day he was to be seen among the little larch plantations, or in the grove of laburnums on the hill — sometimes with lengths of white tape in his hand marking trees to be transplanted (there was no end to that process), or using his pruning-knife to some protrusive branch. But his favourite garden-implement was a short French saw, which was often in his hand for trimming the young trees and for keeping clear the vistas down into the valley. How he dwelt upon the varying aspects of Nature! No two days alike — loveliest in the sunshine of a summer morning, when hills and valley were veiled in luminous haze. "Oh, I am so happy!" was his exclamation, made with glistening eyes. "Sometimes I feel as if I were *too* happy!" He was not a man of many words, and we believe that in his heart he gave thanks to God. In addition to visits from the Russell Scott children, he had the added delight of seeing other little relatives—the grandchildren of his sister Mrs Thurburn, who with their parents, Mr and Mrs Seymour Rouquette, had gone to live at Sevenoaks, and who occasionally came over for a day in the garden. And the little Bullens from the Vicarage were especially

welcome.   A favourite amusement was to climb the
small book-steps in the library, when the youngest,
who was old enough to lisp a few words, held out her
arms and insisted on our geologist placing her on the
very top, while her small brother and sisters sat perched
upon the lower steps.   This was usually followed by
a walk in the garden, when there was rivalry among
the four children as to which two were to walk by
his side and have hold of his hands.

To his Grand-nephew, Geoffrey Scott.   DARENT-HULME, 3rd Oct.

MY DEAR LITTLE GEOFFREY,—We have had to gather your
filberts, and have sent them up by Aunt Isabella.   You can
give the grapes on the top of the basket to mother, and have
a talk with her about coming down.   There are the walnuts
yet to gather, and lots of pears and apples.   Come soon.   How
would next Friday or Saturday do?   Talk it over with Gracie,
father, and mother, and write soon to your affectionate Uncle
Jovis.

You must have had a very jolly time of it at the Lakes.   I
like your drawings very much; but they would be better if you
did not draw in such a hurry, and took more pains about them.
Try next time.

The following letter refers to excavations carried
on, under Mr Harrison's directions, at Oldbury, close
to Ightham :—

J. Prestwich to J. Evans.   DARENT-HULME, 10th Novr. 1891.

MY DEAR EVANS,—I fear there is little chance of seeing you
here, now that the season is so far advanced; so Oldbury must
wait.   Mr A. R. Wallace has paid Harrison a visit, and was
much interested in his collection.   I have a long paper in hand
on the Raised Beaches and "Head" of the South of England,
in which, amongst other questions, I discuss the origin of the
foreign boulders of the Sussex coast, of the ossiferous fissures

of Oreston, and of the Drift in the coast plain and at Eastbourne, &c. It is carrying out very much the views I expressed at Swansea. I fear I shall be considered very heterodox; but I hope it will not be considered of me as Irving, quoting Darwin, says, "that a geologist ought not to live after a certain age." I am thankful, at all events, that I am free from the shackles of Uniformitarianism, and live in hope of loosening their hold on my friends. . . .

His keen attention was given to questions of public interest.

J. Prestwich to J. Evans.   Darent-Hulme, 18*th Novr.* 1891.

My dear Evans,—I read with interest the letters in the 'Times' about the Water question. The mode of proceeding with underground waters is scandalous. The law is in accordance with the ignorance of the 12th century, and it is wonderful that it should exist in the 19th. Geology should be made imperative in our engineers' education.

A. R. Wallace has been to see Harrison's collection at Ightham, and he writes to me respecting the plateau specimens, that he has "not the slightest doubt of their being the works of man," and he found them different from anything he had seen.

To the Same.   London, 4*th Jany.* 1892.

My dear Evans,—I have to-day sent in a long paper of some 140 foolscap pages, which embraces my observations for many years of the raised beaches and "Head," and more especially of many curious phases the "Head" takes inland. I feel pretty sure of my facts, but expect there will be very considerable differences of opinion as to my theory. It will take time to investigate and make its way. I hope it may be read whilst Geikie is President [of the Geological Society]. . . .

J. Prestwich to Sir A. Geikie.
21 Park Crescent, 4*th Janry.* 1892.

My dear Geikie,—Thanks for your note and family news, which it was very pleasant to receive. We came unfortunately to London the very day of the fog, leaving Shoreham in bright sunshine and coming in for four days' night here. I had hoped to have been at the meeting on the 23rd, but was afraid to face the fog and cold. Paris with its clear atmosphere is very enjoyable at the time of the New Year.

I have just sent in a paper to the Society, which I have had long in hand. Of the facts I am pretty sure, but I hesitated long about the conclusions, which are not free from difficulty. I hope it may come on while you are still in office. It is a long tale, but it has been one of much interest to me, and will not, I hope, shock my younger colleagues too much. Hoping you and Lady Geikie are well, and with our united kind regards and best wishes for the New Year, I am, sincerely yours,

JOSEPH PRESTWICH.

J. Prestwich to Sir J. Evans.   LONDON, 14th *Jany.* 1892.

MY DEAR EVANS,—You will remember that in our long walks years ago I always expressed an opinion that the surface of the land seemed to me to show the effects of water-action independently of snow or ice action, but I was not able to give proofs in support of my opinion. Last summer I was so much of a prisoner that I had leisure to work up all my old notes of years past, which have given me an amount of evidence sufficient to satisfy me that the South of England was submerged at a very late geological period. This I have embodied in a paper, necessarily *long*, in consequence of the number of the facts, and have sent it in to the Geological Society. It is to be read on the 10th Feb. I hope you will be able to be present either to criticise or to support. I know I shall be considered very heterodox, but it is not a hasty opinion; I see no other solution of the problem, and fortunately I am not fettered about things possible and impossible. . . .

To the Same.   LONDON, 23rd *February* [1892].

MY DEAR EVANS,—I much doubt whether I shall be able to be present to-morrow. I have been out to-day for the first time, but do not feel up to much. I do not expect my views to be accepted at once, but I give *reasons* and *facts* for all that I advance, and I believe that when dispassionately considered and without the narrowing influence of uniformitarianism, but by investigation of the phenomena on the spot, the solution I propose will be found the one which best answers to all the conditions of the case. I am glad that C. Reid has found glacial striæ on the Pagham blocks. Mr Abbott told me he had also found them on some of the smaller specimens at Brighton. I have shown in my paper that they could not have come from the shores of France or the Channel Islands, but probably from Norway or North Germany. This would agree with and be confirmed by C. R.'s observations. I suppose Geikie is off to the South. I wish I could do the same, and trusting you are keeping well. . . .

Dr H. P. Blackmore to J. Prestwich. Salisbury, 20th *April* 1892.

Dear Professor Prestwich,—I do not know if my thanks are due to you or Mr de Barri Crawshay for a copy of your paper on the character of the plateau implements of Kent. The paper, as well as your previous ones in the Quart. Journ. Geol. Soc., interested me much, and set me thinking over the Gravels of this district: from thinking I set to work hunting, and the result has been far better than I expected. Besides the higher- and lower-level valley Gravels, which have proved fairly prolific in the ordinary types of palæolithic implements, there are two other sets of Gravel, the lower ranging about 300 feet above the sea-level, and the other at from 400 to 500 feet.

The first set, viz., the 300 feet, includes the Gravels at Alderbury, three miles to the south of Salisbury : these I had always thought of Pliocene age ; but two years since, when visiting the pits with Mr Jukes-Browne, I found a rough waste-flake *in situ* which sadly puzzled me, as although only a flake, it to my mind bore clear evidence of human workmanship ; but since reading your papers and seeing the plateau types, the pits have again been visited and hunted over—with the result that plenty of evidence of implements is there. When I say implements, the word would perhaps give a wrong impression, as the specimens found are rather natural or accidental forms of flint that have been taken up, used a few times, and then thrown away—but the evidence of use to any one accustomed to the usual forms of flints is unmistakable. As far as I can yet judge, the early savage only had two ideas in the selection and use of these conveniently shaped stones, viz., hammering and scraping—and this is just what one would have expected. Some years since, the late Professor Leidy gave me a stone scraper which was used by a tribe of North American Indians for dressing buffalo-skins: it was an ordinary smooth quartzite pebble, split in half with the thin sharp edge carefully removed, exactly like the plateau Eocene pebbles described in your paper.

The highest point from which these plateau forms have as yet been found is 486 feet, on the summit of the hill beyond the rifle range: there is, however, another patch of gravel, 510 feet, which I have not yet had an opportunity of searching. With kind regards, yours very truly, H. P. BLACKMORE.

J. Prestwich to Sir J. Evans. DARENT-HULME, 17th April 1892.

MY DEAR EVANS,—It was very pleasant to me to go over your route and recall to mind all the places we had visited together. St Acheul must exhibit a melancholy change from what it was when we first knew it. I have done no field work yet, but am waiting for fine weather to visit two new localities discovered by Mr Bullen.[1] Mr Hale, jun., has come over from the Malay Peninsula with a store of curios of all sorts.

Dr H. P. Blackmore to J. Prestwich. SALISBURY, 3rd May 1892.

DEAR PROFESSOR PRESTWICH,—Enclosed you will receive a sketch of the implement from Burroughs Hill: the shaded part represents the natural crust of the flint.

Mr Bullen has very kindly sent me his Preston Hill specimen for inspection, and I am very glad to have seen it. It is much more finely worked and aged than the one from Burroughs Hill, but I have learnt to pay but little notice to mere surface appearance as far as age is concerned, for many of the later Drift

[1] Rev. R. Ashington Bullen, then Vicar of Shoreham, Kent.

specimens—whose history absolves them from the slightest connection with the family of "Flint Jack"—show marvellously little change, whereas others from the same beds are nearly converted into pebbles by water and wear. We evidently as yet know but little as to the precise action of water percolating through beds of Gravel, either as to staining or whitening. . . .

I hope next week to do some work at a patch of Gravel on one of your highest points, five miles to the N. of this. With very kind regards, yours very truly,　　　H. P. BLACKMORE.

J. Prestwich to Sir A. Geikie.　　　DARENT-HULME, 15*th May* 1892.

MY DEAR GEIKIE,—Many thanks for your letter, and I trust you will not find too much to quarrel with in my paper. I am now continuing the same line of research over France and the south of Europe. I shall there, however, be dependent on the works of others (with the exception of France), whereas in England I am acquainted with the whole of the ground. This is of course a great disadvantage, which it is now too late to remedy.

You must have had a pleasant time in Paris, where formerly I was well-known, but am glad to know that my old friends Daubrée and Gaudry are still to the fore. You do not tell me, however, how you are. We should much like to know, if you can find time to send me a few lines. I am thankful to say we are both well. This quiet country life suits me physically and mentally. . . .

In reply to an inquiry from Mr Harrison we find him writing at this time, "Decomposed flint pebbles are of not unfrequent occurrence in various Tertiaries. They lose their water of crystallisation, and some molecular changes take place which render them white, soft, and friable. These you have sent are from Lower Tertiary (Woolwich and Reading ?) Beds. You speak also of decomposed flints as well as pebbles. These are unusual, but you send no specimen. . . ."

J. W. Hulke [1] to J. Prestwich.

10 OLD BURLINGTON STREET, LONDON, W., 17th *May* 1892.

MY DEAR PRESTWICH,—Warm thanks for your papers on Raised Beaches and on Late Post-Glacl. Submergence, which I have read and read again with very great interest. The variability and fragmentary preservation of these relatively recent beds have for me been great difficulties in getting a good grasp of their time sequence.

I wish our old friend Mansel-Pleydell had been able to give a more detailed account of his discovery some two years ago of elephant remains in a sand-bed which he sketched to me.[2]

I saw many years ago a molar of *Elephas* (from the narrowness of its plates I thought perhaps *E. antiquus*) taken from the Gravel capping the chalk-cliff at Freshwater, I. Wight, close to the "Battery." When I was last at Brook, I. Wight, a few years since, nearly all of the bed under Gravel on cliff-top by the chine, where I had formerly got hazel-nuts, &c., had disappeared by foundering of cliff. The waste of cliffs on the S. coast of I. Wight within my memory has been remarkable. A good instance of this is Shepherd's Chine. When I first knew it, some 25 years ago, it was a narrow gulley crossed by a plank. At its opening on the beach the E. side was a nearly vertical cliff of blue shales with *Septaria*, that I used to dig and break up —they occasionally yielded pterodactylian bones. *Now* the formerly narrow gulley is a wide open dell with sloping banks!

You refer to a former harbour-master at Ramsgate. There was one who made quite a collection of elephants' tusks and molars dredged up off the harbour, and I have myself seen *E.* remains—notably an *os innominatum*, dug up at low tide after heavy ground-swell, between Sandown Castle and No. 1 Battery. As the chalk rock is there at no great depth, these remains may have come out of rubble on its top under the present sand.

---

[1] John Whitaker Hulke, F.R.S., President of the Royal College of Surgeons ; born November 6, 1830 ; died February 19, 1896.

[2] Notes on the *Elephas meridionalis* at Dewlish, Dorset, have been published by Mr Mansel-Pleydell, 'Proc. Dorset Nat. Hist. Club,' vol. x., 1889 p. 1 ; and vol. xiv., 1893, p. 139.

I hope this fine spring weather is dispelling the depressing influenza of the past winter. My wife joins in kind regards to Mrs Prestwich and yourself.—Yours very truly,

J. W. HULKE.

S. R. Pattison [1] *to J. Prestwich.*　　　KENSINGTON, 26*th June* [1892].

MY DEAR SIR,—I had begun, some time ago, to write to you with reference to your very important paper on "Raised Beaches" in the 'Q. J.,' which settled many controversies and raised some others. Your recent Royal Society paper, which you were so kind as to send to me, has given to every one the advantage of your own fuller interpretation, and it is of such paramount importance as to set aside for the moment my personal troubles. I am reminded of one of the late Professor Phillips' last sayings to me—"I believe, Pattison, after all, we shall be obliged to bring back the Deluge."—I am, sincerely yours,

S. R. PATTISON.

When Professor Huxley was made a Privy Councillor the following humorous note from him was in reply to our geologist's congratulations :—

BARMOUTH, *Augst.* 31, 1892.

MY DEAR PRESTWICH,—Best thanks for your congratulations. As I have certainly got more than my temporal deserts, the other "half" you speak of can be nothing less than a bishopric! May you live to see that dignity conferred, and go on writing such capital papers as the last you sent me until I write myself your Right Revd. as well as Right Honble. old friend,

T. H. HUXLEY.

J. Prestwich to B. Harrison.

DARENT-HULME, SHOREHAM, SEVENOAKS, 15*th Novr.* [1892].

DEAR SIR,—No explanation was necessary. Your collection stands upon its merits. Differences of opinion there will always

---

[1] S. R. Pattison, formerly of Launceston, and an early worker on the geology of Cornwall and Devon ; for many years a member of the Council of the Geological Society, and their honorary legal adviser.

be. All you have to say is that Sir J. E. accepts some spec. but rejects others. Let every one judge for himself. I am glad you have ceased field-work for the winter. . . .

J. Prestwich to Sir J. Evans.   SHOREHAM, *2nd December* 1892.

MY DEAR EVANS,—In the short glance at my paper the other day you could hardly have formed an idea of its scope and object. It is not, as you supposed, a paper of minute geological detail, like my paper on the raised beaches, &c., in the 'Journal Geological Society,' but it is a paper in which, following up that line of research, I pass in review all that bears on the subject in South-Western Europe and on the Mediterranean coasts, and *generalise* upon these observations, employing only so much detail as is necessary to illustrate my hypothesis. The detailed papers to which I refer would occupy volumes, and are within reach of the reader. It is also a new departure, and, as such, comes, I think, within the scope of the Royal Society rather than of the Geological Society, from the fact that it involves questions which concern naturalists, physicists, and anthropologists. I am aware that I must expect opposition, as it touches upon questions on which geologists and physicists must differ. All I can wish for is to have the facts fairly considered, and judgment formed on them, and not on assumed postulates founded on very doubtful bases. The votaries of uniformitarianism are, I fear, apt to consider their doctrines as infallible, and to act accordingly. For my own part, I believe that in another half century geologists will wonder that a doctrine so unphilosophical was ever held. Physicists, who pin their faith to a certain rigidity and thickness of the earth's crust, should look to the geological facts before putting geological opinion on one side. I am aware that my hypothesis will appear startling, but if it explains all the facts and apparently discordant phenomena, it surely deserves consideration. As to the facts themselves, I presume I am not saying too much when I claim for myself a better knowledge of them than most geologists. I have decided, therefore, to send my paper to the Royal Society. I have written a short abstract for reading, and that you may see the scope of the paper I send it for your perusal, if you will kindly devote a spare half hour to it.

But before reading I should like you to read the explanations
that have been suggested by others, and to which I have given,
I trust, impartial considerations in the paper referred to—
'Q[uarterly] J[ournal] G[eological] Society,' vol. clviii. pp. 323-328.
You will, I think, see that none of them meet all the conditions
of the case, and most of them ignore the consequences which the
adoption of their views would involve. . . . —Ever yours
sincerely,   JOSEPH PRESTWICH.

J. Prestwich to Sir J. Evans.   19th Dec. 1892.

I have adopted your suggestion to omit reference to the
Deluge, and think you are right.[1] It might have been supposed
that I was working up to that end, whereas I was brought to it
solely by the evidence, and you, no doubt, will remember that it
always struck me that there was something besides river, marine,
and ice action in the superficial phenomena. The [Philosophical]
'Transactions' have not been surcharged with Natural History
papers of late years.

The preceding letters allude to the great Submergence paper by Joseph Prestwich, "On the Evidences
of a Submergence of Western Europe, and of the Mediterranean Coasts, at the Close of the Glacial or so-called
Post - Glacial Period, and immediately preceding the
Neolithic or Recent Period." It was sent in to the
Royal Society on 15th December 1892, and was read
and published in the 'Philosophical Transactions' in
1893. The substance of the following unfinished preface was given in this paper ('Phil. Trans.,' pp. 980-
984) :—

I am aware that in proposing the hypothesis advanced in the
following paper it may be considered that I am taking a retro-

---

[1] The subject was subsequently dealt with in a little work by Prestwich,
entitled 'On Certain Phenomena belonging to the close of the last Geological Period, and on their bearing upon the Tradition of the Flood,' 1895
(Macmillan).

grade step, that I am reviving an exploded doctrine, and that I am ignoring the doctrine of uniformity, which now, it may be urged, regulates geological progress. But I refuse to be judged on such a basis. While admitting as a fundamental truth the proposition of the identity of forces in present and past times, I contend that the exhibition of these forces has been unequal in degree. The contention for this uniformity is based solely upon the value of man's personal evidence, and when the term of this is compared with that term beyond which it does not extend, the propositions are such as to render it comparatively valueless. It is a limited terrestrial measure of distance compared to the measure of our solar distance, and we can no more tell what may have occurred beyond that term than we can tell what cosmical phenomena may have occurred in the vast interval which separates us from our luminary, except on the evidence of the residual phenomena.

Half a century ago Dr Buckland, after considerable investigation, came to the conclusion that a deluge had passed over the land, and that we had in our superficial deposits and the remains of the entombed animals evidence of the fact. Sedgwick and other distinguished men adopted the same view for a time, but it was abandoned in consequence of other evidence of a conflicting character subsequently brought forward. But, while abandoned in this country, that opinion has held its ground on the Continent, and a nomenclature in accordance with that view has been adopted for certain geological deposits, such as *Diluvium rouge*, *Diluvium gris*, and *Alluvium ancienne*.

As may be seen from his letters, Joseph Prestwich held strong anti-uniformitarian views, and yet he could not be classed as a catastrophist in the old sense of the word. Always at work, the autumn of 1893 found him occupied in writing a magazine article, " On the Position of Geology (a Chapter on Uniformitarianism)." This appeared in the ' Nineteenth Century ' for October, and the two following notes to his friend the Rev. O. Fisher have reference to it. It was a declaration of his non-uniformitarian belief, a profession of his geological creed.

It may be remarked that while Prestwich had published very fully his observations on the Tertiary formations and on the Quaternary strata, which immediately preceded and succeeded the Glacial deposits, yet he had not dealt in a similarly comprehensive manner with his observations on the Glacial Drifts. It is true that in many of his papers he had published sections of Boulder Clay and Glacial Gravel, and he contributed much information with respect to them. Nevertheless his views generally on the formation of the Boulder Clays and associated deposits were not given to the public in the same exhaustive manner as were those dealing with the Eocene and Oligocene strata, the Crag series, the Westleton Beds, and the later Pleistocene accumulations. His note-books show how he had followed the Glacial Drifts far and wide, not only in the Southern and Midland counties, but in Wales, in the north of England, in Scotland and Ireland. Indications of his views are given in the second volume of his great treatise on 'Geology,' wherein he remarks (p. 453): "Equally marvellous is the glaciation of the northern counties of England. There also only a few of the higher hills escaped the grasp of the great ice-sheet, the marks of which are perceptible up to heights of about 2500 feet in the Lake district. As the land-ice travelled southward it became thinner, and its traces are gradually lost. The Glacial Drift-beds die out on the hills immediately north of London, whence their boundary passes by Oxford to South Wales." These views show how inclined he was to maintain that the main mass of Boulder Clay was the product of land-ice, although he argued that "the phenomena, as a whole, go to show that the glaciation of Great Britain was not due to a great Polar ice-cap, but was of local and independent origin."

That Prestwich cherished the idea of publishing in detail his views on the Great Ice Age is evident from a tabular statement drawn up in 1892, which gives a scheme for a paper "On the Glacial Series of the South of England." [1]　This task, however, he did not live to accomplish, and the notes remain without the master-hand to mould them into shape, and to decipher the story which they might reveal.

With the return of Easter his thoughts as usual were with his brother geologists, and he followed all their movements. In a note dated 6th April he observes : "I am glad to hear of the Easter excursions continued under such pleasant conditions, but do not approve of the introduction of that relaxing element, fishing. Why, we sometimes had not time to eat fish, much less catch them. Our vicar's little girl picked up a fine flint implement on the beach near Boscombe."

Although Prestwich had at an early date made several journeys with his usual companion to Ightham and to other of Mr Harrison's recently found flint-bearing sites, a long list lies before us of joint visits made with their discoverer and other enthusiastic explorers to the ground where rude implements had been found, beginning with a first joint visit to Ightham and Oldbury, in September 1881, with his friend Fisher. On to 1893 no year passed without frequent and repeated expeditions, when Prestwich was accom-

---

[1] The scheme has been printed in the 'Geological Magazine,' Dec. IV., vol. v. p. 404.

panied by fellow-geologists to these sites, occasionally Mr Topley being his companion, and occasionally Sir John Evans. Latterly Professor Rupert Jones and the Rev. R. Ashington Bullen went with him to review new ground, Mr Harrison being seldom absent from any working party.

The discovery by Mr W. J. Lewis Abbott, F.G.S.,[1] of ossiferous fissures in the valley of the Shode, near Ightham, was naturally of great interest to Prestwich ; and his friend Mr Abbott did not fail to carry to Darent-Hulme the spoils from the fissures for our geologist's examination. They included many mammalian remains, as well as those of birds, reptiles, &c., the small bones of rodents being innumerable. The last visit made by Prestwich to these fissures was in 1893, when he was accompanied by Mr Abbott and Mr Harrison.

J. Prestwich to Rev. O. Fisher.

DARENT-HULME, SHOREHAM, *12th August* 1893.

MY DEAR FISHER,—I am very much obliged to you for the corrections you have made in my MS. With two or three exceptions, I have gladly availed myself of them all. What, however, I particularly wanted your opinion about is whether I have put correctly the opinions of such physicists as Lord Kelvin, Tait, and [G. H.] Darwin. Am I right in saying their estimate of the earth's age is now from fifteen to twenty million years (I know it has varied greatly), and the thickness of the crust from 1000 to 2500 miles ?

I wish I could have gone more fully into the subject, but I suppose a magazine would not care for too long an article. . . .

---

[1] The Ossiferous Fissures in the Valley of the Shode, near Ightham, Kent. By W. J. Lewis Abbott, F.G.S. ; Quart. Journ. Geol. Soc., 1894, vol. l. p. 171. The Vertebrate Fauna collected by Mr Lewis Abbott from the Fissure near Ightham, Kent. By E. T. Newton, F.R.S., F.G.S. ; ibid., p. 188.

To the Same.   DARENT-HULME, SHOREHAM, 24th *August* 1893.

MY DEAR FISHER,—Thanks for your note and references. Lord Kelvin's correction in his address at Glasgow, 1876, refers only to Hopkins's argument about precession and nutation, and does not, it seems to me, affect his previous opinions about the rigidity and great thickness of the crust. Sir A. Geikie gives the thickness as stated by him in 1862. You see I am not touching on the general question, but merely giving what seems to be the opinion held by Kelvin and Tait as to the approximate thickness of the crust—1000 would do for me just as well as 2000.

J. Prestwich to J. Evans.

DARENT-HULME, SHOREHAM, 13th *September* [1893].

MY DEAR EVANS,—A few days since we went to West Yoke (460′), near Ash. There is a very remarkable spread of much worn gravel there, with a considerable number of the rudest possible worked flints and one good pointed form. I am more satisfied than ever of the great antiquity of the Chalk plateau specimens. Next week I hope to visit the several new localities discovered by Mr Crawshay. In one of these of doubtful position he has found 46 specimens. With very much sympathy,

J. PRESTWICH.

The following letter has reference to the ' Nineteenth Century ' article :—

J. Prestwich to the Same.   DARENT-HULME, 22nd *October* 1893.

MY DEAR EVANS,—The very foundation of uniformitarian beliefs is that these terrestrial forces have been alike as now, both in kind and degree, in all past times, and all their calculations of time and denudation have been made on that basis. If you can show any calculations made on a different basis, either in textbooks or papers, I shall be glad: I know of none.

The only exception made has been in favour of volcanic action. But any child could see that volcanic action is spasmodic, and has always been so. But even here the argument is inapplicable.

The energy, so far from being on a par with the present, is, I believe, in the cases of such eruptions as Krakatoa, greater now
than formerly, as I have shown in 'Geology.'

My chronology may possibly err a little on one side (for the
dates are not sufficiently definite), but that of the uniformitarian
errs, I am satisfied, much more than the other. But this does
not touch the essential points of argument. I wish I could
write longer and more clearly, but this is one of my bad
days. . . .

Sir H. D. Acland to J. Prestwich.   OXFORD, *Jan.* 15, 1894.

Alas! most forgiving of friends, I cannot lay my hand on the
beautiful envelope directed to you at midsummer, and carried to
and fro *per mare per terram*, and not fit to send. . . . Everything
here is in restless movement with new-comers, and old ones who
take up questions new to them; and I get disheartened at seeing
things knocked down from sheer want of knowing—would you
were still with us!

The Home [1] for which you did so much is become a *model* institution for *good* and useful work, wisely devised and conducted,
but it needs endowment. . . . God bless you both! Your affectionate and grateful friend,   H. D. ACLAND.

It will have been apparent to the reader that in
amassing the evidence for his Submergence paper,
Joseph Prestwich, without having it in view, was
struck by the fact that his theory of a wide-spread
submergence upheld the Biblical record of the Flood.
Once that the idea dawned upon him he was fascinated,
and sought out all the physical evidence that could be
adduced in support of it. Early in 1894 he sent in a
paper on the subject to the Victoria Institute, entitled,
"A Possible Cause for the Origin of the Tradition of the
Flood," which, as he was unable to be present, was read
by his old friend Professor Rupert Jones, F.R.S. It

[1] The Acland Memorial Home for Nurses, Oxford.

was well received, giving rise to an interesting discussion, and was published in the 'Journal of Transactions of the Victoria Institute' for that year. Its hearty reception tempted him to write a *résumé* of all the geological evidence bearing on " The Tradition of the Flood," and the preparation of this booklet, which did not appear until early in the next year, was meanwhile a pleasant and interesting occupation.

J. Prestwich to B. Harrison.

DARENT-HULME, SHOREHAM, SEVENOAKS, 15*th August* 1894.

DEAR SIR,—Thanks for the copy of your Address, which has interested us both. It might, however, be supposed from it that the geologists were deterred by the height and position. That was hardly the case. It was whether they were worked. I fear you were ill - advised in your selection for the Roy. Soc. It was only the other day that a leading geologist wrote to me saying, "The [your] plateau types selected were very large and rough, and not the most typical ones, like those figured" (in Collected Papers). . . .

You could not have done better than to refer to Well Hill. It is a remarkable spot, which I first visited and [where I] found the chert fragments some 40 years ago, and took Sir J. Lubbock there, who afterwards described it. You should have told your inquirer who asked you why you did not at first write about the plateau implements, that long ago I asked you whether you would not do so. . . .

H. P. Blackmore to J. Prestwich.　　SALISBURY, 27*th August* 1894.

DEAR MR PRESTWICH,—Ever since I heard of the discovery of the plateau type of implement I have been hunting this district for evidence, and have been fortunate in finding plenty to satisfy myself. The main object now is to convince others, and I hope to string the facts of this neighbourhood together shortly, to help the evidence in other parts of England.

As this district was of great use 30 years ago in establishing the presence of man in the river Drift period, so now in what an Irishman would call the advance backwards, Salisbury will prove equally strong, and I trust furnish good evidence to convince some of the sceptics, who don't know what a worked flint is, even when they see it before them.

As far as the fact of the discovery of worked flints in the southern Drift of Alderbury is concerned, make any use you like of the information.

What do you think of the evidence of fire? For the last 20 years I have been hunting in our Drift Gravels for it, but the specimen from Alderbury is the first that has yet turned up. Have you been more fortunate and met with burnt flints in any Drift Gravels under such circumstances that precluded the possibility of their having come from the surface?

Amongst the gravel at Alderbury I have met with a few small pebbles—sea-rolled pebbles, of sarsen stone—quite distinct as regards rolling from the ordinary large sarsen boulders. What old sea-shore do you think they probably came from? The much smaller quartz pebbles are very, very scarce at Alderbury. With kind regards, yours very truly,

H. P. BLACKMORE.

But, alas! Prestwich had soon again to pay the penalty of age, in seeing one after another of those he loved called away before him. The death of his sister, Mrs Russell Scott, to whom throughout life he had been tenderly attached, occurred in August. She was the little sister whom her brother (not two years her senior) used to escort out on Saturdays when the two children were at their respective schools in Paris. In many respects she resembled him, in that quick intelligence and wide grasp of mind so unusual in a woman : it was rare to meet any one so gifted, who at the same time possessed extraordinary sweetness of temper. Her illness had been hopeless and protracted, yet when the end came his distress was not less poignant. "No

Photo by Adams & Stilliard, Southampton.

one knows how much she was to me in early life," was his remark in a note to a friend. Thus for a time the serene happiness of his home was overclouded.

In the autumn of 1894, under Prestwich's personal supervision, Professor Rupert Jones prepared a paper, with diagrams, treating of the plateau implements, their position below the surface, and the derivation of the gravelly deposits in which they occur, from the Chalk capping the Wealden area when it existed as part of a range at least 2000 feet high. This paper was read before a combined meeting of the Anthropological and Geological sections of the British Association on August 10, 1894, and published in 'Natural Science,' vol. v. pp. 269-275. In it occurs the appropriate remark that "it must have been a great pleasure to the veteran geologist, Professor Dr Prestwich, to find that his conclusions (in 1890) as to the Pliocene Tertiaries and Gravels on the flanks of the diminishing island of the Weald fitted so truly, as consecutive history, with his early views (1847) of the probable conditions of the Wealden dome in Eocene times."

The letter from Canon Greenwell, a leading authority on the subject of flint implements, gives his opinion of the plateau implements :—

Canon Greenwell to J. Prestwich.   Durham, 29th Sept. 1894.

My dear Sir,—I am obliged for your paper on the "Flints of the Chalk Plateau," which I read when it appeared in the Journal. I have no objection to your using my name in the reissue as a believer in the manufacture, by some reasoning creature, of the flints in question.

With regard to when they were made, though, so far as I can judge, from the observation of others, they appear to belong to a time anterior to that which produced the ordinary Drift implements, I am unable to express an opinion from personal knowledge of the sites, &c.

But that they have been made with intention I cannot have the least doubt, for I know of no natural agency which has, or indeed could, produce the signs of work so abundantly shown upon them.

I hope some time next year to have an opportunity of seeing the places near Sevenoaks where they have been found. Yours very faithfully, W. GREENWELL.

The following letter from Mr Gladstone is too interesting to be omitted :—

W. E. Gladstone to J. Prestwich.

HAWARDEN CASTLE, CHESTER, 2nd Oct. 1894.

MY DEAR SIR,—I thank you very much for the interesting and able Address you have done me the honour to send me, and I desire respectfully as well as sympathetically to mention a circumstance which has long appeared to me worthy of some notice, and which may have a relation to your doctrine of a larger and late submergence.

I am in no way competent to touch the relation of that doctrine to the tradition of the Noachian deluge.

And it may seem daring for one who speaks from a standing ground supplied by literature, to attempt joining hands with the geologist across the gap which severs him from history and pre-history as commonly understood.

My fact is this: Homer was (in my confident opinion, dictated to me by study of the text) possessed of, and thoroughly possessed by, a tradition, evidently the tradition of his day and people, according to which there lay to the north of the Thracian and Thessalian mountains an open sea; and by this open sea lay, for him, the communication from Western Greece *nominatim* from Ithaca, with an Underworld to which the approach was situated in the East, and was by his great river Okeanos (in his ideas of which river were *probably* mixed together vague notices of the Black Sea and Sea of Azof, the Caspian, and the

Persian Gulf). Of the Danube he knew nothing; but he believed in certain inhabited tracts, which he enumerates, to the northward of the Thracian mountains.

This purely literary fact has led me often, and from perhaps twenty or thirty years back, to inquire from geological friends, who have assured me, as you do, that Central Europe was at a very late geologic period under water.

It was not for me to consider how this tradition stood related to the mountains (of no very great elevation, I think) which sever Central Europe from the Adriatic.

I do not attempt to enter here upon the proof of my Homeric fact, which I think conclusive. But I may mention—is it relevant or not ?—that the Duke of Argyll told me he saw exposed in the fish-markets of Venice sea-fauna (if the phrase may be used) not appearing in the Mediterranean generally, but familiar to him in Argyllshire on the coast of the Atlantic.

Your submergence helps me, because it is south as well as north of the mountains which I named.

Your supposition of the escape of a part of the local population leaves room for the transmission of a geological or Quaternary phenomenon down to (what we call) prehistoric times.

There is a kind of sister tradition, that of the Atlantis; but here it is the ghost of a tradition, for I know of no period in which the Atlantis was the subject of a living popular belief.

I apologise for this intrusion, which you will see is intended in a sympathetic sense. I remain, my dear sir, with much respect, faithfully yours, 　　　　　W. E. GLADSTONE.

From the Same. 　　　　　HAWARDEN CASTLE, CHESTER.

MY DEAR SIR,—One word by way of supplement. What you say of your submergence in no way I think conflicts with the idea that it may have had to do with Homer's European sea. That idea may be compounded of the traditions of several submergences, which (traditions) had coalesced into one, just as I think it almost certain that the Homeric notion of a great circumfluent river Okeanos was made up from partial notices of Eastern (as well as Western) water at the Straits of Yenikale, in the Caspian, and in the Persian Gulf and Red Sea. These things may appear strange; but we have to familiarise ourselves with the position of a race and a poet having extremely narrow maritime experience, and no view or idea of extraneous waters except from very miscellaneous report.   Yours very faithfully,

W. E. GLADSTONE.

A very affectionate letter from Professor Capellini, the distinguished geologist, Rector of the University of Bologna, dated 15th October 1894, informed Joseph Prestwich of his having been elected a corresponding member of the Royal Academy of the Lincei of Rome. The distinction of belonging to this great society was especially prized.   Professor Capellini informed the new member that his election had been carried by a "*splendide votation*," and reminded him that it was the greatest honour in the power of the *savants* of Italy to bestow.

Again at this date are frequent notes addressed to the discoverer of the plateau implements.   Mr Harrison was encouraged to persevere, and it was impressed upon him not to be disappointed should these flint implements not be universally recognised at once.   Joseph Prestwich had more than once fought a battle single-handed, and in the end had always come off victorious. In a note to Mr Harrison of 30th October, he repeats: "I have never had, nor have I now, the slightest doubt about the age and character of the plateau implements. As I have told you all along, it is only a question of time."

J. Prestwich to Professor Jules Marcou.

DARENT-HULME, SHOREHAM, 10*th December* 1894.

MY DEAR M. MARCOU, — Your kind letter of October last found me in bed, where I had to remain a month, owing to one of my attacks.   I am down again now, but not yet allowed to go out.   I, however, go on with my work.   Your account of the Indian traditions of a flood is very interesting, but seems, from what you say, to refer to a more recent date than that of Western Europe. I am glad to know about the ossiferous fissures of Salins. That falls in with my paper.

It is, I admit, a difficult point to account for the absence of marine remains; but, besides the short duration of the flood, it is to be remembered that the breaking up of the vegetable soil by the advancing waters would render them so turbid that, like with the estuaries of the West African rivers in flood, the waters would be deoxidised and destructive to animal life. Further, any marine life carried inland by the waters would be dropped on the surface and subsequently destroyed by atmospheric influences. Mrs Prestwich joins me in very kind regards, and I am, dear M. Marcou, ever sincerely yours,

JOSEPH PRESTWICH.

In January 1895 Joseph Prestwich had the gratification of receiving another testimony of the estimation in which his geological work was held abroad—perhaps in greater estimation abroad than at home. This was his election as one of the Vice-Presidents of the Geological Society of France, he being the first Englishman selected for this honour. It cheered the veteran, then about to complete his eighty-third year, to receive this proof of the constant affection and esteem of his *confrères* in France.

J. Prestwich to M. Albert Gaudry.   LONDON, 14th *January* 1895.

MY DEAR M. GAUDRY,—Many thanks for your letter of congratulation. I can assure you that I feel very much flattered by the honour done me by the Geological Society of France in electing me one of their Vice-Presidents. My connection with my French colleagues has ever been to me a source of very great pleasure, and I have profited much by my studies on French ground. My views on many geological questions are also more in harmony with those prevailing on your side of the water. We are too much tied down here by extreme uniformitarianism. Let me thank you also for the copy of your paper, on the curious new reptile, you lately sent me. When you next see M. Daubrée, kindly remember me to him. We are staying here for the winter, as we find Shoreham too cold. We are both confined to the house, but I am much better than I was last year. Mrs Prestwich sends her kind regards, and believe me to be, my dear M. Gaudry, yours very sincerely and attached,

JOSEPH PRESTWICH.

J. Prestwich to Sir J. Evans.   LONDON, 2nd February 1895.

MY DEAR EVANS,— . . . I am writing a magazine article on the Plateau Implements, in which I wage war against all the Oxford critics, including yourself. I have finished my " Collected Papers," and have another Flood Tradition paper in hand, so we have plenty of occupation during our confinement by cold and snow. . . .

I do not think Skertchly's hypothesis will supersede Richthofen's.[1] Why should the Loess shells be destroyed in China when so many are preserved in Europe ? . . .

J. Prestwich to B. Harrison.   LONDON, 15th March [1895].

DEAR SIR,—Thanks for the sight of the specimen. It is quite immaterial whether it came from the South or the East Coast. The essential is that it is a shore specimen. It certainly *simulates* closely some of the plateau specimens, but it is in fact merely a naturally split pebble of which the outer edges are worn by sea-action. As I have pointed out, some of the plateau specimens are so made that it is difficult to draw the line between Nature and Art. But it is of no use taking such specimens as evidence on either side. What is wanted are well-defined types, of which the characters are *positive* and not *negative.* Let the sea-action advocates show specimens of the [three] types, and then we [shall] attend to their argument. There are many *natural* flints which simulate the palæolithic implements, but they prove nothing. To discuss them is only waste of time. My doctor forbids again my return home for the present, and I am, yours very truly,   JOSEPH PRESTWICH.

---

[1] Paper by Skertchly and Kingsmill, in Quart. Journ. Geol. Soc., vol. li. p. 238.

J. Prestwich to Rev. O. Fisher.

21 HAREWOOD SQUARE, 19*th March* 1895.

MY DEAR FISHER,—How have you been all this severe winter, and how are all your sons ?

We have been spending the winter with my niece Miss Scott, but intend returning home on Friday next. Both of us have weathered the winter well, though it has kept me a prisoner in-doors for the greater part of the time. My sisters-in-law are away at Cannes, and will be away till the end of July. You have of course heard of the death of poor Hulke. It was a great shock to us all, and he will be greatly missed. Evans takes his place as foreign secretary. What are you at work on now ? I have been busy in putting some of my old papers together as "Collected Papers." There will be nothing new to you in them, as you had the separate copies as they came out. I have also a paper for the unbelievers coming out in the 'Nineteenth Century' magazine. I fear that we shall find damage done to our shrubs and trees. I hope your roses have not suffered too much. Mrs Prestwich desires her very kind regards; and believe me to be very sincerely yours, JOSEPH PRESTWICH.

While yet early in the year, four publications appeared from the pen which had been in such constant use, and which was soon to be laid aside for ever. One was 'The Tradition of the Flood,' to which attention has already been directed. The next was the volume of 'Collected Papers on some Controverted Questions of Geology,' which made subjects under discussion readily accessible to the reading public. A reissue, with additions by the author, of the 'Water-bearing Strata of the Country around London, &c.,' was also published, it having regard chiefly to the water-supply of the great city. The fourth publication was an article in the April number of the 'Nineteenth Century' magazine, "On the Greater Antiquity of Man." In this the author traced the changes of opinion that had taken place within the last half-century respecting the age of man on the earth : it was a piece of close reasoning, difficult to gainsay, on the geological age of the plateau implements. The words in which he summed up were : "No traces of older man have been met with on our land, and though elsewhere instances have been recorded, they have either proved mistaken or else require confirmation. Of one thing I feel satisfied, which is that in no other instance do the phenomena exhibit so well as in this part of Kent—the successive geological stages bearing upon human occupation of the land, and so clearly help to establish the Greater Antiquity of Early Man."

The next letter is one from the Duke of Argyll, followed by its answer :—

The Duke of Argyll to J. Prestwich.

INVERARY, *April* 1, 1895.

MY DEAR MR PRESTWICH,—I have been reading with great interest your article on the Antiquity of Man. I have no difficulty about your conclusions as to the human origin of the flints, nor, of course, about the great *submergence* which is involved in the whole of your explanation, for this agrees with my own conclusions from glacial phenomena in this country.

But there are points connected with *time* which are not clear to me. You assume that all the existing valleys have been excavated *since* the high-level Gravels were deposited.

Is this quite certain? I don't know how it is to be proved. Certainly *here* the existing contours must have been *in the main* the same as now before the submergence. All the phenomena point to the ridges of existing hills having been shoals and reefs in the Glaciation sea, and to the existence of valleys as having guided the rock-bearing floe-ice.

Of course in the *re-emergence* of the land there must have been a tremendous "scour" from rushing waters, and this may have effected a considerable amount of excavation. But in our hard and crystalline rocks whole valleys cannot have been thus formed, and all evidence is against it.

The Chalk and Wealden and Greensand beds of the south of England would no doubt yield much more rapidly to the scour of surging waters. But if the high levels were so scoured, how comes it that the very old weapons were not all washed down into the new valleys?

Excuse my scepticism. But I want to know exactly the data on which *time* is calculated as necessary to account for the facts.

To me the main interest lies in the conclusion that a great marine submergence, comparatively rapid and transient, *has* taken place since man appeared. I don't care about the number of years ago. But any *immense* antiquity does not seem to me to be at all proved.—Yours very truly,

ARGYLL.

J. Prestwich to the Duke of Argyll.

DARENT-HULME, SHOREHAM, 14th April 1895.

DEAR DUKE OF ARGYLL,—Pray excuse the delay in my answer to your letter of the 1st instant. On referring to my article in the 'Nineteenth Century,' I fear that I was not sufficiently explicit in limiting my observations to the Kentish area.

I entirely accept your interpretation of the valleys in Scotland. They must be of far higher antiquity. My observations were intended to apply to such valleys as those of the Medway, Holmesdale, and in part to that of the Thames.

The reason why the old implements on the plateau were not all washed down during the re-elevation of the land arose, I think, from the fact that the re-elevation was slow, so that the scour on the high flat table-land was slight; but when the effluent currents became centred in the narrow intersecting valleys, the rapidity of the current and its scouring became largely increased.

Nevertheless, portions of the Drift *a*—which contains the plateau implements—were denuded and worn; and derived plateau implements are found in the reconstructed Drift *b*. *In this district* we have no beds older than *a*, and no valleys older than A, which are newer than *a*, and cannot therefore be older than early Glacial, or may be Pre-Glacial. There is a limit also to the age of *a*, inasmuch as it overlies in place a crag of Diestian age.

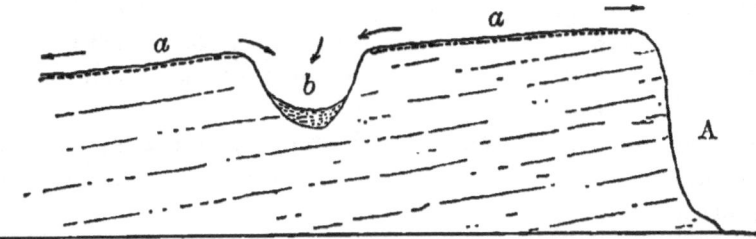

I have gone more fully into the Submergence question and some of its effects in a paper which is just passing through my hands, and will be published by Macmillan.

In the meantime, it will be a pleasure to me to answer any other questions that may arise; and I am very truly yours,

JOSEPH PRESTWICH.

It had become an established practice with the Rev. Ashington Bullen, the Vicar of Shoreham, when absent at the sea-side for a brief holiday, to prosecute inquiries for the veteran. The following letter refers to a visit paid by Mr Bullen to Bournemouth :—

J. Prestwich to the Rev. R. A. Bullen.

DARENT-HULME, 24th May 1895.

DEAR MR BULLEN,—Thanks for notes and particulars. Do not, however, trouble about mineral and structural particulars of the Gravels. I have them all in my note-books. All that is wanted is to supplement them by two inquiries :—

1. Do any implements of the plateau type occur in the high-level Gravels, such as St Catherine's Hill ?

2. Do any fluviatile shells occur in the Gravel referred to the Old Solent river ?

These questions were not mooted when I last worked in the district. Besides St Catherine's Hill you will find the high-level Gravels on Canon Hill and Hampreston Heath, on the N.E.

of Wimborne, and on the high ground E. and N.E. of Ford-
ingbridge.　Probably they are best developed on the hills
between Lyndhurst and Salisbury.　The Gravel on St Catherine's
Hill does not belong to the Old Solent.　The latter forms the
extensive beds of Gravel on the cliffs between Poole Harbour and
Lymington.　I shall be glad to see the specimens of flint implements you have found at St Catherine's Hill, or hear further
about the Solent Gravels; and I am most truly yours,

JOSEPH PRESTWICH.

Another letter of interest from Mr Gladstone, discussing the 'Tradition of the Flood,' is given here.　He
had written on June 9, 1895, to Sir Henry Acland : "It
was a great honour, as I thought, to receive Mr Prestwich's book, and I have put it up for careful perusal
on the voyage.　One curious thing is the way in which
the Deluge connects itself with the unity of the entire
present family of man."

W. E. Gladstone to J. Prestwich.

TANTALLON CASTLE, OFF KIEL, 20th June 1895.

MY DEAR SIR,—I have read with great interest the work which
you did me the honour and kindness of sending me.

The perusal of it leaves behind a lively hope that Geology may
ere long invade the regions of the Noachian tradition, and enable
you and others similarly endowed to learn whether Nature in
those regions tells a tale in any way analogous to that which you
have unfolded.　I am not sure whether I have apprehended accurately your remarks on the Accadian tradition of the Flood.　It
is indeed of the utmost value and importance.　But I cannot
agree with those who treat it as the *original record*, and the
Hebrew account as one altered and adopted from it.　To me both
of them are secondary forms, based upon an older and original
record.　I am able to follow a number of particulars in which
the record on the tablets appears to present marks of a nearer
approach (as I understand) to historic truth.　But there are two
points in which the Biblical account appears not only to be

superior, but superior in a mode indicating nearer resemblance to the primitive record, which may be unknown to us. One is that it is absolutely monotheistic, and the other is its representation of the Deluge as a judgment for sin. If, as some critics tell us, the Biblical text is not simple, but compounded of two separate narratives, this is all the more remarkable. Viewed severally and with regard to the education or evolution of man, the Chaldean record naturally exhibits the inferiority belonging to a state of opinion debased by the innovations of polytheism.—Believe me, my dear sir, very faithfully yours,　　　W. E. GLADSTONE.

J. Prestwich to Sir J. Evans.

DARENT-HULME, SHOREHAM, *6th July* 1895.

MY DEAR EVANS,—Your suggestion that some of the plateau implements might have been formed by *sea* [1] action had become so widely accepted by many geologists and by most anthropologists—the latter of whom have probably never been in a gravelpit in their lives—that I have been moved to write a letter to the 'Geological Magazine' expressing my dissent. It is in general terms, and your name in the matter is not mentioned. I can send you a proof before its publication in August if you should wish, for any suggestions. We both continue fairly well, although I had a bad turn ten days ago, which has obliged me to keep much to the sofa. What a loss the world of science has experienced in the death of Huxley! I had known him ever since his return from his voyage. It is a strange memorial that has been suggested. I hope there will be a better one. . . . —I am, ever sincerely yours,　　　JOSEPH PRESTWICH.

The letter to which reference is made was addressed to the Editor of the 'Geological Magazine,' being headed "Nature and Art," and was published in the August number. A pathetic interest attaches to it, since it

---

[1] Sir John Evans says that the use of the word "sea" in this letter was a mistake. Though he attributes the chipping and bruising of the edges of the flints in question to the turbulent action of water, he never invoked marine action.

was the last appearance in public of any communication from Joseph Prestwich. His first memoir, when a young, hard - working City man, had been read to the Geological Society in 1834 : now, after a splendid record of sixty-one years' continuous original work, his pen for the public was laid aside.

In the letter to the 'Geological Magazine' he refutes the theory of the flint implements from the Chalk plateau of Kent having been formed by natural agencies, and observes : " Had it been possible for sea- or river-action to have produced such forms as those I have figured in Plates V. to IX. of 'Collected Papers,' they should be found in all such shingle of whatsoever age. None are forthcoming." He repeats a former challenge : " [I] am ready to exchange the two volumes of 'Geology' with any young (or old) dissentient, for half-a-dozen shore flints (not derived) of any of the plateau types figured in the five plates above named." No one has come forward or has accepted the challenge. Time will adjudge the verdict, and of it we are not doubtful.

This imperfect sketch of the life of Joseph Prestwich would be still more incomplete without special reference to the affectionate relations which were maintained between him and geologists abroad, more particularly with those in France and Belgium. These friendships were not those of a year or so, or a score of years, but were life-enduring. His position as an Englishman of science among French *savants* was through a long series of years probably unique. In the files of letters from Gaudry, Daubrée, Hébert, and other distinguished members of the Institute, we find Joseph Prestwich repeatedly addressed by the first-named as " *Mon cher maître*," " *Cher et illustre confrère*"; Deshayes wrote to him usually as "*Mon cher et bon Mr Prestwich*," and Desnoyers as "*Monsieur et très honoré confrère.*" Letters from Capellini, the eminent Italian geologist, were couched in still warmer terms, and many similarly inscribed might be quoted from MM. de Rouville, de Vibraye, Boule, Dewalque, &c. Prestwich and Edouard Lartet were on terms of the highest mutual regard. One note from a French academician is given as an example of those delightful letters from France. It is dated less than a year before the end.

M. A. Daubrée to J. Prestwich.　　　　PARIS, *le* 13 *Juillet* 1895.

CHER PRESTWICH,—C'est toujours un bonheur pour moi de recevoir une marque de votre affectueux souvenir et en même temps de constater que vous continuez une activité juvénile.

Aussi, avant d'avoir complètement achevé de lire vos arguments ingénieux et inattendus relatifs à l'intéressante question du *déluge,* je désire vous adresser mes vifs remerciements, aussi que mes sincères félicitations. Comme votre carrière a été bien remplie, et malgré le prix de votre temps, vous vous êtes toujours montré d'une incomparable obligeance ; ce sont des souvenirs que je apprécie d'autant plus que j'avance en âge.

J'espère que votre activité est la preuve d'une santé vigoureuse.

De mon côté, je n'ai pas à me plaindre de ma santé, malgré le malheur qui m'a frappé il y a cinq mois, par la perte de ma chère femme.

Croyez toujours, cher Prestwich, à mes sentiments bien affectueux et dévoués,　　　　　　　　　　A. DAUBRÉE.

Letters from old Oxford students were received from time to time, and gave him keen pleasure. One, to whom he was much attached, was Professor T. W. Edgeworth David, known for his researches in the coal-fields of New South Wales, and for his recent investigations of coral islands, and who now fills the Chair of Geology in the University of Sydney. In

September 1892 Professor E. David wrote to his "dear master" : "Allow me to take this opportunity of thanking you again most sincerely, not only for the very cordial assistance which you rendered me in securing my present appointment, but also for your great kindness to me at Oxford, and the interest in geology and first grasp of its true principles which your lectures and field excursions at Oxford afforded me. I hope that my subsequent work will not discredit your early teaching."

Another student with whom he kept in touch was a Balliol man, now Professor A. P. W. Thomas of Auckland University, New Zealand. Mr C. L. Barnes, author of the 'Rock History' of the earth, was an attached pupil, who wrote to him—and not in vain—for advice and criticism. Another was the Rev. John Hawwell of Ingleby Vicarage, Northallerton, whom he encouraged to persevere in his work among the boulders of Yorkshire. About a year ago the writer of this memoir received a letter from Mr Hawwell, saying, "The one [letter] written to me when I was in the Radcliffe Infirmary, suffering from an attack of diphtheria, to which I fell a victim while undergoing examination for the Burdett-Coutts Scholarship, particularly illustrates the kindness of his disposition, of which I have so vivid and reverent a recollection." Among other old pupils may be mentioned Mr F. A. Bather, of the Geological Department, British Museum, who is distinguished for his researches on the fossil Crinoidea.

CHAPTER XII.

1895–1896.

LAST DAYS.

THE quiet semi-invalid life which had crept on Joseph Prestwich almost unawares was nevertheless a very happy time. It continued to be his practice to walk out a little in the garden before breakfast so as to breathe the morning air and have a look at the vane, always bringing in a rose or pink, or a handful of sweet-scented flowers. Any lady guest found a rose by her breakfast plate, or, when flowers were not within reach, sprays of his favourite lavender took their place, several plants of it being grown near the house so as to be accessible for cutting. The old routine was maintained : after reading the morning papers he adjourned to the library, when longingly he looked at his books and portfolios of MS., which he had been forbidden to touch. Replies to letters and notes were the first occupation, being dashed off in the old rapid style. Sometimes plants had to be ordered for the garden, or some other easy correspondence which could not be termed work. Before lunch, at least an hour (which was always an en-grossing time) was spent in the grounds ; he then often

rested on a bench and made notes of the shrubs marked
for change of position; and at different corners of the
garden considered improvements and alterations which
he had in view.   The route chosen for the afternoon
drive was most often towards some plateau implement
ground, when he was able to contemplate several of
the sites that had yielded the weapons or tools of
primitive man.   These easy open drives in the picturesque country always refreshed him, and in getting
into the carriage a frequent remark with a smile was,
"I have become quite resigned to these lazy ways."
The evening, however, was the time to which he looked
forward, when he liked his wife to read aloud, never
tired of Scotch stories, and appreciating their dry
humour and caustic sayings : it was difficult to maintain a supply sufficient for the demand.   Seeing a
facsimile of the first 1678 edition of the 'Pilgrim's
Progress' advertised, he expressed a wish for a copy,
which was placed on the drawing-room table by his
chair, and at odd moments the marvellous allegory was
usually in his hands.   He had been ever a steady reader
of 'Nature,' and in one of his last evenings downstairs,
while its pages were open before him, his eyes lighting
up, he observed, "I cannot tell you how much I enjoy
'Nature,' it is such a pleasure to me to see what other
workers are doing in other subjects."   While debarred
from his own special books, one which interested him
was 'In a Gloucestershire Garden,'[1] and a list lies before
us of the plants and flowers which were new to him,
and had therefore not found a place in his own garden.
This list had been jotted down in pencil, and was afterwards traced over in ink in a tremulous hand.

In answer to an inquiry made by Mr A. H. Tabrum,

[1] By Canon Ellacombe.

he writes, 12th August 1895, only three months before
his last illness :—

Religion and science constitute two distinct branches of human
knowledge and inquiry. They move in parallel lines, and cannot,
in my opinion, clash. They certainly should not. The one has
to deal with moral questions, the other with physical questions.
You may have seen that I deal with one of the latter in my
'Tradition of the Flood,' recently published by Messrs Macmillan & Co.

Among the last notes in his handwriting is one in
which reference is made to his letter of challenge in
the 'Geological Magazine' :—

J. Prestwich to Sir J. Evans.

DARENT-HULME, SHOREHAM, *2nd Sept.* 1895.

MY DEAR EVANS,—It was a pleasure to us to hear of your safe
return, and of the delightful round you had had—all ground
unvisited by me, but of which I have heard much. I suppose
you secured a bag of the Saxon coins. I suppose you will be at
Ipswich. I have written to Galton to express my regret.

I hope you approve of my letter. It will put the matter to
your followers to the test. You will, I think and hope, have to
give up that leadership, unless you do not wish to be left without
any disciples—at least so I judge from Harrison's gains. This fine
weather suits me, but I have had rather a bad time of it of late,
and have not been allowed to work. I hope that will not last
long. I trust you and Lady Evans are well; and with love from
self and wife, I am, ever sincerely yours,

JOSEPH PRESTWICH.

While conscientious in adhering to the rules enjoined
by his devoted friend and medical adviser, Dr F. C.
Bury, his sanguine and buoyant nature led him con-
fidently to look forward to restored health and capacity for work. But to one who looked on there was

no apparent gain in strength. A visit late in September from Sir John and Lady Evans gave untold pleasure, although he found himself unable to carry out his programme of accompanying them to various sites of the plateau implements. It was after this visit that he felt stronger and better, and, as an intermediate step to geological work, began writing his autobiography, which his wife had often urged him to place on record, and the few pages of which are given in the early part of this volume. With his pen in hand and a sheaf of foolscap before him he lighted up and felt the old power for work. As this was the case, he could not resist breaking ground with a paper "On some Local Freshwater Deposits underlying the Glacial Series in the South of England," which he intended to be the forerunner of a series of glacial memoirs.[1] This last work, unfortunately, is too incomplete for publication. His ruling passion — the love of geology—was, however, unquenchable.

But about 9.30 on the evening of the 1st of November, and after a day when, in spite of repeated reminders, his pen had been longer than usual at work, Joseph Prestwich rose from his chair, while his wife as usual was reading aloud, and going across the room, lay down on the sofa, saying in rather a low voice, "I am not feeling very well." He never complained, not even when in pain and suffering, so it was evident that he was ill. He would not hear of Dr Bury being sent for, saying, "Wait, I am feeling better," and went back to his easy-chair. But the improvement was only temporary, as shortly after he became unconscious for two or three minutes. While a messenger rode off to

[1] A brief account of this MS. is given in the Geological Magazine, Dec. IV., vol. v. p. 405, 1898.

Riverhead for Dr Bury, he had rallied so far as with help to be able to walk upstairs, declining any extra assistance. It proved the beginning of a last illness, when during eight long months he suffered no pain, but lay in a state of extreme bodily weakness. So long as he had strength to listen he liked to have the current news read regularly every morning, and later in the day he again listened to reading.

As Dr Bury expressed a wish for a second opinion, Sir W. Broadbent joined him in consultation and approved of all the treatment: he held out hope, which was clung to at the time, but on looking back it is evident that the physician's opinion was a qualified one.

Soon after this there were anxious fluctuations in the condition of the invalid, which he clearly realised. He expressed a wish to receive the Holy Communion, which was administered to him by Mr Bullen, whose attachment to him was as that of a son. Owing to feebleness of the heart he had been forbidden to sit up; therefore, when seeing the frail form struggle into a strange crouching posture, his wife whispered, " You are in a painful position?" "It is more penitent," was the answer. The solemnity of the scene cannot be told in words.

Rev. R. Ashington Bullen to G. A. Prestwich.

SHOREHAM VICARAGE, *29th Dec.* 1895.

DEAR MRS PRESTWICH,—I sincerely trust that my dear master did not suffer from the intense strain of yesterday afternoon. It was a great privilege to be with you both, and it will abide with me as long as I live. I have always felt very near the dear professor,—now I feel nearer than ever. I would that some of those proud of their spiritual and intellectual attainments could see his deep humility, which, as Montgomery so finely sings in the hymn that was my dear mother's greatest favourite, is " nearest the Throne."

A few days before this date it had been rumoured that Joseph Prestwich's name was one of those in the list designated for New Year's honours, and two of his old kind friends, of whom Dr H. Woodward was one and Sir Henry Howorth the other, thinking to give him pleasure, wrote to inform him of the report. The news gave him unfeigned pleasure—though not on his own account. From weakness which had been alarming he again rallied, and there were even glad symptoms of a little step upward. New Year's morning brought a confirmation of the rumour that he was one of those upon whom her Majesty bestowed the honour of knighthood. One of the earliest telegrams received was from Sir John Evans with hearty congratulations, and "this will help Sir Joseph's convalescence," the words bringing a bright smile to the invalid's face. Throughout the day messages kept arriving from attached friends, each one giving heartfelt pleasure.

But after a few months it was plain that the improvement was not maintained, that on the contrary there was the almost imperceptible decline, and that the frail life hung upon a thread. Yet with that distressingly low pulse there was no actual pain — a mercy for which those who looked on could not be too thankful.

> " But, O my gentle sisters, O my brothers,
> These thick-sown snowflakes hint of toil's release ;
> These feebler pulses bid me leave to others
> The tasks once welcome : Evening asks for peace."

All that the best and kindest medical skill could devise was brought to bear upon his case. Dr Bury

watched for any untoward symptom, and his visit was
eagerly looked forward to as the event of the day.
The tedium of the sick-bed was also lightened by the
frequent sight of near and dear relatives: his sister
Eliza (Mrs Tomkins) was constant in her visits, as was
his attached niece Annie [1] (daughter of Mrs Thurburn),
while his sister, Emily Prestwich, had throughout
his illness remained in the house. There was never
a morning without some letter of affectionate inquiry, the reading of which brought the shining
light into his eyes, none giving keener pleasure
than those from his friend Evans. Again and again
Sir Archibald Geikie sent long letters with accounts
of all that was passing in the geological world, to
every word of which he listened with delighted
interest. "No letter from Rupert to-day?" was
an inquiry often made, referring to his old friend,
Professor Rupert Jones. Then there were the letters
from Sir Henry Acland, expressing, as they ever did,
the old brotherly affection. From abroad, too, came
frequent inquiries, for the news of his illness had
spread. It is not too much to say that these proofs of
affectionate interest coming constantly, as they did,
were a solace and comfort to the frail invalid: they
made him remember that he held a place in many
hearts. It should be mentioned, too, that letters from
Mrs Etheridge invariably cheered him: they always
brought brightness to him, telling perhaps of a step
forward made by some other invalid, something to
think of and look forward to. Then there were the
little visits from Mr Bullen, who occasionally brought
a newly found flint implement in his pocket, and when
it was a sight to see the flash and eager look of delight

---

[1] Wife of General Wm. Percival Tomkins, R.E., C.I.E.

with which it was handled, and how the slender fingers felt it all over, noting the chipping and marks with a smile of approval. Nor must we forget the fresh flowers—his own flowers, which were daily brought to him, and now as ever contributed so largely to the pleasure of his life. The last little tree of which he superintended the planting was the variegated species of the Thuiopsis, the *T. variegata;* and on his more than once inquiring how it had stood the winter, a sprig of the white-tipped foliage was brought to him, when it was characteristic to see the keen interest with which it was handled and examined.

As the spring wore on it was too apparent that his power of listening to reading had become less, and that he was unable to bear the strain of long - sustained attention. At night, when a brief invalid prayer was read—a sentence or two—he roused himself and joined with fervour, and followed also a few verses of a psalm, ending with a hymn, to which he specially liked to listen. He often asked for the hymn, " Jesus, Lover of my soul "; but he was so much affected by it that it was found advisable to substitute another. Dr Bury, always on the watch for any amelioration of his position, suggested his being carried in a recumbent posture into the adjoining library, to a bed placed there. One sad look round at his books—those books which he was never again to open—was given when he was first moved there; afterwards he did not appear to notice them. As no harm was done by this experiment of an hour or two daily in the library, Dr Bury arranged for a move, always in a recumbent posture, down to the dining-room on the ground floor, where, from a couch in the bow-window, the invalid in the daytime could look out on the lawn with its flower-beds, and on the background of shrubs and trees. There is no doubt that this change to a room downstairs gave him immense pleasure, and often as he lay quietly contemplating the flower-borders (his own planning), he sank into a restful sleep. But the sight of that pathetic form in the window was almost unnerving for those who looked on. In the evenings the doors from dining- to drawing-room were thrown open, and to his delight his sister-in-law, Louisa Milne, played piece after piece of the music he liked best. With a wistful smile he remarked, "What with the music and the flowers, I am beginning to enjoy life." Dr Bury's hope was that in warm summer air he might be able to be carried out to a couch in the garden, and this would have been feasible from the dining-room; but, alas! it was not to be. There was a further failure of strength, and an alarmingly low pulse. The music which had given such manifest delight now failed to interest or attract his attention. The end was near: it came before dawn on the morning of the 23rd June 1896.

A few days later the mortal remains of Joseph Prestwich were laid in the churchyard of Shoreham, in the presence of an assemblage of attached friends, many of whom were representatives of the scientific societies of which he had been so notable a working member. The service was performed by his old friend Canon Bonney and by the Rev. R. A. Bullen. A grey granite cross marks his resting-place, with the motto of the Prestwich family inscribed on the base, "In te Domine speravi." It is within sight of his dear home.

Numerous letters of sympathy bore testimony to the place he held as a man of science and to the love he inspired. An extract from one addressed to the writer by Lady Ramsay, widow of the geologist, may be given as an example of many :—

I think I remember telling you when you married that your husband stood on the highest pinnacle of our love and esteem, and those words are as true now as ever, but to those feelings I have now to add the deep grief of parting with, it seems to me, the one last link to the dear old set and the never-forgotten old times, and that parting, the loss of the sweetest, most courteous and high-minded and lovable gentleman of my acquaintance. . . . The memory of dear Sir Joseph will be "sadly kept" as long as I remember anything.

The Master of Pembroke College (Professor Bartholomew Price), who so recently passed away, also gave his testimony :—

Very many friends and admirers of Sir Joseph Prestwich are grieving with you : they feel that geological science has lost the foremost of its able students, and that a man great in all respects has fallen from among them.

M. Gaudry, the distinguished palæontologist, wrote:—

Je suis très affligé d'apprendre la mort de mon illustre confrère, Sir Joseph Prestwich. Non seulement c'était un des plus grands géologues de notre époque, mais ainsi c'était un homme d'un si beau caractère, que tout le monde l'aimait. Le chagrin des savants anglais sera partagé par les savants français, qui avaient pour Sir Joseph la plus profonde estime. . . . L'Institut de France et la Société géologique vont prendre une vive part à votre malheur. . . .

The official letter, addressed to Lady Prestwich by the President and Council of the Geological Society of London, records "their high appreciation of the life-long work achieved by Sir Joseph Prestwich, who for sixty-three years was a member of their body, alike respected and beloved."

SUMMARY OF THE SCIENTIFIC WORK OF SIR JOSEPH PRESTWICH, D.C.L., F.R.S.,

BY

SIR ARCHIBALD GEIKIE, D.C.L., F.R.S.,
DIRECTOR-GENERAL OF THE GEOLOGICAL SURVEYS OF THE UNITED KINGDOM.

THE scientific career of Joseph Prestwich was marked by the long period over which it extended, and by the wide range of subjects within the domain of geology which it embraced. For more than sixty years, with indefatigable industry, he continued to contribute original observations and reflections to the science to which he had dedicated his life. His writings cover almost the whole field of geology. He discussed the various agencies, epigene and hypogene, which are now giving rise to geological changes on the earth. He studied the various geological formations from the Old Red Sandstone to the most recent Gravels, but specially devoted himself to the older Tertiary and the Quaternary series. He gave much thought to the practical applications of geology, and led the way in pointing out the intimate relation between water-supply and geological structure. And lastly, he gave the world the benefit of his ripe experience and long reflection in the text-book in which he took a philosophical survey of the whole realm of geological investigation.

To gain a general idea of the nature, extent, and value of his scientific work, it will be convenient to subdivide his writings according to the several branches of geology which they illustrate. For this purpose we may first consider his contributions to our knowledge of the causes that produce geological changes, and the effects to which they give rise.

From an early part of his scientific studies Prestwich paid close attention to the influence of running water on the face of the land. His interest in this subject was greatly quickened by his observations in connection with the high-level and low-level Gravels of the river-valleys in the south-east of England and the north-east of France. From these deposits he drew the important conclusion that the valleys have been mainly eroded by the rivers which still flow in them. Though this explanation of river-valleys was strongly insisted upon by Hutton and Playfair, and had been demonstrated for Central France by Desmarest and afterwards by Scrope and Lyell, it had never attained wide acceptance among geologists. When it was adopted and enforced by Prestwich on a basis of well-ascertained fact, it came almost with the freshness of a new discovery. He quickly saw its significance in regard to the slow sculpture of the face of the land, and the great antiquity which it proved for the older and higher terraces of Gravel. In his memoir, read before the Royal Society in 1862 [56],[1] he dwelt on the evidence that could be adduced of powerful and long-continued erosion in the valleys by the streams that still flow in them; and he continued to bring forward additional proofs in support of his views [61], until geologists everywhere

---

[1] The numbers within square brackets refer to the corresponding entries in the list of writings given at p. 422.

admitted the validity of his reasoning. There remained, indeed, differences of opinion as to the intensity of the operations by which the denudation had been effected. The followers of Lyell would not admit that the observed facts demanded the existence of larger rivers and more powerful floods than might be witnessed at the present time, while Prestwich was always prepared to find that the geological agents had worked on a grander scale in former times than they do now. But the fundamental fact, that the valleys of the south-east of England and the north-west of France had been carved out by the action of the rivers that drain them, was now accepted without further demur.

To Prestwich, therefore, must be assigned a not inconsiderable share in promoting the advance made during the last thirty years in the investigation of the history of terrestrial topography. He continued to interest himself in the subject up to the end of his life. Some of his last contributions to science dealt with the carving out of the river-valleys around his home at Shoreham and in the neighbouring district of the Weald [123-125].

The geologists of the British Islands have always been foremost in their recognition of the place of the ocean among the agents of terrestrial change. Prestwich followed the national instinct when, in his Presidential Address to the Geological Society in 1871, he seized the opportunity, then offered by the expeditions of the Lightning and Porcupine, to review the progress of inquiry into the life of the deep sea and its relations to geological history [74], while at the same time he called attention to the geological significance of the distribution of temperature in the ocean. This latter department of oceanography especially engaged his attention, and for years he continued to collect the materials, which he finally embodied in a voluminous memoir, read in 1874 before the Royal Society [87], wherein he tabulated all the recorded observations of sea-temperatures from 1749 to 1868, and discussed some of their geological bearings.

Nor did the more active geological operations of the sea escape his scrutiny. Thus he made a careful study of the conditions which seemed to him to have led to the formation of the well-known Chesil Bank. In the account of this inquiry, which he communicated to the Institute of Civil Engineers [89], he combined the results of an investigation of the present action of the tides and currents along the Dorsetshire coast with an examination of the proofs of earlier geological changes in that district. In this, as in so many of his other papers, he was able to bring a wide geological experience towards the elucidation of the problems which he undertook to discuss.

In England, and more especially in the south-eastern counties, the geologist has but slender opportunity of studying the underground operations with which his science deals. In the year 1870 Prestwich spent some time among the volcanic regions of Italy. The writer of the present notice of his labours had the advantage of accompanying him in some of his excursions around Rome and Naples, and recalls with pleasure the keen interest which the veteran geologist took in every phenomenon in the volcanic history of those fascinating districts. He especially remembers the exploration of Vesuvius, the scrutiny of the crater-wall of Somma, and the enthusiasm awakened by the evidence of profound erosion in the gullies that descend from the crest of Somma into the plain to the north—an enthusiasm that was not damped by the torrents of rain that fell as the travellers threaded their way down one of the ravines.

Even had this journey never been made, Prestwich's sound views and wide sympathies in every department of his favourite science would not probably have allowed him to leave the field of volcanic geology untrodden. He had evidently reflected much on the subject before he contributed, in 1885, three short but suggestive papers to the Royal Society. In the first of these he discussed the various recorded observations of underground temperature, and concluded that the rise of the thermometer amounts to an average of 1° Fahr. for every 48 feet of descent. He further suggested that the abnormally high temperatures found in piercing the Alps for the construction of railway tunnels might be the residue of the heat caused by the intense lateral pressure and crushing of the rocks which accompanied the last elevation of the mountain-chain [112]. Pursuing this idea, he was led to speculate on the probable cause of the metamorphism observable among mountain-ranges in strata which, upon the surrounding plains, have undergone no alteration [114]. He connected the change with the great development of heat during the process of mountain-making. Reasoning from the results of Mallet's experiments on rock-crushing, he contended that the effects of this increased temperature would vary with compressibility, some rocks being made three times hotter than others under the same strain. In this way he accounted for the local character of the metamorphism, and for its much more marked development in some strata than in others. In the third memoir [113], he controverted the common assumption that the expulsion of lava at a volcanic vent is due to the expansion of water-vapour contained within the molten rock under great pressure and at a high temperature. But he had formed no original conception of volcanic energy. Following Mr Osmond Fisher's reasoning, he supposed that a thin terrestrial crust rests on a slowly yielding viscous layer within which lies a solid nucleus. The aqueous vapour in volcanic eruptions he regarded as due to the surface and underground waters with which the intensely hot magma of the interior comes in contact, and he believed that the actual cause of the uprise of molten material and the outflow of lava is to be sought in the effects of the secular refrigeration and contraction of this planet, the cooling and shrinking outer shell compressing and forcing out the intensely heated material inside.

It is interesting to note that Prestwich began his geological career by studying in minute and patient detail the coal-field of Coalbrookdale, and that he was thereafter led to explore the Old Red Sandstone of the Moray Firth. This early work was so eclipsed by the brilliance of his later researches among much younger formations, that a later generation of his contemporaries hardly realised the rare excellence and originality of his first great essay. The elaborate memoir on Coalbrookdale [7], presented to the Geological Society when its author was only a young man of twenty, is certainly a remarkable performance. Those to whom it was first addressed can hardly have failed to recognise in its author one of the future leaders of English geology. Selecting an area of about 100 square miles, he carefully mapped its geology on the scale of one inch to a mile. The map was no mere sketch, but an elaborate survey, wherein the outcrops of the several seams of coal were traced, and the positions and effects of all the principal dislocations were represented. The structure of the ground was further displayed in a series of horizontal and vertical sections, while additional details were given in an excellent descriptive memoir, combining a complete account of the stratigraphy and palæontology of the district. The lists of fossils, together with plates of new species, form an important feature in this publication. Not only were the organic remains of the several formations discriminated, but even the characteristic forms of successive horizons were distinguished, and the bearing of the palæontological evidence on the geological conditions of deposit were luminously discussed. This Coalbrookdale monograph must be regarded as one of the classics of English geology, marking a notable advance in the progress of stratigraphy, and serving as a model for the subsequent investigation of the geological structure of our coal-fields. It appeared before the then recently organised Geological Survey had mapped any of those parts of the country, and it is remarkable how closely the mapping of the Survey in subsequent years followed the lines which he had laid down.

But, unquestionably, the most important of Sir Joseph's original contributions to science are to be found in the series of papers which he wrote on the older Tertiary formations of the south - east of England, and on the younger deposits containing the earliest traces of man. This brilliant work was begun, carried on, and completed during the scanty intervals of leisure which he could snatch from a busy mercantile life. Properly to understand its scope and value, we must go back to the earlier decades of this century and take note of the vague and confused ideas then entertained by geologists as to the arrangement and stratigraphical value of the series of deposits that overlie the Chalk. The term London Clay had been applied by William Smith to these deposits from the argillaceous character of their chief member. Subsequently various geologists noticed the occurrence of a group of sandy and clayey strata between the main mass of the London Clay and the top of the Chalk. These were grouped together as Plastic Clay and Sand, but their true stratigraphical value and palæontological interest were hardly recognised. In the year 1846, Prestwich published the first of the long series of papers in which he gradually worked out the true relations of the several members of the series, and brought them into relation with their equivalents in France and Belgium. The story of this evolution of clear order out of the confusion that had preceded Prestwich's researches has been well told by Mr Whitaker, who has followed so worthily in the footsteps of the pioneer whose labours he chronicles.[1] Beginning among the cliff sections of the Isle of Wight [9], Prestwich traversed every part of the Hampshire and London basins, recording his observations on copies of the Ordnance maps, and in voluminous note-books. From year to year he communicated his results to the Geological Society, each paper throwing new light on the history of the geological formations, until in 1854 his great essay on the Woolwich and Reading series [23] added the coping-stone to the edifice he had so patiently reared. He showed that between the top of the Chalk and the base of the London Clay a group of strata, which

---

[1] Mem. Geol. Survey, The Geology of London, vol. i. (1889), p. 88.

he had called the "Lower London Tertiaries," was capable of a threefold arrangement into — 1st, the basement-bed of the London Clay; 2nd, the Woolwich and Reading series; and 3rd, the Thanet Sands. Tracing out the range and general physical features of the middle group, he brought forward numerous sections showing the local variations of the sediments from Hampshire to the east of Kent. He gave ample lists of the fossil contents of the strata, and discussed them in their bearings on the geographical conditions under which the deposits were accumulated. For the first time, the succession of geological events recorded in the oldest Eocene strata of England was clearly stated.

After reducing to order the older Tertiary series of England, Prestwich conferred a still further service on geology by bringing the English formations into line with those of France and Belgium. In a series of elaborate papers [32, 36, 109, 118] communicated to the Geological Society, he established the correlation of these deposits both lithologically and palæontologically, and in so doing became the acknowledged leader in the Tertiary geology of Western Europe.

In the course of his researches among the Eocene formations, Prestwich was necessarily led to take note of the younger Tertiary deposits sparingly distributed over the east and south-east of England. At intervals, from the very beginning of his career, he had made excursions into Suffolk and Norfolk. From 1845 to 1855 he devoted much time to the study of the younger Tertiary deposits of these counties. But he was too much engaged in his Eocene investigations to find time to elaborate his Pliocene notes into methodical form. It was not until the spring of the year 1868 that he was able to bring forward a detailed account of his studies in the form of a memoir on the Coralline Crag [65], followed by another two months later on the Red Crag [66], and by a third in the year 1870 on the Norwich Crag [69]. These three memoirs were delayed in publication, and did not appear until the year 1871, when they were issued in successive numbers of the twenty-seventh volume of the ' Quarterly Journal of the Geological Society.' Though the observations recorded in them by Prestwich were the results of his own sedulous examination of the ground, and though the conclusions he arrived at were founded on his own original researches, these papers made their appearance after much time and labour had been spent in the investigation of the same deposits by other observers. He was perhaps hardly aware to what extent his earlier work had been forestalled in date of publication by the labours of his younger contemporaries. As original contributions to geology, his East Anglian papers have thus not the same originality and freshness that were shown in his series of Eocene memoirs, where he had the ground largely to himself, and published his researches while they were still new and not anticipated by other fellow-labourers.

To one of his investigations in later Tertiary geology reference may here be made as an instance of his sagacity of observation. He had long been acquainted with certain ferruginous sands scattered over the North Downs from Folkestone to Dorking. He recognised these materials to be different from the red flint-drift or loam, on the one hand, and from the outliers of older Tertiary sands and pebble-beds on the other. In 1854 some highly ferruginous parts of these deposits yielded a number of casts of shells which were regarded by some palæontologists as indicating the base of the London Clay. Prestwich, however, assigned them to a much more recent period. He shared the opinion of Searles Wood, who regarded them as probably of the age of the Lower Crag. More recent observations by Mr Clement Reid of the Geological Survey, and the discovery of other and better preserved fossils, have left no doubt that Prestwich was entirely justified in looking upon these remnants of a once extensive deposit as Pliocene.

Outside the ranks of geologists Prestwich was probably best known for his connection with the establishment of the Antiquity of Man, and for his share in bringing home to the English public the enormous importance of geological knowledge in dealing with water - supply and other questions of every - day occurrence.

When in the spring of 1859, at the suggestion of Dr Hugh Falconer, he undertook to investigate the alleged proofs of the occurrence of flint-implements together with the remains of extinct mammalia in some of the old valley - gravels of the north of France, he entered on the inquiry with no very sanguine hope of finding that there was any good ground for the contention of M. Boucher de Perthes, who some ten years before had proclaimed his belief in the remote antiquity of the human race. But the evidence proved so strong as entirely to satisfy him that the French observer, who had met with but scant sympathy or support, was nevertheless right in his main conclusion. It was important to establish the fundamental fact that man was a contemporary of the long extinct mammals whose bones were found lying beside his flint weapons in beds of undisturbed gravel, and further to show that the deposit of this gravel, though referable to a comparatively late geological period, must be older than the present configuration of the ground. Prestwich lost no time in communicating the results of his examination of the Abbeville region to the Royal Society [46]. He cautiously abstained from pronouncing on the antiquity of man, contenting himself with pointing out that though there could be no doubt that man was contemporary with certain extinct forms of elephant, rhinoceros, deer, and other animals, no evidence had yet been obtained to show the chronological value of the interval that had elapsed since the deposit of the gravels containing the worked flints. He himself was at first inclined, not so much to throw the human period indefinitely backward, as to bring down the period of the extinct mammalia nearer to our own day, and to account for their disappearance and for the modification of the superficial topography by some sudden or rapid geological change, which, though transient, was powerful enough to leave its memorial on the surface of the land. As his investigations proceeded he felt the weight of evidence continually augmenting in favour of the long lapse of time required for the excavation of the valleys and for the production of the vast changes in the configuration of the land since the accumulation of the implement-bearing gravels. In his next great memoir, published in 1864 [56], he admitted that "we must greatly extend our present chronology with respect to the first existence of man ; but that we should count by hundreds of thousands of years is, I am convinced, in the present state of the inquiry, unsafe and premature." In this valuable essay, the whole evidence of the valley-gravels and of the gradual erosion of the valleys is marshalled with great skill, and discussed with characteristic clearness and caution. In later essays he admitted that man was living in Glacial or Post-Glacial times which came down approximately to within 10,000 or 12,000 years of our own day [116, 122].

Thus it is to Prestwich, more than to any other geologist, that we owe the establishment of the fact that man coexisted with a number of now long extinct mammals, and that his advent on the earth must be relegated to a far higher antiquity than that which had previously been accepted. While he was engaged in the researches that led to these results, he at the same time greatly enlarged our knowledge of the later phases of the Ice Age, particularly in the river-valleys of the south of England and north-west of France. The term "Drift" has been vaguely applied to a multifarious series of superficial deposits, differing widely from each other in origin and in age. Prestwich strenuously contended for the local origin of the gravels in which flint-implements and mammalian remains occur together. He showed that these accumulations unquestionably belong to the river-systems within which they are found, that they were fluviatile in origin, and were deposited by the streams which still flow in the same valleys. He maintained, however, that the rivers were formerly vastly larger than they are now; that, in virtue of their size, width, and transporting power, they were able to carry downward and spread out over their flood-plains the widely distributed sheets of coarse shingle now remaining; while from time to time they rose in floods of extraordinary magnitude that deposited the fine silt, containing land-shells, which is now to be seen covering all the different gravel - beds. Considerable difference of opinion still exists, however, regarding some of these deductions. Other observers, as remarked above, have been unable to perceive any satisfactory evidence that the rivers were generally more swollen than they are at present, though at exceptional periods of melting snow they may have surpassed in volume any floods chronicled in their valleys during historic time. But Prestwich detected the traces of another transporting agent than that of mere unaided river-water. In the presence of large unworn blocks among the ancient gravels, together with much sharp angular detritus, he recognised the operation of river-ice. Thus all over the south-east of England, where the climate is now so mild, he traced indications that in old times the rivers flowing on the platform of the higher gravels were frozen over; that ice forming along their margins or over their bottoms lifted and carried along the shingle and boulders lying there; and that when these Arctic conditions prevailed, man had already appeared, fishing in the rivers, or tracking the mammoth, the bison, and various extinct forms of deer through the surrounding forests and prairies.

Among Prestwich's contributions to the history of the latest geological changes that have affected the south of England and the north of France, his numerous papers on the so-called Raised Beaches of this region [4, 44, 48, 52, 64, 79, 88, 97-99, 128] deserve recognition. The notices of recent uprise of the land in Britain and on the opposite French coast were based on his own personal observations, and they are of value as records of facts formerly visible, but some of which have been obscured or concealed by the progress of building and other changes. Prestwich, however, carried his deductions far beyond these local limits. He collected a vast mass of evidence from the writings of Continental geologists, regarding what he considered to be evidence of a submergence of Western Europe at the close of the Glacial period [130]. His data ranged from the coasts of Belgium and France to Gibraltar, and embraced the whole wide basin of the Mediterranean. Resting, however, on the testimony of witnesses of unequal value, they lack the directness and coherence of his own personal observations, and the deductions based upon them, though elaborately worked out, have not yet obtained general acceptance. As regards the conclusions drawn by him in some of his later papers dealing with the supposed evidence of changes of level in the South of England, geological opinion is likewise divided [see especially 128]. These papers, though the result of much close personal observation made during the course of many years, were not written out and communicated to the world until the closing years of his life. In the long interval which, in some cases, had elapsed between his labours in the field and the discussion of them in these papers, much had been done in certain directions by other observers. In regard, for example, to the "Head" or "Rubble-Drift" of the South of England, we may share his regret that he was unable to revisit all the ground, and to review his conclusions in the light of more recent research. But it was of great service to the history of geological progress that the actual field-notes and matured opinions of so patient and accurate an observer should have been at last put on record by himself.

One of the most useful services rendered by Sir Joseph Prestwich to the cause of his own science was the active share he took in the practical applications of geology. His labours in this department were manifested in two different directions. In the first place, he, more than other geologists of his day, insisted on the necessity of a knowledge of geological structure in dealing with the question of water-supply. From his early communication to the Institute of British Architects [16] down to his pamphlet on the Oxford water-supply [111], an interval of thirty-five years elapsed, during which he came to be regarded as the leading authority on this subject in England, and his co-operation doubtless added much to the value of the Report of the Royal Commission on Water - Supply, issued in 1869 [67]. It is to be regretted that the maps prepared by him for this Report were never published. In the second place, his early devotion to the coal - field of Coalbrookdale gave him a knowledge of our Carboniferous System, and an interest in its development, which he turned to good use in later years, when he acted as a member of the Royal Commission on Coal. Not the least valuable part of that important and voluminous work was supplied by him in his papers on the quantity of unwrought coal in the coal-fields of Somerset, and on the probability of finding coal under the newer formations of the South of England [75]. In the last-named paper he gave a *résumé* of all that had been ascertained up to the year 1866 regarding the possible extension of the Coal-Measures, and gave good grounds for supporting the conclusions of Godwin - Austen, and for believing in "the high probability of the existence of basins [of coal] under the Secondary and Tertiary formations of the South of England." This opinion, and the reasoning on which it was based, have recently acquired fresh interest and value from the successful borings for coal in Kent.

The main portions of Prestwich's numerous contributions to the literature of geology are to be found in the journals and transactions of the various scientific societies with which he was associated. But he was likewise the author of a number of independent works, the preparation of which gave him an opportunity of ranging over a broader field, and appealing to a wider circle of readers, than that which he reached by his more technical writings. The most important of these separate publications was undoubtedly his treatise or text-book on 'Geology, Chemical, Physical, and Stratigraphical,' in two volumes, of which the first, dealing with the chemical and physical aspects of the science, appeared in 1886 [115], and the second, taking up chiefly the stratigraphical side, two years later [117]. In these volumes, issued towards the close of his scientific career, Prestwich sums up his views on every branch of the science to which he had dedicated his life. Apart, therefore, from their value as contributions to geological literature, they have a special biographical interest in relation to the position of their author with regard to disputed questions in geology, and to the general philosophy of the science. Throughout his life he remained opposed to the extreme doctrines of the Uniformitarian school. He contended that it was impossible to admit that the limited period— — 2000 years at the most — during which man had been recording his observations of nature, could furnish a standard by which the operations of the vast succession of bygone ages could be measured. On the other hand, he never adopted to the full the opinions of the opposite or catastrophic school. He believed that, while the laws of nature are immutable, the relative intensity of different geological agencies may have varied from period to period, and that in seeking for explanations of the phenomena presented by geological evidence we are not to be hampered by any foregone conclusions as to uniformity or variation, but, as in other questions, must frame our hypotheses on an exhaustive discussion of the facts.

He contended that our interpretations should be judged by their agreement with the multifarious questions suggested by the facts, and by the manner in which they satisfy the various conditions of the problems to which they are applied. Neither a Uniformitarian nor an extreme Convulsionist, he was content to accept the guidance of the present condition of geological causation on the face of the globe, so long as it did not involve any contradiction of what seemed to him the obvious teachings of the rocks. But he never shrank from invoking a gigantic flood, or a subsidence or elevation of the land, if such seemed to him the most natural solution of the problems that presented themselves before him. He lived long enough to have witnessed some remarkable oscillations in geological opinion. In his young days a belief was almost universal in former catastrophes by which the surface of the globe had from time to time been devastated. He saw the rise of Lyell into fame, and the overwhelming influence in this country of the Uniformitarian doctrines which that great teacher so cogently enforced. He marked the decline of the extremer form of Uniformitarianism, and the growth of a creed more nearly in harmony with his own.

But it is not from his direct contributions to theoretical questions that Prestwich's name will be enrolled in the list of the founders of English geology. His long, earnest, patient, and sagacious researches among the Tertiary formations will for ever mark him out as one of those to whom geology is indebted for opening up some new chapters in the history of the globe. And when in future years the story of Early Man comes to be written with the fulness of accumulated knowledge, it will be remembered and acknowledged that he was one of the foremost pioneers in that fascinating branch of geological inquiry.

In conclusion, it may not be inappropriate to refer here to the influence which Prestwich exerted on his scientific contemporaries. The writer of these lines, who knew him well for many years, may perhaps be permitted to bear his testimony to the remarkable and perennial charm of his personality. While we revered him as one of the last of the old heroic race of geologists; while we honoured him for the endless enthusiasm and perseverance with which, often in the midst of many hindrances, he devoted every leisure moment to the cause of geology; while we admired him for the infinite patience, the scrupulous caution, and the laborious exhaustiveness of his researches, we loved him for the gentle child-like simplicity of his heart, his unaffected modesty, and his genuine goodness. His bright sunny temperament always found out what was best in those with whom he came in contact. His unfailing sympathy delighted to find expression in active helpfulness. The smile that lighted up his handsome features seemed to reveal at one glance the tenderness and kindliness and truthfulness of his nature. One felt after an interview with him cheered and brightened by contact with one whose serene old age seemed to place him so far above the littlenesses and troubles of life. While his writings will perpetuate his scientific achievements, it should be placed on record that it was not these achievements alone which gave Joseph Prestwich his pre-eminence among his contemporaries, but that he owed this position in large measure to the integrity and charm of his character.

LIST OF PAPERS, BOOKS, Etc.,

By SIR JOSEPH PRESTWICH, M.A., D.C.L., F.R.S., Etc.

1834.

1. On some of the Faults which affect the Coal-field of Coalbrookdale. Proc. Geol. Soc., vol. ii. pp. 18, 19.

1835.

2. Observations on the Ichthyolites of Gamrie in Banffshire, and on the accompanying Red Conglomerates and Sandstones. Proc. Geol. Soc., vol. ii. pp. 187, 188.

1836.

3. Memoir on the Geology of Coalbrookdale. [Abstract.] Proc. Geol. Soc., vol. ii. pp. 401-406.

1837.

4. On some Recent Elevations of the Coast of Banffshire, and on a Deposit of Clay formerly considered to be Lias. Proc. Geol. Soc., vol. ii. p. 545.

1838.

5. Sur les Débris de Mammifères terrestres qui se trouvent dans l'Argile plastique, aux Environs d'Epernay. Bull. Soc. Géol. Fr., vol. ix. pp. 84-95.

1840.

6. On the Structure of the Neighbourhood of Gamrie, Banffshire, particularly on the Deposit containing Ichthyolites. Trans. Geol. Soc., Ser. 2, vol. v. pp. 139-148.
7. On the Geology of Coalbrookdale. Ibid., pp. 413-495.
8. On the Occurrence of Mammalian Remains in the Lower Eocene Deposits of Epernay, Marne. Mag. Nat. Hist., Ser. 2, vol. iv. pp. 187-194.

1846.

9. On the Tertiary or Supracretaceous Formations of the Isle of Wight, as exhibited in the Sections at Alum Bay and White Cliff Bay. Quart. Journ. Geol. Soc., vol. ii. pp. 223-259.

10. On the Wealden Strata exposed by the Tunbridge Wells Railway. [With John Morris.] Ibid., vol. ii. pp. 397-405.

1847.

11. On the Occurrence of *Cypris* in a part of the Tertiary Freshwater Strata of the Isle of Wight. Rep. Brit. Assoc. for 1846, Pt. 2, pp. 56-58.

12. On the Probable Age of the London Clay, and its relations to the Hampshire and Paris Tertiary Systems. Quart. Journ. Geol. Soc., vol. iii. pp. 354-377.

13. On the Main Points of Structure and the Probable Age of the Bagshot Sands, and on their presumed Equivalents in Hampshire and France. Ibid., pp. 378-409.

1849.

14. On the Position and General Characters of the Strata exhibited in the Coast Section from Christchurch Harbour to Poole Harbour. Quart. Journ. Geol. Soc., vol. v. pp. 43-49.

15. On some Fossiliferous Beds overlying the Red Crag at Chillesford, near Orford, Suffolk. Ibid., pp. 345-353.

1850.

16. On the Geological Conditions which determine the relative Value of the Water-bearing Strata of the Tertiary and Cretaceous Series, and on the Probability of finding in the Lower Members of the Latter beneath London Fresh and Large Sources of Water-supply. Proc. Roy. Institute of British Architects, July 8, 1850.

17. On the Structure of the Strata between the London Clay and the Chalk in the London and Hampshire Tertiary Systems. Part I. The Basement Bed of the London Clay. Quart. Journ. Geol. Soc., vol. vi. pp. 252-281.

1851.

18. A Geological Inquiry respecting the Water-bearing Strata of the Country around London, with reference especially to the Water-supply of the Metropolis. 8vo. London. Pp. 240.

19. On the Drift at Sangatte Cliff, near Calais. Quart. Journ. Geol. Soc., vol. vii. pp. 274-278.

1852.

20. On some of the Effects of the Holmfirth Flood. Quart. Journ. Geol. Soc., vol. viii. pp. 225-230.

21. On the Structure of the Strata between the London Clay and the Chalk in the London and Hampshire Tertiary Systems. Part III. The Thanet Sands. Ibid., pp. 235-264.

1853.

22. Sur la Position géologique des Sables et du Calcaire lacustre de Rilly (Marne). Bull. Soc. Géol. Fr., Ser. 2, vol. x. pp. 300-310.

1854.

23. On the Structure of the Strata between the London Clay and the Chalk in the London and Hampshire Tertiary Systems. Part II. The Woolwich and Reading Series. Quart. Journ. Geol. Soc., vol. x. pp. 75-170.
24. On some Swallow Holes on the Chalk Hills near Canterbury. Ibid., pp. 222-224.
25. On the Thickness of the London Clay ; on the relative Position of the Fossiliferous Beds of Sheppey, Highgate, Harwich, Newnham, Bognor, &c. ; and on the Probable Occurrence of the Bagshot Sands in the Isle of Sheppey. Ibid., pp. 401-419.
26. On the Distinctive Physical and Palæontological Features of the London Clay and the Bracklesham Sands ; and on the Independence of these two Groups of Strata. Ibid., pp. 435-454.
27. On the Correlation of the Lower Tertiaries of England with those of France and Belgium. Ibid., pp. 454-456.

1855.

28. On the Origin of the Sand- and Gravel-pipes in the Chalk of the London Tertiary District. Quart. Journ. Geol. Soc., vol. xi. pp. 64-84.
29. On a Fossiliferous Drift near Salisbury. [With JOHN BROWN.] Ibid., vol. xi. pp. 101-107.
30. On a Fossiliferous Deposit in the Gravel at West Hackney. Ibid., pp. 107-110.
31. On a Fossiliferous Bed of the Drift Period near the Reculvers. Ibid., pp. 110-112.
32. On the Correlation of the Eocene Tertiaries of England, France, and Belgium. Ibid., pp. 206-246.

1856.

33. On the Boring through the Chalk at Kentish Town, London. Quart. Journ. Geol. Soc., vol. xii. pp. 6-14.
34. Note on the Gravel near Maidenhead, in which the Skull of the Musk Buffalo was found. Ibid., pp. 131-133.
35. On the Correlation of the Middle Eocene Tertiaries of England, France, and Belgium. [Abstract.] Ibid., pp. 390-392.

1857.

36. On the Correlation of the Eocene Tertiaries of England, France, and Belgium. Part II. Quart. Journ. Geol. Soc., vol. xiii. pp. 89-134.

37. On some Fossiliferous Ironstone occurring in the North Downs. [Abstract.]   Quart. Journ. Geol. Soc., vol. xiii., 1857, pp. 212, 213.

38. The Ground beneath us : its Geological Phases and Changes ; being Three Lectures on the Geology of Clapham, and the Neighbourhood of London generally.   8vo.   London.   Pp. 79.

1858.

39. On the " Haggerstone."   Geologist, Vol. i. pp. 113, 114.

40. On the Occurrence of the Boulder Clay, or Northern Clay Drift, at Bricket Wood, near Watford.   Ibid., pp. 241, 242.

41. British Localities of Fossil Mammalia.   Ibid., pp. 251, 252.

42. On the Boring through the Chalk at Harwich.   Quart. Journ. Geol. Soc., vol. xiv. pp. 249-252.

43. On the Age of some Sands and Iron-Sandstones on the North Downs. Ibid., pp. 322-335.   [With a Note on the Fossils by S. V. Wood.]

44. On the Westward Extension of the Old Raised Beach of Brighton ; and on the Extent of the Sea-bed of the same Period.   Quart. Journ. Geol. Soc., vol. xv. pp. 215-221.

1859.

45. Sur la Découverte d'Instruments en Silex associés à des Restes de Mammifères d'Espèces pérdues dans des Couches non-remaniées d'une Formation géologique récente.   Paris, Comptes Rendus, vol. xlix. pp. 634-636, 859.

46. On the Occurrence of Flint Implements, associated with the Remains of Animals of Extinct Species in Beds of a late Geological Period, in France, at Amiens and Abbeville, and in England at Hoxne.   Proc. Roy. Soc., vol. x. pp. 50-59 [Abstract] ; Phil. Trans. for 1860, 1861, pp. 277-318.

47. Flint Implements from the Drift.   Athenæum, Dec. 3 and Dec. 10, 1859.

1860.

48. Letter on the Boulders and Gravels of the Gower Cave District, and on a Raised Beach to the West of Gower.   (Appendix to Dr Falconer's Memoir on the Ossiferous Caves of Gower.   Palæont. Mem., vol. ii. p. 536.)

49. [Note on the Bone-cave at Brixham in Devonshire.]   Quart. Journ. Geol. Soc., vol. xvi. pp. 189, 190.

50. Description of the Gravels from Spitzbergen collected by Mr Lamont. Quart. Journ. Geol. Soc., vol. xvi. pp. 438, 439.

51. On the Presence of the London Clay in Norfolk, as proved by a Well-boring at Yarmouth.   Ibid., pp. 449-452.

52. On a Raised Beach in Mewslade Bay, and the Occurrence of the Boulder Clay on Cefn-y-bryn.   [Abstract.]   Ibid., pp. 487-491.   [Appendix to paper by Dr Falconer.]

1861.

53. On some New Facts in Relation to the Section of the Cliff at Mundesley, Norfolk. Geologist, vol. iv. pp. 68-71.
54. Notes on some further Discoveries of Flint Implements in Beds of Post-Pliocene Gravel and Clay ; with a few Suggestions for Search elsewhere. Quart. Journ. Geol. Soc., vol. xvii. pp. 362-368.
55. On the Occurrence of the *Cyrena fluminalis*, together with Marine Shells of Recent Species, in Beds of Sand and Gravel over Beds of Boulder Clay, near Hull ; with an Account of some Borings and Well-sections in the same District. Ibid., pp. 446-456.

1862.

56. Theoretical Considerations on the Conditions under which the Drift Deposits containing the Remains of Extinct Mammalia and Flint Implements were accumulated, and on their Geological Age. On the Loess of the Valleys of the South of England, and of the Somme and the Seine. Proc. Roy. Soc., vol. xii. pp. 38-52, 170-173 ; Phil. Trans., 1864, pp. 247-309.
57. Report on Wines, Spirits, Beer, and other Drinks. International Exhibition, 1862. [Reprinted for Private Circulation by permission of the Society of Arts.]

1863.

58. On the Section at Moulin Quignon, Abbeville, and on the Peculiar Character of some of the Flint Implements recently discovered there. Quart. Journ. Geol. Soc., vol. xix. pp. 497-505.
59. The Antiquity of Man. Athenæum, April 25, 1863.
60. The Human Jaw of Abbeville. Ibid., June 13, 1863.

1864.

61. On some Further Evidence bearing on the Excavation of the Valley of the Somme by River-action, as exhibited in a Section at Drucat, near Abbeville. Proc. Roy. Soc., vol. xiii., 1864, pp. 135-137. Reprinted in 4to, with notes.
62. On the Quaternary Flint Implements of Abbeville, Amiens, Hoxne, &c. ; their Geological Position and History. Proc. Roy. Instit., vol. iv. pp. 213-222.
63. The Brick-earth with Elephant Remains at Ilford. Geol. Mag., vol. i. pp. 244, 245.

1865.

64. Additional Observations on the Raised Beach of Sangatte with Reference to the Date of the English Channel and the Presence of Loess in the Cliff Section. Quart. Journ. Geol. Soc., vol. xxi. pp. 440-442 ; Phil. Mag., vol. xxx. pp. 378, 379.

1868.

65. On the Structure of the Crag Beds of Norfolk and Suffolk, with some observations on their Organic Remains. Part I. Coralline Crag. Quart. Journ. Geol. Soc. [Abstract], vol. xxiv. pp. 288, 289.

66. On the Structure of the Crag Beds of Norfolk and Suffolk, with some observations on their Organic Remains. Part II. The Red Crag of Suffolk. Quart. Journ. Geol. Soc., vol. xxiv. pp. 460, 461 [Abstract]; Phil. Mag., vol. xxxvii., 1869, pp. 146-148.

1869.

67. Royal Commission on Water-supply. (Appointed 1866.) Report of the Commissioners. 1869. Maps.

68. Metropolitan Board of Works. Reports on the Boring Operations at Crossness. (Appendix C. 1868.) 1869.

1870.

69. On the Crag of Norfolk and Associated Beds. [Abstract.] Quart. Journ. Geol. Soc., vol. xxvi. pp. 281, 282 ; Phil. Mag., vol. xi., 1870, pp. 137, 138.

70. A Fact relating to the Crag-pit at Thorpe, near Norwich. Geol. Mag., vol. vii. p. 539.

71. Notes on Earthquakes. Ibid., pp. 541-544.

72. The Thames Subway. Nature, vol. i. pp. 280, 281, Jan. 13, 1870.

1871.

73. On the Structure of the Crag Beds of Suffolk and Norfolk, with some Observations on their Organic Remains. Part I. The Coralline Crag of Suffolk. Quart. Journ. Geol. Soc., vol. xxvii. pp. 115-146. Part II. The Red Crag of Essex and Suffolk. Ibid., pp. 325-356. Part III. The Norwich Crag and Westleton Beds. Ibid., pp. 452-496.

74. Deep-sea Life and its Relations to Geology. Address to the Geological Society. Ibid., pp. xlii-lxxv.

75. Report of the Commissioners appointed [in 1866] to inquire into the Several Matters relating to Coal in the United Kingdom; including— Report on the Quantities of Coal, wrought and unwrought, in the Coal-fields of Somersetshire and Part of Gloucestershire, pp. 33-70 ; and Report on the Probabilities of finding Coal in the South of England, pp. 146-166. Rep. Royal Coal Commission, vol. i. Fol. London.

1872.

76. 'La Seine.' Review by J. P. of 'Le Bassin Parisien aux Âges Anté-historiques.' Par M. Belgrand, Inspecteur-Général des Ponts et Chauseés, Directeur des Eaux et des Egouts de la Ville de Paris. Nature, vol. v. pp. 337-380, March 14, 1872.

77. Denudation of the Mendips. Nature, vol. vi. pp. 60, 61, May 23, 1872.
78. Our Springs and Water-supply, and our Coal-measures and Coal-supply. Address to the Geological Society. Quart. Journ. Geol. Soc., vol. xxviii. pp. li-xc.
79. On the Presence of a Raised Beach on Portsdown Hill, near Portsmouth, and on the Occurrence of a Flint Implement on a High Level at Downton. Quart. Journ. Geol. Soc., vol. xxviii. pp. 38-41.
80. Report on the Exploration of Brixham Cave, conducted by a Committee of the Geological Society, &c., J. Prestwich, Reporter. Proc. Roy. Soc., vol. xx. pp. 514-524 [Abstract]; and Phil. Trans., vol. clxiii., 1873, pp. 471-572.
81. On the Probable Extension of Coal-measures in the South-East of England. Popular Science Review, vol. xi. pp. 225-243.

1873.

82. Our Coal-supply. Review of Professor Hull's Coal-fields of Great Britain, and of the Report of the Commissioners appointed to Inquire into the Several Matters relating to Coal in the United Kingdom. Vol. I. London, 1871. Manchester Guardian, Feb. 7 and 19, 1873.
83. Building Stones. Review of Professor Hull's Treatise on the Building and Ornamental Stones of Great Britain and Foreign Countries. Ibid., Aug. 8, 1873.
84. The Depths of the Sea. Review of Professor Wyville Thomson's Depths of the Sea. Ibid., Dec. 1873.

1874.

85. On the Geological Conditions affecting the Construction of a Tunnel between England and France. Proc. Inst. Civ. Eng., vol. xxxvii., 1874, pp. 110-145.
86. Translation into French, 1874, of the Structure of the Crag Beds—Les Couches du Crag, par Dr Michel Mourlon.
87. Tables of Temperatures of the Sea at Different Depths beneath the Surface, reduced and collated from the Various Observations made between the Years 1749 and 1868. With Map and Sections. Proc. Royal Soc., vol. xxii. pp. 462-468 ; and Phil. Trans., vol. clxv., 1876, pp. 587-674.
88. Notes on the Phenomena of the Quaternary Period in the Isle of Portland and around Weymouth. Quart. Journ. Geol. Soc., vol. xxxi. pp. 29-54.

1875.

89. On the Origin of the Chesil Bank. Proc. Inst. Civ. Eng., vol. xl., 1875, pp. 61-79.
90. The Past and Future of Geology. Inaugural Address, Oxford, 1875. 8vo. Macmillan & Co. Pp. 48.

1876.

91. On the Geological Conditions affecting the Water-supply to Houses and Towns, with special Reference to the Modes of supplying Oxford. 8vo. Oxford. Pp. 48.
92. On the Mineral Water of the Artesian Well at St Clements, Oxford. Read before the Ashmolean Society, 1876.
93. Thickness of the Oxford Clay. Geol. Mag., Dec. II., vol. iii. pp. 237-239.

1878.

94. On the Section of Messrs Meux & Co.'s Artesian Well in the Tottenham Court Road, with Notices of the Well at Crossness, and of another at Shoreham, Kent; and on the Probable Range of the Lower Green-sand and Palæozoic Rocks under London. Quart. Journ. Geol. Soc., vol. xxxiv. pp. 902-913.

1879.

95. On the Discovery of a Species of Iguanodon in the Kimmeridge Clay near Oxford; and a Notice of a very Fossiliferous Band of the Shotover Sands. Geol. Mag., Dec. II., vol. vi. pp. 193-195.
96. On the Origin of the Parallel Roads of Lochaber, and their bearing on other Phenomena of the Glacial Period. Proc. Roy. Soc., vol. xxix. pp. 6-21; and Phil. Trans., vol. xvii., 1879, pp. 663-726.

1880.

97. On a Raised Beach in Rhôs Sili Bay, Gower. Rep. Brit. Assoc., Swansea, 1880, p. 581.
98. On the Geological Evidence of the Temporary Submergence of the South-west of Europe during the early Human Period. Rep. Brit. Assoc., Swansea, 1880, pp. 581, 582.
99. Sur la Plage Soulevée de Sangatte. Bull. Soc. Geol. de France, 3e Série, vol. viii. pp. 547-552.
100. Note on the Occurrence of a new Species of Iguanodon in a Brick-pit of the Kimmeridge Clay at Cumnor Hurst, three Miles W.S.W. of Oxford. Quart. Journ. Geol. Soc., vol. xxxvi. pp. 430-432.

1881.

101. On the Strata between the Chillesford Beds and the Lower Boulder Clay. The Mundesley and Westleton Beds. Rep. Brit. Assoc., York, 1881, p. 620.
102. On the Extension into Essex, Middlesex, and other Inland Counties, of the Mundesley and Westleton Beds, in relation to the Age of certain Hill-gravels and of some of the Valleys of the South of England. Rep. Brit. Assoc., York, 1881, pp. 620-622.

103. Some Observations on the Causes of Volcanic Action. Rep. Brit. Assoc., York, 1881, pp. 610-613.
104. Letter on Section at St Edward's School, Summertown, Oxford. Reprint from St Edward's School Chronicle, Dec. 12, 1881.
105. An Index Guide to the Geological Collections in the University Museum, Oxford. 8vo. Oxford.

1882.

106. On the Occurrence of the *Cyrena fluminalis* at Summertown, near Oxford. Geol. Mag., Dec. II., vol. ix., 1882, pp. 49-51.
107. On a Peculiar Bed of Angular Drift on the Lower Chalk High Plain between Upton and Chilton. Quart. Journ. Geol. Soc., vol. xxxviii. pp. 127-134.

1883.

108. Notes relating to some of the Drift Phenomena of Hampshire : 1. Boulders, Hayling Island ; 2. Chert *débris* in the Hampshire Gravel ; 3. Elephant Bed, Freshwater Gate. Rep. Brit. Assoc., Southampton, 1882, pp. 529, 530.
109. On the Equivalents in England of the "Sables de Bracheux," and on the Southern Limits of the Thanet Sands. [Abstract.] Ibid., pp. 538, 539.

1884.

110. A Letter on the Oxford Water-supply. Clarendon Press, 1884 (April).

1885.

111. Oxford Water-supply. Letters and Report. 8vo. Oxford, Clarendon Press. Pp. 12.
112. On Underground Temperatures, with Observations on the Conductivity of Rocks, on the Thermal Effects of Saturation and Imbibition, and on a Special Source of Heat in Mountain Ranges. Proc. Roy. Soc., vol. xxxviii., 1885, pp. 161-168.
113. On the Agency of Water in Volcanic Eruptions, with some Observations on the Thickness of the Earth's Crust from a Geological Point of View, and on the Primary Cause of Volcanic Action. Proc. Roy. Soc., vol. xxxviii., 1885, pp. 253-260.
114. On Regional Metamorphism. Proc. Roy. Soc., vol. xxxviii., 1885, p. 425.

1886.

115. Geology, Chemical, Physical, and Stratigraphical. Vol. I. Chemical and Physical. 8vo. Clarendon Press, Oxford.

1887.

116. Considerations on the Date, Duration, and Conditions of the Glacial Period, with reference to the Antiquity of Man. Quart. Journ. Geol. Soc., vol. xliii. pp. 393-410.

1888.

117. Geology, Chemical, Physical, and Stratigraphical. Vol. II. Stratigraphical and Physical. 8vo. Clarendon Press, Oxford.

118. Further Observations on the Correlation of the Eocene Strata in England, Belgium, and the North of France. Quart. Journ. Geol. Soc., vol. xliv. pp. 88-109.

119. Congrès Géologique International : Discours du President [1888]. Reprinted in Compte Rendu du Congrès, 1891, pp. 20-31.

120. The Atmosphere of the Coal-period. Geol. Mag., Dec. III., vol. v. pp. 238, 239, 334, 335.

1889.

121. On the Recent Discovery of the Remains of the Mammoth in the Valley of the Darent. Geol. Mag., Dec. II., vol. vi. pp. 113, 114.

122. On the Occurrence of Palæolithic Flint Implements in the Neighbourhood of Ightham, Kent, their Distribution and Probable Age. Quart. Journ. Geol. Soc., vol. xlv. pp. 270-294.

1890.

123. On the Relation of the Westleton Beds, or Pebbly Sands of Suffolk, to those of Norfolk, and on their Extension inland : with some Observations on the Period of the Final Elevation and Denudation of the Weald and of the Thames Valley, &c. Part I. Quart. Journ. Geol. Soc., vol. xlvi. pp. 84-117. Part II. Ibid., pp. 120-153. Part III. On the Relation of the Westleton Shingle to other Pre-Glacial Drifts in the Thames Basin, and on a Southern Drift, with Observations on the Final Elevation and Initial Subaerial Denudation of the Weald, and on the Genesis of the Thames. Ibid., pp. 155-181.

124. The Elevation of the Weald. Geol. Mag., Dec. III., vol. vii. pp. 479, 480.

1891.

125. On the Age, Formation, and Successive Drift-Stages of the Valley of the Darent; with Remarks on the Palæolithic Implements of the District, and on the Origin of its Chalk Escarpment. Quart. Journ Geol. Soc., vol. xlvii. pp. 126-160.

126. The Saiga Antelope in Britain. Geol. Mag., Dec. III., vol. viii. p. 190.

1892.

127. On the Primitive Characters of the Flint Implements of the Chalk Plateau of Kent, with reference to the Question of their Glacial or Pre-Glacial Age. With Notes by Messrs B. HARRISON and DE BARRI CRAWSHAY. Journ. Anthrop. Inst., vol. xxi. pp. 246-262.

128. The Raised Beaches, and "Head" or Rubble-Drift of the South of England : their Relation to the Valley Drifts and to the Glacial Period ; and on a late Post-Glacial Submergence. Quart. Journ. Geol. Soc., vol. xlviii. pp. 263-343.

1893.

129. The Position of Geology. (A chapter on Uniformitarianism.) Nineteenth Century, October 1893, p. 551.
130. On the Evidences of a Submergence of Western Europe, and of the Mediterranean Coasts, at the Close of the Glacial or so-called Post-Glacial Period, and immediately preceding the Neolithic or Recent Period. Phil. Trans., vol. 184, pp. 903-984.

1894.

131. The Great Japanese Earthquake. Geol. Mag., Dec. IV., vol. i. pp. 191, 192.
132. On the possible Marine Origin of the Loess. Ibid., pp. 237, 238.
133. The Southern Drift. Ibid., pp. 476, 477.

1895.

134. Collected Papers on some controverted Questions of Geology. 8vo. London.
135. On Certain Phenomena belonging to the Close of the last Geological Period, and on their Bearing upon the Tradition of the Flood. 8vo. London.
136. A Geological Inquiry respecting the Water-bearing Strata of the Country around London, with reference especially to the Water-supply of the Metropolis, and including some remarks on Springs. (A Reissue, with Additions by the Author.) 8vo. London.
137. The Greater Antiquity of Man. Nineteenth Century for April.
138. Nature and Art. Geol. Mag., Dec. IV., vol. ii. pp. 373, 376.

POSTHUMOUS.

1898.

139. The Solent River. Geol. Mag., Dec. IV., vol. v. pp. 349-351.
140. Memoranda, chiefly on the Drift Deposits in various Parts of England and Wales : being Extracts from the Notebooks and other MSS. of the late Sir Joseph Prestwich. Ibid., pp. 404-417. [Communicated by Lady Prestwich, and edited by H. B. Woodward.]

LIST OF SOCIETIES

SIR JOSEPH PRESTWICH BELONGED.

Fellow of the Royal, Geological, and Chemical Societies of London.

Associate of the Institute of Civil Engineers.

Correspondent of the Institute of France (Academy of Sciences).

Member of the Geological Society of France.

Honorary Member of the Imperial Geological Institute of Vienna; of the Royal Academy of the Lincei of Rome; Royal Academy of Sciences of Belgium; Anthropological Society of Brussels; American Philosophical Society; Pontifical Academy of Rome; Helvetic Society of Natural Science; Vaudois Society of Natural Sciences; Literary and Philosophical Society of Manchester; Belgian Society of Geology, Palæontology, and Hydrology; Imperial Society of Emulation of Abbeville; Imperial Geological Society of Hungary; Geological Society of the North of France; the Yorkshire Philosophical Society; the Edinburgh Geological Society; and the Geological Society of South Africa.

Corresponding Member of the Geological Society of Cornwall, and of the Society of Natural History of Boston, U.S.A.

INDEX.

www.ingramcontent.com/pod-product-compliance
Lightning Source LLC
Chambersburg PA
CBHW032010110726
47901CB00004B/1034